The Confessions of Noa Weber

The Confessions of Noa Weber

a novel by

Gail Hareven

Translated by Dalya Bilu

MELVILLEHOUSE

BROOKLYN, NEW YORK

S

The author and Melville House wish to thank David Stromberg whose kind assistance made this book possible.

Passage from *Eugene Onegin* by Alexander Pushkin, translated by Charles Johnston (Penguin Classics 1977, Revised edition 1979). Copyright © Charles Johnston, 1977, 1979. Lines from "When a Stranger Comes to the City" from *The Penguin Book of Hebrew Verse* edited by T. Carmi (Allen Lane, 1981). Copyright © T. Carmi, 1981. Lines from "How Can I See You, Love?" Copyright © David Vogel, trans. Arthur C. Jacobs in *Holocaust Poetry*, New York, St. Martin's Press, 1996.

Melville House Publishing
145 Plymouth Street
Brooklyn, NY 11201
www.mhpbooks.com

Book Design by Blair and Hayes

ISBN 978-1-933633-37-4

First Melville House Printing: February 2009

Library of Congress Cataloging-in-Publication Data
Har'even, Gayil.
    [She-ahavah nafshi. English]
    The confessions of Noa Weber / Gail Hareven ; translated from the Hebrew by Dalya Bilu. -- [1st English ed.]
        p. cm.
    Includes bibliographical references.
    ISBN 978-1-933633-37-4
    I. Bilu, Dalya. II. Title.
PJ5055.23.A75S5413 2007
892.4'36--dc22
                                    2007046685

A CALM DISTANCE, A PANORAMIC VIEW

The city of J lies at the top of the hills of J. That's how I'd like to begin my story; at a calm distance, with a deep breath, in a panoramic shot focusing very slowly on a single street, and very slowly on a single house, "this is the house where I was born." But you'd be making a fool of yourself if your J were Jerusalem, since every idiot knows about Jerusalem. And altogether it's impossible to talk about Jerusalem any more. Impossible, that is to say, without "winding alleys" and "stone courtyards," "caper bushes" and "Arab women in the market place." And I have nothing to say about caper bushes and stone courtyards, nor do I have the faintest desire to flavor my story with the colorful patois of colorful Jerusalem characters, twirling their mustaches as they spin Oriental tales.

Nor do I intend to mention here the hills of J, in other words the Judean Hills. These hills always depressed me with their thick history and the thin trunks of their pine trees, and the picnic leftovers scattered over the dry pine needles. And anyone who didn't spread out a picnic blanket and open a picnic basket surely trailed behind their scoutmasters there in the footsteps of Judah Maccabee and Uri Ben-Ari and the continuing saga of Jewish heroism, which I somehow managed to forget, however hard they drilled it into my head.

Of all the things that preoccupy my thoughts, not a single one happened to me between the thorny burnet and the arbutus tree, and so from now on I'll do without the geographical features, the ancient human landscape, the black goat and the briar, with all those details that compose what is referred to as the panoramic view. And even if once upon a time, a great many years ago, I went for walks in the forests of J, it definitely isn't worth the effort of distancing the camera for the sake of those ancient neckings. They're about as riveting as the autumn crocuses. Or the spring. Or whatever you call them. The truth is that I wasn't really born in Jerusalem, either. I was eight when my parents left the kibbutz—for seven years after that we lived in Tel Aviv—and if I began by saying, for example, "I was born in the Emek Hospital," you'd come right back: "Ahaa, of course, my two sisters-in-law gave birth there too," and immediately want to talk to me about "that amazing midwife, the one with the faint mustache, worth more than all the doctors put together, you don't mean to say you've never heard of her?"

It isn't my personal problem as a writer. It isn't my personal problem that a person who was born here can't open with the words "I was born"—because so what? So you were born, good for you, you were born, okay, and then what? Because after "I was born" has to come an adventure story that will take the first person far, far away from his birthplace, and how far can you really get from here? To the Far East on the beaten track of the ex-warriors from the Golani Brigade? To Uman with the nutcases of the Bratslav

Hassids to their rabbi's grave? And however far you went you'd end up meeting someone who knew your cousin's cousin. Not interesting. Not interesting at all.

Not that I'm complaining, God forbid. The facts of my birth and upbringing have nothing to do with what follows here, and even if they did, you need calm and composure to distance the camera like that; calm and composure and a sense of historical perspective, and as far as my situation is concerned, I clearly suffer from a severe lack of both.

For the record I'll simply mention here that I was favored by the luck of the draw. I grew up well fed and protected, and that's another reason why where and how I "came into the world" is not a matter of public interest. People who've survived a holocaust, who were born into a world that no longer exists, they can begin their biographies with "I was born." The heroes of nineteenth century novels begin with "I was born," my heroic father can begin his story with "I was born." Not me. My early history is too boring, it fails to provide any explanation for what happened to me in later years, and I have never felt the urge to examine it or whine about it. Nor do I now.

In any case, it's no great loss, and if the right to say "I was born" has to be paid for in dire catastrophes, stepfathers, orphanages, and picking pockets in the marketplace, I say, "No thanks," and choose to enter this story at the age of seventeen, where the real me begins:

Me and my love for Alek—which against my better judgment I experience as transcendence. Me with my dybbuk—which is the only thing that gives me a sense of space.

Forty-seven, that's how old I am now; forty-eight in September.

FORTY-SEVEN

Forty-seven years old, and in my twenty-something years as a writer it's never happened that I wrote a story in the first person. Not that I haven't felt like sending the heroine of my books, that paragon of perfection Nira Woolf, to hell, and sometimes I've had the passing thought that maybe one day in the future, in some sober, even-breathed maturity, I would change my genre. I've had thoughts along those lines, but it's never, ever occurred to me to push myself into the story, and what's more, to puff and pant it in the first person.

I enjoyed writing my detective stories, I enjoyed the status they gave me—writing thrillers isn't a bad profession, especially when they have a surplus value in the educational and political sense—and when I took care in various interviews to clarify that I had "no other literary pretensions," it wasn't a total lie. And it still isn't a lie.

In one of the newspapers' holiday supplements there was an interview I gave for the release of my latest book, *What Did Mrs. Neuman Know?* In this book Nira Woolf sets out on the trail of a network of pimp slave traffickers importing Russian sex slaves, "and the trail leads her from the suburbs of Moscow to the Israeli Ministry of Interior, up to the highest echelons of the Israeli police," as the blurb says on the back cover. I came out of the interview okay: I managed to get in a few shocking statistics about the trafficking of women, and with my well-known sensitivity to sociopolitical issues—let the envious eat their hearts out—I spelled out enough of a sociopolitical agenda for a holiday supplement.

Since I know my own political agenda quite well, I have to admit that as soon as I opened the newspaper it was actually the picture that grabbed my attention. It was a cruel photograph, even though I don't believe that the photographer or the editor meant me harm on purpose. I looked like a weird little girl turned into a wooden doll. Because of the angle of the shot, my feet were enormous, my seated body was hidden behind wooden calves gnarled with veins, and above my knees was a dark face surrounded by unkempt witch's hair, with wide-open eyes popping out of their sockets. I can only blame my own stupidity; I shouldn't have let them photograph me on the steps of my house in the spring light in running shorts and red sneakers without any makeup. Once, I could have gotten away with it, but not now, not at my age.

• • •

One of the pieces of nonsense they feed people is the idea of "times of life crises"—adolescent crisis, forties crisis, fifties crisis, end of the millennium syndrome crisis—book shops and newspapers are full of this shit, and there are people who actually live their lives from manual to manual as if age and time were explainable. Somehow I have never thought seriously about age, and now too, ever since that photograph, it's not about the age of forty-seven that I think, but rather about the ages to come.

Let's say Noa Weber is suddenly sixty-eight. A bony body full of the opinions of a militant old lady, climbing tip-tap up those same old stairs. An old body full of opinions entering its old house, and lying down on the same old bed to give its feet a rest. And when this Noa Weber finally lies down, what exactly runs through her brain's worn-out connections? Does she polish up one of her correct opinions? Reflect compassionately about one of the victims in her books? Does she think about reforming society and justice for all? Definitely not. Just like now, Noa Weber thinks about him. She thinks about him, and wrinkles twitch around the dry mouth that still moans, and a hand blotched with liver spots moves down to her gray pubic hair. Sixty-eight years old, and still her heart goes out to he who is gone and to that which is gone, and still her body arches at the memory of his touch. Wretched, wretched, wretched Noa Weber, wretched her love that is beyond time and place, wretched her sparse pubic hair with the white skin showing through.

Noa Weber is old and moaning. Noa Weber is forty-seven and moaning. For years she's been moaning, and there's nothing new in her moans or her fantasies, and the self-disgust isn't new either.

Sometimes you have to stick your finger down your throat and vomit up the disgusting insides of the self . . . sometimes you have to increase the nausea in order to get rid of the disgust. . . .

The light of the computer screen is the best disinfectant.

• • •

For years this itch has been coming and going in me, like a gravitation toward suicide, like a yearning for purification. Like a demon that whispers to me: Now, now, imagine them all . . . put them into a hall, row after row . . . Miriam, Talush, your parents, Hagar, Osnat, friends and fellow citizens, all your readers, and all the fucked-up activists and employees of the fund. Seat them in front of you one by one, and then snigger yourself to death before their eyes.

To confess to the finish . . . to confess till it finishes me off . . . to talk about him, to talk about myself, to talk so I won't have to bear it any more.

To talk until I can't stand myself any longer. To talk, to talk, to talk myself to death—this is apparently why I'm standing here before you today.

Forty-seven years old. My daughter will turn twenty-nine this summer, and this story certainly isn't meant for her. Children, I believe, don't need to know the whole truth about their parents, and a gasping confession without any perspective won't make her any the wiser. In any case she's smarter than I am, or perhaps not smarter, but clearer and more sensible. Her mouth is always where her heart is. I need my daughter, the first row in my imaginary audience, while Hagar is clearly in no need at all of my imaginary striptease.

All my Nira Woolf novels have great beginnings that lead straight into the plot. I put a lot of thought into my opening sentences. The opening sentences and the closing sentences. That's the kind of orderly plot in which I'd like to package myself and my love; to lead my madness along until it leaves me, to lead it and myself along like a story to the end.

A PANORAMIC PICTURE

I told you to forget about a panoramic view, but there's one panorama at least that I can offer you. A panoramic picture of the disease I've been dragging around with me for almost thirty years. The picture that comes up on the computer screen after midnight is at its brightest between two and four in the morning, and fades gradually towards dawn, Israel time:

LAA—Love Addicts Anonymous—holding hands on the web. Lovesick ladies from the East Coast to the West Coast, from Europe to Australia, entering the forum for therapeutic encounters. All of them fell in love suddenly, once and for all. And through winter, summer, autumn, and spring they cling to the one and only love that never lets them be.

Women who love too much, is how they define themselves. Women addicted to love. Women whose neurons have been screwed up by their unhealthy loves.

Since discovering the LAA forum, whenever my own neurons begin to go berserk, I enter the web site. I call myself Adele there, a private joke which I have never explained to my sister sufferers and which I never will. Adele, after Victor Hugo's pathetic floor-rag of a daughter, who followed some nothing all the way to Marrakech and went so crazy because of him that they had to put her in the loony bin. The Adele H. of Israel. Very funny. But the women-who-love-too-much wouldn't find it amusing, none of them would laugh.

Maybe women who love too much have no sense of humor and maybe they just have no idea about Israeli names and how unromantic they are. Take Sarit for example. Can anyone imagine Sarit throwing herself under a train? Or drowning herself in a river? Which river, exactly? In the shallow trickle of the Jordan? Or perhaps in the fish ponds of some kibbutz? No, the most Sarit could do is give a revealing interview to the mid-week supplement of one of the tabloids. Some names simply impose an anti-romantic discipline on their owners: Pazit. Sarit. Yossi. Amit. Try fitting them into an old love song by Alexander Penn, for instance, "My plain winter coat and the lamp on the bridge, / An autumn night and my face wet with rain. / That was the first time you saw me, remember? / And it was as clear to me as two and two / That I was in love with Amit, and Amit was in love with Pazit, / Yes, it wasn't any good, it was gloriously bad . . ."

Gloriously bad. I actually understand these words. And they are the ones that creep up from my tailbone to my collarbone, in complete contradiction to my logic which tells me that bad can't be glorious. And that all this romantic bullshit is basically a conspiracy against the female sex.

I said that lovesick females from all over the world meet at night on the net, and that of course was an exaggeration characteristic of my state of mind. Africa is silent. China is silent. Japan is silent. India is silent. No Russian soul comes onto the screen to seek support from her sisters. But what do I know about love in Chinese? Or in Japanese? Or in the multitude of Indian languages? Nothing. I simply have no idea how women there love.

In Russia, on the other hand, I'm positive that there are a lot of broken hearts. Judging by their literature and our translations of it, every second heart there is gloriously badly broken. So why are they silent on the net? Even if we limit ourselves to English speakers capable of corresponding, taking into account the tens of millions of Russian women, some of them should definitely have found their way to the group. Hey, you over there, in Kiev, in Saint Petersburg, in Tobolsk, in Baku, in Tallinn, let's hear from you. Haven't you heard of the revolution? Haven't you heard yet? Of course you have. So come on, girls. Stand up now and confess. What's going on with you there? What's the meaning of this silence? Isn't there even one of you who's sick of her bondage? Let's hear one Russian soul at long last admit the depressing folly of feeling. One Natasha who'll come forward and type the ritual admission on her computer keyboard: "1. I am powerless over love, I am addicted to it and my life has become unmanageable." "2. I have come to believe that only a power greater than myself can restore me to sanity." And, "3. Seeking recovery, I turn my life and will over to the group and to the care of God as I understand Him."

Love like ours is a progressive disease, in the opinion of our nocturnal forum. In acknowledgement of this fact we are called upon to stop and make a searching and fearless moral inventory of ourselves. To admit to ourselves, to our sisters, and to God—"as we understand him"—the many wrongs we have done because of our addiction. To humbly ask Him to remove our shortcomings. And then to make a list of all the people we have harmed in the lunacy of our love, apologize to them in detail and make amends to them all.

Sandy from Seattle abandoned four children and her husband for a certain clown, a real honest-to-goodness clown who put on a performance at her son's seventh birthday party, and who now thinks he's doing her a favor when he agrees to see her once every few months. Debra from Dallas got out of jail a year ago after making a childish attempt to poison her alcoholic's wife. Terry from Toronto jams up the mailbox, the fax machine, and the telephones of her lying ex with endless hysterical messages, and he's about to sue her for the damage she's caused his business, but all the silly cow can think about is what it'll be like to see him in court and how exactly he'll look at her there.

Sandy from Seattle, Debra from Dallas, Betty from Boston, what imbecilic names they choose for themselves. As if they've entered a contest for Miss World, and are about to be called onstage in their bathing suits. And now, ladies and gentlemen, please welcome dopey Debra from Dallas, senile Sandy from Seattle, and number fifteen on our list, brainless Betty from Boston. Here they are, our gorgeous girls, stepping up one after the other in the nakedness of their cute little souls.

Women who love too much are supposed to regret the fact that they were so dependent and so addicted, to regret it profoundly and to apologize profusely. As far as regret is concerned, I don't know: but apologizing is another matter, and if anyone asked my opinion I would say that most of the group doesn't need to apologize to anyone. Not as a matter of any urgency at any rate. Somebody screwed these screw-ups, most of them got beaten and betrayed, insulted and humiliated by the scum they fell in love with, and nevertheless they gave them their hearts and souls, and quite often their property too. So you can despise them for it, it's definitely possible to despise them, but apologize? Let their lousy men apologize first. And let them change the whole system before anything else.

From what I've come to understand, a woman joins the group when in general terms the whole love-thing begins to seem unprofitable to her. She reaches this understanding a little late in the day, but in the last analysis that's what it's all about: the cost exceeds the gain, the balance of energy is upset, the psychic economy is on the verge of bankruptcy. That's the way they talk on the site. So is it any wonder, girls, that most of our members come from the strongholds of capitalism? And is it any wonder that nearly all these Protestant ladies with hemorrhoids in their souls talk about "investing in a relationship," about "profit" and "waste" and "loss"? Okay, I don't object. I think in these terms too, at least once a day.

When I enter the forum, I identify myself by my pseudonym, say hi to everyone, and then sit in my corner in Jerusalem. The women who love too much allow me to sit in silence while they give me the benefit of their experience, which is certainly very kind and gracious of them. The women in LAA permit me to watch the proceedings from my corner and grow in strength, until such time as I am able to move myself and my fingers and come forward with the whole sad story of my addiction. Debra from Dallas, Sandy from Seattle, Ursula from Utrecht, Terry from Toronto, Chelsea from Charleston, Beatrice from Bern, all the regulars sit patiently on their hemorrhoids and wait for me to admit at last that, yes, I too am suffering from the same progressive disease, and I too am powerless over love, and that only a power greater than myself can restore me to sanity. But I have no intention of giving them this satisfaction and confessing on the Internet.

Because the fact is, dear friends, that there may be "brothers-in-arms" but there are no "sisters-in-love," and my devotion to Alek doesn't give rise in me to any consciousness of sisterly solidarity. Certainly not with dopey Debra or senile Sandy. Eternally sudden, self-absorbed, ardent, and grandiosely megalomaniac, the monster of love sees itself as unique and alone in the cosmos, and Noa Weber doesn't have even a drop of empathy for the romantic folly of her fellows.

I remember that, when my daughter was still small and I had already begun to love her, I was overwhelmed by a powerful feeling of solidarity with other mothers of small children, whoever they may be. Mothers in the park. Mothers at the nursery. Mothers everywhere. In nineteen seventy-five or -six, I would sit and gnaw at my fingernails in front of those black and white images televised from Vietnam, then in the dark go into the room where Hagar was sleeping on her stomach with her bum in the air and listen to her breathing, covering her head with the palm of my hand.

But maternal love is one thing and romantic love is another, and all I can say is that romantic love certainly doesn't fan the flame of humanism in me.

CONFESSING

A few times I almost confessed to the girls in LAA. "Forgive me, sisters, for I have sinned."

"How have you sinned, sister?"

"I've distorted, I've lied, I've pretended to be someone I'm not. I've lived like a slave and an idolator in secret, while boasting of a freedom I didn't possess. For almost thirty years one feeling has served me as a justification for a lack of feeling. I loved something I should have loathed, and I didn't love what was worthy of being loved enough."

Women who love too much aren't very interested in metaphysical sins of this nature. Squandering their child's college-savings fund, throwing acid at the legal wife, abandoning their bodies to violence, self-imprisonment, subsidizing their man's drug habit by prostitution, catatonic depression, drunk driving, these are the kinds of practical sins that preoccupy them, and in comparison to them my sins of thought and feeling turn white as snow. Well, maybe not quite white, but you could certainly say they pale in comparison.

It's not the fact that I have no sensational sins that prevents me from confessing to the group. The problem is the language. They are all guilty of "co-dependency," they all want to free themselves of "harmful relationships" and make themselves fit for "meaningful relationships." They are all trying "to develop their spiritual aspect," to "grow emotionally," "to be in touch with their feelings"—whatever the hell that means—and all of them without exception believe in the liberating effect of archaeology. As a consequence of this belief they carry out energetic excavations in their family history, and on bad nights I definitely find their stories gripping. Senile Sandy from Seattle, for example, had an alcoholic father and an alcoholic grandfather, which in her opinion and that of the group explains the "co-dependency" she has with her clown. Brainless Betty from Boston has no history of alcoholism in the family, but she had a neglectful mother who to this day is still a compulsive overeater. And it's certainly touching to read how little Betty used to hide the bread in hopes of saving something for her school sandwich from her mother's nightly kitchen raids. Except that according to Betty's and the rest of the group's logic, a mother who loves food sentences her daughter to a lifetime of compulsive love, and at that point I stop being touched and begin to laugh.

On a number of occasions I was tempted to make the girls happy and join the party at last by cooking up some sort of terminal explanation for my case. An eloquent etiology of my disease. Ready? Yes, they're all ready. So what happened to me, girls, is that my father was hardly ever at home, my heroic father was in the army with men and other women, he was with other women a lot, and I never had a real home either, because the first eight years of my life I spent in the children's house on a kibbutz. Allow me to confine myself for a moment to the story of the kibbutz.

Kibbutz, girls, do you have any idea of what a kibbutz is? No, of course you don't, because the only people who know what a kibbutz is are those who grew up on one, like me. If there are any Jewish souls among you, if you grew up on the propaganda of the Jewish National Fund, kindly forget the fishermen spreading their nets, the female tractor driver and the suntanned women picking oranges and smiling photogenic smiles from the tops of their ladders. A kibbutz, my sisters, is not a poster, and even though the children's house covered in ivy and bougainvillea looks like the Garden of Eden in the photographs, that's what the island in *Lord of the Flies* looked like in the beginning, too.

The children's house . . . let me tell you about the children's house. In this house with the red-tiled roof, I was abandoned every day to the violence of my peer group, and every night to my loneliness. Eight years times three hundred and sixty-five days equals . . . You can work it out yourselves, but the sum is the number of nights that I was abandoned by my mother.

Eight times three hundred and sixty-five days of violence and ridicule, and eight times three hundred and sixty-five long nights of anxiety and fear, taught me to hide my neediness. When I ran away from the group to my parents' room, my mother would lose no time in taking me back. When I complained, she pretended that she didn't hear or told me to be strong and pull myself together. And I, it seems, was a good pupil, and gradually I stifled my tears until the weeping was silenced inside me and turned into quiet despair. That's how they taught me to associate love with abandonment, and that's how they got me used to the idea that love is not a refuge.

Only now, my sisters, that I, Adele H. from Israel, sit here in our nocturnal group, do I suddenly have the insight that with so many abandonments behind me—I've already counted them for you: three hundred and sixty-five times eight—with so many abandonments, it's clear why before I reached the age of eighteen I turned myself into a Natasha (*natash* being Hebrew for "abandon"), and why I have remained abandoned ever since.

This kind of description, which is definitely not complete fiction, but only partly false, this kind of description would immediately reward me with an international wave of empathy. The trouble is that what I need is contempt, not empathy, and certainly not the empathy of blockheads.

A parody of self-interpretation will not bring me the self-disgust I'm looking for.

I say a parody of self-interpretation, partly because my childhood wasn't as miserable as I described it, but mainly because I, in contrast to my sisters-who-love-too-much, do not believe that my dybbuk has a "psychological background." My father, my mother, and Yochie the kibbutz children's caretaker, have no part in this story, and if not for the psychobabble they hear on the television or read in the newspaper, it would never have occurred to the love-addicts of LAA to shove their parents into the picture, either. Think of Romeo and Juliet, for instance: it's true that Romeo and Juliet had parents, and logic demands that before the play begins they had some kind of childhood too, but nobody would seek the reason for Juliet's love in Mrs. Capulet's eating disorder, the love came of its own accord, the love seized hold of her, the love made her what she was. And in the face of such a lightning bolt only an idiot would insist on asking, "Why?"

So even if I could easily offer a psychological explanation for my dybbuk, and not only just one but a few, in this matter you won't get even a hint of a clue from me. Accept it, dear reader, or not; here I stand, and this is not a psychological novel.

And if, like some stubborn interviewer, you go on nagging me about the "why," I'm prepared to throw out the hypothesis that on the second of July, nineteen-hundred and seventy-two, somebody put a love potion into my coffee. It was black Turkish coffee, and I drank it from a thick glass purchased in the Machaneh Yehuda market in Jerusalem. The kind of love potion imbibed by Tristan and Isolde, who as far as I know had no psychological reasons for their love either.

JULY THE SECOND NINETEEN SEVENTY-TWO

Nineteen seventy-two was an eventful year. Richard Nixon defeated McGovern. Bobby Fischer defeated Spassky. The Pope visited China. Brezhnev was taken for a ride on Apollo 15. Terrorists poisoned the pandas in the Washington Zoo. I'm not being serious here. I could have done a bit of research to refresh my memory, but I don't leave the house now, and what do I need research for? I've already warned you that there isn't going to be any historical panorama here, only me, me and my life, that in the summer of '72 received its present form.

I can't describe what I was like before the second of July, but if it's really necessary, think of a formless entity of a girl. Naturally I did various things, like most of the people around me, and voiced opinions like them—more emphatically than most, as a matter of fact—but these deeds and words did not shape the entity I was into any particular form.

Because what can you already say about a seventeen-year-old girl? That she's a good student, but not a nerd? That she's athletic? That she collects stamps? I didn't collect stamps. That her relations with her parents are strained and her relations with her younger sister a little less so? Open any teen magazine and you'll find hundreds of girls described in precisely the same terms.

When I say formless, I mean mainly in the bodily sense. My measurements haven't changed much since then, only my style of dressing has undergone changes; in the summer of '72 I went about mainly in batik skirts and Arab kaftans, and my sense of my body underneath them was as loose and fluid as the garments. In hindsight, that body seems to me like a sea mollusk without edges, as if it hadn't been properly packed into my smooth girlish skin.

Of course I didn't think of myself in those days as a formless mollusk. In April I began to fuck and in May I discovered how to come. The earth didn't shake, even though I wanted very much to convince myself of a certain tremor, but in any case at the beginning of July, with the experience of about ten orgasms behind me, I saw myself as a model of decadent sensuousness, Liza Minelli playing Sally Bowles.

I began to fuck, I say, but in those days in our school nobody "fucked," not even the boys. "Going to bed with," we called it politely, or "going all the way," or best of all: "making love." And since I had "made love," or more precisely in order that I could at long last "make love," I was naturally obliged to assume that I was "in love." My boyfriend's name was Amikam, and he too was officially in love.

In order to "make love" we would go for hikes in the countryside on holidays and weekends. On ordinary weekdays, we would go to the Jerusalem forest, a place which should more properly be called the Jerusalem woods, and it was all as nice and delightful and enjoyable as it was supposed to be, except for an alarming weariness that sometimes overcame me on the way back. This weariness sometimes came over me without any connection to anything: a gray heaviness that poured in and overpowered me so that I had to sit down on the curb. My head like a hot sponge, my eyelids stuck together, hearing the cars go past, smelling asphalt and gasoline, and losing my limbs that refused to take messages from my brain. How many times did it happen? Five or six, I don't remember, but I do remember Amikam's hands massaging my shoulders, invading my bra and retreating with the noise and heat of another passing car, the hands of a boy trying to awaken Sleeping Beauty.

Sex is supposed to wake you up, love is supposed to wake you up, but me, a healthy and athletic young girl—first in the thousand- and two thousand-meter races—it put to gray sleep. We surmised that it was because of the pill, and since we were both about to be drafted into the army, and didn't expect to see much of each other after that, even though we would "still be a couple," be faithful to each other and so on, we decided to forgo the contraceptive pills I had very responsibly started to swallow a month before we "went all the way." Today it's clear to me that getting rid of the pills was *inter alia* a promise that I would remain faithful to him, faithfulness being a subject on which we conducted lengthy and solemn seminars during this period. Should we give ourselves a chance to "experience relationships with other people"? Should we "free each other" before we began our army service? Did "a love like ours close us off from other experiences"?

At the beginning of the summer we went together to see the movie *Cabaret*, and came to the common conclusion that it was about repulsive people in a sick society, and that it was no wonder that the Germans ended up doing what they did after such appalling decadence. We weren't lying, this was our honest opinion about which we both agreed, but an hour after we left the cinema it happened that I came on to him with a new, provocative boldness, and while I was busy doing so I also fantasized that Amikam was Michael York and that I was lying between him and a decadent German baron who was embracing me closely from behind. What Amikam's fantasies were I don't know. Perhaps the suppleness of Sally Bowles, perhaps the firmness of the German baron, or perhaps he didn't fantasize at all. Everything seems possible to the same extent. What do I know about him? In any case it was good that night, except for the attack of weakness afterwards, which is the only one that I can place in the context of a specific event.

AMIKAM

Was killed on the Golan Heights in the first week of the Yom Kippur War. He was my first boyfriend, with whom I "made love," and that should be important. He was my boyfriend for two years. I can conjure up his appearance in words: very tall, shoulders sloping slightly forward, black hair on a chest that never got a deep tan, black hair on fingers strumming a guitar—"I'm just a poor boy . . ."—brows frowning in concentration like a little shelf jutting from his forehead, a prominent Adam's apple. I can describe him in words, but I can't really see him. He isn't present, and although I feel guilty towards him, there isn't enough substance in the memory to torture and chastise me. His ghost doesn't haunt me at night and I have never had nightmares about him.

What is there to say about a seventeen-year-old girl? What is there to say about someone who was nineteen years and three months old when he died? He was a good student. He was an outstanding soldier and an outstanding tank commander, or so I was told. Amikam read two newspapers every day, Amikam wrote a fine essay on *Escape from Freedom* by Erich Fromm, Amikam was a counselor in the Zionist Socialist youth movement Hashomer Hatzair, he liked Joni Mitchell and Joan Baez, he couldn't dance and he could fix things, and everything he did he did seriously and with concentration, with the tip of his tongue between his teeth, his black brows frowning. Once, when I tried to remember his touch, I thought of a wooden board.

I didn't go to his funeral. When he died Hagar was already there, a baby of five months, and I was detached from my surroundings owing to my madness and my motherhood and because of the melodramatic pose I had adopted. I heard about his death weeks after he fell and it was too late to pay a condolence call to his parents. And anyway, how would I go? With the "accident" baby in my arms? I didn't even fit the role of the ex-girlfriend, their son's first sweetheart. And, in any case, they bore me a grudge.

I don't intend to dig up what happened with Amikam, the way I treated Amikam. Such things happen, when I did what I did I didn't know that he was going to get killed, and, anyway, it isn't him I've been carrying around for the past twenty-nine years. Amikam comes into this story only because one evening he took me to an apartment on Usha Street, in the old Jerusalem neighborhood of Nachlaot, where I still live today.

THE SECOND OF JULY

Amikam related to politics with the same thoroughness and deliberation with which he prepared for his final exams, with which he mended a coil in the electric heater, with which he "went all the way" with me. When he was asked about his political views he was in the habit of replying that he "saw himself as part of the New Left," and for months before his conscription he was engaged with the question of whether he should "go even further to the left," in other words, left of his parents who were active in MAPAM, the Zionist-Socialist United Workers Party.

Amikam took me to Usha Street because a graduate of the youth movement who had "gone even further left" told him about an interesting group that met there in the evenings. History students. Activists from poor neighborhoods. Artists. Students at the Bezalel Academy of Art. And so on. I didn't want to go. In arguments I couldn't get out of I showed the proper degree of enthusiasm, but the truth is that politics interested me less than they did Amikam, and the thought of entering a strange house with a group of people older than myself embarrassed me. We lived mainly among our peers, and the world of the free spirits who had already completed their army service seemed to me like a vague and distant dream. A magical stage which would no doubt arrive, but which we were still too callow to be fit to enter. I knew that I would be ashamed of my very presence in their space, and I knew that I might very well, however unjustly, also be ashamed of Amikam. And nevertheless I went. I went because I was his girlfriend. And I went because the next day we were due to take our final exams in literature; and on the pretext that we were going to study late into the night, I received permission from my mother to sleep over at his house, in his sister's room.

Thirty-six steps of an external stairway led to the apartment on the second floor. I didn't count them then. Forget the prophecies of the heart: No premonition told me that for the next twenty-nine years I would go up and down them about seventy thousand times, a few hundred of them with a baby carriage; no tingling of my toes hinted that I would wound my exposed big toe four times on the rusty can holding the sick jasmine bush that refused to die; that in certain moods I would decide to change the soil and plant a new bush there, and in others I would plan to drag it to the dumpster, and that I would never do either; I had no inkling that I was to see the top of the shaky iron banister covered with a strip of snow, and that its unsteadiness would worry me from time to time, and that about this too, I would do nothing.

Entering the apartment was as embarrassing as I had imagined. The noise inside was so loud that the students/artists/neighborhood-activists did not hear us knocking, and when they finally opened the door it turned out that Amikam's acquaintance "who had gone even further left" wasn't there. The bearded man who opened the door identified himself as "Hamida," and when we said together "What?" and "Sorry?" he barred our way and demanded to know whether or not we recognized the right to self-determination.

His real name was Yoash, and Yoash, as an expression of his right to self-determination, had gone to the Ministry of Interior and demanded to have his name changed to "Hamida." The Ministry of Interior, for its part, had argued that "Hamida" was the name of an Arab woman, that a Jewish male could not call himself "Hamida" on the grounds of fraud and imposture, but Yoash insisted on his right to call himself whatever he liked, and his correspondence with the Ministry of Interior and with the lawyers he badgered to represent him for nothing, as a public service, filled a shiny orange folder which he took with him wherever he went. I learned these details later; at the threshold, the exchange was confined to Amikam's declaration that we did indeed recognize the right to self-determination, a slogan which served as the "open sesame" that let us in to the apartment.

Amikam and I sat on a mattress while a passionate debate about the Organization of African Unity stormed above our heads. Anyone listening might have gained the impression that the question of whether Africa should unite would be determined on Usha Street, and if so, around what principles, for example whether the spread of Islam was a stage that could be skipped, or whether "we had to go through it." Someone lectured with astonishing knowledge about colonialism and Liberia, colonialism and Cameroon, colonialism and Ethiopia, Somalia, the Congo, Congo-Brazzaville, Burundi, and I remember thinking that I should know something about all these places; my father traveled a lot to those parts of the world, to make devil-knows-what connections and to negotiate all kinds of deals. The business he had entered a few years before was called the Agricultural Development Corporation, and from then on the hall table was covered with shiny brochures in English and French, with photographs of a black man driving a red tractor, and a black scientist holding up a test tube like a wine glass and flashing a white smile from ear to ear. During all his years on the kibbutz my father had never worked in agriculture, except for the seasonal mobilizations it was impossible to get out of, and his partners in the enterprise had retired from the army only a little while before he did so himself, but to this day he continues to insist that "although the company had expanded its interests from grain storage to heavy equipment and other areas of aid," it had never sold anything shady to any shady regime. What do I know? What did I know then? Only that from the day he became a civilian the house filled up with all kinds of junk from Africa—families of carved elephants, masks inlaid with mother-of-pearl, stinking leather gourds—and nevertheless I couldn't place Liberia on the map. But why am I dwelling on my father? And who cares about Liberia? And what do I care today about which theoretical organizations that group was debating then? I didn't sit down to tell nostalgic tales about the Jerusalem folklore of student radicals in Nachlaot in the seventies—and here I am already dragging in "jasmine bushes" and "Bezalel" and "Yoash-Hamida"—and with this kind of decor, in a couple of pages I'll have turned myself and my life into something affected and anecdotal. It's very easy to present yourself as a charming bunch of anecdotes, but it wasn't for the sake of being charming that I sat down to write, nor was it to capture the "period" and its "atmosphere," which in any case I have no desire to remember.

It took some time before anyone paid us any attention. We sat down low and looked at the sandaled feet of the debaters taking the floor opposite us, and in the air was a strong scent the name of which was then unknown to me. Patchouli, I later learned.

Amikam looked as if he was concentrating hard, the tip of his tongue between his teeth, trying to focus on one of the discussions out of the several taking place simultaneously. Simultaneity wasn't his strong point, but nevertheless he managed to turn to look at me and scowl when I lit one cigarette with another; despite the nausea induced by the unaccustomed amount of nicotine, I was chain-smoking. The person who addressed me in the end was a very fat girl, with a vast heaving bosom and agitated gestures, someone swaying above me and enthusing about her experiences at a "La Mama" workshop. She wanted to know what I did; I said I was in the middle of my final exams, I was being drafted in November, and of course I didn't know yet what I was going to do in the army. It was one of those moments when for no evident reason an interval of silence suddenly comes into being in all the conversations being conducted in the same space at the same time, so that everyone heard me saying: "What I'd like most is to be an operations room clerk in a commando unit and the thing I most dread is being stuck in an office in Tel Aviv." This was not the right thing to say to a girl just back from six months in New York in a "La Mama" workshop. And it wasn't the right thing to say in that place. The owner of the heaving bosom puffed out her already swollen cheeks, holding back her laughter, and in the embarrassing silence a "tsss" of ridicule was heard from the direction of the kitchen.

"It's important to me to contribute," I added, in a panic, aware of the looks recognizing my panic. The only matches left in my matchbox were burnt.

"Contribute to whom? Contribute to what?" A boy in ostentatiously ugly thick black glasses looked both amused and irate. I tossed my bangs out of my eyes and, without any idea of what I was about to say, avoided the question in a defiant voice, with a statement that was completely new to me: "Obviously if I can't really contribute, then I'd prefer not to serve at all." Without looking at Amikam I felt him turning his head, and this was also the moment that I saw Alek.

"There's nothing funny about what. . . . " He was standing directly opposite me, leaning on the kitchen door frame, the leaning hand holding a closed book, with one finger inside it marking his place.

"Noa."

"What she says isn't funny. Her voice doesn't make me laugh." His pronunciation was very clear, with almost no trace of a foreign accent, except for certain soft vowels; only his pronunciation was excessively clear, separating the words; and when he paused they waited for him to continue. "Noa is a woman," he continued at his leisure, "you don't laugh at what happens to a woman. An authentic person would understand what she's saying . . . what it means . . . and what her voice is saying to him. . . . What is it saying?" he repeated the question obediently echoed back to him by one of the girls in his audience. "It's saying that she needs to be freed. It's saying that a man has to marry her, and all the other girls who are beginning to think like Noa. There have to be men to go with all of them to the Rabbinate and free them from the army by marrying them."

AND THEN HE SAID TO ME AND THEN I SAID TO HIM

I reread the "he said and I said," and "then he asked me, and then I answered him"—the description is accurate, but nevertheless I can't find even the nucleus of an explanation of what happened afterwards in it. Perhaps I should have run the moments like a silent movie. A very young woman sits on a mattress on the floor, hugging her knees and smoking. The camera follows the woman's look, a look from below, takes in bits of detail: dirty toes, thick ankles, cutoff jeans ragged at the edges, a heaving bosom, a jaw moving in speech, a jaw moving in mastication. An orchestra accompanies the pictures with a cacophony of sound and suddenly stops. The young Valentino, he was so young then, stands in a relaxed pose in the frame of an open door. He has black hair cropped as short as a convict's, he is wearing a very white tee shirt, and is standing far enough away so that the woman's look, still from below, can take him in at full length. The man speaks, without marked expressions, without gesticulations, a restrained foreign body, and when he stops talking the orchestra begins to play again, but now the music has one clear theme. The man lingers in the doorway and his look rests on the girl, who is fiddling with a packet of cigarettes. After a long moment he reaches out his hand and beckons her to him with two fingers. The girl gets up and goes to him, he lights her a cigarette, and they both disappear into the kitchen.

Love can be described as compulsive thinking. The thought buzzes and buzzes like an insect stuck to a wet picture. And in the days to come I would be stuck on two gestures from the opening scene:

The man signals "come here" with his finger, and the girl gets up and comes. It's the kind of gesture with which you beckon a child. Or a servant. Or a waitress, if you haven't got any manners. Is the girl not aware of this? And how she is. And nevertheless—oh, the shame of it—she gets up. Not "in spite of" the gesture but because of it. Let's admit that the nonchalant movement of the finger turns her on, as if it's moving between her legs.

The foreign man looks into her eyes, and with a foreign gesture he lights her cigarette. And afterwards too, in the kitchen, he keeps on watching her and offering her a light, instead of giving her the lighter so that she can light up herself.

Compulsive thinking latches on to details and dwells on them as if they hold enormous significance which cannot be grasped in a moment. It keeps returning to them again and again as if there is still something left to understand. The more I think about the meaning of these gestures the sicker I get of my thoughts and of myself for thinking them. Mulling over the subtleties of gestures and their erotic nuances like some idiotic character in a genteel English romance.

You won't find any such absurd courting rituals in my Nira Woolf stories. No *luuuve* and no brooding thoughts. Not with Nira. Since she's my character and I invented her, obviously I constructed her according to my taste: my heroine would never go in for such nonsense as "and then I said to him" and "and then he kept quiet and didn't say anything." And nobody would beckon my heroine with his finger—"come here." Because if anyone ever uses that gesture in my books—and I don't think anyone will—it will only be Nira herself. She'll beckon and the man will come, and they'll fuck on the carpet before anybody can say Jack Robinson. And she won't spend too much time thinking about it afterwards either, because my James Bond with the perfect female body has more important things to think about.

Nira Woolf conducts herself according to my beliefs, and I don't conduct myself according to them, and although I can argue in my defense that at the age of seventeen I didn't know what I believed yet, that argument lost its validity a long time ago.

I can imagine Nira Woolf listening to my "he looked at me" and "he went on looking at me," stroking one of her monstrous cats under its chin, flexing a muscle in her arm and yawning with boredom. At some point she would cut me short and say: "Okay, okay, okay, I get the point, so what happened? Did you fuck on the carpet?"

Yes, I went to bed with Alek that night, not on the carpet but in his carved wooden bed that I still sleep in to this day.

I could have written that in the way my heroine would have approved of, in other words, wittily. I could have mocked him and the foolish girl I was until Nira Woolf split her sides laughing. But that's not the reason why I sat down to write.

THE MARKETPLACE OF ANECDOTES

The temptation always exists to be flippant at your own expense in the marketplace of anecdotes and then to go around with your hat and collect the laughter. Everything's a joke nowadays, everything's a laugh, it's the fashion. So that feeling seriously has become utterly and completely pathetic. A kind of social impropriety which only a real blockhead would be guilty of. You won't usually catch me making this kind of *faux pas*, because I am a polite person, I have self-respect and I don't want to cause embarrassment either. And since I'm such a classy gal, everything about me is classy too. In other words, in the framework of the anecdote and the shtick, the best thing about a good shtick is that like a hawker in the marketplace you can dish it out to people like a tasty morsel of yourself.

So I could sell you this wild shtick about how I got turned on by Alek, and how from the thing we had together I got pregnant, and how afterwards I got back into that whole scene again; and it'll all be terribly flippant and witty, how I'll laugh at her, and for a few moments perhaps I'll even feel healed, because I'll be really capable of laughing at "her," who by then is already not completely me.

The truth is that emotional seriousness involves not a little stupidity. The stupidity lies in that toad-like inflation itself, as if vis-à-vis all the terribly painful and terribly important and terribly, terribly terrible things happening in the world, Noa Weber jumps up and croaks out loud: Listen, listen, look, look, I too have something terribly painful and terribly important to tell. Something about my tortured soul. Something about my delusions.

Nira Woolf, for example, would not make that mistake, because my Nira is first of all a moral being, and it's quite clear to her what's important and what's not. Fighting for the rights of dispossessed Arabs, defrauded patients, oppressed women, abused children, and so on, exposing the "system," saving the innocent and stamping out evil—that's important. But pining and whining about *luuuve* when your heart's broken, all that's just self-indulgence and nonsense as far as she's concerned.

"Your heart aches because of some man?" she would say. "Nonsense, darling, just hypochondria, a little twinge you've decided to blow up out of all proportion. But never mind, sweetie, if you want to feel sorry for yourself, you go right ahead. And I hope you never know what real pain feels like."

SO WHAT IF

So what if the soul stole its trembling from a body trembling with terror? And what if the aching of the heart was plundered for metaphorical purposes from those suffering the agonies of real pain? And if I say: there is no soul, there's no such thing, the trembling soul is nothing but literary bullshit, will the trembling of that non-existent entity stop? Like hell it will.

Because what does it help me to know that the heart is a muscle, just a blood-pumping muscle, if my heart still goes out to him, and the bloody muscle still yearns and swells?

IN SHORT, WHAT HAPPENED

Noa: Where are you from?

Alek: You don't want to know. Too many places.

Noa: What places?

Alek: It won't mean much to you. I was born in Sverdlovsk, later we lived in Moscow, Warsaw, Paris, and there were a few more on the way. A Jew's story.

1) He made me coffee in a thick glass and served it on a saucer. Afterwards he opened the iron shutters and watered the pink geranium on the bars. In spite of all the glasses and plastic bottles piled up there during the evening, the kitchen looked clean.

2) When he filled the *finjan* with water to make coffee he put his book down on the marble counter. It was a German book. Alek said that when he finished everything he intended doing, next July, in one

year exactly, he was going to fly from here to Heidelberg, and I, without any justification or logic, felt a little vacuum of surprise and insult opening inside me. "Heidelberg?" I asked, and Alek said: "Why not? All kinds of interesting things started from there. And anyway, I have a scholarship for Heidelberg."

3) People who were in the kitchen before us gradually left, and those who came in after us took what they wanted and quickly went out again. Because of us.

4) I asked him what he meant when he talked about my voice, and Alek said: "It has to do with slavery and also inner freedom. People, as you know, speak in several voices, you can distinguish by the sound and the content." When I said "an operations room clerk in a commando unit" he heard the foreign, banal voice, we all have foreign voices like that that speak from our mouths and they are what make us slaves. But when he heard me suddenly say that perhaps I didn't want to serve in the army at all, something changed, and for a moment he thought that he was hearing my authentic voice. Like a clean note.

All these are distant memories, twenty-nine years is a long time, and I remember exactly only because in the days and hours that came afterwards I returned to them again and again and again, like learning a lesson by rote.

I remember that although I didn't really understand what he said, it seemed to me that I understood, and in any case I had no desire to break the atmosphere of clandestine understanding in which we had wrapped ourselves. Because of this atmosphere of secret, self-evident understanding it seemed we were only talking for the sake of talking and that there was actually no need for words at all.

Perhaps because of our lengthening silences, perhaps because the others began to leave, perhaps because he had spoken before about voices—I suddenly became aware of the record which had apparently been playing for some time in the background. Not the Rolling Stones or Pink Floyd or Led Zeppelin, and not Joni Mitchell. Not Judy Collins or Dave Dee, Dozy, Beaky, Mick, and Tich. Something completely different was playing there. Something I'd never heard before, the angelic voices of women singing to God.

A MUSIC SEMINAR

The months to come were, among other things, a concentrated seminar on music, or to be more precise on Alek's forty-something records. My musical experience up to then consisted of one year of recorder lessons on the kibbutz, shrieking community singing on bus trips, and Amikam's not absolutely tuneless vocal accompaniment to his guitar strumming.

With my lack of any musical education I had no possibility of identifying the "irony" Alek found in Stravinsky, of relating to his "inner freedom" or his "playfulness," nor to compare different performances on the music programs on the radio. But nevertheless I learned what I could as quickly as a dog, both because of the sensitized senses of love, and because I had no choice, a simple matter of conditioning. I very quickly learned that Schubert's symphonies fulfilled the role of elevator music for him, something played in order to hear neither the music nor anything else. And with the Fifth or the Eighth Symphony in the background, pulled over his head like a helmet, it was better for me not to be seen or heard if I didn't want to see a blank face or hear a formal voice, flat to the point of sarcasm, answering me.

One degree further than Schubert—I'm talking about degrees of torture here—were hours of Sibelius, with a couple of works by Dvořák thrown in. Because they were the sign that Alek had opened the sluice gate of despair, not reading, not working, just lying in bed and smoking. If anyone knocked at the front door, he wouldn't answer. Would he be angry if I opened it? Would he be angry if I didn't? Because if there was anyone at the door it wasn't me they were coming to see. Nobody came to see me.

My musical conditioning was such that to this day it's enough for me to overhear a couple of notes from a radio, or the window of a house, for my whole body to react immediately. Or sometimes it happens the other way around: first the body reaction and the images return, and only seconds later do I become aware of the sound stimulus in the background. One morning last summer when Hagar was visiting I woke up with an old joy, smelling a whiff of the Flex shampoo that I didn't have in the house and hadn't bought for years. A Debussy piano sonata was playing and announcing a morning of the *good morning to you* kind, a morning promising a day of cheerful well-being in our abode. Soon the winter sun would warm my shoulders in the kitchen. "Yesterday I bought us strawberries in the market," and "Why don't you slice some bread? Should I put cream and sugar on the strawberries?" And at those moments of waking my whole body was invaded with a sense of youthful joy, until a woman's voice on the "Voice of Music" interrupted the fantasy and identified the stimulus.

Of the forty-something compositions constantly playing then in the background, I taped only one in the days to come, and it too I only play very rarely, in a kind of bitter surrender to sweetness. *Gregorian Chants* was written on the brown record sleeve.

The low pealing of a single great bell, low voices slowly gathering as if coming from a great distance, and the sense of infinite space opening up a window open to the rain opens to . . . and slanting rain wets the gas ring and nobody cares. Alek embraces me from behind and puts his hand on my rounding belly. I listen, closing my eyes and putting my hand on my flat stomach, and like then, with my head falling back, I slow time down on the waves of the slow singing over an infinite expanse. Like then, I slow time down, delaying and at the same time waiting for the return of a certain note and a certain moment. Because before he goes back to his room Alek turns me round to face him and his face is completely open. He turns me to him and looks at me as if he admits everything, and as if he is thankful for everything, and a great grace envelops us both.

For some mysterious psychological-biographical reason rooted in the distant past, in those days he associated church music with erotic feelings, as if religion permitted sex, and as if sex had no value unless it connected you to the wings of angels.

It's difficult for me now to think of this religious eroticism in its raw, youthful, "consumer" incarnation; to think of how we "consumed" this music, to think of all the tours of churches we "consumed." His favorite was the one in the Garden of Gethsemane, and the descent on foot from the Mount of Olives. He never touched me there, but when we stood there I knew how he would touch me later.

It's strange to think of that particular music as a "substance" to be consumed, but that's how I opened up to him then, by "using" this "substance." That's how I felt I was opening up. And the world actually opened up again and again, in this mystical pretension, as if the contact of body with body brought us into contact with something greater than we were. Bringing down Bach's "Joy" on us, bringing down joy on all the world.

Because we were really into it, boy were we into it: with the heavenly sex, with sex and heaven, and the Kyrie eleison, oh God, have mercy on us, oh Agnus Dei, save us, yes, yes, just so, *sanctus, sanctus, sanctus*. Until we came together on this pretentious trip. On the third movement of Bach's Mass, on the first night.

We came together, I say, but the truth is that the first time only Alek came, while I had the mental equivalent of an orgasm. Our movements weren't yet sufficiently coordinated, the coordination came later, and somehow coming wasn't in the least important. A faint orange light illuminated the room from outside. An orange light illuminated his face. And the sight of his slender face looking tortured in the light was important.

Something in me was no doubt screwed up before that, and Bach is not to blame for the fact that from the beginning I fucked Alek, from the beginning I cleaved to Alek, as if I was seeking salvation.

IF YOU ASKED ME TODAY

My daughter turned twenty-nine this spring, and she's almost eleven years older than I was then. Sometime or other, when she was serving in Training Camp 12, I think, she began talking solemnly about something she called my "spiritual needs," and whenever my daughter returns to the subject of her "spiritual needs," we get into a fight. However hard I try to stop myself I can't suppress the aggression this combination of words arouses in me. Once, six or seven years ago, she tried to explain to me something about the "spiritual need," or maybe it was the "cultural need," because of which she chose to study Judaism, and in response to this I remarked that "If we're already talking about needs, haven't you noticed that the toilet paper in the bathroom's finished?" Afterwards, for a month, consistent as usual, Hagar ignored my attempts to butter her up and refused to speak to me, and when in the end she relented, I almost pushed her into a renewed silence when I remarked that "needs" sounded like the jargon of politicians or social workers.

Since in the end I satisfied her needs by financing her studies, we ended up with a fashionable agreement to disagree. "Tolerance," they call it.

Today my daughter is studying in New York, for the rabbinate, God help us, and intends to take responsibility for the "spiritual, religious, and cultural needs" of others. From time to time she sends me papers, articles, or little sermons she has written, and in all of them God appears, with complete naturalness, in one form or another. "Redemption" and "the soul" are frequently featured too. Chaos neatly packaged and filed in a clear card-index with an enlightened message. Social justice, relationship, community, responsibility, love, and peace.

"Wasted on me," I write to Hagar, "I was born deaf to God and the sublime, eternity, the soul and redemption, and I definitely regret it. If you want your mother 'to accept you as you are' you'll have to accept me as I am, and stop looking for my nonexistent religious sentiments. I have no such latent sentiment, I have never had them, and, if you ask me, the world would look a lot better without eternity, redemption, and so on." I refrain from adding that her god of social justice bores me, and that her "congregation" that comes to get a taste of "Jewish spirituality" before Saturday brunch makes me sick.

What would my daughter say about the sexual-religious sessions in the course of which she was created? I sometimes wonder if their shadow is sailing in her blood.

If you were to ask my opinion today, that is to say my official opinion, then fucking is for fun, fucking is for the simple joy of it, and all the rest, dear sisters, is pure and total bullshit. That's what I think, that's what I think I think, but if that's what I think, how come certain sounds make my fingers breathe? And how come I revive the pain inside me as willingly as I revive the pleasure? And how come for years I haven't found any fun for its own sake in fucking for its own sake?

I can mock Alek's bands of angels until tomorrow, I can talk about the ostensibly illegitimate way he used church music in order to "create an atmosphere" conducive to getting me into bed. And in fact, perhaps not only me. So what? Others used protest songs against the war in Vietnam, or against the atom bomb, or against capital punishment, as a smooth slide into bed, and that's not the point. A musical accompaniment is only an accompaniment, and it accompanies what exists without it too.

The point is that with Amikam I waited for the earth to shake, which is bad enough to begin with, and with Alek I expected even more, I went even further, from bad to worse. The earth wasn't enough for me, suddenly there were the heavens above too. And with all my soul I longed for that heaven to open, and even though I don't recognize the existence of that heaven, for a moment it seemed that it had opened and that *lux, lux, lux perpetua* was illuminating my soul, whose dubious existence I don't admit to either.

I should have written to my daughter: At the age of eighteen you were much wiser than me. You knew how to identify your evil instinct, and to tame it like a cute puppy whose name is "need."

"God," my daughter repeatedly explains to me, trying to appease my anti-religious feminism and annoying me with the increasingly educational tone taking over her letters, "my God isn't a man." And she also writes: "If you would find the time to read at least a few chapters of the collection I sent you (from your last letter I understand that you haven't read it yet) you would discover that in our culture God has a feminine aspect, too. And this feminine aspect can be stressed in study and developed in interpretation."

My darling daughter, my sweet and kosher Hagar, first cuts off God's prick, and then fakes a religious orgasm, and in English what's more.

But my daughter with her castrated God—does she really believe in His existence? I've never been able to understand it—my daughter with her emasculated Sublime, divested of both His prick and His wrath, will never turn love into religion or confuse a man with God like her mother did.

THE WINK

When most of the guests had already left, Amikam came into the kitchen. "Are we going?" he asked me. When I try to remember his face, it's the way it looked then that I remember: frowning, worried, slightly downcast, not looking me in the eye.

A devil got into me. Or I grabbed a devil by the tail and jumped onto its back. I swear, a minute before I opened my mouth I had no idea what I was going to say. "We're not going, you're going. You're going and I'm staying." He didn't deserve such a slap in the face. He had never done anything to justify it. Or the cold smile that appeared on my face when he failed to react immediately. Out of the corner of my eye I saw Alek leaning against the marble counter, hugging himself with one hand and smoking with the other.

And Amikam left. For some reason I turned to the window and watched him going down, down, down the steps. I didn't know that he was going to die. How could I have known? Who was I to know? Even the head of military intelligence didn't know that a war was going to break out. And in any case Amikam's death has nothing to do with this scene, and the death does nothing to change the nature of the deed. But what exactly was the deed? What did I think I was doing? A cold, arrogant gaiety bubbled inside me like an unfamiliar drug, and my voice too was new in my ears.

Strange that I felt no guilt for that gratuitous cruelty, only shame, a cringing shame, especially for the gesture that came afterwards. Because when Amikam was already at the bottom of the stairs he turned his head and looked straight at the window, and when his eyes met mine, suddenly and for no reason, in a kind of clownish grimace, I winked at him. As if we were both party to some kind of practical joke, as if it was only a joke, and as if he had some part in this trick I was playing. A thousand years have passed since then, and to this day when I remember it that grimace distorts my face. An unformed seventeen-year-old putting on—what character exactly? One minute I was the reckless Sally Bowles, the next minute I was somebody else, and the next the devil knows who.

In those days, as far as I can remember, the phrase "no big deal" was not yet part of our vocabulary, but that's what that clownish grimace of a wink was apparently meant to convey to Amikam. "Relax, I was only joking, it's no big deal." But it was a lie. It was a big deal, and I knew it even then.

Because it's a fact that seconds afterwards I turned to Alek as if I'd proven something, and as if I was now worthy.

A lot's happened since then, a whole history has happened since then, more important things than a stupid wink, than some whim of no significance whatsoever. Only my fixated brain would be capable of latching on like that to a momentary grimace, and I still have to cover my face with my hands and wait and wait, quietly, quietly, quietly, until the spasm passes.

A few words nevertheless about what happened afterwards. Love has its own cruel and banal laws, and in the wake of my scorpion bite, as if doomed by these laws, Amikam was truly poisoned. It was no longer a matter of feeling "the right thing" for a boy and a girl to go to bed together. And it was no longer a matter of a "healthy, normal feeling." He haunted me, he felt haunted by me, in spite of and in opposition to his declared contempt for me. How predictable are these shameful moves—first he waited for me to come and explain and apologize, I could see the tense anticipation and the anxious awareness of my presence, I saw it in his posture, even when he engaged himself in conversations at the school gate before and after exams. And when he saw that I had no intention of approaching him, because what could I say, he came up to reproach me, and when I still had nothing to say except for I can't help it, he haunted me.

For months he wrote me from the army, scornful and imploring letters, delving and searching for words that would change my heart, clinging to the hope that somewhere, in some nook or cranny the magic words existed, and all he had to do was search diligently to find them.

But there were no such words because no such words exist, and when his letters arrived I was already enmeshed in my misery and I read them and threw them away without being touched by them. In love, I think I have already said, there is no solidarity, and his clumsy, stilted style—and also, I have to confess to my shame, his spelling mistakes—embarrassed me; they embarrassed me as if they were a parody of myself and my own unique love. In any case, I thought, it isn't me he loves, but the capricious, reckless character I was playing then. Like falling in love with a character in a movie.

On several occasions he lay in wait for me outside the house. And once he popped up in the rain and barred my way. "So this is what you want, so this is how you like it," he hissed at me as he pushed me against the fence. His hair was wet, his face was wet, and his teeth were clenched over me. My pregnancy was already showing and my five-month belly was crushed against the trousers of his uniform. He had received a twenty-four-hour pass on the pretext of needing to have a wisdom tooth extracted, and after the tooth which didn't need to be extracted at all had been extracted, straight from the dental clinic, with half his jaw still numb, he came to wait for me in the street. I learned all this later, from another letter he wrote me, and this too did not touch me.

I don't want to think about him. He's not my fault, and it's not my fault that his expression looked ridiculous to me. As ridiculous as the way he grabbed my hands and held them behind my back, as if he was copying some manly gesture he'd seen in the movies, only the imitation was too transparent, like an actor in a bad audition. I shook him off without any difficulty. Without any difficulty because at this point I had nothing to offer in any case and nothing to give. Not to Amikam or to anyone else who wasn't Alek.

FRAGMENTS

He asked: "Are you expected at home? Should I take you home now?" And I said: "There's no need, I'm allowed to stay over, I've got my final exams in literature tomorrow." He was amused by the literature exam. "What are you being examined on?" "Tons of stuff. The poets of medieval Spain, Tchernikhowsky, Bialik, Leah Goldberg, Amir Gilboa, five Agnon stories, *Pere Goriot(??)*, *Crime and Punishment*, and that's not all. I like *Crime and Punishment* best, in my opinion it's the most profound, except for the character of Sonia which isn't very convincing." This amused him even more. I didn't yet know that Alek was studying Comparative Literature. "Interesting . . . why don't you find Sonia convincing?"

"Because she's too one-dimensional, too saintly, as if she isn't a prostitute at all. It's obvious that no such prostitute exists."

"You mean that Dostoevsky failed with her from point of view of social realism?""

"I mean that a prostitute can't be a saint."

"And you know this, that a prostitute can't be saint," he stated, without a question mark. I didn't know what to say to him, and I simply repeated like a literature teacher that Sonia was "a one-dimensional character, much more one-dimensional that Raskolnikov."

He pulled on a pair of pants and got up to make us tea. I remained naked. "If you have an exam tomorrow, you must sleep," he said and pulled the sheet up to my chin.

How did I come by the illusion that I "understood him," having only the vaguest notion of what he was talking about?

"Only someone with an individual voice of his own can describe what is impossible to describe," he quoted to me once, I don't know from where.

Alek turned off the reading lamp and went to his cubbyhole of a study, the little room where I am writing now. In the light coming from his room and the light of the street lamp coming from outside, I could still see things, and everything I saw gave rise in me to a feeling of wonder, as if something very wonderful and joyful were dancing and twinkling in all the objects in the world. As if something beyond comprehension and steeped in magic pervaded everything, and I had only just found out. An old wooden cupboard, a mirror in a wooden frame hanging on the wall, a picture of a pale green demon woman reflected in the mirror, the bamboo armchair with a white bedspread thrown onto it. And a chilly breeze sharpening the edges of my body, the touch of the sheet and the configuration of the cascading fabric on the armchair.

Wide awake, more wide awake than I had ever been in my life, I sensed everything with my gaze, and it seemed to me that my eyes could feel textures: the lingering touch of a fold of pale cloth; the dry touch of a pile of books; the hooked green touch of the she-devil's fingernails; the cold green touch of her figure in the mirror and the curly cold green of her hair. Below her, four patterned floor tiles, patched into the yellowish floor, the tendrils of a vine gaily twining over them.

With this gaze came the sensation that I was filling my body, that I was inhabiting all of it, and that I had been given a form. This was me-my-body, and these were my edges, and beyond them was living air. I extracted my hands from under the sheet, I twiddled my fingers in front of my eyes like a baby, and laughed softly with their movements.

Hello, hello, this is me in space.

At some point I got up and went to Alek. I stood behind him and put my hands on his shoulders. He didn't turn around, just held one of my hands with his and went on writing with the other. On the desk the German book I had seen before in the kitchen lay open, together with a German-Russian dictionary.

"What are you doing?" A question that in the days to come I learned not to ask.

"If I'm already going to Heidelberg, I should learn German."

"Tell me more."

"More about what?"

"More about the army. You were in the army weren't you?"

"Once a million years ago I studied medicine for half a year, so they made me medical orderly in the Golani Brigade. Logic of the Israeli Defense Forces."

"So why shouldn't a girl serve in the army?"

Alek sighed, turned round to face me, and sat me naked on his knees.

Woman (flirtatiously stubborn, arching her neck back and distancing her face from his kisses): No, explain to me....

Man (kissing her neck, slipping his hand between her legs): Explain to you what? You know everything.

Woman: But still ... explain....

Man: What can I explain to you? What? A soldier is a slave (turning her face towards him and giving her a deep kiss), a soldier is a slave (another kiss with his eyes closed), and a woman in the army is ... how do you say it? Slave of the slave.

Woman (with her eyes closed too): A bondmaid.

Man: Right.

ALEK'S FRIENDS

Alek wasn't keen on presenting his biography in an orderly fashion: "It doesn't matter now," "that's prehistory," "it wouldn't mean anything to you anyway." So that it took me months to put the facts of his CV together, and a lot longer to begin to understand something about them. And indeed, what could I understand from a sentence like "My mother's husband is Polish by origin, and because of that in '58 they let us leave." Because what did I know about it? I loved Dostoevsky and to a lesser degree also Tolstoy, they "spoke to me" and for some reason I assumed that I understood them. I liked the "Russian songs" we sang in the youth movement, until I saw that Alek detested them. And

I was fascinated by the tales my father used to tell about the "Russian lunacies" of the early days on the kibbutz. My mother would purse her lips whenever he told these stories. She was born on the kibbutz and he wasn't, so: "Not everything has to be talked about. Some things are better left alone."

Apart from that, there were the almost daily articles about the "Jews of Silence" and a lot of arguments about the dropouts at the transit station in Austria, and one graffiti on Gaza Street next to the Prime Minister's house: "The Russian Jews want to go home? Let them go home." To put it plainly, I didn't have what's called a background, I didn't know a thing, not about the country Alek called his "prehistoric motherland"—France he sometimes referred to as his "historic motherland"—and not even about a mother's husbands. I didn't know anyone who had a "mother's husband."

Alek wasn't any keener on explaining the facts than he was on revealing them, and in this he was completely different not only from Amikam but in fact from anyone else I knew. Questions like "If you were already studying in Paris, why did you actually come to Israel?" would make him close up completely.

"I thought this was a country of Jews," "The students there, in Paris, didn't really understand. They didn't have any clue about what their slogans meant. It was clear from the outset that the Communists would take over the whole thing, it couldn't have happened any other way." Sometimes he would produce sentences like this, but I didn't know what to make of them, even though I tried to look as if I understood. Somehow I grasped that Alek's politics too were different from those of the crowd that hung around in his house, but nothing in my education had prepared me to actually understand what he was saying.

More than twenty years later, in '93, when I came to him in Moscow, he began to talk to me about Russians and Russia, and he continued to do so in the six further visits I paid him. Perhaps the changed times made it easier for him to explain, and perhaps he needed the years of our common history to trust me. Perhaps he was also influenced by the fact that in these meetings he was the host, and therefore the guide by force of circumstance. In any event, one of the many things I didn't understand in '72 was how much of an Israeli I was in his eyes. And that "Israeli" meant foreign. It was enough for me that his Hebrew was almost flawless, it was enough that he had spent six months on a kibbutz and then served in the Golani Brigade, to take it for granted that he understood everything as I did. And more than that, that he understood me as I did.

Close to my final exams in Bible studies—an exam in which Alek showed a surprising interest—I adopted the verb "to know" as it is used in the Book of Genesis as part of my inner language: What, for example, did Adam know about his wife Eve? He didn't ask, investigate, clarify things to enable him to "know about" her, and nor did she, for her part, "know about" him. Adam knew Eve his wife, and Eve, so I decided, knew Adam. And this primordial knowledge, whatever its meaning, seemed to me the highest level of relationship. A kind of pristine knowledge, preceding words and names. An illumination that does not need biographical data, and is always felt as a miracle.

And even today, years later, I'm not sure that this subliminal knowledge was a total illusion. That is to say, if I were asked my official, rational opinion, it would be that it is impossible to know someone whose language you don't speak, whose memories you haven't investigated, whose associations are all foreign to you. A man for whom sounds and smells, words and tastes and concepts are associated with images about which you haven't got a clue. That's my opinion, I have no argument to contradict it, and nevertheless, in spite of my irrefutable opinion, what is it that happens when he turns my face to him, when he looks into my face, when I look at him while we're fucking? What else can I call it but pure knowledge? And a kind of recognition, as if we were predestined to know, and that nothing else is possible for me.

With the passing of the years, the more I thought about it, the more clearly I saw how much bullshit is involved in this kind of "knowing." "He looked into her eyes until he saw to the depths of her soul." "And then, in a moment of grace, his soul was revealed to her." "They were soul mates," and all the rest of that romantic novelette rubbish. So he fucks me with his eyes open, so I look at him without fantasizing, so I come at the same time as him without taking my eyes off him, so—what does it mean?

I say: It's sentimental crap, I think it's crap, it's clear to me that it's crap, and nevertheless, against my better judgement, I still feel it as a miracle, and I am still full of the grace of that knowledge.

I say that I had and still have a deep sense of knowledge, but this subcutaneous knowledge did nothing to abate my curiosity. I wanted to know everything—no detail was too trivial for me—and every detail I accumulated immediately split up into lots of new details charged with magic that also split up at the edges into radiant new reflections of light. Alert as a stalker, I spent my days watching him, me, us, trying to learn things from every word and gesture. This was a new, focussed activity that demanded all of me and concentrated all of me, very far from the soft, dazed state usually associated with lovers. And even now, when I recall those memories, it still seems to me that there is yet something to be learned in this story.

In the evenings the house would often be full of people. Looking back it's clear to me that he didn't regard them as friends or even like them, but for some reason he simply put his place at their disposal. Sometimes he would make them coffee, sometimes he let somebody else wash glasses or grapes from the market and serve, for the most part he seemed to observe them and their arguments from the side.

In the living room behind me—though for some reason I feel as if their scenes took place somewhere else—they chewed over the third world and the cultural revolution, capitalist technocracy and the tyranny of tolerance, artistic fetishism and the right to violence, and suchlike subjects. Menachem Levy wanted to burn down all the museums. Menachem Becker agreed to burn down the lot—except for Van Gogh. And with sentences like these they would burn entire evenings. Becker was a Trotskyite and Levy was a Maoist, or maybe the opposite, in any case I didn't know the difference, I just sat on the mattress and soaked up Marcuse and Sartre, the Red Brigades, the Rage Brigade, and urban guerrilla warfare.

Alek intervened only rarely, and when he did they listened to him. Once, I remember, it happened when they were arguing about Godard, what he was actually saying and exactly what kind of revolutionary he was. They appealed to Alek because Dalit had heard from somebody that he had met Godard and interviewed him for a student newspaper in Paris. And Alek, with demonstrative reluctance, said that Godard's political opinions were of no interest to him, nor were Mao's sayings in *La Chinoise*, nor what Godard thought about Mao's sayings. He had interviewed Godard because he was asked to do so, it was a job, there were people who thought that this was the way to write in a newspaper and these were the questions that should be asked, but they were in a house now, not a newspaper. "Of course Godard is a revolutionary, from ideological point of view the worst kind possible, but Godard is nevertheless the Schoenberg of cinema, and the important thing is the revolution an artist makes with his camera, and all the rest is just rubbish for politicians."

Sometimes when Alek finished speaking he would turn around and disappear into his little study or the kitchen. Sometimes in his absence they would go on arguing about what he said, but this was one of the occasions on which he silenced them. Not because they agreed with him, but because he had the halo of someone who had been a student in Paris and met Godard. I knew that Alek realized this, and that he despised them for it. And I also knew that they felt his contempt, and that the scorn only strengthened the spell he cast over them.

Now, looking back, they seem very young to me, forgivably young. "Abroad" was further away then than it is now, and certain abroads, like Paris, had a glamour then that it took years to dispel.

Most of the regular participants in the group were men, except for Dalit from "La Mama" who would always make a tempestuous entrance. He treated Dalit nicely, he never ignored her arrival, and it was the same with all the pretty faces with the plucked eyebrows who would turn up with someone or other, stick around for a week or two, and then be replaced. When they didn't come with a guy, the pretty girls would come in pairs, and huddle together like goslings waiting for someone to stick a worm in their beaks. Alek would clear the records or the occupant off a chair, make sure that the pretty face was comfortably seated in her short mini, and he never failed to ask her name and if he could get her anything. Occasionally a female made of sterner stuff would turn up, like for instance Osnat law-and-order who actually succeeded in forcing her way into the discussion. I admired this woman. She had an exquisite jaw and black, unplucked eyebrows, she would turn a chair around and sit astride on it, leaning her arms on the backrest and harangue us: "So ask yourselves—whose law and order? Law and order that serve what? That serve whom?" Because she impressed me, I assumed that she impressed Alek too, until I looked at his face.

In the morning I threw a neutral remark into the air anyway, to check out his reaction, and Alek raised his eyes from his book and gave me a long, faintly amused look. "I've known too many woman of this type," he said in the end and went back to his book, pinching his cigarette as usual between his thumb and two fingers.

Ten or maybe twelve years later, in the home of friends in Tel Aviv, I came across Osnat again. She taught in the history department at the university, published articles in the newspapers, she still turned her chair around, and she still smoked the same short Chinese pipe. Since she failed to recognize me and remember me from then, I felt free to touch the erogenous zone and remind her of "that crowd from Nachlaot." "Oh yes, them, sure . . . they were fucking male chauvinists, too, just like everyone else in those days." Beyond this sweeping generalization it appeared that the group had not remained in her memory, and we actually became quite good friends.

Opinions I heard on those evenings seeped into me gradually, and even though I lacked the intellectual background to understand them,

I started trying on ideas like a young girl trying on a dress: not in order to see if it fits her, but to see who it turns her into and who she looks like when she puts it on. "What's the difference between the actions of Black September against us and our bombing in Jordan?" I threw at my mother's back one evening during the weeks when I was still going home. "They hurt civilians and we hurt civilians. They took our athletes hostage in Munich, and we treat Jordanian civilians as hostages; so tell me why what Israel does is called war and defense, and what Black September does is called terrorism?"

• • •

"It's a good thing your father isn't here to hear you talk like that," my mother said grimly, draining the water from her steamed vegetables into the sink. "If you, Noa, don't know the answer to that question yourself, it would be better if you kept quiet and didn't shame yourself by such talk. We know very well who's influencing you, who's putting that nonsense into your head." My mother, unlike me, has never felt the need to try on opinions, and in this she resembles my daughter far more than me. My mother is a dietetic nurse, my daughter is about to become a rabbi, and they both relate with the same degree of seriousness to what goes into the mouth and what comes out of it.

Looking back, even though I agree in general with Osnat's verdict regarding the group's male chauvinism, it's clear to me that the seeds of my feminist views were planted during that period. At the time I didn't take any notice of the way they behaved towards women, it wasn't too different from the way my father or any other man I knew behaved, they certainly didn't count women among oppressed population groups, and neither did it ever occur to me to do so. And nevertheless questions like: "Law and order—that serve whom?" registered in my mind and left an impression, and years later, when I constructed the character of Nira Woolf, I gave her some of Osnat's gestures, and some of her views regarding the law.

("When Nira Woolf gives the sex slave her pistol, in order for her to use it, she is actually killing them both with one bullet: the slave trafficker and the oppressed woman. So that after the shot we are left with the body of a man, a dead female slave, and a living woman. She who was previously a slave and who is now a liberated woman." From my last interview about *What Did Mrs. Neuman Know?*)

Alek, as I said, didn't talk much, but before I finish with the folklore of those days in Nachlaot, I'll just mention one outburst of his. The discussion was not particularly lively—about the indifference of the Israeli student, the Sorbonne commune, the occupation, police brutality and the right to violence—and they were rehashing the subject of "the suppression of thought" again when Alek suddenly began to talk about the Prague Spring. I won't try to recapitulate everything he said, because more than I remember the content, I remember the tone. He sat slightly bowed in his chair and spoke quietly, without looking at any of us, speaking as if he was telling a very personal story, and one sentence kept coming back like a lament: "It was beautiful, the Prague Spring, it was beautiful, and I like a fool actually began to believe that the world was going to let it happen."

When the story was drawing close to its end, Alek raised his voice, glaring at us suddenly with a strange hostility: "Half a million Russian tanks crushed Czechoslovakia. They trampled the students, they trampled artists, they destroyed a hope that you'll never understand. People like you, who talk about repression, have no idea of what kind of freedom people were fighting for there." He stood up with a distorted face, close to tears or violence, and what happened afterwards was very much like flight.

In the space of ten minutes everyone had left the house, except for me and Hamida-Yoash, who took him to the kitchen and sat there with him until three in the morning emptying a bottle of vodka. The drink silenced Yoash and made Alek talkative and less sparing of gestures. "... It's the talking ... that's the problem, I can't stand the talking, not just Menachem's, the two Menachems, with them it's relatively easy, because they come right out and call themselves communists. I mean the others, all the others who haven't got faintest idea of what they're talking about," he lashed out at both of us, or maybe only at Yoash. "Even you, who're a friend and genuine human being, even you're like a communist. You all know best, you all know what's good for everyone, and you're all ready to drag us by the hair into a bright future. Forgive me, I apologize, I'm not just drunk, I'm pathetic, but I can't stand it physically, physically."

And nevertheless he treated Yoash differently from the rest. Alek needed money, I don't know if Yoash really needed his help in his work, but from time to time, at an evening's notice, he would ask him to come and paint a house with him. House-painting days were always good days. The pickup honking its horn outside early in the morning, and at dusk the two of them returning cheerful and spattered with whitewash, unloading vast quantities of meat and vegetables, and taking over the kitchen to cook and drink. I wasn't allowed to join in the cooking, it was a ritual with no room in it for a woman, and they sent me to "go for a little run outside." But when the meal was ready, at the table, my presence was very desirable. I loved sitting there between the two of them, happy and hungry from the running, bathed and shampooed after it, like an honorary member of the male fraternity. They filled my plate, poured me water, sliced me bread. "Hamida is my true friend," he would sometimes say, and examine me to see if I understood the meaning of the word. "I can see," I would answer seriously. More than once it happened that while we were sitting at the table somebody knocked at the door, and Alek would put his finger to his lips and signal the two of us to be quiet, ignoring the record player that betrayed our presence in the house. But there were days when he didn't even open the door for Yoash.

MARRYING NOA

I don't remember who began the teasing, but it was Danny Hyman who turned it into a running joke. Hyman was a law student, a man with small limbs, stiff movements and the pronunciation of a radio announcer. I detested him instinctively, and he for his part never threw a word in my direction. From time to time when they talked about freedom, and they talked a lot about freedom, Hyman would tap an American cigarette on its packet and point out that, "The trouble is that all we do is talk and talk, and nobody's prepared to do anything." Then he would stick the cigarette in his small mouth and add: "Alek, for example, thinks that we should liberate girls from the army. So why doesn't he marry Noa and free her from serving in the army?" After he had repeated this a few times, "Why doesn't he marry Noa?" turned into "Why don't we marry Noa?" or "Yeah, sure, and now let's go and marry Noa," a line that could be fallen back on by anyone wanting to put an end to any tedious debate, with the highly amusing conclusion that we were all impotent anyway.

I had no idea that Alek took this teasing seriously, until the afternoon after Yom Kippur.

The preceding twenty-four hours had not been easy. At this point I no longer needed excuses for not going home, but this week my father had flown in for a visit, and in order not to aggravate the tension that had started to accumulate, I presented myself for the meal preceding the fast, which in our case, needless to say, preceded nothing. When my mother set about polishing the sink, and my sister Talush's friends called her to come out to skate in the empty streets, I said a hasty goodbye and left. I ran most of the way from Ramat Eshkol to Nachlaot.

Alek had given me a key the first week, but when I saw a light on in the house I didn't use it, I knocked, and this was the first time that Alek opened the door and stood aside without touching, letting me in as if I was his roommate. "Is this not a good time for you?" "It's fine. You can come whenever you like. That's what the key is for." And he retired to his little study as if he was dividing the rooms up between us.

To my astonishment, Alek fasted, shutting himself up for the evening and the day and drugging himself on Sibelius, played softly so as not to disturb the neighbors. I spent the time staring at the pages of a book, sleeping and daydreaming alternately, disturbed by the lack of the routine sounds that divided the day into clear units of time and notified the body of its functions. There are three synagogues near the house, and in the bedroom the sounds mingled, with one prayer rising and then another, and all the time the subterranean current of Sibelius, coming to the surface only in the hot, heavy silence of the afternoon break, and giving rise in me to a miserable little whimper that punctured my trance.

At the end of the day, when the music stopped, Alek still didn't open his door and I fell asleep again, and when I woke up sweating in the middle of the night I discovered that he hadn't come to bed, that he must have gone to sleep on the sofa in his room.

I saw him again only the next day at noon, when he came in with a few of the regulars. The academic year was about to begin, and they were angry about some survey courses they were obliged to take and some teacher whose contract hadn't been renewed, for reasons which were only too clear: because of the way he talked about Dayan and because of that joke he told about Golda Meir. The heat wave had not yet broken, and they all looked worn out by the heat. Someone I didn't know suggested going on strike or publishing a statement, and this time it was Dalit who said: "Yeah, sure. You'll all go on strike, just like you'll all marry Noa." Alek was standing opposite her, clenching one fist in another in front of his chest, cracking pecan nuts which Yoash had brought from his parents' farm. A silence must have fallen, because I heard the sound of the crack, and then his voice saying: "Marry Noa . . . okay . . . Noa, do you want to get married?"

ALEK ASKED

Alek asked: "Do you want to get married?" And he didn't add, "to me."

But at the same time he said: "Do you want to get married?" and not "Do you want me to exempt you from serving in the army?" Which is perhaps a slightly different question.

Did I want to be exempt from army service? Until I met him it wouldn't have occurred to me for a minute not to be drafted, and apart from one classmate who had polio, I didn't know anybody who avoided army service, including those present in the room, including Alek himself.

The idea of serving in the army of occupation and oppression didn't bother me particularly, what troubled me was the new awareness that the IDF was about to oppress me. Girls from my year who had been drafted in August had already concluded their basic training and been sent to all kinds of bases to serve as clerks. And somehow it was clear to me that the new me couldn't be sent anywhere to serve anyone. That I would simply get up and run away if they tried to squeeze me into some asbestos office. It had no connection to ideology, or only a tenuous connection—my criticism of women's service in the IDF developed years later—I only knew that I wouldn't be able to bear it: I wouldn't be able to bear being sent away from Jerusalem, and I wouldn't be able to bear being sent away from Alek. Because I didn't have an ounce of attention to invest in anything that wasn't charged with my love.

Jerusalem was charged with love for me. The map of the city was imprinted in me with illuminated areas where the air grew bright and the vibration of my inner waves intensified, the concentrated areas where we had wandered together, and the further I receded from them in my imagination, the grayer I grew inside, disappearing from myself into the gray, flat nothingness.

Alek was going to leave for Germany in July, I had no doubt that he would leave, but until July there was still more than nine months to go, a short time, a long time. I couldn't consent to this time being taken away from me. Love had mobilized my entire being, love ruled me like a tyrant, and love would allow for no other master.

I reread the last couple of paragraphs and it's all true: I couldn't imagine myself leaving Jerusalem, I couldn't part from Alek, I wanted to buy more time, true and true and true, but there's one simple and shameful thing I haven't yet said. I loved Alek, and therefore I wanted to marry him.

GOING TO THE RABBINATE

I didn't look at him or at anyone else when I said: "Yes, I want to." And the next thing he said was: "Okay, then let's go and do it now, just tell me where to go."

At that moment he was a king, he was their prince, they admired him more than ever, and some of that admiration was directed at me too, so that the doubts as to whether we were "really going to do it" were addressed to us in the plural. For a few minutes "you" meant both of us, and that "you"—the crazy, impulsive, glamorous, free-spirited you—was intoxicating. At the first words of doubt Alek threw the cracked pecans into the basket, and on the spot, accompanied by all of them, we set out for the Rabbinate on Havatzelet Street.

I recall the movement with which he aimed the pecans and hold it in my imagination, and Alek in his white tee shirt looks like a boy, slender and cropped. He was then twenty-eight, almost as old as Hagar today. But even today when the touch of his thinness sometimes feels like the touch of old age—and only rarely like the touch of a slender boy—he is still the same Alek who clenched fist over fist, and so he will apparently always remain, never mind the metamorphoses of his body.

Dalit, Hyman, and two others I barely knew, dropped out on the way on various pretexts. Perhaps things had gone further than they intended, perhaps they had been infected by some other embarrassment, but three of them, surrounding the pair of us like tipsy bodyguards, accompanied us into the Rabbinate building and testified that they had known us from early childhood, and that they knew beyond the shadow of a doubt that Alexander Ginsberg and Noa Weber were single. And when the officials of the Holy One Blessed Be He began to inquire as to the exact date of Alek's arrival in Israel, it turned out that one of our witnesses was also a Ginsberg, just like Alek, and this Ginsberg quickly improvised all kinds of fibs about the family connection, about uninterrupted correspondence and frequent visits in Paris. "Alexander Ginsberg," babbled the ginger-haired Ginsberg, imitating the gossipy tone of the clerks, "Alek, as we call him in the family, is a confirmed bachelor. To such an extent that his mother began to worry that she wouldn't have any grandchildren, and my mother told her, send him to Israel, and you'll see that he'll soon find himself a nice Jewish girl to marry." And we all smothered hysterical giggles.

Alek was surprised to discover that we couldn't finish what we had come to do on the spot. The men were sent outside, and I was sent to have a talk with the rabbi's wife as a necessary preliminary to setting the date.

In the years to come I told the story of this interview countless times, it became part of my anecdotal stock-in-trade, which I polished up from time to time, perfecting the details of the scene, the asides and the timing. Now I'll be brief and stick to the facts: A short woman with her hair covered in a brown snood greeted me from the other side of a scratched office desk and without any preliminaries began to explain to me what a mistake it would be to bake my husband a chocolate cake every day, even if he hinted that he wanted it and even if he demanded it, because you get tired of even the best cake if it's served up every day. She reminded me of my mother with her nagging about the proper eating habits—"Chew, Noa, chew before you swallow."—except that my mother is a thin woman, and this one had a double chin tucked in over a swelling bosom. In my innocence I replied that I didn't know how to bake, and only when she sighed, and I, suddenly embarrassed without my male support group, stared at the bucket someone had left by the door, only then did I realize what the woman was talking about.

In the face of my surprising naiveté she abandoned the culinary metaphors and asked for details about my menstrual cycle. Was it regular? How long did it last? And when exactly was it due? I thought about the four who were presumably waiting for me outside, about Alek's impatience, and about what I would have to tell them in a few minutes, and with this to inspire me, as soon as I realized where all these questions were leading, I whispered that there was a problem, you understand, we have a problem because I'm pregnant. That's why we have to get married as quickly as possible, a quick, discreet wedding...perhaps right here in the Rabbinate? My face burned with a shame whose origins were different from what the rabbi's wife supposed.

Overflowing with concern she waddled with me to the clerk, who set the date for ten days' time, right after the holiday of Simchat Torah. "Light Sabbath candles," she recommended in parting, "forget the past, and explain to your husband that this is the time to make a new beginning and fortify yourselves with tradition. It's important to him too for his child to grow up like a Jew, why else did he come to Israel?. . . The mother is the foundation of the home, the wife is the foundation of the home, you'll see how your husband will respect you when you make him a Jewish home. You'll make him a Jewish home, and he'll make you a queen."

The really crazy joke in this story, the joke I never tell when I'm delivering the shtick, is that while I was inventing my urgent dilemma for the benefit of the rabbi's wife, the first cells of Hagar were already dividing inside me. And that I didn't have the faintest idea that I was pregnant.

I LOVED HIM

I loved him and I yearned to marry him. Even worse, I yearned for him to marry me, to take me to be his wedded wife, to sanctify me.

The rabbi's wife's double chin, the nagging tone of the clerks, the desks piled with cardboard files, the mop bucket—these details helped me to cover up my true desire for him to single me out to have and to hold, forever. The decor bespoke a seedy bureaucratic secularity, and I welcomed the ugliness. Since the marriage was not a true marriage, it was better this way, I thought, in all the ugliness of reality, in the harsh summer light, without any atmospherics to soften the facts, without any illusions. It was right, it was fitting, I was happy with it.

I loved him. And Alek wasn't in love with me. And in spite of my youth, I did not give way to the temptation to interpret various gestures of his as possible manifestations of love. I did not count my steps to the refrain of "he loves me, he loves me not, he loves me, he loves me not . . ." And even when I read between the lines—lovers will always read between the lines, they are never satisfied with the manifest content—I did not deceive myself by discovering signs of a feeling he did not possess. I loved him, and precisely for that reason, I knew that he didn't love me.

In the nature of things, according to the rules of the game laid down from the start, I did not try to hold seminars with him about the nature of our feelings for each other, their origins and destination. I saw that I aroused his curiosity, I saw that the curiosity and the enjoyment bordered on amusement, and as far as I was able I tried to join in the style of provocative flirtatiousness stemming from these feelings. To behave as if we were brother and sister up to some naughtiness.

It took me years to understand that in Alek's eyes I, Noa Weber, was the ultimate stranger, foremost because I was a woman. And for all his experience with the members of my sex, to this day he still tends to attribute a kind of alien mystery to us—as if we belonged to a completely different species, governed by incomprehensible inner laws, which a man, however hard he tried to penetrate the mystery, would never succeed in deciphering.

Beyond that—and this was something that was harder for me to understand—not only were we from different cultures, but he was the immigrant and I was the "WASP." Not just a WASP, but a descendent of the "Mayflower" in Israeli terms, forty-eight on my father's side, the pioneers of the early twenties on my mother's side. Which in itself was a reason for curiosity and investigation.

But nevertheless, in spite of the strangeness, it was clear to me that the cloak of naughty flirtatiousness I wore and the ideological reasons I spouted, did not deceive him. Alek knew that I was possessed, he knew it very well, and he chose to marry me nevertheless. Why did he do it?

Twenty, no, nearly twenty-one years later, the first time I went to visit him in Moscow—Hagar had already completed her army service—it happened that I asked him. In January one of the European newspapers he worked for sent him to write a series of articles on the upheavals in Russia, and Alek invited me to join him, and we were there together for a whole week.

One night I was standing in the hotel opposite the wide window sill, drunk with sex, sleeplessness, and vodka, and looking down from the thirty-sixth floor at the configurations of the cracks in the ice on the river below. Alek had parted the heavy curtains for me, climbed up, and opened the upper section of one of the tall double windows, and the icy air cleared my breathing body.

From the moment I had landed, my sense of distance had gone haywire, and at that moment it seemed to me that I could have put out a finger and touched the cracks in the ice, or the white marble of the parliament building on the other side of the river and the six-lane road. Something opened inside me, something opened and spread and adapted itself to the vast dimensions of the place. Alek lay on the bed behind me and smoked. I was electrified, I had wings, I was too awake even to lie down beside him. The height stimulated me. And ghosts of previous guests in the Stalinist tower, people who were once alive and were now dead. The privileged of the regime. The dead man on holiday who hung his suit up in the closet, the dead man who sat writing opposite the mirror, the dead man who, like me, dried his wet stockings in the bathroom—who were they? What nightmares did they have here on this bed? What nightmare did they imagine in detail when they were awake?

I thought: If somebody pushed me out of the window now I wouldn't fall. Weightless, I would glide over the city like a bird.

There is a pose that may well only exist in old movies: a man and a woman exchange important declarations while standing not face to face, but face to elegant back. If I'm not mistaken, a lot of the dialogue in *Casablanca* takes place this way, and I apparently had a romantic echo of that kind in my head when I asked Alek: "October '72 . . . I didn't ask you then, but why did you propose marriage to me?" I imprisoned the cold air inside me until he answered me, and when he answered I could hear the smile in his voice. "Maybe I wanted to see how far you would go with it." It was clear that he wasn't talking about my politics. "Did you have any doubts?" I asked.

"Yes, I think I did."

"It's no big deal."

"What do you mean?"

"That it all seems very small to me."

"It all seems small to you . . . if you say so. I remember things differently."

"What do you remember?" Alek sighed and didn't reply. "What? Tell me," I turned around to face him. "What do you remember?"

"I think it was hard for you."

"So what if it was hard? Maybe it wasn't hard for me at all. Maybe that was exactly how I wanted it."

"Really?" He examined me with narrowed eyes.

"Yes, really. Why are you laughing?" I asked, laughter in my voice too, and I sat down on the windowsill with my profile to him.

"You're beautiful."

"You don't believe me."

"Actually I do believe. That's beautiful too."

"What? What? What's beautiful?" The click of a lighter, and no answer. I put my hand on the window pane, tilted my head slightly, and with three fingers blocked the river. "You're wrong. It was never hard for me, not really," I said and examined the new window picture, "and on Wednesday too, when we say goodbye and I get on the plane, it won't be hard for me."

"If it isn't hard for you, good. I'm glad."

I freed the river and hid the road. "Have you noticed that someone could shoot straight into the President's residence from here?"

"There's already been a shooting here. But in the opposite direction. During the August putsch a photographer was shot in the window here. What are you doing there?"

"Looking at things," I answered like an intoxicated child. "You know what I think? I think I have a lot of strength. You know how much strength I have?"

"Enough to stop a bolting horse and enter a burning house."

"You're making fun again."

"I'm not making fun. Nekrasov wrote it. He wrote it seriously."

"Try me."

"How?"

"I don't know."

"You want me to try your strength? That's what you want?"

"Yes."

The next movement looked like a response to my "Yes," it was impossible to think anything else. It was close to three o'clock in the morning, and Alek got up and got dressed, and as he put the key to the room in his pocket he said, "I'll be back. Don't let anyone in."

HOW FAR ARE YOU GOING WITH IT

The Moscow Alek was the same person, but nevertheless different. When he met me at the airport, at first glance he looked tired, and only afterwards, in the taxi, I realized that the eyelids which were beginning to droop a little gave him a new look of weariness or sad resignation, but that this deceptive expression was contradicted again and again by a lively smile, because Alek, at least during my visit, was as intoxicatingly alert as I was. Not only did he play the gentleman more attentively than ever—I already knew exactly what these gestures were worth—but from the moment he picked me up at the airport he made it clear in many little ways that, more than acting as my tour guide, he intended to be my bodyguard here. In the street he was careful to take my arm so that I wouldn't slip on the ice. He tied the strings of my fur hat under my chin, carried my handbag, chose for both of us the moment to leap into traffic and cross the road. In addition to all this, he insisted, to my surprise, that I accompany him to all his meetings at the Journalists' House, and to apartments steeped in the smell of smoke and wet old clothes, all of them either too cold or overheated. "I'm an egoist," he said one night as we descended stairs stinking of cooking and urine in the dark, "maybe I shouldn't have told you to come."

"Why?"

"Nobody knows what could happen here."

"I like not knowing," I said.

"Really?"

"Really."

"You're like a little girl," he said and pressed me against the wall, laughing and strangely excited. And when he removed his lips from my neck he lifted his head, looked up as if he was searching for something, and added: "This smell, I didn't think I could get used to it again. We had a whole life in stairwells like these."

"So what did they say could happen here?" I asked as he led me downstairs. He translated very little for my benefit during the interviews. "What could happen?" He replied: "History could repeat itself, or not repeat itself, and both possibilities are frightening. Moscow is paradise compared to what's happening in other places. Already people have no gas, no food, no salaries, no pensions, no nothing."

I was completely dependent on him, dependent on him physically as I had never been anywhere else. I needed him in order to ask for another cup of lousy coffee at the hotel, in order to open the window I was unable to budge, to cross the street safely, even to understand the dialing instructions and call Hagar in Israel and go on lying to her—when he summoned me to him, I lied to Hagar and told her that I had been invited to Moscow to lecture on behalf of the Jewish Agency, and I stuck to this story on my subsequent visits too. I have to admit that I enjoyed the helplessness, the total dependence on Alek, and for some perverse reason I even enjoyed the fear. In February of 1993 normal people didn't go to Moscow as tourists, and it didn't even occur to Alek to take me to any of the tourist sites. Under the splendor of the snow there were filthy tenements and palaces, patched with dark squares of boarded-up windows. Passive lines of people stood in the clouds of steam at the entrances to the Metro; bookshelves, clothes hangers, shoe closets, kitchen cabinets, glass-fronted sideboards were emptied for sale. In all of Alek's meetings the warnings were repeated: don't go there, don't let her go, don't do this, that, or the other thing. Despite his Russian and his connections, they lumped us together as naive foreigners who needed to have the dangers pointed out to them.

At night I had the recurrent fantasy that the airport was closed, that the television screen was blacked out, that the silence meant the telephones were disconnected and tanks were blocking the roads. Alek: "The screen won't go black. You'll know that it's happening when the television starts giving us *Swan Lake*."

What would I do if he was torn away from me? If he went out to get something or clear something up and didn't come back, if he was thrown bleeding onto a street corner, if he lay with his body broken in a hospital or a jail, if he was sent to the infinite expanses of the East? I doubted I would survive. Or perhaps I would survive but I would never return to the world. I would be tossed by the tidal wave of history into some other mutation. I would wander the Metro platforms, a demented beggar, mumbling my pleas in broken Russian.

Alek didn't leave me alone for a minute, until "You want me to try your strength?" when he got up and went out.

I think about the dramatic "Try me" that came out of my mouth and I fill with self-loathing. What feeling was I dramatizing there? And what response was I longing for? For him to say to me, "Get thee out of thy country, and from thy kindred, and from thy father's house, unto a land that I will show thee"? For him to test my love with some sadistic trick? To make me wait and wait for his return, until I sang over the domes of Moscow, "If crying is forbidden I will not cry"? Now it occurs to me that I identified cruelty with testing, and confused being tested with being chosen. He would choose me in order to try me. He would try me and then I would be the chosen one. Look at me, winged and electrified, I can do anything. I'm stupid Noa Weber, a chosen people of one woman.

Alek came back after fifteen minutes. "Aren't you cold yet?" and he carried me to bed and lay me down and stroked me until my whole body arched, but he didn't get undressed. Twenty more minutes passed, maybe half an hour, until there was a knock at the door.

The night before, it happened that we talked about the prostitutes. They hung around in the lobby at all hours of the day and night, standing on stiletto heels next to the telephones, or sitting on leather armchairs under the fresco of a sturdy peasant woman, gigantic as a goddesses, carrying sheaves of wheat. And I in my stupidity didn't realize that the women in brief mini skirts and fur coats were whores. How could I have known? I didn't know the first thing about prostitutes, except the ones in the movies, and in any case the way that some of the Russian women we met were dressed and made up seemed whorish to me. Amused by my lack of perception, Alek said that next time one of them called our room to find out if it was occupied by a single man, perhaps he should invite her to come on up, so that I could satisfy my curiosity without staring in the lift, like I did. "You can use it in your book," said the man who had never read even one of my books.

When he got up to answer the knock at the door it occurred to me that when he went out he had invited one of the whores in the lobby to come up to our room. In order to test me—how? Doing—what? Interviewing her? Making love to her before his eyes for his enjoyment? Watching him fuck her? Watching her give him a blow job? From the moment he got up until he closed the door maybe sixty seconds passed, but during those sixty seconds I imagined with utter clarity all three latter possibilities, and in my imagination I did not rebel or protest against any of them.

Even in my glittering mood, even in my self-intoxicated, hallucinatory state, I knew that it was only a fantasy, and that nothing was going to happen. Whose fantasy? Not mine and not Alek's, but a kind of morbid symptom of an implanted virus, the pornographic mental product of a pornographic industry. The product of the male sex industry. While I only added the words "a pornographic mental product of the sex industry" later on, I definitely remember that in real time, too, in some corner of my mind, I thought to myself: "This is an alien fantasy."

But in real time this self-criticism was not in the least effective, and the fact is that in the following seconds I froze like a rabbit in the bed, riveted by the horror of the loathsome trial about to come through the door. And even when I heard it was a man's voice, my thoughts went on turning round and round in the same area: I'm naked and Alek's dressed, I asked to be tested and now the test is at the door, waiting to come into the room. And I'm not getting dressed or doing anything to stop it.

HOW DID I GET HERE

But how did I get here, and what am I doing in the Ukraine Hotel? I was about to report on my wedding day, that is what I intended on doing, but now that I'm already in Moscow, I may as well stay there a moment longer, until the end of this particular story.

Alek closed the door and came back inside with a bottle of vodka in his hand. He put it down between the double windows, to cool it, and then he got undressed and climbed into bed. Aroused as I was, I couldn't fly again. Carefully I touched the little wrinkles around his eyes, I covered his heavy eyelids with my hand, it was the first time in our history that I left my body to lie with him, and distanced my soul for fear that he would read my thoughts.

Another few lines on this subject, before I return to the matter of our marriage. I said that the test of the prostitute was only the mental product of the pornography industry, which is of course an easy and convenient solution. Too easy and convenient. Because what am I saying by it? I'm saying that it wasn't me hallucinating, it wasn't me fantasizing, but some wicked corrupt people who came and put these fantasies in my head.

Sexual fantasies, I think, are a rather banal subject, because when you come right down to it, how many of them are there? We are all fed by the same junk, and however many junk fantasies there are, there's no problem cataloguing them. They're catalogued in the video libraries. They're catalogued on the sex sites on the Internet. They're catalogued in the tabloids and in the brothels.

I don't use pornography, I have never been tempted to enter one of those sites, and nevertheless it's clear to me that I'm polluted too—it simply can't be otherwise. The pictures, the images, and the symbolic gestures are everywhere.

I have no idea how people thought about sex before cinema and television. It's clear that most people didn't read the Marquis de Sade or *Moll Flanders* or anything of the kind, so that if pre-cinema man had fantasies about sex they were evidently his own personal fantasies, taken from his private memories and personal experience, and not some polluting germ male industrialists shoved into his brain.

Today nobody has a chance of developing a virgin fantasy any more. Even if they've never opened a *Penthouse* or watched *Nine 1/2 Weeks*, however hard people try to protect themselves they get infected by perversion anyway, because the system insinuates it even via the most ostensibly innocent places. Including family favorites. Take for example the women in the movies of the forties and fifties, the way they hit the man on his chest or back, hitting and hitting hysterically, until their hands gradually come to rest and the blows turn to caresses. Look at Rhett Butler carrying Scarlett O'Hara upstairs to the rape she's asking for, listen to her singing happily afterwards, and tell me what to call it if not pornography. Look at the way Howard Keel spanks the shrewish Kathryn Grayson in *Kiss Me Kate*; remember how Clark Gable tames Claudette Colbert in *It Happened One Night*; remember how the spineless Adele H. sends a whore to her officer to make him happy, and how that revolting pervert in *Breaking the Waves* sends his wife to fuck. . . .

And that's quite enough, there's no need to look-remember-and-see, not now, because without in any way belittling the importance of the foregoing lecture, I didn't undertake to lecture here on sexuality and the cinema, on the cinema and patriarchy, on patriarchy and capitalism. Because this isn't a public debate, and that's not why I sat down to write.

The crux of my problem is that it's clear to me that this whole lecture is one big excuse. Because even if the masochistic virus was implanted in my mind, it's still my mind, mine and nobody else's, made up of a combination of transplants just like anybody else's. So that even if I babble on here for hours about the influence of the media, it will not negate the knowledge of the polluted self or blur the sickening awareness that of the entire catalogue of fantasies, my sick mind chose to replay the one I regard as the most humiliating of all: a man amusing himself, a woman victim, and a whore.

WE MARRIED IN OCTOBER

In October I married Alek, and there was no way I could avoid telling my parents. My mother, to be precise, because that week my father was out of the country again. In childish embarrassment I put it off until almost the last moment, two days before the wedding, so that in the end I did it in the worst possible way. Years later, and for quite a long time, I regretted my rudeness towards her, but it didn't happen at once, far from it.

Supper at the Webers'. Batya Weber, my mother, cuts up a cucumber, a tomato and a hard-boiled egg on her plate, smears a slice of bread with low-fat white cheese, and arranges everything in bite-sized pieces before she begins to chew. My sister Talush studies the shape of the egg as she rolls it around and around her plate. The transistor radio is on in anticipation of the seven o'clock news.

"I have news," and in the same breath, "the day after tomorrow I'm getting married." An atavistic maternal glow spreads over my mother's face before she takes in the words "the day after tomorrow." Mazal tov, Batya, mazal tov, Benjy, what's this we hear? Your daughter's getting married? A little young, isn't she? So, where's it going to be? On the kibbutz? In a reception hall? Tell us everything. And who's the groom?

On the stock exchange of Usha Street it was a story worth its weight in gold, not just another anecdote, but a full blown production, and in days to come I capitalized on it shamelessly, blunting the embarrassment and guilt with a mockery that improved with practice. Think of this woman, that is to say my mother, Batya, with her socialist upbringing in the children's house on the kibbutz. Her parents turned their backs on their bourgeois families, Grandpa left the shtetl, Grandma ran away from the family home in Kraków, they cleared away rocks, sweated in the fields, burned with malarial fevers, and all for what? For the revolution, right? To create a new man for us here who would live in a new, just society. There was an article about it in the paper only last week, I don't know if you saw it. A new man, a new family, a new form of relationship—that's what they wanted and that's what they talked about. And what did we get instead? *Fiddler on the Roof,* back to the shtetl with violins, mazal tov, comrades, mazal tov, our little girl's getting married and grandchildren come next.

"Don't start jumping for joy. It's only a fictitious marriage," I said quickly.

"Fictitious?" the knife was still in her hand. "But what does that mean, fictitious?"

"It means that I'm getting married at the Rabbinate the day after tomorrow, and later on I'll get divorced. Not that marriage means anything to me in the first place, it's just a primitive custom, but in any case this marriage isn't for real."

"Really? Is that so? One of the boys from the kibbutz married an illegal immigrant from Europe in a fictitious marriage, and afterwards they got divorced. But since then, as far as I know, we managed to chase the British out of the country."

"I don't intend to go to the army."

At some point she asked me if "he"—she never called Alek by his name—if "he" was "giving me drugs." At another point she bemoaned "what would people say" and how she was going to tell my father. And when, on the verge of a childish hysteria I hadn't planned for at all, I denounced her, my father, Zionism, the army of occupation, and the oppression of the Palestinians—she ordered Talush to leave the room so that I wouldn't "influence" her. "We know very well who's influencing you," she said.

With the Beatles's "She's Leaving Home" in the background, with frames from *Five Easy Pieces* and refrains from the Israeli version of *Hair* in my head, the two of us played our roles in this little historical melodrama with facility and total identification. Only I wasn't leaving home to go to San Francisco with a flower in my hair, but because I wanted to get married. To get married to a man I would rather have died than told my mother how much I loved him.

The truth is that it wasn't at all clear to me that I was leaving home, until my mother finally came out with the inevitable lines: "If that's what you think of us, if that's what your espresso generation is like, then perhaps there really isn't anything for you and your generation to look for here. And if you're old enough to get married, then perhaps you're old enough to earn your living as well," at which point I went up to my room, threw a few clothes into my rucksack, threw a nasty "I'm sorry for you," at the alarmed Talush, and left the house.

How much sincerity was there in this stormy scene? I don't know. It's possible to play a part with feelings of absolute sincerity, and when I arrived at Alek's with tears pouring down my face I had no sense of theatrical exaggeration. In other words, I was sure that the rift with my family was final and absolute.

"What happened?" he asked at the door, and immediately took me into his arms, which immediately brought on a fresh bout of weeping. "What happened?"

"I can't do it," I groaned when he closed the door behind us.

"What can't you do?"

"Get out of the army. My mother, my parents, if I don't go to the army they'll throw me out of the house, and at the moment I'll simply have nowhere else to go." We were still standing in the hallway, and Alek stroked my head with concentrated gentleness. "All my girlfriends are going to the army and I don't want to go to my Granny Dora on the kibbutz."

"Noichka, Noichka . . . yes . . . "

I buried my head in his shirt, and with my head under his chin I felt the smile suddenly spreading over his face. A slow Alek smile with closed lips. "You don't want to be in army?"

I shook my head.

"Okay, then you won't," and he raised my face to his. "Your mother and father...those are rules of the genre, you know," he said holding my cheeks and pulling them into a smile, "that's the way it is, Noichka, everything conforms to the rules of the genre." And when he took his hands away the smile remained on my face. When he wanted to he could always effect this change in me, from total identification with my feelings, to a kind of light-hearted, mischievous observation of myself.

"You don't want to be drafted?" he asked again.

"No," I answered, this time out loud.

"And you want me to marry you?" My face was completely exposed. I knew what he could see in it, I knew what he was asking, I could deceive the whole world, but not him, and I didn't want to deceive him anyway.

"Yes, I want you to do it."

"Good, if that's what you want, then that's what I'll do. I gave you a key, have you got the key? I want you to use it always. Will you use it? I'm leaving the country in July, and then too ... you can stay here as long as you need to."

How easily female tears turn into sexual arousal, not only of the male comforter but also of the weeping woman. The woman's panties were already pulled down, one melting was turning into another, and Ravel's *Bolero* was beginning to swell in the background when the man said: "And you'll manage, and you'll be all right, because that's how it is in your story. Everything according to rules of the genre, right?"

ON THE MORNING OF MY WEDDING

On the morning of my wedding I went to the Old City and bought a white dress. I didn't think that I was buying a wedding dress, but suddenly, as if for no reason, I just coveted a white *galabiyeh* flapping on a hanger in an alleyway, and it was only afterwards that it occurred to me to wear it to the Rabbinate.

"They expect a white dress," I said meekly to Alek who examined me in silence before we left the house. "If they don't like the way we're dressed they might throw us out, and we'll have wasted our time for nothing."

With the dress in my hand I strolled in the direction of the church of the Holy Sepulchre, simply because this was one of the places I went with Alek.

I've already mentioned that he loved churches, they acted on his soul, and when I stood in the church at his side, I understood that his admiration wasn't only aesthetic. "That's a nice picture," I let slip once in one of the alcoves opposite the sooty face of the Virgin Mary. "I like it."

"It's horrible icon," he replied impatiently from the side, "most of the paintings here are horrible."

"You think so?"

"It's not a question of what I think. They're simply horrible, but it really doesn't matter. Church isn't a museum. And from religious point of view maybe bad art is preferable."

Sometimes he would hurry through the halls—in Gethsemane, in the Dormition, in the Holy Sepulchre, there were two Saturdays when we walked as far as the Church of the Nativity in Bethlehem—and then, "That's it, let's go get some coffee." Other times he would linger in one of the corners, standing erect and somehow obedient, his hands folded in front of him on the zipper of his jeans, not focused on any of the objects around him, and nevertheless somehow very focused indeed. It seemed as if he were capable of standing there for hours without moving a muscle, as if he had been trained to wait in silence, and the sight made my heart contract. I tried to impose a similar stillness on my own body, I tried not to shift my weight from foot to foot, to relax my shoulders, to relax my hands, as if by succeeding in doing so, I would know what was happening inside him. It seemed to me that if only I emptied my mind and cleaned out my body, Alek's thoughts would seep by some magical osmosis into the void formed inside me, where they would take shape as the picture, the memory, the ancient experience that he was seeking. Because for some reason it seemed to me that he was searching for something inside him, not actively but the opposite; that he was stilling his thoughts and making room for something to rise up inside him, as if he were trying to call it up and waiting for it to come.

As always, I had to piece bits of information together. "My mother lives in this," he said to me one night as we descended the Mount of Olives in the direction of the onion-domed church. "Lives in it?" "In Jesus."

"Is your mother a Christian?"

"She's a Jew. She's a Jew in her own eyes, and everyone who sees her sees a Jew."

"Sometimes when we walk here I try to imagine what it would be like to believe that—"

"You can't."

"Just to imagine, what it's like to really believe that Jesus—"

"Impossible. People like my mother, and all her friends from the sixties, they don't believe 'that Jesus,' they believe *in him*, which is completely different. They believe in Jesus, and 'believing that Jesus' only comes—or doesn't come—afterwards."

"But you would like to."

"What?"

"Know how it feels? To believe?"

"No, certainly not." He lied, and after a few steps he added, "You and I, we don't come to these questions from the same place. It's not a question of what a person wants at all. You don't choose the direction of the movement of your soul. I don't choose the direction of mine. There's nothing you can do about it. So the most a person with intellect can do is to curse all the way, to yell at his soul: Why did you take me here? And why did you take me there? It's normal, it just doesn't really help, all that yelling."

The moon whitened the stone walls lining the path and cast long shadows behind us. From a distance the city returned to its primeval sounds. A dog barking and a dog replying. The voice of a woman calling over rhythmic metallic blows. Far-near sounds as if we were walking in a country village. I wanted to linger longer, not to go down into the field of vision of the new city. But Alek took hold of my elbow, hastened his steps and said dryly, "Such talk . . . the direction of the movement of the soul . . . don't trust a man who invites you to come up to his apartment to listen to Vivaldi, and don't believe a man who talks to you about God."

So on the morning of my wedding I bought a white dress, and with the dress rolled up in my shoulder bag, without really thinking, I arrived at the church of the Holy Sepulchre. Straight from the autumn heat into the cool halls below and the dim little room with the single icon hanging in it, the one that Alek loved and belittled.

To this day I have no explanation for what happened there. I was very tired and very alert. I was high on the smell of the incense. Dazed by the transition from glaring light to gloom. I really don't know, but I remember how the flickering candlelight lent a strange life to the young Madonna's face, and I remember how quietly and gradually the longer I looked at her the more present she became to me, until she was more real than the tourists moving overhead. She was a timeless Mary, the one who received the annunciation and the one who gave birth, the one at the foot of the cross and the one ascending to heaven to be the bride of God. All the paintings I had seen with Alek combined in her, just as if she was a familiar personality and the object of private memories beyond time. So present to me was she in her infinite serenity, that it came about that I smiled, not to myself, but at her.

What is there to say about this scene? I was eighteen, in other words still an adolescent, and stretched to my limits. And even at those moments I didn't think of "revelation"—in other words I knew all the time that the flickering figure was only a mirage—but I had a terrible need, and the need radiated out of me, and projected the figure out of the picture, where it twinkled and shone at me until it came about that I addressed it. "Make it be true," I begged, and by true I meant me and Alek.

All kinds of alien words, alien wishes, whispered in me then. It embarrasses me to remember them now. I wished, with all my heart and soul, I wished for it to be "true" and "pure." I asked to be "cleansed." I asked to fall asleep and wake up bathed and washed in light, free of the dross of speech and of buffoonery and of lies. I was ready to endure pain, to be scoured by it, and I begged for grace. The devil knows where I got all this from, but the yearning was so physical and absolute, and the tenderness flowed and ebbed and flowed from her so powerfully that I relaxed my knee and started to kneel. Yes, that's exactly how it happened, that's what I did: I relaxed one knee, sent the other one backwards, and I was on the point of kneeling in front of the icon when something grabbed me in the middle of the movement, sent a shiver of disgust through me, and made me stand up straight.

For a minute longer I stood there, concentrating on purpose on the grotesque artistic clumsiness of the gesture of kneeling, and I let the self-loathing pour through me and fill me completely. For one more minute I examined the rather blackened face of the Madonna, with its expression of autistic sweetness, and only then I turned to go. "Comedian," my Grandma Dora's word came back to me, "comedian, comedian, comedian," and to the hammering of this word, "comedian," I made my way through the crowd of tourists and pilgrims to the door of the church.

URGES AND IMPULSES

When she completes her studies Hagar will be a rabbi, and when she finds herself a congregation she will also marry people. In the framework of her tireless efforts to educate me, she recently sent me a collection of articles about the importance of "rites of passage" and the enlightened alternative ways of celebrating them. I read my lucid daughter's lucid contribution, and paged disinterestedly through the rest of the collection, and the next morning I sat down to compose a careful maternal response. I praised the quality of the production and the editing, thanked her for the illuminating analysis of the components of the marriage ceremony and especially the interesting interpretation of the apparel of the bride, expressed my not completely sincere wish that the numbers of religious people like her fellow students would grow in Israel, too, and only at the bottom of the page made the barbed comment: ". . . I still have my doubts as to whether anthropologists can serve as priests."

"Understanding the meanings of the rites we perform doesn't turn us into anthropologists," my daughter answered in a hasty e-mail, "our awareness doesn't contradict our faith, and as far as I'm concerned it only strengthens it."

If I had told Hagar the story of the morning I got married—which I have no intention of doing—she would have seen it as conclusive proof both of my need for ritual, and of my repressed religious feeling. And she would also have said that if I had been married in a Jewish ceremony that was "progressive" and "meaningful," rather than in the Rabbinate, my feet would not have led me to a church. But that's not the point, it's something else entirely, which I can't explain to her: I'm not denying the existence of the religious impulse, who am I to deny it, I'm only denying the existence of a godhead to which this impulse is directed. And I'm certainly not convinced that my intelligent daughter really believes in God.

She certainly possesses an urge to believe. It's not clear to me where it comes from or why, but it's there—maybe this desire is genetic, maybe she inherited it from her parents. But the desire to believe is not the same as belief itself, and my daughter's garrulous religiosity is in my eyes only a self-indulgent courting of a bad impulse. An act of buffoonery, exactly like my almost kneeling in front of a badly painted icon of the Virgin Mary.

I didn't understand much at the ages of seventeen and eighteen. Since then I've come to understand a little more, and when I recall things that Alek said, and even more so the way he stood there in the church, it seems to me that the religious impulse was aroused in him then to a degree or in a manner that he still needed to fight, and it was only for the sake of this war that he went to church. Liberating the experience in order to overcome it and emerge as someone who had triumphed over himself.

And what was I doing there? The Christian God was Alek's God, the specific god that Alek didn't believe in. But a god you don't believe in is still a god, and so it happened that when I was pining for Alek's love, I went and prostrated myself to his gods.

I have already made it clear, I think, that I find no touching charm or beauty in this—though this is not absolutely the truth. However much I despise myself for my attacks of religious epilepsy, I despise my daughter, without any justification, more. Despise not only her convenient, dietetic, easy to digest religion, but she herself, for the small, civilized instinct that she cultivates by will. Hagar is of course not deserving of this contempt, and who am I to despise my honest daughter, immeasurably more honest than I.

Since Hagar's new Jewishness isn't only an aspect of her life, but something that determines it more and more, the diplomatic dishonesty in our relationship will no doubt grow greater over the years. With her grandmothers, astonishingly enough, Hagar has found a common language, and her preoccupation with religion has only increased the love that they both feel for her anyway. My mother is capable of spending hours nodding in admiration as my daughter lectures her on Jewish culture/Jewish renewal/new ways of interpreting Jewish traditions, etc. Meekly she agrees that a great injustice had been done her by her parents who robbed her of "her roots," "her culture" and "her Jewish bookshelf," and glowing with pride she occasionally accompanies her granddaughter to Saturday morning services at her progressive synagogue.

As for Grandmother Marina, Alek's mother, it seems to me that she is happy that her granddaughter is showing an interest in "spirituality," even though she has no idea of the nature of this "spirituality," and although no serious discussion is possible between them, both because they have no common language, and because of the vast cultural gap between them.

When her father invited her to visit him in Paris, after she was discharged from the army and after my first visit to Moscow, Hagar was still at the beginning of her "Judaization" process, full of conceptual doubts and willing to sit up until the wee hours of morning debating such questions as "What is Jewish identity?" and "Is Judaism a religion/nationality or a culture?" In her debating style she sometimes reminds me more of Amikam than of her father. In the ten days she spent with her grandmother in Paris the child did not find an answer to the vexing question of whether Grandmother Marina, who had secretly converted to Christianity while still in Russia, could be considered a Jew.

I understood that all kinds of relations who were strangers to her and also strangers who weren't related to her at all, enveloped her in warmth and love there, fed her as if she were a baby, accompanied her everywhere she went so that she wouldn't get lost in the big city, and that no serious clarifications took place, either with Alek or with Marina. Alek waited for her outside when she went into Notre Dame Cathedral, and at the same opportunity remarked, by the way, that in recent years his mother's church attendance had fallen off. A couple of times Marina said grace in Russian when they sat down to eat; over her and her husband's double bed hung a triangle of beautiful icons—what the husband, Jenia's, position was on these matters I do not know, for some reason he was seldom mentioned, as if he didn't count—and when they parted at the airport Marina covertly made the sign of the cross over her granddaughter's head. These were all the clues that Hagar received, and she had no idea what to make of them, but for a while it seemed that her tendency to set the world in order in the same way as she tidied her room had been swallowed up in a torrent of sense impressions: the smell of cheese and roasting chestnuts, the taste of new foods, the giddiness of the wine to which she was not accustomed, an exhibition of paintings, a statue, the view of a street framed in a café window.

Hagar talked without stopping, and a little rodent inside me devoured it all to the last crumb, while I kept my eyes and hands busy sorting the washing, folding the washing, cutting up the salad, so that she wouldn't see and wouldn't guess at the depths of my abject longing to feel the touch of the air around her father.

In my imagination I followed them to the Louvre "to see the Impressionists," and only after she piled on the details and digressed in various directions did I discover that she went to the Louvre not with Alek but with "a terribly interesting friend of Grandma Marina's, an artist who's actually an American, but she's been living in Paris for years." And I felt a similar secret shame at the description of the "amazing picnic in the Bois de Boulogne," which I only discovered later had not been attended by Alek.

To my complete and utter surprise it seemed to me that Grandma Marina had captured Hagar's imagination and thoughts more than her father—or perhaps she had enabled her to avoid thinking about her father and her relationship with him. "You know that at Granny Marina's, people phone up at one o'clock in the morning as if it's the middle of the day." "The most amazing thing is that Granny's gorgeous, you should see her, she's got legs that look as if they reach all the way to her neck, much better than mine." Or: "I don't understand how come Grandma Marina, with her gift for languages, never took the trouble to learn English." The stream of her chatter flowed on and on, and I drank it in thirstily, until she gradually returned to her old boring ways, with questions like: "So in your opinion, can Brother Daniel, a Christian priest who claims to be Jewish, be considered a Jew just because he was born one?"

I HAD REACHED THE MORNING OF MY WEDDING

I had reached the morning of my wedding, in the month of October, in the year 1972, and as far as possible I shall try to stick with this chronology, without getting ahead of myself or digressing at every thought that pops into my head. But if I'm going to talk about my wedding, there is an impression I must correct first: when I mentioned the consolation fuck Alek gave me after my leaving-home scene I didn't say that it was our only fuck since the day we presented ourselves at the Rabbinate.

It is clear to me, and it was clear to me then too, that Alek, to the best of his nonverbal ability, was trying to clarify himself to me: don't mistake me and don't deceive yourself, we're talking about a fictitious marriage here, and you don't fuck a woman you're married to fictitiously in every corner of the house, and you certainly don't stroke her hair and look into her eyes before, after, and during the act.

Alek, being Alek, was incapable of not offering me his home after I was "thrown out by my parents who demanded that I go to the army," but the fact that I was living with him only complicated the situation. If I hadn't been living there, maybe he wouldn't have abstained from me entirely, but living together was too much like proper married life and he was therefore obliged to draw the line.

"Obliged to draw the line"—I am presenting his abstinence as if it stemmed from an explicit decision. I would like to believe that it came from some deliberate decision, on principle, which was the only reason he kept away from me even though he still desired me greatly. It would be nice to believe this face-saving explanation, very nice, but I know very well, and I knew very well, that it isn't so. I haven't got a clue whether Alek "decided" to abstain from me, maybe he "decided" and maybe he didn't, but in any event it is clear to me that most of the time he didn't need any "decision" to depend on or remind himself of. The simple truth is that the farce of the marriage, the political act of the marriage—whatever we call it—produced a sense of complication and turned Noa Weber into an oppressive presence on the ground. It didn't happen in a minute, it didn't happen in a day, and in the terrible months of chilliness there were still moments of warmth, but the process was very rapid.

So what could Noa Weber do? What could I do? I could have picked up my peacock's tail and returned to my parents' home, married or single, they would have taken me back. I could have gone to Grandma Dora on the kibbutz. I could have gone to the recruiting center and volunteered to serve in the army even after I was married. I could have "confronted Alek and discussed the situation openly," as the wise advisors in the agony columns in the newspapers always say, or, in the same spirit, I could have taken myself to a psychologist who would "help me to untie the knot." I could have and could have and could have, but the problem of course is that I couldn't. That is to say that from the chemical point of view there was simply no possibility of my detaching myself from him. Just as there was no possibility for me to change my soul, or to cut myself into pieces. I loved him. In other words, he had infiltrated my very depths and then spread through all my cells, and changed my being until I was no longer mistress of my love. It wasn't "my" love. It didn't belong to me, I belonged to it and was ruled by it. Or perhaps I belonged to him and was ruled by him. I don't know.

I'm not denying all responsibility, but I feel I can definitely claim diminished responsibility; and so in the end I did the only thing I could do, which was to efface myself so that my presence wouldn't be oppressive. Light as the wind, playful as the wind, that is what I tried to be. Soft, pure air, a perfect cirrus cloud floating in the kitchen sky.

It's easier to describe on the practical level. Alek was and remains a tidy man. I am still untidier than he is, but from the minute he cleared three shelves in the closet for me, I adapted myself to his standards of order and even more so: not a crumb on the chopping board, not a hair in the bathroom sink. Shrewdly I avoided playing the role of the housewife Alek was certainly not interested in, but I did my best to behave like the perfect roommate. When I polished off the cheese I was quick to replace it, when a bulb burned out in the bathroom I refrained from calling him to change it, and I never used up all the hot water, things like that, and looking back I can see that it was all nonsense. I can't imagine Alek resenting having to change a light bulb, or complaining about the cheese, but nevertheless I was careful.

Beyond all this was the perpetual question of the choreography of our parallel lives. Alek settled into the study, I without a word was given the bedroom, and when Alek closed his door, I closed mine too—so far it was clear. But what am I supposed to do when he's sitting in the kitchen? Is it a let's-peel-Noa-an-orange morning, let's tell her the name of the quartet playing on the radio, improve her mind with a little "Nietzsche, Ivanov, and the Dionysian principle," and chat to her about romantic triangles in Russian literature? Or is it the beginning of another day when we don't raise our head from the bed or the book even when the door bell rings? Does he want me frivolous now, passing airy remarks? Is my silent presence acceptable to him now? And at this moment—what? And what about the moment after it? Will it drive him crazy if I move? Open the tap? Chew? Breathe in his den?

Alek was and is a man of expansive gestures, but the gesture with which he opened his home to me was too expansive even for him.

WEDDING

Three people accompanied us from the house: Yoash-Hamida, the ginger-haired Ginsberg, and the revolting Hyman, and at the entrance to the Rabbinate we were joined by the acne-scarred Maoist with another guy I didn't know, whom Alek apparently didn't know either.

Until they were ready to marry us, we were all asked to wait in the corridor. Alek, a pale prince, graceful, disdainful, leaned on the doorpost, while Hyman took over one of the offices and conducted all kinds of debates. I remember couples sitting on a bench like patients in a queue at the free clinic, the screaming of a woman outside, all kinds of people passing between us with rapid steps carrying cardboard files, all of them staring at the woman in the white dress: what's she doing here? Staring at the woman pacing to and fro in a white dress, in other words, me. One man—he sticks in my mind—walked past with floral slippers on his feet.

Money passed from Yoash's wallet into the drawer of one of the clerks, a note was written, and then we were sent to an empty hall upstairs, to wait for them to prepare the marriage contract and collect ten men for a prayer quorum. Everything registered in my mind in partial pictures, like quick peeks through the blindfold in a game of blindman's bluff: stacked towers of orange plastic chairs, a glimpse of a blue nylon scroll, which was the rolled-up wedding canopy, the sight of a shoe crushing a cigarette end on yellowing floor tiles. Three people gathered opposite the rabbi next to a table in the corner, crowded, sullen voices asking and answering in the corner, feet receding from the table, a stir spreads through the room, and then a pair of hands take hold of the pole of the canopy as if it were a flag. And all this time I kept my eyes lowered and I didn't look at Alek, but even without looking at him I knew his location and his movements. A concentrated prince, captive among the hand-wavers.

Two women approached me, neither of them the rabbi's wife I had met on the day we came to register, two other women. They asked me my name, they asked me pityingly about my family, if I was expecting anyone else to come, and when the rabbi came up to demand the note from the mikveh, they gave him my name in Yiddish, and it was only from their gestures that I understood what they were saying, that the poor girl was pregnant. The arrogance of our group abated, or perhaps it did not penetrate to these kindly, pious women, because their fingers kept touching my shoulders and my hair, as if I were in need. They straightened the neckline of my dress, they smoothed and stretched its folds, they brushed a lock of hair off my forehead, and then with increasing boldness they affectionately kneaded my arms. If we had met in the street the next day, I would not have recognized them, but together they arranged a gauze kerchief on my head, so I would have a wedding veil, they called me "the beautiful bride" and wished—it sounded like a promise—that all would be well.

When the canopy was spread a command was given, and the two women took a firm, final grip on my arms and began to lead me round and round the groom in what felt like a kind of slow torture. "This is so you'll forget all the others," one of them breathed warmly into my ear.

Although I'm not tall, they were shorter than I was, actual dwarves, and with every step I was conscious, to the point of gut-twisting revulsion, of the grotesqueness of this circular movement in threesome, of how I disappeared for a few steps, and immediately reappeared in Alek's view, with no possibility of escape. Straight-backed as a novice model, pulled by the arms, one shoulder drooping and the other raised, unable to even them out, my face distorted, unable to relax my expression. On the next round, here it comes, on the next round I'll slip past him with nonchalant, jaunty grace, I'll smile ironically, and again I am under his all-seeing eyes, and everything is even more crooked than before.

In all my life up to then I had attended four or five weddings, no more; the children of my parents' friends, married on a platform on the lawn opposite the kibbutz dining hall, or in a hotel. For Alek this was his first Jewish wedding, but somehow he succeeded in deciphering the Yiddish-accented "Behold thou art sanctified unto me with this ring" and to repeat the words, and when he repeated them, for a moment I didn't recognize his voice, and it seemed to me that somebody else was repeating them so that he would understand. One of the strangers present in the room.

Is it possible, as my daughter claims, that a person has a kind of genetic memory in which the ancient texts are imprinted? I don't have a genetic memory, I don't believe in it, it's nonsense, and nevertheless there was a moment, when he put the ring on my finger, there was a moment when all the pains of self-consciousness vanished and shame disappeared. For a few moments I was absolutely innocent, sanctified, sanctified, sanctified, blushing, raising my eyes at last from the white of his shirt to his naked face, with my hand held in his, and all of me loose and unraveled as if we were alone together. Let my right hand forget its cunning, Alek, let my tongue cleave to the roof of my mouth, if I forget. No joy, no gladness, no rejoicing, no jubilation, and nevertheless, my beloved husband, I will not forget.

As soon as we got home I removed the thin band from my finger, left it in full sight on the window sill in the kitchen, and there it remained until after Alek left. Before he put it on my finger, the ring had warmed up in the repulsive Hyman's shirt pocket, through the blur of my kerchief-veil I saw it being removed from there. I imagined that he had reminded Alek it needed to be bought, or that he had been asked to buy it, and in any case even if it had not been purchased with Hyman's money, I could not wear it. I was only married to him fictitiously, but the fact that Hyman had bought the ring prevented me from developing any kind of fetishistic relation to it. And that too is perhaps for the best.

FETISHISM

The truth is that I had no need of the ring as a fetish. First of all because I was surrounded by everything of Alek's, I was living in his house after all. And even after he left and took his clothes and most of his books with him, even after he removed the black comb from the bathroom shelf and the shaving brush from the sink, even after he gave all the records to Yoash, I was still surrounded by things related to him: the curtain he had hung in the bedroom, the blanket with which we had covered ourselves, shelves he had put up, a bed and another bed and empty drawers. The house was charged with his movements and his touch, and recharged with them on each of his visits, and even though with the passing years—before I restored everything to its former state—I'd changed many things, and so did Hagar (carpets, television, a new closet, an air-conditioner)—all these did not banish his spirit.

In romantic movies and novels it was once the fashion to make a big fuss about a single object: "my mother's cameo ring," "the packet of his letters," "her fan," "his baseball bat," her picture, his picture, his underpants. In our day, I think, people are rather ashamed of this fetishism, but I can actually understand how one can become attached to a single object, and if I failed to do so it is only because so much was haunted by Alek in any case.

Sometimes I think, it's the weather that does it for me. It's the smell of the rain. It's the warm wind. It's the sight of the softened light refracted from the stone, like it was then. It's the taste of the air that's exactly like it was then when I went out in the evening for a run. With them and because of them come the longings, and the sense of his absence which makes him desperately present. Because there is nothing that makes someone more present than absence. And with moderate fluctuations in intensity, he is still absent-present to me most of the time.

But what did I just say? The warm wind and the softened light refracted from the stone give rise to my longings? In the last analysis that's romantic bullshit too. Setting the feeling in "the softened light refracted from the stone" to make it more photogenic. I loved Alek under the ugly neon of the hospital too, and in all kinds of other lights that can't be poeticized.

Warm wind, cold wind, drafty wind, wind with a whiff of diesel oil, and no wind at all, they can all do it to me, and my love stirs within me with every change in the light and every movement in the air. Occasionally, I have to admit, it feels like grace, his presence suffused in everything. My awakened senses. The objects quickened into life. The touch of everything he touched. Alek's spirit in inanimate objects.

WHEN YOU GIVE BIRTH AT THE AGE OF EIGHTEEN

When you give birth at the age of eighteen, you have no choice but to explain yourself: So tell me, didn't anybody teach you about contraceptives? An intelligent girl like you, didn't you realize that you were pregnant? So how come you didn't have an abortion? Weren't you afraid that you were going to ruin your life? What on earth were you thinking?

I began to invent excuses while I was still pregnant, clearly aware that I was lying, and when I didn't have anyone to tell them to, I told them to myself: Look, my period was never regular. Listen, in October I bled (true, a little spot of blood which I didn't really think was a period). Understand, we did use contraceptives, but nothing is a hundred percent effective, by the time I realized what was happening it was already too late to have an abortion. These were my first rationalizations, and they were all intended to explain to the world that I wasn't an utter fool, that I was a rational person, that I had worthy goals in life and that I had no intention of losing control of my life. Because this, of course, is what teenage pregnancy means to the public: irresponsible stupidity and losing control over your life. And if you don't want to be seen as a stupid fool who has lost control over her life, you have to inform people what happened in your underpants when.

Over the course of the years, as Hagar grew up, I began to tell, especially to my girlfriends, a slightly different version: My period was never regular, blah-blah-blah, when I found out it was already too late, blah-blah-blah, Alek actually wanted me to have an abortion, an abortion would have suited his convenience—but why should a woman do something just because it's convenient for a man? It was my pregnancy, my body, my reproductive system. Understand me, girls, in the end I wanted the baby, and as far as I'm concerned the father had nothing to do with it.

Girls: What, you really didn't think of letting him share in the decision?

Me (so arrogant, so heroic): No, I didn't. From the outset I didn't think it was any of his business, and I gave him to understand as much.

Girls: And you weren't afraid? To be a single mother at that age?

Me: Of course I was afraid, obviously I was afraid, what am I, an idiot? But I decided that if that was what I wanted to do, that's what I was going to do.

A girl (suspicious): And you really had no feeling for him?

Me (in an amused voice): No feeling? Look, of course I had a certain feeling. That is to say, we were quite close, and all kinds of things happened between us, obviously they did, because otherwise I wouldn't have gotten pregnant. But the pregnancy was much more important to me than the being-in-love bit, and the being-in-love bit was over anyway.

The bottom line of all these conversations, and later on in my life of a number of newspaper interviews:

A woman needs a husband like a fish needs a bicycle! "Okay . . . maybe there are some fish who need bicycles, I'm not judging them, I only hope that this is a problem that evolution will solve . . ." Me, in one of those interviews. Sometimes I sound exactly like my Nira Woolf.

Long live the eternal, true, pure, and meaningful tie between a mother and her offspring, to which no other love can compare.

Telling Hagar the story of her conception and birth was the most complicated. Because what could I say to the child? My daughter, my marriage to your father was only fictitious? What's fictitious, Mommy? My daughter, I never loved your father? So how did I get born to you, Mommy? You should know, my daughter, that your father didn't love me and that he didn't want you either.

You may say that I could have told her the truth, that the truth is best, and the truth is actually an excellent story to tell a child. You want the truth? Here it is. The truth, my child, is that I loved your father, that I still love him, I loved him so madly that I never imagined for a moment, I couldn't have imagined, getting rid of his child. The truth, my darling daughter, is that at first you were only a fetish to me, the object most charged with Alek, something that would remain after he disappeared into wicked Germany.

You should know, my little one, that if I had become pregnant by somebody else, Amikam for instance, this story would have ended completely differently, in the gynecologist's trash can. That's what you would have done to me, Mommy? Killed me and thrown me into the trash? Go confuse a little one of three, four, or five with philosophical arguments along the lines of: If you had a different father you wouldn't be you and you wouldn't exist at all, so that your claim that you could have ended up in the trash is meaningless. You go and put a three-year-old to bed with arguments like those.

Apart from which, even though when she was small I was not yet a fully-fledged feminist, a declared feminist I mean, I was instinctively averse to raising a little girl on the basis of the drugged love of a man. I think that what was at work here was a protective maternal instinct to distance her from my addiction, joined by the simple motive of pride. I didn't want her to know that her mother was a downtrodden doormat. A worm eaten up by longings for a man who was her father.

I didn't want her ever to see her mother eating the leftover scraps of affections from his table. I wanted her to have respect for me, and I had no intention of passing on my weakness to the younger generation.

Over the years, therefore, my version for Hagar was composed as follows: Your mother and father were very young when they met, and even when people love one another, it's not a good idea to marry so young. So Daddy loved you? Yes. And you loved him? Yes, but not like I love you; you, pumpkin, I love always and forever, because that's the way mothers love their children. And fathers? Fathers what? Fathers don't love their children? Fathers do love their children, but sometimes somebody has a child when that somebody isn't ready to be a father yet. When that somebody is still a bit of a child himself.

The idea of her father's immaturity sank into Hagar's mind, so that when she was five or six years old, during the period when Alek was living in Israel again, she once asked me: "What do you think, do you think that Daddy is more mature now, or less mature, or the same?"

"And what do you think?" I evaded her question with a question.

"I didn't ask you what I think," my logical daughter replied, "I asked you what you think. I know what I think."

"You know better than I do. You went for a walk with him, not me."

TELLING ALEK THE NEWS

By the end of October I more or less knew that I was pregnant, and in November, right after my birthday, I went to be examined. I didn't tell

Alek about the test and I didn't have to tell him about the results either. A few days after my visit to the gynecologist, and after I had already obtained the results from the lab, he found out for himself. It wasn't the first time I threw up, and I always tried to do it quietly. I knelt down and bowed my head over the toilet bowl, but early on this particular morning when I emerged from the toilet with my mouth full of nausea, Alek was standing opposite me in the passage.

A similar scene takes place in a lot of movies and television series. A woman tells her lover that she's pregnant, a pregnancy which all the circumstances known to the audience lead them to believe is unwanted, and at these moments we always see the woman in close-up: the camera lingers on her facial expressions, on the nervous movements of her hands, and then draws it out to keep us in suspense. What's going to happen, what's going to happen now? Will the lover's face light up in joyful pride when his paternal instincts are unexpectedly aroused? Will he reject the woman rudely? Will he meanly cast doubt on his paternity of the child she is bearing in her womb? Offer her money for an abortion?

In my case there were no lingering moments of suspense. And before either of us uttered a word, questions and answers passed between our eyes. As still happens to this day, it seemed that everything was conveyed before it was spoken. And nevertheless he asked, and nevertheless I answered. "I'm pregnant," and immediately added, "but it doesn't concern you." I had prepared the position, the words, in advance, I had worked on them for hours, but saying them out loud for the first time, standing weakly in the toilet door, they sounded quite pathetic.

"How doesn't it concern me?" He spoke almost without moving his lips, in a dry, disgusted tone. This gave me a second chance to speak my piece.

"It doesn't concern you, because I definitely don't want anything from you," I replied and went into the bathroom to brush my teeth. This time I had been more successful, the words "I don't want anything from you" had come out without any female hysteria.

Strange how small sounds and movements can have an effect: from the moment I pronounced these calm, uplifting words, from the moment I closed the door behind me, the fact that I had said the words and closed the door, and the knowledge that Alek was waiting outside— these little things filled me with a feeling of power. I remember, I brushed my teeth in front of the mirror, I brushed my hair thoroughly, wet air came in through the window and banished the last of my nausea. All that remained was the rather pleasant, disembodied feeling that comes after vomiting. I inspected my face in the gray light and I liked what I saw: absolute detachment and calm. As if I had been enveloped in a chilly halo, as if a cool blue halo had enveloped my heart. I love you, I thought, I love you infinitely, and you, my love, relax, relax, because none of this has got anything to do with you.

And thus, like an Ayn Rand heroine, I came out to him at my leisure, washed and combed, with the gestalt mantra tasting of peppermint toothpaste repeating itself in my throat: I do my thing and you do yours, because you're you and I'm me. As far as I remember, this nonsense of I'm me and you're you was a big hit in those days, people repeated it all the time, and always as if it were an amazing, original discovery flung at their interlocutors in order to open their eyes to a vital truth. But in those moments in the bathroom this piece of nonsense gave me strength. And I mean strength. I was an independent personality capable of anything, and I went out to him like a resolute goddess of free will.

Afterwards we sat in the kitchen. "It has nothing to do with you," repeated the independent, all-powerful personality, "you're leaving for Heidelberg in July and I . . . I'll do whatever I like." I couldn't even pronounce the sentence "I'm going to have the baby," it sounded so embarrassing to me.

"You have to be realistic," he said and made me lemon tea without being asked. "Normal human beings should be realistic, and you're not being realistic now." "Realistic?" I sneered, suddenly sure of my strength. "Since when, exactly, Alek Ginsberg, have you been a realist?" I was great, no doubt about it, I didn't only impress myself, I impressed him, too, because he flashed me a smile and seemed to reassess me. "So you still love me?" he asked quietly. "I love you." He looked at his fingers which for a moment touched my face, and on his face there was a new and strange expression of humility. "I can't be anybody's father," he said.

"I know that."

"You know that," he repeated.

"Yes, I know, and I also know that you're leaving, and I don't want anything from you."

"You don't want anything or you're not asking for anything?" He always had the shocking ability to put his finger right on the spot.

Was it the madness of love that led me to think that although he was afraid of being bothered, he was somehow also fascinated and even delighted by the whole thing? I'm still sure that it was Alek himself, not the illusions of love, who secretly made me think so. By his expression. By the fluctuations in his voice. By the movements of his fingers. As if he were conducting two conversations with me at once. In one language he says to me, with that lip-narrowing disgust, which looks to me like self-disgust, again: "If you want . . . to end it, Gido—remember him?—the redheaded guy who was with us at the Rabbinate . . . he's doing his residency at Hadassah, he could tell us where go to." And in the other language he applauds the madness, the holy and actually rather surprising madness of Noa Weber.

"Forgive me," he says in the end in a gentle voice, "I shouldn't have spoken like that. A man has no right to tell a woman what to do about her pregnancy."

BEING REALISTIC

I, to the best of my knowledge, am a realist, but how realistic I was at the age of eighteen it's hard to say. If one of Hagar's girlfriends from high school had come to me, if Hagar herself had come to me, and said: (a) I'm pregnant, and I'm not going to have an abortion; (b) I'm in love; (c) he doesn't love me; and (d) he's leaving the country in nine months time—I would have made her see reason right then and there. First I would have knocked the nonsense out of her and then I would have accompanied what remained of her to a reputable gynecologist to have an abortion.

Yes, and just how do you think you'll manage with a child? Have you got any idea of what it means to be a single parent? What makes you think that you'll be able to study and work at the same time? And where exactly will the money come from? And the strength to get up at night? And when the child suddenly gets sick, which happens quite often, and you're all alone, and there's nobody else to take care of him but you...or if you get sick, or heaven forbid if you break your arm, and that happens too, have you any idea of the stress, the anxiety, of being without any safety net at all? Now explain to me exactly what you have in mind. That your parents will bring him up? That your parents will support you both until you grow up and stand on your own feet? Aha, very good, you say you want to be independent. So tell me, exactly how much money have you earned in your life up to now? A hundred shekel as a babysitter? And apart from babysitting, my dear, have you ever taken care of a baby in your life?

Since no friend of Hagar's ever came to ask my advice about an unwanted, in-these-circumstances pregnancy, I never had a chance to test the effectiveness of this rebuke. On me, in any case, it didn't work. And I could no more consider getting rid of the fetus than Mary could have sat on a rock in the hills of Nazareth to consider getting rid of Jesus. Which isn't to say that I thought I was pregnant with the Messiah or any such psychotic delusion, but that the pregnancy itself was sacred to me. Sacred not because I decided that it was, I didn't decide anything, it was simply self-evident to me.

The word "sacred" is difficult for me, it's difficult for me to use it without mockery, without being witty at my own expense, but I don't have any other word, and even today and even now, I can still relive the feeling of hard grace that came with my love and was embodied in the developing fetus.

Since I was young but not entirely stupid, or not entirely detached from reality, I was scared stiff, and the fear naturally increased the closer the due date approached. And although I may not have had a serious grasp of what it meant to be a single mother at eighteen—I couldn't possibly have known—I can testify that I certainly tried to guess. In other words, at first I just wondered vaguely, and later on

I imagined, and then I imagined more, until towards the end I spent most of the day and night agonizing over completely realistic worries, which, especially after darkness fell, appeared insolvable. It would be reasonable to assume that the worry would banish the grace, but this did not happen, and throughout that winter I existed as if on two planes: one of fearful thoughts going round in circles—birth, hospital, pain, baby; money, profession, baby, money; birth, pain, pain, profession, loneliness, parents, baby—and another plane, on which I had as if been chosen to be blessed. Blessed I say now, and blessed I thought then too, but there was nothing saccharine-sweet in this consciousness. No bliss-azure-skies-plump-cherubs. It was more like a mission or a sign that marked me out, like a burn on my skin, which could not be denied even in great fear. What I'm trying to say is that grace does not banish the fear, but on the contrary, grace can be terrifying.

I HAVE TO TALK ABOUT MONEY

I have to talk about money, a few words at least. Because if I'm boasting about the courage with which I accepted the pregnancy—which in a sense is what I'm doing—it must be remembered that the courage demanded of me wasn't so very great. And in order to deflate my heroism a little, I must give an account of the economic circumstances, as they say, in which I cultivated my love.

"Cultivated my love," I say, "cultivated my love." To the best of my knowledge I never "cultivated" it. And I only said so in order to needle myself and be sarcastic at my own expense. It would be much more accurate to say: the economic circumstances in which I loved.

When I left my parents' home in an adolescent tempest, all I had was a small savings account at the postal bank. A little money I received for my bat mitzvah, money I saved from babysitting and counseling at summer camps, and the symbolic dollars my Aunt Greta sent on my birthdays. Since I deluded myself that the rift with my parents was final, and since I had been brought up to work, that same week I applied to the labor bureau, which sent me to an old bed and breakfast in the suburb of Talpiot. Until the end of the month of February, when I could no longer hide my pregnancy and I was fired, I worked there from quarter to seven in the morning to quarter to four in the afternoon. Two Arab women from East Jerusalem cleaned and tidied the upstairs rooms, and I, looking more presentable to the proprietors, laid the tables, cut up vegetables, fried omelets, poured drinks, served meals, and in general provided the guests with "homey service." At eleven o'clock, when breakfast was over, I mopped the floors in the dining room, the lobby and the stairs, and all I had to do after that was to sit and answer the phone. The work was relatively easy, the owners, an elderly couple, were quite friendly until they fired me—at that period I did not yet have a clue about "legal rights"—and there isn't the slightest justification to see me as the pregnant-servant-heroine. I certainly am not trying to present myself as such. And even if it happened that I was overcome by weakness or nausea while frying the omelets, these attacks were not severe and passed quickly.

My difficulty with the work was different. I have to admit that the smell of the frying in my hair and of the detergent in my clothes, and all the "go, do, bring," were quite damaging to my self-image. It's true that I was brought up to work. I was taught that all forms of work were deserving of respect, but even on a kibbutz scale this was close to the bottom of the ladder. Service work. Not productive labor that a person could be proud of, definitely not something that brought credit to the kibbutz. And let's not forget that while I was busy not bringing credit to the kibbutz, Alek was plowing through Nietzsche with the help of a Russian-German dictionary, poring over his mysterious Soloviev and his symbolist poets, or catching the eye of his teacher, the poet Leah Goldberg, in class. I know that he tried to attract her attention in class, she interested him, I guessed that he interested her, too, and this too did nothing to add to my sense of worth.

What Alek's financial situation was I did not know, and it never occurred to me to ask. That is to say, I knew that sometimes he had money, because then he took taxis and threw money around at Fink's Bar, and that shortages of cash would last until he got fed up and he would go to work with Yoash. Further details I learned only later, after he left, and after the repulsive Hyman came to inform me of my legal husband's intentions and of my rights: As of this moment, Alek, even if he so desired, is unable to pay child support, you have to understand this, and since he is abroad in any case, my advice to you is not to enter into a fight because you won't get anything out of it. At the time, as you probably remember, I advised you to talk to him in order to secure your position, but there's no point in crying over spilt milk now. Under the circumstances, and if we're already talking, have you got some arrangement for the child already? They're looking for an extra girl to work in our office in the mornings, and if you're interested I'll be happy to recommend you. Just take into account that you'll have to learn to type, because presumably they didn't teach you to type at school, ha ha ha.

I didn't understand if Hyman had been sent by Alek or if he had appointed himself to the task, if he was trying to represent me or my husband, and the truth is that I wasn't interested, either. At the end of all the talk he informed me that Alek had paid a deposit for the apartment in which I was living, and that I could go on living there as long as I wished. Hyman also tried to hint that it would be a good idea to "regularize the situation" and draw up a written agreement, but neither then nor in the future did I have the faintest desire for any kind of "written agreement." Perhaps simply because there was no need for it, perhaps because a contractual procedure of this kind didn't fit in with my lofty standards and exalted love.

Over the years, partly through Hagar, I discovered that Alek was not a complete beggar, at least not in terms of his home. From bits of stories I pieced together it transpired that Jenia, Marina's husband, evidently a capable man, had had a hand in some textile business in Poland, and he had not only made a profit but also succeeded in getting the money out of the country, and afterwards, in France, he had made more. I don't know if Alek took money from him, perhaps he had managed to save something during the period when he was a student with a job in Paris, perhaps he received money from the state as a new immigrant to Israel. The important thing from my point of view is that even before he enlisted in the army he acquired the apartment on Usha Street and renovated it, and it was in the course of the renovations, by the way, that he met Yoash. The quarter of Nachlaot had not yet become fashionable then, prices were relatively cheap, and as a result of all of the above it came about that I and my daughter had, and still have, a home. This fact was not yet known to me when I decided to have the baby, but even without it, I can't deny that I made my leap of faith with a safety net spread out beneath me. A safety net consisting of parents, I mean, and with parents like mine there was no real possibility that I would turn into an abandoned-pregnant-maidservant-heroine. Even in my mental state of adolescent melodrama, I think that I knew this.

A few words about my parents' situation. After leaving the kibbutz we lived austerely for a while, without property or savings, on the salaries of a nurse and an officer in the standing army. The change came two years later, when my father left the army and started to exploit the connections he had made on various sales and acquisitions missions in order to broker private arms deals.

Connections are Benjy's strong point. Connections and a kind of greedy lust for life, expressed among other things in overpowering energy and dynamic industriousness. My father, Benjamin Weber, is a man whose sense of responsibility borders on megalomania, who slaps everyone on the back and looks after everyone. "Everyone" came to Talush's bat mitzvah and he went to "everyone's" celebrations, flashing them, me, all of us, the cheerful, bright blue looks of a tanned, wrinkled little boy. After the Yom Kippur War, and again after the Labor Party lost the elections, and after his heart attack, and when Bibi Netanyahu rose to power—he seemed to have emptied out, with his shirt empty at the shoulders, to have turned into a nostalgic whiner who had lost his back-slapping cheerfulness and his natural ability to fix things with a couple of phone calls. But whenever we thought that old age had finally caught up with him, he pulled himself together, jumped back into the saddle and returned to his hail-fellow-well-met ways.

What is important here is that in the winter of '72 my parents were already "doing well," as they say, that afterwards they did even better, and that even if this were not the case, they would never have abandoned their firstborn daughter to the streets or the social services. Would I have persisted in my madness and my pregnancy without this safety net? Not having been put to the test, I don't know, but the bottom line is: I believe that I would have.

ONCE I'M TALKING ABOUT MY PARENTS

Once I'm already talking about my parents, I may as well mention two shameful events connected to them which took place during my pregnancy. When I was in my fourth month, it was in December, I dropped into my mother's clinic, she worked then in the old Sha'arei Tzedek Hospital, and informed her of my situation—Hello, mother, how are you? I got married in a fictitious marriage and now I'm pregnant.

To the best of my recollection I didn't plan this visit in advance, I didn't plan it and I didn't decide on it, but on my way home from work, I simply went up to see her as if on a whim. From the heights of my maturity today I can admit that I was miserable and frightened and I needed a mother, but then I didn't admit this even to myself, and armored myself instead in a kind of conceited, annoying calm. My mother, in spite of all the advice she read in women's magazines, my mother, a veteran nurse, with a table of the principal nutrients on the wall over her head, and a table of calories under the glass on her desk, my mother couldn't find a word to say. She simply sat there speechless, and I can't say that I blame her. I blew in out of nowhere, impermeable and intoxicated with myself, albeit in need, desperately in need, but not of her and her touch—of him, who made any other contact impossible.

That same evening, in the street below, someone put his hand on the horn of his car and kept it there. And when our neighbour Miriam poked her head out to complain, and Alek emerged from his room, I saw my father's white Alfa Romeo from the kitchen window.

"It's my father," I said quietly, "I suppose he wants me to go down." Chivalrous by education and principle, Alek offered to go down with or without me. Judging by his tone it sounded as if there was nothing out of the ordinary in the street scene taking place below, or in the one that was about to take place. As if this was the way of the world and the way of fathers and everybody knew it. "Put on a coat at least," he said, mildly amused, "here, take mine," and he draped it round my shoulders.

Wrapped in Alek's coat, while its owner took up a position at the window, I went down to my father. When I opened the gate for a moment his eyes were at the level of my stomach, and he immediately jumped out of the car. "Get in," he shot at me, "we're going home, first thing tomorrow morning your mother's taking you to Zvi's clinic."

"It's too late."

"Don't you tell me that it's too late."

"It is too late, one; and two, I'm not going with you anywhere."

My father kicked the tire and let out a curse in English aimed at Alek. "Why are you cursing him? What's there to curse about? What do you want him to do? To marry me? He's already married me. I'm a married woman." I could have made do with these lines, they were quite good, but I couldn't resist going on: "And, all together, what right have you got to talk? You didn't marry Yifat, and 'that man,' as you call him, did marry me." When we were still living on the kibbutz, one of my father's volunteer activities was to prepare the twelfth-graders for the army, and Yifat from the Swallow Group, some of the kibbutz members said also Dalia from the Dawn Group, apparently received his personal attention. At home nobody ever mentioned these stories, or even hinted at them, as if it might God forbid hurt my father's feelings, but in my group there was a girl whose sister worked in the kibbutz clinic, and according to her my dear father arranged for a friend of his at the Tel Hashomer Hospital to perform abortions on both of them.

All this happened shortly before we left the kibbutz and invites the construction of some bombastic theory about my subconscious hostility towards my father, which is of course nothing but love in disguise. About the incestuous jealousy I felt for the girls he had fucked, an incestuous jealousy which was the sole reason . . . except that this interpretation doesn't hold water, and is completely beside the point. I love Alek. Full stop. I loved Alek, full stop. I was impregnated by Alek, full stop. And my father's activities have nothing to do with it. As a child his behaviour embarrassed me. And later on it angered me. As an adult I accumulated fluent reasons to explain to anyone ready to listen why it was abhorrent, and I went on condemning and denouncing until I reached a height of maturity where my feelings were joined by a kind of compassionate affection as well.

But all these emotional and ideological developments with regard to my father, all this textbook psychological growth, had absolutely nothing to do with my relationship with Alek.

My love watches me from the window. My father looks at me through his superfluous sunglasses, and his mouth is suddenly slack and drooping. My love and my father, my father and my love. Reality brought them together this one time, in this one scene. My mind, however, never made any connection between them, and the same goes for my subconscious mind. I'm sure of it, you have my word for it, and it's my word that counts.

"And I already fixed up a job for you in the army as a company clerk," said my father, and no doubt wanted to drive away with screeching brakes, but the Alfa refused to start. He almost exhausted the battery before it moved. But still he let the window down to have the last word: "Just tell him, in my name, that I'm going to find out everything about him," and then he stepped on the gas.

WRETCHEDNESS

That was my last big scene, and the further we advanced into winter the lower I sank, without being able to raise myself or my spirits. I couldn't even go out to run, and running had always been a part of my life. It seems to me that I discovered jogging naturally, long before it became fashionable, and I kept it up after it went out of fashion too. Until recently, running has helped me keep to my daily ration of five cigarettes, as well, and it's only rarely, like this Passover, that I let myself exceed it. I liked, and I still like, the effort, the stretching of myself beyond the point where you think you've reached your limit. And still, to this day, I go on pushing myself past the stabbing pain in my ribs and the pain in my legs, for the sake of the miracle that takes place when you don't break, when the pain vanishes, and you grow light to yourself and you feel as if you can carry on gliding through the air forever. But already at the beginning of the pregnancy I found that I was short of breath, I was too tired after work, in the evening I felt sleepy, and I stopped running.

Beginning with the fifth month I could no longer hide my condition, not even under the *galabiyehs* I wore, and my swelling stomach and undisguised wretchedness embarrassed everyone who came to the house. And they came in droves, flocks of guests who dropped in almost every evening and sometimes stayed until the wee hours of the night. Alek entered into a kind of sociable trance, and in that freezing February-March there were weeks that looked like a never-ending party. *Rhapsody in Blue* playing on the record player, stacks of dishes piled in the sink, used tea bags on the marble counter, cigarette ends in empty bottles of brandy, vodka, and Sprite. People sprawled in every corner of the house, including his room. Someone squatting on the stairs, wrapped in a red banner bearing a picture of Che Guevara, filling the stove with kerosene while the wind made the banner billow around him. Someone dead to the world on my bed, his muddy shoes dirtying the corner of the mattress. A smell of kerosene, and rain and smoke and orange peels on top of the stove, never grass, because even at the height of his sociability Alek would send the joint-rollers outside, with the apology that he couldn't stand the smell.

There was a certain Shmulik who turned up with a guitar and the entire repertoire of the youth movement and the kibbutz, and suddenly this too didn't bother Alek, who up to then hadn't been able to stand "those Soviet songs." Or maybe it did bother him, because a murderous, demented expression spread over his face as he joined in and sang as if to spite himself, sang with them, to them, in Russian.

I said before that I was a source of embarrassment. In practice most of the guests ignored me, they didn't even know that I lived there, and the ones that knew me didn't know what to say. I stuck out like a sore thumb, like a kind of walking hump, a hump that was liable, God forbid, to attach itself to their own backs. Sometimes Dalit from La Mama would ask in a confidential-compassionate voice: "Should I make you a cup of tea?" Or: "Are you sure we're not stopping you from sleeping?" And in my misery I was glad even of these little pats.

Once, on a gray early evening, outside, I remember, a niggardly snow was falling, Hyman sat down next to me on the mattress, and when he put his arm around me in a comradely manner, as if we were sitting round the campfire, and slipped his fingers into my bra, I didn't even protest. I was chain-smoking then, one cigarette after the other whenever I wasn't feeling nauseated, and that gray evening, with Hyman's arm around me, Alek suddenly bent down and removed the cigarette from between my lips. "That's enough. You're smoking too much." By such crumbs of attention I was nourished then, and with them I sustained my love. Love does not need very much to sustain it.

Another time he came home in the morning, it was already after I had been fired from my job, and I was just sitting in the kitchen. And I was hurting so badly then that I couldn't even raise my head. But Alek came up and stood behind me, and stroked my nape, the sensation of that particular touch is imprinted in me to this day, as if my nape remembers, and then he pulled me to my feet and went on hugging me gently from behind. "It's hard for you." "It is," I admitted in a low voice. "Yes . . ." he whispered to me, "yes, Noichka, it's hard." As if a common destiny had been imposed on both of us. A common destiny . . . even today, when I no longer believe in that kind of predestination as I did then, sometimes against my better judgement, I still sense its existence.

When he turned away and went to his room, I, moved to the point of tears, thought of a poem by David Vogel we had studied for finals. "How can I see you, love, / Standing alone / Amid storms of grief / Without feeling my heart shake?" I returned again and again in those days to that poem, which continued: "Come, / My hand will clasp your dreaming / Hand, / And I shall lead you between the nights." But I was only his fictitious wife, married to him only by law and by the law of my love, and most of the time I stood "alone amid storms of grief" and his heart did not shake. And his hand did not clasp my hand to lead me between the nights.

Only one single time, one single night in that winter, when my stomach was not yet very big, he got into bed with me. He didn't fuck me, he didn't even take off his pants, he only undressed me naked and worked on me until I came in tears. And he held me a little longer against his chest, until perhaps he thought I had fallen asleep, and then he got up and went away.

I didn't want to come like that. I did want to come, the fact is that I did come, it's only in pornographic movies that a woman shudders and comes against her will, and he finished me off completely with that unselfish sex, I finished myself in that beggarly sex, under the generosity of his mouth and hands, trembling, rising and falling, not holding my head above water, swallowing black water, sinking in waves of humiliation. And in all that time I knew that he was really trying to do me and my body good. And in the days to come, too, like a dog I would fawn on the accidental touch of his hand, and arch at the memory of a caress.

You could say that in that winter I lost my self-respect, you could say so—but that wasn't the way I felt, at least most of the time. And with the feeling of humiliation, with my wretchedness and pink, running nose, in my madness I invented a new kind of respect for myself. Like a private code of chivalry. Like setting myself a martyr's test, at the conclusion of which I would present myself to receive a medal from the Order of Faithful Lovers. No nagging. No clinging. No whining. No expectations and no demands. This was the motto inscribed on my shield. And with all my strength I tried to comply with these commands. Because if I was sentenced to being a beggar, then at least I would be a beggar with an ethical code.

Vogel's weren't the only lines of poetry in my head, there were all kinds of others, too, and without any other books at hand—Alek's were in Russian, French and German—I absorbed myself in the material from my high school literature courses to such an extent that I still know some of it by heart. For hours I held myself spellbound with the poems of Alterman's *The Joy of the Poor*, with the eternal absentee coming to the woman "to join her behind the glass," with the stranger coming to the city to "stand in the gate, and guard your sleep," with his hidden voice demanding: "And you, now swear by God that you / will draw strength from your miseries." With his voice promising "like fire and spear I shall give you / comfort, I shall fill you with inhuman / strength," until "before all is lost I shall / brace you for the time / I the remem- / berer, I the witness."

I knew that Alek didn't love me, I've already said so, and with a surprising maturity I did not delude myself with thoughts of lightning suddenly striking him. Somehow it was clear to me that people don't suddenly fall in love with someone who in any case is getting under their feet all day. And nevertheless I wanted something, I longed for something. To be significant in his eyes. To be important to him. To be woven into his heart in a way that could never be unraveled.

Of all the poems I read then the most perverse was an old English ballad we studied in the first year of high school, called "Childe Waters." In this ballad, which I don't remember by heart, even though I've read it many times, the pregnant heroine cuts off her hair, puts on a page's costume and accompanies her lover when he sets out to find himself a bride. Childe Waters rides and rides on his horse, the lovelorn girl walks and walks barefoot at his side, and after many verses in which he rides and rides and the damsel walks and walks through thorn fields and rivers, they arrive at a golden palace in a great city. When they are already inside the palace the cruel Childe Waters sends the fair Ellen to bring him a whore from the street, and to add to her humiliation he also commands her to carry the whore in her arms so that she won't dirty her feet. Ellen does as the knight commands, and while he rolls around in bed with the whore she has brought him, the chivalrous pregnant woman goes to sleep in the stable.

I admit that I was really turned on by this sad ballad then, even though I already had some idea that it was stupid and sick.

In my imagination, I think, I saw myself as the descendent of all these lovelorn literary women, their sister in an order of unrequited love. Armed with my limitless love, armed with my passivity, possessed of great strength in my way, and "Not all is vanity, my dear / not all is vain," and "Strength has no end, my dear, / only the body that breaks like clay."

Clearly I was trying to glorify my wretchedness, obviously I was trying to glorify my wretchedness, what else? But this glorification held me to a certain standard of dignified behavior, and it may have saved me from an even worse wretchedness, and from actually crawling like a worm. I mean that "If you tell me to go I shall go, / If you tell me to stay away I shall stay away," is preferable, after all, to "please don't go, no, don't go, I can't stand it, I can't take it, no, Alek, please, please don't...."

So it's true that I painted the banal bad as "gloriously bad" to myself, but it's also true that the "gloriously bad" helped me to get through another miserable hour and another miserable morning. And therefore, however ridiculous I find this romantic pose today, and for all my crushing feminist critique of those poems, I remember how at a certain point in my life they simply helped me to cope. And how in the end, after I gave birth and Alek left, what saved me from total collapse was precisely the romantic pose.

IF YOU TELL ME TO GO

Among all the marvelous qualities I bestowed on my heroine Nira Woolf I also gave her a musical gift and an exquisite contralto. For the most part she only plays to herself at night, improvising jazz both in order to relax and in order to think about her current case, but once I let her sing a completely different song. This happens in the last scene of

Dead Woman's Voice, the sixth book in the series, whose grim plot centers on the attempt to cover up a case of incest. The raped daughter of the senior officer in the security services kills herself before the book begins. The senior prosecuting attorney, the rapist father's mistress, who is completely subjugated to his will, kills herself in chapter sixteen, after he thrusts a revolver into her hand. And in the last scene, the intern who was trying to blackmail the father lies bleeding on the steps to Nira's house, while the chief villain himself lies bound at her feet.

Throughout the book my Nira is mainly interested in the servile behavior of the mistress-lawyer, and at the end, after the mystery is solved and the police are already on their way, she sits down at the piano and sings to the villain lying on the floor with his hands and feet tied painfully together behind his back, in the so-called "banana knot," Alterman's "Song of Three Answers": "Everything you ask and wish / I shall be happy to do / I shall never lack the strength / To do as you wish me to." Nira Woolf's back is turned to the cruel villain who tried to trap her, too—first to seduce her with his charms and then to murder her—her warm contralto grows louder from line to line against a background of sirens, and only when the police are already in the room does she turn around, without even looking at him. A private joke of my own, I would say, but what kind of a joke is it in fact?

My darling Hagar, who is not a great admirer of my books—she considers them "shallow"—actually praised this scene, although she remarked that "for her taste" it was "too far-fetched." My daughter, who from time to time sends me articles about "The image of the woman in . . ."—all her articles seem to me the regurgitation of the same slogans—my daughter appears to have been born with an innate immunity to the germ of romanticism and to have subsequently enlisted in the medical corps dedicated in deadly earnest to its extermination. Not for her own personal benefit, since she does not seem to be in need of it, but for the good of the population at large.

Hagar's preoccupation with "the image of the woman" began in high school, at the same high school I attended myself, with the same literature teacher and regarding the very same works that I myself studied.

"To say to a woman 'be to me a god and an angel,'" she once wrote in one of her more successful compositions, "is like telling her that she isn't a human being!!! Bialik has no right to dictate to a woman what she should be!!!" On behalf of these well-put sentiments, with all their angry exclamation marks, and others like them, my darling often quarreled with her literature teacher. Thanks to her congenital immunity she seems to be completely deaf to certain notes, so that they simply fail to have any effect on her at all, or else they activate only her sense of justice and social anger. A justified anger, I have to say, an absolutely and completely justified social anger.

But for the second of July 1972, but for Alek, perhaps I would be as pure and innocent as she is today.

"In my opinion Sonia is a superficial one-dimensional character," wrote my darling vehemently when they studied *Crime and Punishment*, and she added arguments far more compelling than any I had to offer at her age. All kinds of explanations about the connection between the *kedosha*, the saintly woman, and the *kedeisha*, the temple whore, and how "the patriarchal culture produced them both."

In my day the combination "patriarchal culture" did not yet exist.

When I read the essay she left lying on the kitchen table, with the usual mark of *100* written on top of the page, it suddenly seemed to me that this red-inked hundred referred to my age, so infirm of mind did I feel. Muddling memories, he stood there like that and I lay there when he said and then I said. . . . My arteries so clogged with memories that I didn't have a drop of strength to speak, and in any case there was too much, much too much, and it was too late to explain anything.

When she praised the last scene of *Dead Woman's Voice* my daughter told me—she was twenty-five then—that I had done well to "expose the falsity of that text" and that it was "important to educate the public to understand how chauvinistic that song is."

My good darling is right, we have to educate, we have no choice, and I educated her, I had no choice, and she with her marvelous purity is the perfect creation of my educational endeavors.

Even if I were given the chance to bring her up all over again, I wouldn't change a thing.

I DO MY THING AND YOU DO YOURS

The first time I saw Tamara was on the eve of Purim, when all kinds of people dropped in on us on their way to the big party at the Bezalel Academy of Art, and already in that half hour I knew that something had happened or was going to happen between her and Alek. It's hard to say exactly how such things are grasped, but I think that I knew not because of the way they looked at each other, but just the opposite, because of the way they avoided looking. He didn't make room for her to sit down. He didn't pour her a drink. None of his usual chivalrous gestures towards the pretty faces who would show up at the house.

Tamara—not Tamar but Tamara—was as affected in my eyes as her name. She had dressed up for the party in a gold sari, and if she had removed her steel-rimmed glasses, with her long black hair and dark, slightly asymmetrical face, she would have looked like one of Gauguin's women. A thin Gauguin. Although she was as Israeli as I was, a Jerusalemite from the well-heeled suburb of Rehavia, she surrounded herself with a kind of aura of foreignness. She was studying comparative literature with Alek, and she talked through her nose in a would-be European accent, although it was impossible to say which Europe exactly.

On that first evening she showed up with a friend draped in a sheet supposed to be a toga, who came back on the following days, but the minute I set eyes on his pampered mouth and receding chin, and took in the pair of them together, I knew that I couldn't expect any protection from him.

The pregnant Cinderella was not going to the party, even though a number of people asked me if I wanted a ticket. With my big belly and scratchy tights under my *galabiyeh*, and my feeling of vulnerability, I had no intention of exposing myself to the particular torment of Purim. I waited for everyone to leave with their costumes and rattles, so that I could go to bed at last and be by myself. But when I was alone I was subject to another torment, no less intrusive than the noise of the merry-making, and from which I could not hide in bed, because it was even more savage lying down.

From the beginning, the beginning of our relationship, that is, I knew that this torment would come. In other words, I had no reason to assume that Alek would abstain from other women, and in spite of my own limited experience, I was certainly able to recognize his. I knew on my skin how every movement of his with me, every kiss and caress, bore the memory of previous contacts, and I knew it so precisely, that it sometimes seemed to me that the memory of these previous sexual encounters had entered into me by osmosis, and I could actually see the images. I was seventeen and eighteen in our first year, and he was twenty-eight. And to this day I have this feeling, as if I can guess via the sex what kind of woman he was with before. As if our love-making made all the others present.

Today I don't care any more, I think I don't care, but that lofty indifference was acquired with effort and passed through all kinds of stages on the way, the one being the stage of the gestalt mantra: I'm me and you're you, I do my thing and you do yours. Now I think that this slogan serves as a theoretical rationalization for abuse, but for some strange reason I used this rationalization then to justify my own mute suffering: this is what I chose, this is what he chose, that's how he is, that's how I am, and if I don't get up and leave, I have to bear it. And with dignity.

As far as Alek is concerned, by the way, I don't think he ever had any desire to abuse me or any other woman. In all our years together he was discreet about his other women, perfectly discreet, but never secretive in a manner that spoke of guilt.

With me and also presumably with them, he behaved as if polygamy was the most natural thing in the world. And with the passing of time, without anything being said, he succeeded quite well in making me internalize the notion that the demand for sexual fidelity was tantamount to emasculation.

So I would never put my Nira Woolf, for example, into any kind of exclusive relationship, let alone a total commitment. And if the curtain comes down in *Suitable Service* with a passionate sex scene with the decent military advocate, at the opening of *Daggers Drawn* she already has another man in tow.

Looking back, the hardest thing was waiting for the inevitable to happen, for another woman to appear, and so perhaps, however perverse it may sound, when Tamara came into the picture it was a kind of relief.

Jealousy craves knowledge, as if knowledge of the details has it in its power to liberate the obsessive preoccupation, and at a certain point, two weeks or more after the party, I needed to know so badly that I went up to talk to her. It was in our kitchen, and she was making tea for the owner of the pampered mouth and a few others.

Me (leaning against the marble counter next to her): I wanted to tell you something.

Tamara (obviously alarmed): Yes, of course . . .

Me: About you and Alek.

Tamara: What? Oh . . . what about it? (A quick glance in my direction, and then lowering her head as she pours the tea into the mugs on the tray.)

Me: I just wanted you to know . . . and for Alek to know, too, that this is his house. And that nobody tells him what to do in his house.

Tamara (More alarmed than ever. The lenses of her glasses are covered with steam): I don't understand.

Me (Pulling the cardigan more tightly around my body. My hands folded above my high stomach.): I don't know what you've been told about us, but you should know that Alek and I are only married fictitiously, because I didn't want to go to the army.

Tamara: Oh, but you're mistaken. It isn't like that. You're completely mistaken. There's nothing between me and Alek. Rani (or Dani) is my boyfriend.

Me: What I wanted to say is that you don't have to behave like a couple of thieves, because that's what's unfair to me. And if you really want to know what hurts me, then that's what hurts me. It insults me that you try to hide it.

In the course of this dialogue I suddenly realized what it means to be crazy: I attached myself to her like some crazy beggar woman seizing the sleeve of a passerby in the street, and I clearly sensed how she instinctively recoiled in fear. Instinctively she wanted to pick up her heels and run away from me, not because I had "caught her out" and "discovered her secret," but because of what I was, which could be dangerous. And nevertheless I could not stop. As if only the explicit confirmation that it had happened and was happening would bring me relief. The devil knows what kind of relief, because I didn't have even the vaguest notion of what I would do when I knew. When I knew for certain. When I knew what for certain? That he was fucking her? How he was fucking her? Slowly and looking at her to see? What her little breasts looked like when he rolled her on top of him; how he wound her long hair around his hand and smiled at her; if he kissed her eyes and stroked her back too when she fell asleep on his shoulder?

Above all, I think, I wanted it to be different with me. To know that something different happened to him with me. Because it was impossible that it could be the same with me and this phony Gauguin fake.

It sounds funny, but what aroused my jealousy most, even more than the imagined sex, was the fact that Tamara knew French and was studying

Russian. That she sat next to him during classes and afterwards, gossiping about Leah Goldberg and reading Verlaine and Baudelaire, and Bely, and Blok, and Ivanov, all the poets he could only tell me about. That he talked to her about "Schopenhauer's perception of music" and what exactly an important thinker called Eduard von Hartmann thought, and what exactly someone else, I can't remember who, said. For some reason it was clear to me—a crumb of consolation—that he talked to her, while all she contributed to the conversation was her affected cultured expression. I brooded a lot about how he made her laugh with all kinds of misquotations and never had to interrupt with "that I really can't translate."

Of course I never found the certainty I sought. And after Purim, when Alek's trance of sociability calmed down a bit, he simply started to stay away from home more and more. Once when I came back from work the two of them were sitting in his room with the door open, and he had his arm around her shoulder. "Noichka . . . come and join us. Tamara's tried to translate something we read in class here, and with my Hebrew I can't even tell her how it sounds." He said this quite naturally, without removing his arm from her shoulder that had turned to stone. And then, too, what hurt most of all in this scene was the apparently trivial fact that he called me "Noichka," a name that up to then had been reserved for only the most intimate moments between us.

TWENTY-NINE YEARS LATER

Twenty-nine years later, the jealousy was no longer alive. It died down after the shock of the birth, and after he left and came back and left again, and I went to visit him abroad. Perhaps I grew accustomed to being one of a number of Alek's women. And perhaps the distance and the longings dulled the other pain. From the outset I should never have allowed myself to be jealous, for what right did I have to be jealous of him? And for lack of any alternative, what I wanted above all was only to believe that I was in some way special to him. That something not given to others was given only to me.

With more than twenty-nine years behind us, I am entitled to believe that I am, indeed, special to him. That my perseverance has borne fruit, and there is a place reserved exclusively for me in his heart. But at what price?

Now too I do not think that I fell in love with a man unworthy of me, and that if only I woke up from a twenty-nine-year-old dream I would to my horror see a donkey's head. Alek turned fifty-seven in December, and still, with his angular thinness and his graying hair, he is more worthy in my eyes than any other man, and so I know he will always remain. The problem isn't that he's unworthy, but that perhaps it isn't worthy to love anyone the way I love him.

I said that the birth and everything that followed it dulled my jealousy. But it happened a few times that it bit me again, and I didn't succeed in loosening its teeth immediately.

My Hagar (aged six): What do you think, that Daddy is more mature now, or less mature, or the same?

Me: You know better than me. You went for a walk with him.

And thus from my worried daughter I learned that Ute was about to give her a baby brother. This was in '79, after Alek had returned to Israel as a correspondent for Radio Luxembourg and a couple of

European newspapers, and I was already leading the life of a mistress. Waiting for him to phone me. Not phoning him. Deserting my job on all kinds of pretexts to keep appointments with him. Looking for babysitters for Hagar, simply in order to accompany him when he went to cover a demonstration. Arranging for another mother to pick Hagar up from kindergarten and waiting for him bathed and ready at home, afraid that the phone would ring and it would be him, to say that he was sorry but he couldn't come. Maybe next week? I'll call you. . . . The whole humiliating package.

Soon after Alek's return, I had dropped in for coffee at Yoash's picture-frame shop on Agrippas Street, and he said to me: "She's a restorer, he met her in Paris. Her name's Ute." I already knew this, but Yoash, bending over his work table, went on, more slowly than usual and surprisingly hostile: "The way Alek tells it, she came to the newspaper office to pick up a parcel her cousin had left there for her, and a second after she entered the room he already knew that he wanted to have children with this woman. Do you believe that? Or is he just rewriting history?"

Alek and Yoash didn't see a lot of each other at this time. Perhaps the political atmosphere strained relations between them: the rise of the right to power that appalled Yoash and pleased Alek the foreign correspondent—"Changing the government is always a good thing"— and perhaps there was some other reason. I didn't see a lot of Yoash, either. But that Friday morning, for no particular reason, I dropped into his shop for a cup of coffee on my way to the market. Or perhaps the reason for my visit was that I had already met Alek since his return, and I wanted to hear what Yoash knew, and to feel I was touching him again through someone who might have met him too.

"He wanted to have children with this woman." The sentence cut right through my stomach to the sound of the cardboard splitting in two as Yoash slowly and intently sliced through it with his box-cutter knife. I already knew about Ute, but I didn't know this, and suddenly I understood that in my foolishness I had seen my pregnancy with Hagar and the night of her birth as a kind of covenant between us.

BIRTH

On the night of the tenth of June I woke up with wet panties, a strong feeling of nausea, and a pain no worse than the pain that had been coming and going intermittently during the previous days. As soon as I woke up I knew that it had begun, and I was completely unready.

When my sister Talush was born I was not yet six, and all I remembered of the event was that my mother went away to Afula and returned five days later with the baby, and how for some time my father would take me to the children's house to put me to bed, because my mother had gone to feed the baby. All my girlfriends today gave birth in their thirties, and from their prenatal courses, and from the stories they told and retold afterwards, I learned things I had no idea of even after I had already given birth myself. Contraction length, dog pants, dilation, epidural, Pitocin, head presentation, breech presentation, vacuum, forceps—an entire vocabulary of combat experience that could certainly have been useful. Only once, when I was already in my ninth month, I paged through some manual in Stein's Bookshop, and the black-and-white photographs disgusted or alarmed me to such an extent that I closed it immediately. And so I came to give birth in a state of total ignorance, with only the vaguest notion of what was happening to me.

They say that women forget the pain of giving birth, which is absolute nonsense and I don't know why people keep repeating it. Because what does it mean to remember pain? You remember pain in exactly the same way as you remember pleasure, which is also not exactly re-experienced with the memory, and nevertheless is implanted firmly in your body.

It was dark in the room and I was feeling too nauseated to get up and look for clean panties in the closet, so I simply took off the wet ones and went on lying half naked on the bed under the piqué blanket. Alek's door was shut, he had returned after I had already fallen asleep, and for some stupid, stubborn reason I got it into my head that whatever happened, I was on no account to wake him up. Maybe he had come home late from Tamara. Maybe he was with Tamara now. He had never hidden behind the door with Tamara, and the couch in his room wasn't big enough for two, but nevertheless this piece of idiocy stuck in my head, that the two of them might be there together now, and that nothing on earth would make me call him or knock on the door.

You could argue that my stubbornness was actually an expression of anger. That instead of punishing him I punished myself, and that what I was really doing was trying to make him feel as guilty as I could: "Look how much I love you, and look what you're doing to me." Maybe. I don't know. I only know that together with the thought that he was in the room with Tamara, I was afraid of the possibility that he wasn't home at all, that his door was still closed from the day before, and that I was mistaken in thinking that it had been open when I went to bed.

Apart from which I have already said that I was unprepared, and waking Alek meant admitting that this was it, it was beginning. So even though I really knew it was beginning, at the same time it seemed to me that if I didn't wake him up, perhaps I would fall asleep again and somehow or other I would wake up in the morning as if nothing had happened.

I don't know how much time passed in this way until, at a certain point, I tried to reach the bathroom to vomit, and in the darkness I threw up on the passage floor. When I squatted down with my bare bottom to clean up the mess, a whine like a dog's suddenly escaped me and took me by surprise. This whine seems to have breached the dike, because after it, and when I returned to sit on the bed, I gave myself up entirely to self-pity and tears. I wailed and rocked, rocked and wailed, even though the contractions were not yet of an order that could not be borne in silence.

Through closed lids I saw the light go on, and even before I opened my eyes I located him standing in the doorway.

"Noichka . . . has it started?" For some reason I shook my head, but Alek took no notice of my denial. "What a swine I am," he exclaimed and punched the doorpost with his fist. And even before I recoiled from the violence of the gesture he was already at my side, tucking the blanket around me, embracing me tightly, brushing a sticky lock of hair off my face, whispering tender words to me in Russian: "Shhh . . . shhh . . . shhh . . . *devuchka . . . harosheya maya* . . . shhh, child, don't cry."

Nothing will help me, because even today this memory is dear to my heart, and all I have to do is remember Alek, concentrating intently, holding me between his hands, one hand on my breast, the other between my shoulder blades, imprisoning the sobbing inside me—all I have to do is remember it and I melt. As if the importance of those moments is far greater than everything else. Very slowly, as if we had all the time in the world, he helped me to steady my breath and pull myself together, and then he gathered me to him gently and rocked me slowly. "It's all right . . . *vsyo harasho* . . . it's all right, don't be afraid." Nothing will help me— because even now, when I think of complete and utter consolation, it is personified for me in that cradling in his arms and his voice whispering "don't be afraid." Because with that touch and that movement I felt that I was being lapped by a wondrous oceanic sensation, being filled with a sweet oceanic sensation, which was utterly and completely consoling. To this day, whenever I feel the need of consolation, I try to conjure up that sensation, and mostly I only succeed in touching its edges.

The sheet was wet with the amniotic fluid. I was sticky and stinking of vomit, I hadn't even brushed my teeth, and nevertheless he gathered me up and held me in his arms.

ALEK WASN'T DISGUSTED

Alek wasn't disgusted by me. On the contrary, he was completely absorbed in me. Not as if he were rushing to the aid of some "emergency" but as if he was intensely moved, and yet he was able to perform all the necessary operations without fear, without being paralyzed by this intensity of emotion.

I can't say why I love Alek. My love is not a function of any one of his attributes, not of those that I admire, and certainly not of those that are not to my liking. And nevertheless, when I think of my sexual addiction to him, I attribute it at least to a certain extent to his attitude towards the body. I say his attitude towards "the body" and not "my body," because it is perfectly clear to me that this attitude, which is an essential part of Alek's nature and being, is not reserved for me alone, and that he treats other women in the same way.

In the four years that he was in Israel with Ute, and I played the part of the classic mistress, I fucked not a few other men. In order to keep my balance, I think, and to even the score. But in all these experiences, and all the experiences that came later, I never met another man like him. I'm not talking about the fact that fucking someone you love is a completely different experience, and I'm not talking about his repertoire of sexual stunts, either. I've met a few sexual athletes in my life, the kind who've read all the manuals and wear your orgasms on their chests like medals, and without denying the pleasure I had with them, with Alek it was different.

The thing is that Alek really loves the body, he loves the body as if he's never seen a movie in his life, or a TV commercial; he is free of the external eye and aesthetic perception. It's difficult to explain properly, because Alek actually likes looking, but it seems as if the sights penetrate him and are beautiful in his eyes and gladden his heart not in the conventional way, not because of "what they look like." Somehow, almost always when sexual moves are initiated, he seems to undergo a transformation; he fills then with a kind of wonder, and seems to be intent only on guessing and serving—not because it swells his ego, even though in some way of course it swells his ego, of course it does—but the main thing is that he is entranced. Entranced—perhaps this is the right word, as if we are the first people in the world to perform the act, sinking deeper and deeper into it, and the spell is so potent that my external eye too closes until I am all body and until the body vanishes.

Sometimes I think that it is this transformation that drives me crazy. Sometimes I like to look at him in public. To look at his restrained public movements, and then to remember their opposite.

On a number of occasions I have heard Alek describing an old woman as "beautiful," or an official beauty as "not interesting," and altogether it seemed that most of the conventional ways of judging women had passed him by. For example, he likes women's perfumes, and knows how to distinguish between them, too, his favorite is "White Shoulders," on my neck at least, but in our first month together, when we once emerged from the shower together, he took the deodorant out of my hand, put it back on the shelf, and said: "Not yet, with your permission, we haven't finished yet," and it wasn't an empty gesture. Over the course of time I really became convinced that this clean man really loved the odors of my body, and in our day and age maybe this is enough to win a woman's heart.

I remember how on my fourth visit to him in Moscow, it was summer then, we were already in his apartment in Ordenka, and I had forgotten my razor blades at home. And since we're talking about Moscow here, there was no way I could just walk into a shop and buy one. In the end I found a packet of razor blades in a bookshop, in a locked display case next to Ajax cleaning fluid, but before I did so, the stubble that had sprouted on my legs during the course of the week did not stop Alek from rubbing his face on them and smiling to himself as if he was innocently delighting in the new touch.

Thanks to running or genetics, or perhaps to the fire of my madness, my body is what is referred to as "well preserved," but it is very far from being the body of a seventeen-year-old girl. Before every trip to visit him there is a certain moment in front of the mirror when I take note of the changes, but Alek without words somehow manages to persuade me that they only make me more interesting, and to the signs of aging that appear on my skin from one visit to the next he relates the way a woman is supposed to relate to a man's scars of honor.

In recent years, ever since my first visit to Russia, I began to attribute this identification with the body to the landscapes of his motherland, perhaps because it was very pronounced over there. He always enjoyed feeding me, but in Moscow it seemed that the simplest act of eating gave him immense pleasure, as when he raised a forkful of food to my mouth and said: "Taste this, see how you like it," and never took his eyes off me as I bit and chewed, and kissed me without being ashamed of the taste of food in his mouth.

"In Israel the food is tasteless, in Paris they know how to cook the best, but food only has a real taste here." Perhaps because I saw Moscow through his eyes, and through the rest of his senses, I too began to sense the "real taste of food." Like the taste and the smell of the sex, which were sharper there than anything I had known before. I had never lived my body as I did there, and it had never dissolved and evaporated as it did there.

All this is true, the truth as far as I am capable of formulating it, and still it revolts, it disgusts me, it utterly disgusts me to have to put the sex with him and my body with him into words. "The sights penetrate him," "he undergoes a transformation," "he is intent on guessing and serving." Why do I do it? Because only in this way can I exorcise the demon and smear it like tar with treacherous phrases. Smear it and smear it until I make myself sick.

BIRTH

When he thought I had calmed down he said: "I'll go down and call Yoash now to come with the pickup," and I clung to him and said: "No, don't go. I don't want to. I don't want to drive," and then he stroked me a little more and raised my chin and gave me a look that brought a reluctant smile to my lips. "Five minutes," he said, "five minutes and I'll be back with you again."

By the time he returned I was already dressed and I had also cleaned myself up a bit. I still felt nauseated, but I was already able to think of the drive without wanting to throw up. On the way out to the pickup he draped his brown corduroy shirt over my shoulders, and, wrapped in his shirt with his arm around me all the way, I rode between the two men to the hospital to give birth to Hagar.

The drive to Hadassah Hospital in Ein Kerem took maybe twenty minutes, and when he put me in the nurses' hands my mood was already greatly improved, as if I had been infected by Alek's festivity, and had risen to the importance of the occasion. And nevertheless he lingered a little longer, gazing at me in admiration, as if at the ultimate mystery, and then he kissed me gravely on the forehead, as if he were sending me on some important mission. "*Ti molodetz*," he said to me before he left.

Months later I asked him: "What's *molodetz*?" "Say it again . . . ah, *molodetz*. Where did you hear that word?" he was suddenly curious.

"Someone said it to me."

"*Molodetz* is . . . hero, person who overcomes. You say this of a man, but it may also be said of a woman. It could be said about you, that you are *molodetz*. The someone who said it to you, he said it about you?" I didn't answer. It was a few weeks after Yom Kippur, the two of us had invaded Yoash's apartment in Yarkon Street, and instead of answering I asked him if he had heard anything more about Yoash, who was still in the agricultural buffer zone on the other side of the Suez Canal.

A birth is a birth, millions of women all over the world give birth every day in worse conditions than I did, and I really have no intention of turning my delivery into something heroic. After being handed over to the nurses the usual procedure began, what was then the "usual procedure." I know from my girlfriends that a few things have changed since then. They gave me a nightgown, shaved me, gave me an enema, lay me on a bed in the labor room, stuck an IV into my arm, and attached me to a monitor to wait. On the other side of the screen was an empty bed, and beyond that empty bed a woman with a middle-aged voice was wailing fearsomely. At a certain point, when I had already lost my sense of time—they had taken away my watch—they wheeled her out, and after that there were other voices belonging to other women. From time to time a relation came in to visit one of them, and every few minutes the midwife came to see "how we're coming along." Two or three times she accompanied me, tottering and hanging on to the IV stand, to the toilet.

In years to come, when my friends began comparing the tales of their deliveries, I understood that I had apparently made good progress, i.e. at a normal pace, for a first birth. What I especially remember is the fear of how much worse the pain could get that came with every wave of contractions, and the graph on the monitor representing the climb from contraction to contraction, like an abstract threat of torture. How much more could I take? The same pain, presumably, was experienced by all the women beyond the screen, and by every woman in the world who has ever given birth, and it is of no particular interest, at least in the context of the story that I am telling here.

What is pertinent to the story is my perverse feeling that I was somehow handing myself over as a willing sacrifice for the sake of something of surpassing importance, which was not only the baby about to be born. Suffering pain and nausea and shivering with cold—for some reason I felt cold all the time—my mind filled with confused, hallucinatory images of ancient rituals, in my folly I saw the daughter of Jephthah and the daughter of Montezuma, and somehow it all connected to Alek and his kiss on my forehead, as if he had sent me to the sacrifice.

Pain is pain is pain, what else can be said of it? But I hadn't resolved to "bear it with honor" for nothing, my gritted teeth and clamped jaw were connected to the thought that Alek was somehow watching me, and this is what he expected to see. To see me "bearing it with honor." As the hours passed I gradually lost all control over logic, until at a certain point it seemed to me that Alek himself had inflicted this agony on me, and since he had inflicted it I accepted it, breathing quietly, barely sighing, and hugging his corduroy shirt.

Ten years ago, after my sister gave birth to her twins, a few of her girlfriends were visiting her at home, and, as was usual on these occasions, reminisced like war veterans about battles waged in the delivery room. One of them, orange-haired and ample-bosomed, was burping Noam on her shoulder, and at the same time making us all laugh with reports of how she had made her husband suffer during her labor, and how she had screamed at the top of her voice. "I had a ball, believe me, I really went to town, people must have heard me screaming miles away."

"Didn't they give you an epidural?" "You bet they did. Right at the beginning I screamed so loudly that they didn't have a choice, they came running to give it to me. What am I, a wounded soldier, to lie there and suffer in silence? How many opportunities do I have in my life to scream? So the minute I get the chance I do it with all my heart."

In the midst of all the joking and laughter, I envied the funny redhead, who appeared to me the embodiment of female mental health.

The story of my own delivery I kept to myself, of course, even after Talush threw out "In comparison to Noa our stories are jokes for children. My sister gave birth in the Middle Ages."

Perhaps people have a kind of reflex that makes them try to endow pain with significance, but how could I explain to this group of women hilarious with anarchic mirth—laughing at their husbands, joking about the hospital, bad-mouthing their mothers, giggling at themselves and their newfound motherhood—how could I explain to them the perverse meaning which I had given to pain? This meaning belonged to another world, very far from the living room heated for my sister's offspring, and though I was sitting there in that living room, it was also far from me. What happened to me during the birth was that I began to think about pain as a kind of sacrifice I was making for Alek, as if I had surrendered myself to pain for his sake. And to my sorrow I must point out that this warped idea was quite detached from the knowledge that at the end of the process I would have a baby. In other words, I didn't think that I was suffering for the sake of the child, the way that women in labor are at least supposed to think, but found a point in the pain itself, a point which was somehow connected to Alek. And thus with every contraction that racked my body, I imagined that I was taking the pain and offering it up, dedicating it, I have no idea to whom, all I know is that this dedication was connected to some absolute of love. As if all I had to do was take it upon myself, and I would be rewarded in the end by absolute love, which was not simply Alek-will-love-me, but something more tremendous. Something infinite.

At some point, I think it was already afternoon, the midwife came in and after examining me—"Good girl. Not yet, but we're coming along nicely"—she asked me if I wanted them to "give me something." Of course I wanted them to give me "something," but I didn't know what this "something" was, I only understood from her voice that it would lessen the pain. In my defense I have to say that even in my warped mental state I didn't wish myself still more pain, and I was very frightened of the pain to come.

Looking back I suppose they must have given me Pethidine, and that while it dulled the pain it somehow increased the hallucinations, because at that point I really went completely off the tracks.

Although the curtains in the room were closed, light still came in, and in addition they had left a light on over my head, on which my hallucinations became fixed. At first I imagined that the light was growing stronger, and at the same time that the shape of the lamp was changing and becoming limitless and unfocussed like the sun. The spreading sun/lamp warmed me and banished the cold shivers, and gradually it came to seem that it was this that was banishing the pain from my back and stomach. As if a sweet warm light were seeping into me until my whole being was full of light, from top to toe, and still it went on welling up and filling me. Gratefully, I let go of Alek's shirt, and silently thanked the lamp, that is to say the sun, that is to say the face which had begun to appear inside it and which I really cannot describe, except that it was surrounded by a halo like a figure in an icon or that it was itself the aura of something else hidden in its light, which was far more radiant and present than a figure in an icon. The face was very clear, like that of a very familiar personality, clearer and more vivid than any familiar personality...and nevertheless like a familiar personality, and nevertheless, for some reason, impossible to describe. All I know is that this figure revealed itself to me like love, and that with its appearance I felt completely loved, as if I had been made one with my love and now it was inside me, and I dwelt safely within it forever, or something to that effect. . . . And it was still somehow connected to Alek. As if I had prostrated myself before it like a supplicant, and been promised that my yearnings would be fulfilled. And as if the light was the happiness filling me to overflowing.

It was with the sensation of this superabundance of light, I think, that the change started, and the same thing that was pouring and pouring into me began to arouse my fear. It seemed as if the light was converted inside me into some other substance, and although it was still light, this dense light was crystallizing inside me into something hard and blazing. The light grew stronger, the sun grew hotter and hotter, and the face of the figure turned into a burning presence. And the heat increased even further, until I felt the burning light on my skin, in a minute it would be inside me, melting my bones, boiling my blood, turning the fluid in my eyes to steam. Glued to the bed I pleaded with the figure to withdraw its light, whether it was an expression of wrath, or simply the annihilating effect of its powerful presence, which was growing more powerful all the time.

Like a frightened child I covered my face with the shirt and folded my hands on top of it, but even thus, with my eyes closed, the harsh light and heat increased to terrifying proportions. And only when it seemed that I could bear it no longer, the light and the fear gradually began to grow dimmer.

Three times this experience returned. A benevolent light converted into a burning one, dying down into sweetness, sweetening my blood, pouring into me with infinite gentleness, and then intensifying and hardening inside me and above me with blind indifference.

In days to come, when Talush was getting ready to give birth, I read in one of her manuals about the existence of a defined stage, before the appearance of the major contractions, when it sometimes happens that for a few minutes a woman enters something like a psychotic state. Since in the middle of this hallucination I was rapidly wheeled into the delivery room, I imagine that this is the stage I was in, and that the "stage" and the Pethidine produced their effects on me. But neither the "stage" nor the Pethidine can explain the specific content of my hallucination, and the way in which it was related to Alek and the obsessive thoughts of love that accompanied me throughout.

After the birth I did not give the experience much thought. The baby's presence and Alek's absence were more compelling, and it was only half a year later, on one of our invasions of Yoash's apartment, that I told Alek. Not what preceded the hallucination or followed it, but only the visionary delusion, with his presence expurgated. Alek, his hands clasped behind his neck, listened as if what I was telling him was the most natural thing in the world, and although it was interesting, even very interesting, there was nothing strange or surprising about it. "It happens that a person dreams a dream that seems not to belong to him," he said quietly, as if stating a fact, and reached under the blanket for the packet of cigarettes. There was no mystical mumbo-jumbo or gush in his reaction, and this made it easier for me to talk. "That's exactly how I feel," I said, "although it wasn't exactly a dream . . . but that's what it felt like, as if I dreamt somebody else's dream." "Except that now it's your dream, too," he replied with a smile, and pulled me onto his chest.

As I lay resting on him like this, I thought that there really was nothing to be done with this alien vision, which was like a strange object bequeathed me as a legacy by some primeval mother. I didn't choose it, I didn't ask for it, it simply fell on me as if from another world, and now it was mine. Like this love.

It was morning, a pale winter sun shone into the shutterless room. The portable electric heater didn't work very well, only one of the coils was working. But Alek got up and piled all the blankets he found in the closet on top of us, and between the hot and the cold we were content.

NIRA WOOLF

Nira Woolf is forty-five, this is her age in my first book, *Blood Money*, and at this excellent age she remains in the books that follow. The setting in which she operates changes from book to book—Israel at the beginning of the eighties is not the Israel of today, even as the arena of a detective story—but my fighting lawyer doesn't change, only the causes she fights for change in accordance with the period. In *Blood Money*, which was about the plunder of Palestinian land, through patients' rights in *The Shattered Man*, through children's rights in *The Boy Who Didn't Know How to Ask*, through sexual harassment in the army in *Compulsory Service*, through the shocking corruption in *Birthright*, through the fear of AIDS in *The Stabbing*, up to the militant feminism of the last four years: *Dead Woman's Voice*, which as I may have already mentioned turns on a case of incest, and *What Did Mrs. Neuman Know?*, in which my feminist lawyer does battle with a ring of traffickers in women.

When I started writing about Nira I was twenty-six years old, and when I started to imagine her I was even younger, and forty-five seemed to me a venerable and dignified age. An age at which nobody calls you a "girl" any more. Although the way I constructed Nira, nobody would have dared to call her a "girl" at the age of twenty-six either.

From the outset it was clear to me that my combative lawyer was single, that she had no children and no longings for children, or needless to say for a husband, either. The mother of children is not free to jump into her car and fly to the murder scene when a phone call wakes her up in the middle of the night, nor can she rush around with a revolver ready to fire. And in general, children bring up a lot of questions I had no desire to deal with on the page or the computer screen. For instance: Who looks after them when their mother is running around with a revolver? A nanny? And who takes them to school at quarter to eight in the morning? And what happens when the disappearing client, the one who's suspected of murder, suddenly turns up at the house? And on what Afghan carpet can my Nira have a spontaneous fuck when the plot approaches its suspenseful climax? The one with the toys strewn over it?

When I wrote *Blood Money* I didn't know that it was the first in a series, and I wasn't even sure that it was a book at all. But in the following books, too, I was not tempted to give her a child, because how would this child suddenly arrive on the scene? Could I allow her to get mixed up with gangsters when she was eight months pregnant? From a feminist point of view it might actually be amusing to send a woman with a bad attack of heartburn to the Supreme Court on a case, and make her whip out her gun on the way to the hospital to give birth. The critics would scream their heads off. Especially those who always attack me on the grounds that "Nira Woolf isn't a feminist heroine, but a macho man disguised as a woman." But even assuming that I made her pregnant just to annoy the critics, what then? Nira Woolf lies helplessly in the delivery room and waits for the dilation to grow big enough for them to give her a shot at last? The midwife raises and parts Nira's legs? The midwife bends down between our heroine's legs to make the cut?

In a general outline of the next book I thought of giving Nira a ward or an adopted child. I even knew who the little girl was. The daughter of Anna, a foreign worker who substituted for Mrs. Neuman's regular nurse for a week, and who was the sole beneficiary of the surprising new will dictated by Neuman to Woolf. "Sasha" I would call the child orphaned in *What Did Mrs. Neuman Know?*, and in the exposition describing the background to her adoption I would briefly relate how the kind-hearted lawyer traveled to Kharkov to find the nine-year-old who had become the beneficiary herself (after Anna's body was discovered on Palmahim Beach in the previous book), and how it came about that my heroine returned to Israel with the little orphan in tow.

The trouble with this idea, which I liked in itself, was with the limitations it would impose on me in the continuation of the series, assuming I wanted to go on with it. Nira Woolf could remain forty-five forever, it was the age she was meant to be and I had no problem with it, but the little girl could on no account go on being nine years old in book after book, because that would be ridiculous. I couldn't possibly send her to the fourth grade every year, make her mourn her mother in every new book, and let her be stuck with difficulties in Hebrew forever.

The trouble with children is that they have to grow up, and I have no idea how to deal with the literary problems presented by this fact. So that in the end it appears that Anna's orphan will have to be left to grow up by herself in Ukraine, nameless and outside the plot of this book.

THE DAY AFTER GIVING BIRTH

The day after giving birth I felt fine. Stupidly happy in a way that makes me cringe with embarrassment to this day.

In the afternoon, a couple of hours after they transferred me to the maternity ward, they brought me the baby. A nurse put her into my arms, and I—forgive me, whoever's job it is to forgive—looked at my daughter for the first time and the first thought that crossed my mind was: so small and so perfect, he won't be able to help loving her.

Her head was covered with a lot of black hair, and I rejoiced in this downy hair, and in the wrinkled little face, and the tiny hands imprisoned in their sleeves, only because I felt that Alek would have to surrender to this tiny softness. And when I put her to my breast in the first clumsy attempt to feed her, I silently rejoiced in fantasies of how he would fall in love with her. But it wasn't the loving father she would gain that I was thinking of, it was the crumbs of this inevitable paternal love that would no doubt fall into my own lap. After all, it was from me that this sweetness came, and it was impossible for it not to project itself onto me. The baby slept, she didn't want to wake up and suck, I still hadn't seen the color of her eyes, and I arranged my hair becomingly on the pink pillowcase, and thought how charming the two of us looked, Madonna and child.

If I had given Nira Woolf a child, I wouldn't have let her have it by a man she loved. A sperm donation might have fit the bill, except for the repelling nature of the procedure, and if she had wanted a child she would have been more likely to choose a man for a one-night stand according to the probable quality of his genes. What would have suited her best, I think now, would have been a virgin birth, and I would have given her one without any qualms: the possibility of replicating herself by herself without the assistance of a man. Except that a miraculous event of that nature belongs to a different genre than the one I write in. And even though my thrillers are far from being realistic, they are not amenable to this kind of supernatural event.

A newborn baby is a wonder, and children should be rejoiced in for themselves from the moment they are born. They should be loved simply for what they are, and not thanks to another love. And I did not love Hagar in this way. With time I did begin to love her, of course; the heavy-headed, well-tempered infant, the logical child suddenly fired up over questions of justice and injustice, the young girl sprawling on the floor to paint bad slogans for demonstrations and asking me to put her hair up in a ponytail because her hands were full of paint. I loved her as she deserved to be loved, but from the outset the feeling was tainted.

Don't get me wrong, if I had been faced with the kind of dilemma people like to pose in youth movements—you and Hagar and Alek are cast away in the desert with only one water canteen; or, if you could only rescue one person from a fire—I have no doubt what my answer would be, and it would be sincere. I wouldn't hesitate for a second, and that is not the point. The point is the despicable way I sometimes looked at her, and still sometimes look at her, through Alek's imagined eyes. Like the way, for instance, when she was six months old and her face was covered with a red rash, I was afraid of his reaction, as if he might be repelled by her appearance, and this repulsion might somehow be projected onto me. And the way when she was five years old, and he would sometimes take her for walk, I would wash her little jeans and dry them on the stove so that she would look cute for him. The way I inspected my teenaged daughter with a cold eye before she flew to Paris. And the way I tried to guess from her stories upon her return if he was charmed, and to what extent, and by what precisely, so that I could learn the secret. I knew very well how loathsome these thoughts were, and nevertheless before she set off to visit her father and grandmother in Paris, like a pimp I bought her a bottle of his favorite White Shoulders perfume, in the hope that in some unconscious way she might remind him of me. If only she would have hated it, but she didn't hate it, my daughter was delighted with her mother's gift, without having a clue about what I was up to, because the overt message I gave her was the opposite of my true wishes: "You're allowed to decide that you don't like him"; "You shouldn't have any great expectations of him or his mother. Think of it simply as a trip to Paris without any strings attached"; "I'm sure they'll welcome you with open arms, and you don't have to make an impression on anyone there," and so on and so forth until Hagar said: "Stop it, Mommy, relax, I'm not five years old, and this time I have no intention of letting him upset me. My main feeling is one of curiosity . . . to meet my roots."

Luckily for us Hagar does not resemble me or Alek, and if she resembles anyone, it's my father: in her clear, unshadowed, round-eyed regard, the way she purses her mouth, and the stubborn cleft in her chin. Whether she bears any resemblance to Alek's parents I have no idea.

ALEK DIDN'T COME

At the visiting hour on the first day Alek didn't come, and I put off my expectations to the second day. Perhaps he was sitting for an exam at the university, perhaps he had promised to work with Yoash and he couldn't get out of it, perhaps he had fallen asleep after a sleepless night and when he arrived at the hospital they wouldn't let him in. For some reason I didn't think of Tamara, perhaps because the events of the night had made her pale into insignificance in his eyes, or so I believed, and therefore also in mine.

Without any logical reason I fell asleep in a kind of daze of happiness, and in the certain knowledge that he would come tomorrow. At the beginning of August he was supposed to present himself in

Heidelberg, I did not imagine for a moment that he would cancel his trip, but the weeks before us, like the parting itself, were indelibly stamped by the covenant of the night of the birth.

The next day legions of visitors passed through the room, bearing flowers, bags, magazines and plastic bottles. My bed was the middle one of three, and even when I drew the curtain around it, I couldn't shut out the voices coming from all directions. Improvised vases overturned and spilled water on the floor, the two chairs in the room were dragged to and fro. "Excuse me, is this so-and-so's room? . . . Mazal tov . . . what time was the birth? . . . Mazal tov . . . it's so cute. . . . How are you feeling? . . . Is this so-and-so's room? . . . You're still a little pale. . . . How much does she weigh? What can we bring you? Should we call the nurse?" Twice a man opened the curtain and immediately apologized, and once a toddler snuck in and hid and was immediately removed with a gentle rebuke.

My solitariness did not bother me, not at this stage. It set me apart, it enabled me to concentrate on the one person whose presence I desired, and all the comers and goers seemed to me like extras in a movie, an accompaniment to the main plot that was mine. Only mine. To my right and my left lay women who had just given birth just like me, women who had lives just like me, perhaps more interesting than mine, but I was barely aware of their existence. And when the babies were brought in for us to feed, I did not respond to any conversational feelers. A kind of game developed between me and the nurses: they opened the curtains around my bed and I closed them, they opened them again, and I closed them again, hiding behind them and putting on a Madonna face, as if the stitches didn't sting like hell whenever I went to pee.

Five visiting hours went by in a waiting that was like a concentrated doing, until my strength ran out. I yearned for him to come so intensely, I imagined him so vividly, that I felt as if the yearning itself would bring him to me. Like a beamed message, a call that could not be ignored. Because he had to hear it.

Waiting, like concealed internal bleeding, gradually brings about a kind of anemia, a completely tangible loss of strength. And in the hospital I felt for the first time how this concentration—here he comes, in a minute he'll come, in a minute he'll be standing in the door—slides me slowly into a tearful impotence. I should have hated the person who made me feel like this, not because he was to blame, but simply because of the feeling itself and because of survival instinct. But my survival instinct didn't work, not in the hospital and not later on. And the secret expectation became a part of my being. Like a chronic pain that awakens with changes in the weather. I have no idea what failing causes it, but for the most part I think that this failing is not in me and my mind, but in the nature of love.

I remember a picture from my last visit to Moscow, it was in February of this year and we were standing in the street next to the Patriarch's Ponds waiting for a friend of Alek's to pick us up for a late lunch. When we left the house in the morning the temperature was minus ten, and towards midday it dropped even further. The sky turned gray, low and damp, and from the moment that we stood still the snow lost its glamour, and I felt very cold, especially my feet. Twice Alek went to the little booth next to the ice rink and bought me a ghastly cup of hot coffee, but even with the styrofoam cup in my hand I couldn't stop moving back and forth. "If you're already moving, then lift your leg like this," he said and demonstrated a few high swings of the thigh, "it will warm you more." But Alek himself did not shake a limb. For an hour and a half we waited there, his friend was caught in a traffic jam, and for most of the time he stood there without a hat, in infinite patience, his shoulders slightly stooped, as if he had been trained all his life to wait. At some point a little old lady in a black flowered headkerchief stopped next to us. She raised a wrinkled fairytale face to us, with bright blue, benevolent fairytale eyes, and rattled off a couple of sentences that brought an affectionate smile to Alek's face. "She says it's obvious you're not used to the weather," he said when she walked away, "she says I must take you home and give you black bread and drippings. Black bread. She says it must be a black and not white." "I'd eat anything now, never mind what, I'm dying of hunger." "Dima will come soon, and then we'll eat properly. Unless Anushka spilled the oil, of course. . . ."

"Anushka?" "You didn't read *The Master and Margarita*? You did read it? Take a good look at that bench. On that bench Berlioz met the devil."

I went on shaking my limbs, stamping on the slushy snow on the pavement, skipping onto the fresh snow piling up next to it, and breathing into my gloves. And the next time I approached him he took hold of my hands to rub them and said: "I don't think you have problem with weather. You should see yourself with snow on your eyelashes. I think you just don't know how to wait. They didn't teach you to wait, over there in Israel?"

As often happens to me with Alek, the sentence took on a meaning beyond the concrete complaint. No, they didn't teach me to wait.

You taught me to wait. I taught myself to wait. I taught myself until I became such an excellent apprentice that I didn't even cross off the days any more. Women excel at this activity. Thousands of years of history, a long genealogy of spinning wool and waiting at the window lies dormant in our blood just waiting for an opportunity to break out. I noticed this when after a regrettable developmental delay I finally acquired a circle of women friends. And when I finally started to listen to other women—all of them, by the way, strong and successful—I discovered that not one of them had escaped the experience of intensive inaction. But I had taken it further than any of them.

In my book *The Stabbing* I have a nice little scene in which the doctor who is a client of Nira's comes late to a meeting. "I'll say this once and once only," says the lawyer Nira Woolf after he gets into the car. "I'll say it once, and there won't be a next time. I don't care why you're late; I don't care if you were locked up in the laboratory; I don't even care if three hooligans in white chased you with syringes full of poison. Anyone who comes late for an appointment robs me of my time, and I don't take robbers as clients. And by the way, since I've broached the topic, from the beginning I noticed that you have the look of a serial latecomer." A clever woman, my Nira, especially in view of the fact that she suspected this serial latecomer from the beginning of being the person who had falsified the results of the AIDS test.

With all my woman friends who had wasted their time waiting for a man sooner or later the natural instinct that distances people from pain kicked in, and they all liberated themselves in the end from brooding about their relationships with variations on the lament: "What an idiot I was." I on the other hand never regarded waiting as a waste of time, perhaps because I never had the same expectations that they did—for him to "show that he was serious," "leave his wife," "move in together," etc. You could say that I expected "less" and in a certain sense that would be true, except that what I yearned for always seemed to me to be "more," and perhaps this is the essence of the disease.

The hospital was a shock-treatment, a concentrated dose of waiting, worse than anything I had experienced up to then, in the hours when he was away from home, the hours when he shut himself up in his room, or even in the month of May when he was called up for emergency reserve duty and released only two weeks later. Later on, over the course of the years, I learned that it is possible to conduct all kinds of relationships with waiting. Sometimes I turn my back on it flirtatiously and amuse myself with something else; sometimes I confront it and fight it by fanning the flames of self-disgust so as not to wait, not to wait, not to wait any more; and sometimes I convert my anger into its opposite and let myself go completely. I don't spin my wool, I don't glean the straw, I just lie down and let my personality bleed out of me until I reach a state of such emptiness and helplessness that I can hardly rise to my feet again.

Most of the time waiting accompanies me like a kind of presence, which only goes away under defined conditions. Like this Passover, for example, when I know that Alek has taken his wife and Mark first to Prague and from there on to Germany, to meet Daniel and Ute's parents. On days like these when the phone rings and I pick it up, and a second of whispering silence announces a long distance call, I expect only the voice of Hagar.

"And you, wait for me to return, wait well. . . ." Not one of the works that glorify the waiting of women was written by a woman, and nonetheless the woman waits well. I wait very well.

IN THE HOSPITAL I THOUGHT

In the hospital I thought that I was seen as a snob, but the nurses apparently saw something else, too, for on the fourth day the head nurse said to me: "Someone will come and talk to you," and in the wake of this obscure sentence, immediately after the midday feed, the social worker appeared from behind the curtain. Her name was Deborah Rubin, I remember because for most of the talk I kept my eyes fixed on the nametag pinned to her white uniform. Her face has been wiped from my memory together with the faces of all the other women in the ward, but I remember a salt-and-pepper braid coiled round her head, the glint of her gold spectacle frames, and most of all the way she sat there, as heavy and authoritarian as Queen Victoria. She did not fit any preconceived idea I had of a "social worker," she looked severe and intelligent, and she frightened me from the get-go. Looking back I think that the fear helped me; it pierced the dullness and weakness and forced me to pull myself together, to respond and to act.

"Officially you're supposed to leave tomorrow, but we're asking ourselves if it would be right to discharge you." A cacophony of paranoid thoughts clamoured in my head: They've found me out. They're not going to let me go. They'll let me go, but they'll take the baby away and give her up for adoption. What nonsense had escaped me when I was having that vision? And what else did I say? And what else did I do? I shouldn't have shut the curtain, because that's what annoyed them, and now they're going to take their revenge. I should have gotten up for meals when they called me and not stayed in bed. I should have acquired a toothbrush and not stolen toothpaste from my neighbour and brushed my teeth with my finger. She must have noticed, the miser, and told on me: "She hasn't even got toothpaste. She's completely out of it. How is someone like her going to look after a baby?" For the first time I experienced the cunning of the mad, a quality that I developed strongly later on.

"But why? What's wrong? Everything's fine, really . . . it's just that I'm young so it's a little difficult," I said to the social worker, but Queen Victoria was not impressed, as evidenced by her silence, and by the way she lowered her spectacles from the bridge of her nose. "I'm thinking of your situation. . . . Each of the women here comes from a different situation, and I would like—if you agree to tell me—to hear something about yours . . . ," she said in the end, and her authoritative voice turned the mild ending of the ellipses into an order.

"My situation . . . is that . . . I'm happy, naturally. Naturally I'm happy, naturally. It's just that I haven't completely recovered yet."

"Did you have a regular birth?" She forced me to concentrate and fall into step with her.

"Regular?"

"Was there anything unusual about the delivery? A vacuum? Forceps? Did anything else happen that you can think of?"

"No. Nothing."

"Nothing . . . and nevertheless . . . we would like to know: if you're discharged tomorrow, if you go home, what will you be going back to?"

"Home," I answered stupidly, folding the sheet with Alek's shirt underneath. And then I had a sudden inspiration and said into the silence: "My husband's on reserve duty, perhaps I should have told you at once. My husband's on reserve duty in the army, and that makes things a little difficult for me, too, him being in the army now."

"Didn't they let him know that you've given birth?"

"I think that . . . they must have probably informed him already. But he's serving in Sinai, in some hole in Sinai, so maybe it's taking them a long time. Yes, of course, it must be taking time, but he'll definitely come soon, today or tomorrow."

"Your husband, my dear, is entitled to forty-eight hours leave," she informed me with a hint of rebuke in her voice, "even the army understands how important his presence is to you now. And what about your parents? What about your family and his? Where are they in all this?"

"My husband is a new immigrant," I replied, and what next? Should I tell her that my parents were abroad? Someone here in the hospital staff might recognize me. Maybe they already had. The whole world knew my parents. They would catch me out in a lie and then they would definitely take my baby away from me. Or send me to the psychiatric ward. Alek didn't come, he didn't come, but I wanted to go home to Alek. It was only when she said the words "about to be discharged" that I understood that this was indeed what I wanted. And now this was the only thing I wanted: to get out of here, out of this nightmare, to go home, to see Alek, to be with Alek, when everything would settle down and I would be okay. "My parents were very unhappy about my marriage," I improvised. "They thought I was too young to marry, they wanted us to wait, and for me to go to the army first. The truth is that since the marriage they've more or less broken off relations with me."

The ring of truth in these words finally convinced the social worker. "Things change when a baby is born," she said, "I've seen it again and again. Perhaps you should try to make contact with your parents in spite of everything. I'm not promising you that it will succeed, nobody can make any promises, but maybe you'll be surprised." I promised her I would think about it, and she gave me a card with her room number and phone extension. She said that she would be in her office all the next morning, perhaps before I left I would like to come up with the baby and say goodbye, and I could phone her from home as well, if I thought she could be of any help. I was about to relax with the thought that the conversation was over, but Deborah Rubin was not yet satisfied. "And when you get home, who will be with you until your husband returns? Who is there to help you? Who's getting everything ready for the baby? A woman who's just given birth shouldn't be by herself, certainly not a sweet young girl like you." To this I hastily replied that we had tons of friends, my husband and I, they simply didn't know that I'd had the baby because there was nobody to let them know, but as soon as they knew—they would do whatever needed to be done, that is to say, my husband would definitely do whatever needed to be done first, but they would do it too afterwards.

"By the way, my child, you haven't told me yet what you're going to call the baby. Have you already decided on a name?" the social worker asked as she stood up to go.

"A name . . . of course . . . ," I paused for a moment, "she has a name. Hagar. Her name is Hagar."

Until that moment not only had I not chosen a name, I hadn't even thought properly about names, only that at some stage I would have to solve this problem too.

I don't know where the name came from, but from the moment I said Hagar, it was clear to me that this was her name, as if she had come into the world with it. My daughter Hagar. Baby Hagar.

NAMES

Since I was legally married, she was registered at the Ministry of Interior as Hagar Ginsberg, daughter of Alexander and Noa Ginsberg.

It was only when I went to register her, when she was already almost a year old, that I discovered that the Ministry of Interior was kept up to date by the Rabbinate, and that without my knowledge they had changed my name from Weber to Ginsberg, which meant that as far as the state was concerned I had been Ginsberg now for over a year and a half without anyone taking the trouble to inform me. When the situation became clear to me, I didn't even try to find out whether I could change it. On my first ID card, which I had received just before I got married, my name was given as Weber, and I simply continued to sign my name and introduce myself as Noa Weber. The struggle for the right of married women to keep their maiden names was unheard of then, I had no ideological reasons against taking my husband's name, but because it was "only a fictitious marriage" it had never occurred to me to use his name.

Whenever the subject of the name came up, for example before the elections in December '73, when my mother noticed that the voter's notification they sent me was addressed to "Noa Ginsberg," it led automatically to talk of divorce—"Really, Noaleh, isn't it about time you resolved the matter and asked him for a divorce?"—I would say, "I haven't got the strength to take care of it now," and "I'm in no shape to make contact with him now," and it was only at the end of the seventies, when I was already working for the human rights fund, that I adopted the avant-garde position: I don't care what my name is at the Ministry of Interior, and I'm not interested in their opinion regarding my marital status. As long as there's no separation between state and religion in Israel, we should take no notice of their registrations, and the more anarchy we create the better. My name is Noa Weber, I'm as single as I ever was, and I have no intention of entering into negotiations with some official in order for him to confirm my true identity.

In 1984 things became a little more complicated, after my bag was stolen with my ID card inside it. The new ID they issued me was in the name of Noa Ginsberg, and the same went for the passport I obtained at the end of the eighties. As a result, to this day I have to explain myself when I sign checks—the name printed in my checkbook is Noa Weber—but all my plane tickets are in the name of Ginsberg, and Ginsberg is my name at airline check-ins.

The fact is that at the end of the eighties I could have registered myself again as Weber, without requiring a divorce or waging a legal battle—other women had already won the battle—and the other fact is that I failed to do so.

Openly I mock the "bureaucratic joke" of my name, and say that "I haven't got the strength for the Ministry of Interior," but what I haven't told a soul is that because of this "bureaucratic joke" that I am ostensibly cultivating for anarchist reasons, I have wasted more than a little time on solving problems with the Income Tax and National Insurance authorities. My "bureaucratic name" is like a secret, illicit thrill, a thrill I feel whenever I get official mail from the government.

My daughter appears like me as Weber. At the daycare I registered her as Weber, friends and neighbors have known her as Weber since the day she was born, and the questions began only when she entered the education system, where she appeared under the name registered at the Ministry of Interior. In '91, when she turned eighteen, she asked to be registered under the name of Weber on her ID card, and to both of our surprise, her request was granted after filling in a single standard form.

"I belong to you more than to Alek. I even belong to Granny and Grandpa more than to him," she kept on explaining, as if anyone needed an explanation. During that period she was preoccupied by thoughts of Mark and Daniel, the half-brothers she didn't know, once every few years she would begin to brood about them, and it seemed to me that adopting my name was an act intended to put an end to this futile preoccupation. "I even belong to Granny and Grandpa more than him. . . ." But I belong in secret to Alek. And in the secret of the bureaucratic joke I am still called by his name.

• • •

Alek, as I said, is spending Passover or Easter with Ute and the children in Germany, and in my inner language I call such times my "white days." White days because of their clarity, uncolored by any expectation. As if the mind has retired and is free to take up all kinds of hobbies.

At times like these not only the suspense of concrete expectation declines—for there were long periods, years, during which I had no expectations of any concrete contact—but it is as if Alek has removed his withdrawn gaze from me, and for days or weeks I hardly see myself through his eyes.

A great silence reigns over this Passover, as if the street has emptied of its inhabitants. In recent years quite a lot of well-off people have moved into the neighborhood and they have apparently all gone away on vacation. Once, it was different here on religious holidays.

My parents are in London, Talush is with the children on the kibbutz, my women friends—who almost all have young children—have been swallowed up by family affairs, Hagar is spending the holiday with a girlfriend in Boston. On the eve of Passover she called to wish me a happy holiday, and until she returns to New York I don't expect even an e-mail. I haven't annoyed her enough for her to write to me from Boston.

In the mornings the air is still clear, a uniform blue sky without a scrap of clouds is painted strongly over the clean white and green of the street, and only towards midday, when it begins to grow hazy, a kind of sensuousness invades the air, presaging the heat wave.

What Did Mrs. Neuman Know? is already in the shop windows, and until the more or less anticipated reviews appear, thoughts of "the next book" remain unfocused. I sleep a little, wake up early, and go early to the grocery, even though there is nothing I need, or need early in the morning, on the half-empty shelves. The short morning walk does not banish the gloom of awakening, and the transparency of the air and the view only ferments my self-loathing. Yesterday on the way home the outside stairs of the houses looked to me like tongues sticking out.

"White days" I said . . . but this time around my mind refuses to divert itself with hobbies, and when I wake up I feel depression covering me like a heavy blanket that I push off, but after an hour or two it returns, and drives me back to bed.

For two weeks I haven't gone out to run, writing has become the backbone of my day, as if it has taken the place of running, or any other activity keeping me upright, but it is only after dark that I can summon up the energy to sit down in front of the computer and poison myself with an unreasonable amount of cigarettes.

What am I doing? What do I want? What have I taken it on myself to want?

Forty-seven years old, Alek turned fifty-seven this year, and never again will I see how he has changed, and how to me he is unchanged, to me he is never changed as he comes towards me at the airport.

Timelessness is an illusion. Timelessness is a derivative of love, a derivative of faith, a concrete derivative of a state of mind which I no longer have any idea what to call. Alek, according to his age, could already be a grandfather, Hagar at her age could turn me into a grandmother, and eternity is nothing but an illusion. There is nothing timeless in me or in him or in us or in anyone.

What am I doing? Telling. For there to be a beginning and an end. For there to be an end.

What did I take upon myself to want?

He will never look into my eyes and bring to my lips that familiar smile which acknowledges everything and wipes out everything.

I'll never try on a new dress and think: I'll wear it when I walk with him, if I walk with him in summer in the street.

There will never be a summer for us. Never in any summer will I walk with him along foreign streets, with their desperate squalor and their desperate splendor that I seem to know from some previous incarnation. And never will I experience again the consciousness of infinite expanses where everything seems pointless but love itself.

Love will never expand me.

The one right body will never come to me.

GOING HOME

I promised to parcel myself out in the proper order, even though I have no idea what I will do with this parceled self when I bring it to the end of the story.

In the meantime: Hadassah Hospital, maternity ward. Deborah the social worker has gone, and I collect myself around a new wish, to go home, home to Alek; fortified by my mad cunning, I go to the newborns room, ask the nurses to show me how to give the baby a bath. "I'm so sorry I missed the demonstration, I didn't feel well." Prattle any nonsense that comes into my head, with them and the other women in my room and their afternoon visitors; picking sentences out of the air of the room, fermenting them in my mouth, and bubbling over in an exaggerated gush: "Show him to me ... show her to me ... show me how you ... what a cutie ... oh, what a sweetheart ... what a little darling!" Broadcasting youthful maternal energy and joy.

After supper I lurked in the corridor until the nurse with the mean face left the nurses station, and then I asked the one with the nice face to let me use their telephone. "I'm not supposed to, so do it quickly." With Yoash on the phone I was brisk and cool, and suddenly he was the one gushing and hardly letting me get a word in edgeways: "Wonderful news . . . I never got a chance. . . . I had that renovation, and you know what it's like with the year-end audits . . . so Baruch says to me . . . I'll tell you . . . how Baruch . . . yes, sure . . . I'll come tomorrow . . . sure thing . . . in the morning, with pleasure." I didn't ask him about Alek, somehow it was clear to me that he didn't want to be asked, but in any case, I thought, I would know tomorrow, and what could Yoash really tell me? What did he know? He would think that I was taking advantage; but the way I arrived at the hospital, without telephone tokens or money in my purse, I needed him. I simply couldn't think of anyone else.

Yoash showed up at ten o'clock in the morning, appearing in the corridor in his eternal overalls, with his ungainly walk, and without the Hamida file under his arm. But then, when we were already on our way to the infants a new obstacle popped up: in my stupidity it hadn't occurred to me that without something to wear, they wouldn't release Hagar from the hospital. Dear Yoash looked as if he was delighted with the situation—to this day, I think, nothing pleases him more than the prospect of "driving the authorities crazy."

"Idiot that I am," he said to the nurse and hit himself on the forehead, "idiot, idiot, idiot . . . forgive me, Noa, I'm an idiot. How you got such an idiot for a brother I don't know, but I forgot the whole parcel at home." He went off for an hour, I waited on a bench in the shade at the entrance, and when he came back he was carrying a few swollen bags, whose contents he spread out with a conjurer's pride before the astonished eyes of the nurse. A pile of tiny white garments, a pile of diapers, a tube of ointment for the baby's bottom, a cloth clown with bells on its head, a yellow rattle, a parcel of paper bibs. One by one he whipped them out and showed them, and in the end, with a triumphant flourish, he fished out three pacifiers and hung them around his fingers. "In case she loses one. My sisters were always throwing their pacifiers out. You know what it's like with pacifiers. They're always vanishing and you can't find them and it's a big mystery, one of the greatest mysteries in the universe."

All the way out he didn't stop chattering. Like some dopey spy he boasted of how he had cut all the price tags off the garments, "so they wouldn't suspect me of only just buying them." And only after he brought the pickup round from the parking lot, and only after he helped me climb in with Hagar, and only after he got in himself and inserted the key, only then did he lean back and ask without looking at me: "So where am I taking you?"

"Home," I replied, but it was a question more than an answer, because I already knew that there was bad news in the offing.

"Home . . . Alek said you'd want to, that's to say, that you can if you want to. Listen, there's something I have to tell you. Alek . . . brought forward his trip. What I mean to say is that he's leaving today." Since I was silent Yoash went on talking, and his voice—I remember his voice—grew rude and abrupt, almost hostile: "In any case, you know, he had to be there in August, and if you ask me, with all due respect to you both, all of this is a bit too much for him. Seeing the baby, I mean. Seeing her—it's too much for him." And when I remained silent he went on: "Alek thought that perhaps you might want to get in touch with your mother in spite of everything."

"I want to go home," I said. "I want you to take me home." And we drove to the empty house.

I don't remember feeling anything, I don't remember thinking anything, I was like a hollow body propelled into motion by a push from an invisible hand. When we entered the house—I held Hagar, and Yoash opened the door—I was surprised to see everything in its place, but this too was at a remove, like a kind of curiosity outside myself. At the fringes of my mind I was apparently expecting to see empty rooms and bare walls, and in these same margins I noted to myself that everything was the same as before. Only later on, whenever Hagar fell asleep, I examined and re-examined every inch of the house. The record player was standing in its place, the records—I discovered afterwards—he had given to Yoash. The bookshelves in his room were empty and striped with dust. I found some of the books later in boxes in the storage space under the roof. His shelves in the closet were bare. His desk was cleared. In the drawers there were only a few pins and a pen without a refill. No crumpled note in the wastepaper basket. And no note anywhere. He didn't take anything from the kitchen, there was a big sack of potatoes stuffed into the wicker basket, and a few packets of sausages and cheese and seven bags of milk in the fridge. Perhaps he thought that this was what babies drank. Perhaps he thought that this was what a nursing mother needed.

Yoash: I really have to go now. Are you sure you're okay?

Me: It's okay.

Yoash: Are you sure you don't want to get in touch with your parents? I can get in touch for you, if you like.

Me: It's okay.

(And then, when he was already standing at the door, it seemed to me that I read something in his slightly averted face, or perhaps in his raised shoulders, or perhaps in the way he twisted his feet.)

Me: Yoash? You said Alek was leaving today? What time is his flight?

Yoash: What time is his flight . . . is it important? What difference does it make to you, in fact? Okay. Okay. Don't look at me like that, just don't look at me like that. His flight's at 4:20, which means that at half past one, in another . . . forty-five minutes I have to pick him up and take him to the airport. From my place.

FROM A DISTANCE

From a distance of twenty-nine years I don't feel a drop of pity for that girl. Not because "she got herself into it"—people "get themselves" into all kinds of trouble and they still deserve to be pitied—I don't feel any pity for her because of the blank expression on her face, rejecting the hand reaching out to her even from the distance of these years.

Blankly she moves about the rooms, barely glancing at her baby daughter lying on the big double bed. Nothing moves in her even when she finds the envelope he left on the kitchen table. There are six hundred and fifty shekels. He cleaned out his bank account, put the money into the envelope, licked it, closed it, and put it under the salt shaker, without even writing her name on it.

Now she sits down in the wicker armchair in the living room, looks at her watch and tries to trap the movement of the minute hand, hypnotizing herself not to blink and miss the second that it moves. The baby is sleeping, if she wakes and cries maybe she won't hear, and if she does hear maybe she won't react. The time is thirty-three minutes past one, thirty-four minutes past one. They have already loaded his luggage onto the pickup. Gone back to get the shoulder bag and sunglasses. Locked the door. Detached from feeling she senses his departure from the city like a change taking place in the nature of matter. He's leaving, he's getting further away, already he's at the turn in the road descending from the city, still close, in another two and a quarter hours he'll be on the plane. She notes the change in matter with every breath she takes, as if the touch of the air is different and objects are less present. She follows his departure as if she has been made responsible for studying the effect of his departure on matter, which is fading and becoming thinner as the minutes go by.

I don't pity her, because she is wrapped up in her belief, and she still believes that she has no salvation outside his love.

And if I try to leap into the picture, to reach out to her and break the tension, she'll bite my hand to stop me from disturbing her hypnotized concentration.

She's suffering, true, and in the hours to come when her sorrow runs riot, she will suffer more, but for the time being there is no sign that she wants to keep the sorrow at bay. I want to make the sorrow go away. And she, the mad girl, receives it into her. She won't let me rob her of it.

The days that followed, until the rescue team arrived, are difficult to reconstruct in an orderly way, and in fact also the weeks after them. Somewhere before I mentioned the kibbutz education that I refuse to see as the seedbed of my sickness, and the fact that I functioned then I attribute precisely to that despised education. "Pull yourself together, control yourself," was the message of my childhood, and I did my best to conform to it. I was always taught that in all circumstances it was important to function, and perhaps thanks to this I functioned, a strange, partial functioning, but functioning nevertheless.

Hagar was what in days to come I learned to define as an easy baby; contact with the world did not dismay her, it did not invade her or disturb her, she slept for hours on end and cried only when she was hungry. I did not concentrate on her, I did not smell her head, I did not wait for the seconds when she opened her eyes in order to inspect their color, but when she cried I put her to my breast exactly as I had been told to, and somehow or other I also changed her diapers, although I didn't clean her properly. Most of the time, I remember, I sat next to her on the double bed where I had placed her in the beginning; I sat—because of the fear that if I lay down a last barrier inside me would be breached, and I would drown in what burst out. I don't remember day and night, but I do remember that I piled up the pillows at the top of the bed and propped up against them like a sick person I dozed and woke without distinguishing clearly between one state of consciousness and another. Only once in the dark I know that I got up, took a pail and cloth and for some reason began to wash the floor. It would have been better to wash myself and Hagar, because we were both no doubt in need of bathing by then, but that's what happened and that's what I did. And in the meantime the soiled diapers accumulated in a bag, without my giving a thought to what I was going to do when the clean ones ran out.

My sleeping and waking states were visited by all kinds of sensations and hallucinations, some of which still come back today. The pain cutting through my diaphragm, because of which I can't lie down. The grayness crawling over my body and threatening to cover me completely if I lie down. Fragments of myself floating in the cavities of my body like lumps of broken ice.

Looking back it is clear to me that I put my daughter into a situation that could have been dangerous, and I don't take any credit for the fact that we emerged unscathed.

HANDS OF MERCIFUL WOMEN

Hands of Merciful Women is the name of a painting I once saw in an art book; the painting itself did not remain in my memory, but the name stuck in my mind. Most of the actual good in my life came to me at the hands of women, and if I could choose whom to love with all my soul, I would choose a woman and not a man. With the passage of the years I have learned to love my mother and my daughter, and I love my girlfriends, but in my opinion I should love them differently, because even if I can't do without the folly of "he-makes-me-come-alive" and "I-can't-live-without-him," the feeling of love should be directed towards those I can't live without in reality. And in reality the man isn't there, and the hands of merciful woman always appeared in time.

When I was still pregnant, towards Passover, it was my sister who appeared like an angel on a bicycle, accompanied by a tiny little friend who turned out to be her classmate. Perhaps she had been sent by my mother to put out feelers, I didn't ask, but in any case Alek wasn't home, and I seated the pair of them in the living room and put on a show for them. They sat close together on the mattress, like two little birds, looking around with birdlike curiosity at everything, and when I went into the kitchen to make them tea—there were no cookies in the house—I heard the tiny friend whisper: "If she only got married to get out of going to the army, how come she's pregnant?" And my sister answering with a pride that brought sudden tears to my eyes: "That's how it is when you've got a bohemian sister."

Those were bad days, the days before Passover, days of Schubert symphonies, when nobody talked to Noa; Hagar lay high and pressed on my diaphragm, I only dragged myself out of bed when the little girls knocked on the door, and nevertheless in my capacity as the bohemian big sister I put on a Gershwin record for them, drew them out with amused superiority—what's new at school and what's new in the youth movement—and threw out anarchistic remarks about this and that. In the course of putting on this act of a free-spirited woman of mystery my mood somewhat improved, but Talush somehow saw through me, or maybe not, but in any case, for whatever reason, she turned up again the next day on her own behalf, and took out of her jeans bag two papayas and a giant pineapple that our father had brought back from Africa, and a few bars of chocolate from the airport, all of which she had swiped from our parents' kitchen. "You probably have to eat a lot if you're pregnant," she said, and her face was bright pink, and her nostrils and upper lip trembled, as they do to this day when she's excited.

On the third evening after my return from the hospital, I think it was the third evening, the downstairs neighbor Miriam Marie, who now that she no longer lives downstairs is regarded by Hagar and myself as a member of the family, and who up to then hardly impinged on the fringes of my consciousness, knocked on the door. She realized that a baby had been born, and came with a plate of cookies to congratulate me, and after seeing me she went downstairs again and came back with a little pot of chicken and rice which without asking she put on the stove to heat up.

Before this I had hardly exchanged more than a couple of sentences with her, in my eyes she was just one of the extras cast to play a bit part on the margins of my drama, but it quite soon became apparent to me that Miriam had taken in more than a little of the drama, and that her understanding of what was happening with me was closer to reality than anyone else's. So close to reality that in the future, whenever Alek showed up, I was afraid that she would see him and despise me. So that when she moved to Maaleh Adumim on the outskirts of Jerusalem to be close to the grandchildren on the way, I felt relieved. And even though I missed, and still miss, the warmth of her closeness, I was relieved to be rid of her look.

Miriam Marie. If I was a real writer and a proper human being, I would have written her story and not mine, because whichever way you look at it she's the true heroine and I'm the phony. When she came up the first time she was forty-four, only a little younger than my mother, but she looked years older. She hasn't changed much since then, as if her appearance had been fixed at a certain age, before old age and after the stage at which femininity, consciously or unconsciously, is directed towards men. Today, too, when she dyes her hair with raven black henna, wears three-piece outfits of cheap gaudy velvet and "artistic" brooches pinned to her bosom, she gives the impression that she is only dressing up to broadcast her feeling of well-being to the world.

When I met her she had one son, called Avi, who was already studying for his master's degree in education. When the boy was seven she had been abandoned by the husband—"the engineer" she sometimes calls him scornfully, though he really was an engineer—who ran away to France with a relation of hers. A little girl of sixteen from the immigrants transit camp in Talpiot. The main outlines of her story she told me that first evening, I think, holding Hagar securely while she bustled about the kitchen. "If I ever tell you the story of my life . . . ," she said. Or perhaps she didn't tell me everything then, as I sat with her weak and dizzy in the kitchen, and my memory is filling in the details from later installments. How he abandoned her to her fate as an *aguna*, a woman whose husband's whereabouts are unknown. How the rabbis over there searched for him, how it took them nine years to find him. And how she, with very little Hebrew, went to work, first as a cleaning lady, then taking a course to qualify as a kindergarten teacher's assistant, which didn't pay enough to care for the child, so that even with the steady kindergarten job she always took on extra work. Over the years I heard these stories again and again: how she managed to put food on the table, how she made sure that Avi went to school, and how in the end she moved to the center of town just so he would get into a good high school. "All his reports were ten out of ten, ten out of ten for everything. One day I'll show you, you'll see what they write about him there. But the principal didn't want to let him into the gymnasium, just because he was from Nachlaot. Every day I went to the municipality and sat there to make them look me in the face, and in the end what do you think? They took him, they didn't want to, but they did. Just because of my character, that I don't give in." What I remember clearly is that at some moment of that monologue I suddenly wanted a cigarette badly. I hadn't smoked since the birth, and suddenly for some reason I was dying for a cigarette, so that although I knew I wouldn't find one, I got up and began opening all the empty drawers in the house, one after the other. When I had despaired of the closet, with my hands still fumbling inside it, Miriam came and stood behind me, my daughter folded in her arms. "You shouldn't be left alone," she said. "It's not normal. There are women that get a psychological depression from it. Believe me, I know what I'm talking about." Then she put her hand in her pocket and offered me a packet of Europa cigarettes. "Promise me you won't smoke next to the baby."

In time I began to respond to this woman with the admiration she demanded and richly deserved, but on that first evening I didn't have the strength to utter a word, as if the road from their origins somewhere inside me to my mouth was too long for me to lead them along it. Nevertheless I was grateful that somebody was talking to me.

When she came to me she already knew that Alek had left—"that one of yours with the eyelashes" she called him—and when she placed the plate whose steam made my face damp before me I somehow understood that she was offering me her biography on a steaming plate as well. That she was laying her past before me not only as "a personal example of willpower and character," but mainly in order to make this spoiled young girl open her mouth at last and give her a clue as to her situation.

When Miriam's husband went off with his teenage mistress and with Miriam's gold bracelets, she had nobody to lean on: her father was already sick when they arrived in the country, her mother had three more young children at home, and in comparison to these facts I know that my unhappiness was like a pampered parody of distress.

A pampered parody of distress—that's what I was then, and that in many ways is what I still am today. And then, too, when she asked me straight out over a cup of tea where my family was—Wasn't that your father who hooted for you downstairs then, driving the whole street mad?—I knew how ridiculous I was in the comparison between us: she a penniless immigrant, and I the daughter of parents who may not have been rich, but who were getting richer all the time, and who had never lacked for connections or the sense that the country belonged to them.

I have no idea whether Miriam loved her man before he ran away, or how she loved him, I never dared to ask. History as she tells it begins on the day he deserted her, and from the beginning of this history he is referred to in derogatory terms. Perhaps she called him different names once, and perhaps not, but in any case it was clear that she would not be sympathetic to the kind of reckless madness that led "that poor girl" to run away with her husband.

"You could make a movie out of my life," she sometimes says, with absolute justice. If I had to choose a heroine, I would definitely choose her, myself I don't even see as a candidate, but if that's what I think, and I really do think so, then how is it that to this day I still feel that I have a certain advantage over her? Not because I am better educated, not because I know more words, but only because in my folly love makes me superior in my own eyes. As if it has exalted me to some lofty pinnacle, as if I have been branded by a hallucinatory fire, and as if I have been privileged to touch what she and others have not touched.

Miriam Marie loves her son, her daughter-in-law, her grandchildren, two of her brothers and most of her nephews and nieces. She loves most of the toddlers in her nursery school, and some of their mothers. And to my good fortune, I don't know why, she loves me too and she loves Hagar. When Miriam says that someone loves, she almost always adds proofs to her statement; practical proofs, not cliches about feelings: "You should see how he helps her," "the way he looked after her," "he would do anything for her." "His heart goes out to her," or "her heart goes out to him" are phrases which do not appear in her lexicon, and certainly not "soul mates combining into one androgynous creature." In all the years that we have known each other, I have never heard any such highfalutin drivel from her.

Miriam is occupied with real people: the asthmatic Itamar, Dror who is about to be drafted, Yaron and Liron who are building a house; whereas I am occupied with the fictions of my books, and with my ever-present absentee. And from this point of view as well I believe that she is superior to me.

But what do I really know about her fantasies and her nights? I know nothing, and I have no right to patronize her in this way.

After I had given her a few mumbled details about my situation, she pronounced that I had to "forget everything that had happened" and turn to my parents, because "what do quarrels mean now? This sweet little baby is their granddaughter, wait and see what they say after they see her." I promised her that I would think about it, and I realized that she wouldn't leave me be, and she didn't, even after my parents showed up.

PARENTS

My parents showed up the next day. Without thinking about it I had given my name as Weber in the hospital, and one of the nurses who knew my mother made the connection and got in touch with her. I have already said that my parents know everybody and everybody knows them, and it was only to be expected that they would hear the news, sooner rather than later. I think that they had prepared themselves for it, for as they told me afterwards with a reasonable degree of resentment, when the nurse phoned my mother was able to hide her ignorance of the fact that she was a grandmother from her. She didn't repeat the text to me word for word, but I can imagine it: "Our Noa . . . she's so stubborn . . . got it into her head that she didn't want any visitors . . . you know how it is, it's so important to them to be independent . . . she feels fine . . . everything's fine . . . the difficulties are behind us . . . we're looking to the future."

I could easily write the memory of their appearance at my door as a "shtick," and to tell the truth I actually did so a number of times over the course of the years: little Talush, a scouting party of one little girl, is sent to knock on my door. My mother takes up her position as back-up halfway down the stairs. My father sits in the getaway car without switching off the engine.

When it transpired that the "Russian nihilist," as Grandma Dora called him, was gone, the family gathered round me, and in a matter of minutes, without any overt negotiations, formulated an agreed version of the state of affairs. Our Noa came under a bad influence, our Noa was kidnapped by the wicked wolf, and now that the wicked wolf is gone, the past is forgotten and we're "looking ahead to the future." My father, who apart from the embarrassments I'd caused resented the scene in the street, found it a little difficult to accept this agreement, but from the moment the Weber team made it into the apartment, and from the moment it transpired that Noa Weber looked the way she looked—in other words, a mess—it was clear that Mother Batya would take command. Armed with my new cunning of the mad I was relieved at not-having to answer any questions about "that man," that I was not being required to pay with a confession, and weak as I was I surrendered myself to their efficient care. Because at that stage I really did feel sick. Sick and very frightened.

My mother was at her best, performing her role as a nurse, and although her experience with babies was not great, she applied herself fearlessly to the operations of bathing and diapering. Methods of suckling, pacifiers for and against, and ointments for diaper rash supplied us with sufficient subjects of conversation, and the rest of the time we dealt with my "recovery"—of my body, that is. I was a good patient, just as my mother was an excellent nurse. Lying between clean bedclothes, my shampooed hair on the raised pillow, my hands on the blanket, I did whatever I was told. When I was told to eat, I ate. When I was told to drink juice, I drank juice. When I was led to the bathroom, I washed myself. Days and nights ran into each other, and my memory from then is mainly of a sensation of dripping; drops of milk and blood and tears that didn't stop flowing from the moment they started taking care of me. Dripping into the shower water. Dripping into the steam of the soup.

The tears were genuine, I didn't have the strength to stop them, but at the fringes of consciousness I was also aware of the fact that crying helped me. The child is weak and traumatized. Leave the child alone. Don't remind her, don't ask any questions. Can't you see that she's suffering enough as it is?

Talush was sent to fetch and carry, my father dropped in every day "to see how you're getting on," and my mother took leave from work and took over the house and reorganized it. I accepted everything with mute, grateful nods: when she converted Alek's room into a nursery, when she brought the rest of my clothes from home and arranged them in the closet, when she ordered Yoash, who came to visit, to "give a hand" and move the table here and the closet there—she didn't let him go even when he provoked her by asking her in the name of the principle of self-determination to call him Hamida. She called him Hamida, and still insisted that he help her move the closet. Even when she asked my permission to remove Klimt's dead floating women from the kitchen wall—"that picture gives me the creeps"—I nodded.

My part in the new agreement was easy, I accepted it willingly: no more cheekiness with my parents, and no more ideological deviations. Our Noa has learned her lesson, and sadder but wiser she has come back to us. Sadder and wiser, and the roots of her hair hurt. Until then I never knew that the roots of your hair could hurt, but this is one of the strange things that I discovered. It hurt me even to cut my nails, and with every sip of soup I took I heard a wave breaking inside my ears.

Only once did I voice any opposition, and this was on the evening they first appeared, when my mother proposed taking me and Hagar home with them. I don't know if my first burst of tears prevented a big argument, or if they weren't so keen on putting the two of us up in the first place, but in any event, the result was that for two weeks or more my mother slept in Alek's bed.

I didn't explain the reasons for my objections; in days to come my mother noted that "that was a sign to me that you were recovering, and that it was important to you to stand on your own feet"—but the real reason was different, completely different, it was the feeling of the gaping void around which I was crystallizing. The feeling was and still is completely physical. And under my swollen breasts I then felt the void all the time. As if an amputated internal organ was still hurting me. And in my heart I sobbed that Alek, Alek, Alek was hurting me.

The stronger this feeling grew, so too did the idea that as if by some law of nature the void had to be filled with what accorded with it, in the only manner that accorded with it; in other words, I began to believe that Alek would return. Of course I also formulated more reasonable and realistic reasons for this belief to myself, such as: "He has a daughter he will want to meet one day," or "Alek may be angry with Israel, but he's not indifferent to it"—they proved to be correct more quickly than I imagined—but at the basis of the belief was the feeling of a void, and Nature abhors a vacuum, doesn't it?

Since I believed that Alek would return, I had to remain on Usha Street to wait for him, nothing could prevent me from waiting for him there.

I don't know where I got this romantic nonsense from, as if I were the heroine of a black-and-white movie, waiting for my lover in the place where the war had parted us, but even if anyone had ridiculed me along these lines, or said that Alek was perfectly capable of opening a telephone directory and locating me, there were no words in the world with the power to move me from my stubborn refusal to budge. Alek would return here, and I had to be here when he came.

When this irrational certainty crystallized inside me, I buried it inside me and wrapped myself around it in the dark, drawing secret strength from my madness. When Alek came back he would find me worthy of him. I had to make myself worthy of him.

IN A CROOKED WAY

Much of what I am today stems in a crooked way from this wish to be worthy in his eyes, equal in power to his imaginary power. At the beginning this ambition related mainly to basic functioning: to start taking care of myself and of Hagar so that he wouldn't despise me, to gradually limit my mother's presence; and gradually more and more ambitions were added, until my will to prevail was extended also to the area of my mood, in which I also began to see a measure of my strength. Alek was doing his thing in Heidelberg, I was doing mine in Jerusalem. Alek was not suffering from "psychological depression," therefore I too would hold my head up high.

At first, of course, I pretended: Get up. Stand up straight. Lift up your chin. Raise your eyes from the pavement. Take a deep breath. Straighten your shoulders. Stretch your neck. Look up. Go out to run, at least for a few blocks. Until the pretense took over, and with my chin up and my eyes on the horizon, I really did begin to feel better.

Most of my achievements over the years I measured under the imaginary gaze of Alek's eyes, and to this day it remains fixed on me in both small and great events. I remember for example the gradual change that took place in my appearance in the first year as a law student, when I began to wear buttoned shirts and for the first time in my life went to a salon. The lightheaded feeling that came with my shoulder-length haircut and the touch of air on my nape like a new nudity were connected to his touch in my mind.

I remember my first staged court case, it was a damages case, the show I put on in order to impress precisely the person who wasn't there, and the paradoxical way in which his imaginary gaze helped me to relax, as if the imaginary audience of one enabled me to ignore the real one. Alek's imagined gaze steadied my voice and my arguments, and concentrating on it distanced the lecturer and class in front of me, turning them into the spectators of a play not really intended for them.

The whole episode of my legal studies was connected to the imagined eye of Alek, and my desire to impress him. Actually, Miriam too played a part here, a far from inconsiderable part, for from the start she urged me to study. My father offered to get me a job with one of his friends "until we see what's happening with your life"—translation: "until you meet someone normal and marry in a normal way." My mother said that a profession was definitely important for a woman, too, and "in my situation"—in other words, as a single parent—teaching could fit the bill, and only Miriam insisted that I had to "believe in myself," and set up a meeting for me with the only lawyer she knew, the mother of a toddler who had attended her nursery school the year before, who she still sometimes babysat for in the afternoons.

In those days there were not yet television series about glamorous and neurotic female lawyers, but Miriam very much admired this lawyer, who was dealing with a protracted court case about building in the yard on her behalf, and she made up her mind that law was the profession for me and nothing else would do. For months she kept at me: "You've got a head on your shoulders," and "You know how to talk," and "You were lucky to go to high school, don't waste your luck," and for months

I kept at my parents to agree and for the assistance they were unwilling to provide—"A plan, Noaleh, must first of all be realistic"—until Aunt Greta arrived and contributed her share and compelled my father to contribute his. In all this time Miriam kept on at me, but what really decided the issue was the thought of Alek.

For almost a year I worked in a little soup restaurant that catered mainly to art students. It was relatively pleasant work, in a relatively pleasant place. The owner of the establishment, Tami, is a friend of mine to this day. And nevertheless when I served the customers, some of whom I recognized from Alek's social evenings, and most of whom did not recognize me, I began to feel like Cinderella. As is usual with students, they worked at all kinds of odd jobs, but according to their definition and also their self-perception, they were something else: the future of Israeli academia, the future of the local avant-garde, activists in all kinds of left-wing and protest movements; even Tami was studying part time for a degree in economics. Only I was a real waitress. A mother, waitress, and a vegetable peeler. Sometimes I would imagine Alek coming into the restaurant and sitting down next to the window with some female intellectual, and then the humiliation was insufferable. So that after a few months of peeling carrots and wiping tables, I was determined to "make something" of myself, and when Miriam continued to insist that "something" meant lawyer, I decided to think so, too.

My idea of the profession was of course absurd: a combination of Robin Hood and Clarence Darrow, doing justice and solving all Miriam Marie's problems with the municipality. Two days after the beginning of the academic year I realized how grotesque this image was. But without an alternative direction, I continued to study law.

Sometimes during interviews I feel a kamikazi urge to crash into the truth. The bit about Clarence Darrow and social justice sounds good, even charming, I've used it a number of times, but I take good care to censor all the rest.

Interviewer: So how did it happen that you went to study law?

Feminist writer: It was a coincidence. With women, you know, things happen by chance. There was a man I wanted to impress.

Interviewer: Did you want him to fall in love with you?

Feminist writer: I knew I didn't have a hope.

Interviewer: But surely he must have been impressed. . . .

Writer: He didn't even know I was studying. You see, he wasn't in the country at all, there was no contact between us. I just imagined that he was looking at me all the time.

Interviewer: And afterwards?

Writer: What afterwards? There is no afterwards. There is no earlier and later in love. When he felt like summoning me, I went to be his mistress. That's the way it still is.

What's missing in this confession is the benefit I derived from his imaginary gaze. Apart from the intense color of the world, apart from the sharpening of senses that comes with love, apart from the increased energy, there was also a specific benefit, a lot of specific benefits: what I described before as "holding my head high." Under Alek's imaginary gaze I couldn't be a floor rag. And so in some strange way his gaze helped me push the baby carriage nobly up Tiberias Street when a heat wave had already pushed me out of the house, and helped me drag myself out of bed in the dark to light the kerosene stove in the kitchen and summarize "The Development of the Concept of Good Faith in German Law."

The funny thing about it is that Alek, to the best of my knowledge, doesn't give a damn about the way I or any other woman looks when she pushes a baby carriage, and studiousness was never one of his qualities. And nevertheless I mobilized his gaze in order to brush my teeth, dress properly, get onto the bus, photocopy legal precedents and understand what exactly Reuben and Simeon had done to Levi.

"NOT THE LOVELORN MAIDEN"

In the winter when we were still living together I found a copy of *Eugene Onegin* in a second-hand book store, and on good days I amused Alek by learning whole stanzas off it by heart, to which he would respond by quoting from the poem in Russian. Pushkin in his eyes was the prince of princes; the "poet of the golden age" was beyond any criticism or irony, which gave the poem such magical status in my eyes that in his absence I would read passages from it to myself out loud. The symbolists he was working on had not been translated into Hebrew—or if they had I never succeeded in finding the translations—and Dostoevsky he hated, so I was left with Onegin, who I saw as a key. Another way of touching Alek.

From reading it so many times I absorbed the story into myself to such an extent that when I fantasized about the return of my man, I imagined the scene in the words of the poet. When he returned I would be someone impossible to ignore. When he returned, a new Noa Weber would be revealed to his eyes. "Not the plain, timorous, dejected / and lovelorn maiden whom he'd known" but Noa Weber, a duchess who not only "never shivered, / paled, flushed, or lost composure's grip—/ no, even her eyebrow never quivered, / she never even bit her lip."

Even at the height of my fantasy I never deluded myself that in the light of my new incarnation my Onegin would suddenly fall in love with me. But when I sat poring over "Constitutional Law" at night, and when I stood up in my first staged trial to defend Levi against Reuben and Simeon, and when I walked into my literary editor's office for the first time to talk about the manuscript of *Blood Money*— vulnerable and nervous as a child of eight on my first day at the town school—I mobilized his imaginary gaze, I sensed his imaginary eyes on me and heard his imaginary words: "could it be she . . . or had he dreamed? / the girl he'd scorned in what he deemed the modesty of her condition, / could it be she, who had just turned / away, so cool, so unconcerned?" And upon my word it made me noble. In my eyes at least.

The motif of the late return it's called: when she languishes in love, he is indifferent or amused. And when he languishes in love, she no longer responds. In non-literary reality I don't know of a single case where this trick worked. Later on I did make a number of genuine attempts not to respond, but in those first years all my Duchess fantasies were directed towards a very different end than that of *Eugene Onegin*. I wanted to meet him "cool and unconcerned" only so that he would strip me of my false indifference. I wanted not to flush and pale only in order for him to make me flush and pale again. It's true that I wanted him to admire my small and great triumphs, but it's also true that in my imagination I saw the lawyer's gown as one more garment that he could strip me of.

NIRA WOOLF

"Female lawyers are sexy," says Dr. Miles to Nira Woolf as he accompanies her on the courthouse steps, "I like strong women." "Forget it," replies my heroine. "Forget what?" asks the charming doctor. "Forget what's in your head. I'm not interested in egos that want to lay feminist lawyers," and neither of course in idiots who have no respect for a woman's achievements, but this Nira Woolf doesn't say.

In this world there is no Noa Weber who did not go to Usha Street on the second of July 1972 so that I have no control group for myself. Perhaps even without Alek the drive to achieve would have appeared in me, I don't know, but what's certain is that the initial urge was connected to Alek. To the desire to awaken his admiration and the desire to please him. In other words, it wasn't some nobody who was in love with him, and it wasn't with some nobody that he went to the Rabbinate, but with someone who was somebody. Someone whose love was a credit to him, because it was only with him that she turned into a floor rag.

Blood Money, the first in my Nira Woolf series, came out in 1982, and from then on the straightening of my spineless back proceeded at a considerable pace. But I'm putting the cart before the horse again, because in the summer of '73 the era of holding my head high was far in the future, and I was still busy with the emergency patching up of Noa Weber, who cried a lot then; she cried day and night without any shame. I was only ashamed with Miriam, but Miriam retreated before my mother, telling me tactfully that I was welcome to visit her with the baby whenever I wanted to. My crying was real, my helplessness was not a total lie, and nevertheless there was an element of bribery in it. As if I was buying myself time with hysterical behaviour.

I remember how underneath the hysteria I imagined myself coming out cold and sober on the other side, and at the height of my depression, weeping between the starched sheets, I knew very well what I was doing, and what was happening inside me and around me. In the time that I bought with my weakness I allowed myself to indulge in all kinds of wild schemes. I would slip out of the house, take a taxi at dawn to the airport, and just as I was, without luggage or money, get on a plane to Heidelberg. I would join the foreign service or the Mossad, and they would send me to Heidelberg. I would get out of bed, go somewhere or other, and then I would walk and walk and walk until I fell. A small item in the newspaper would say: Young Israeli woman found dead on street in Heidelberg. Or a small item in the newspaper would say: The body of a young woman was found lying in the church of the Holy Sepulchre, cause of death unknown. I had these visions, not of actual suicide, but of walking and losing myself on my way to him, losing myself until I came to his door, and then perhaps he would let me in.

In the end of course nothing of the sort happened. My suicidal tendencies are limited, my Adele H. qualities are restricted to the realm of fantasy, and in reality there is little chance of my turning into Victor Hugo's retarded daughter. But the fantasy of turning into someone like her did not go away as I grew older, and it still happens, too often and for too long, that I think about Alek and feel that ignominious urge to lose myself rising in my heart again.

HAGAR

In the weeks after giving birth to her I hardly thought about her. When they gave her to me to feed I fed her. When they handed me a soiled diaper, I dropped it into the trash. When my mother gave her a bath, I stood next to the bath, and when she put the baby in my arms I held her. I didn't deny her, I wanted her to exist, and at the same time her presence seemed to me like a temporary matter. As if sometime someone would come to take her, and then I would be able to devote myself entirely to the one who wasn't there.

Maternal love, they say, is a part of nature. From the moment you lay eyes on your baby the instinctual programming begins to operate, and the feedback with the cub gives rise to infinite devotion and inevitable tenderness in you.

I love Hagar. She makes me happy, she even makes me proud. With time I developed the devotion, the tenderness, the pleasure and so on and so forth, so that even in her absence she occupies my thoughts. If I were put to the test, to the best of my knowledge I would say: My life for hers. But such theoretical tests are not necessarily proof of love.

In reality, I raised her and took care of her to the best of my ability, with all the unavoidable mistakes of a too young and very busy mother, mistakes that do not necessarily stem from coldness.

What I'm trying to say with all this beating around the bush is that I didn't fall in love with my daughter in the same way as I fell in love with her father, and I never had the same stunned sense that the feeling was inevitable with her as I had in relation to him. I learned to do the things that a mother has to do, and as I did them the feeling developed, and this is the reason why it is precisely maternal love that seems to me a matter of choice. I never chose to love Alek.

When she was a little girl Hagar said to me more than once: "When I grow up I'll only have children when I love someone and marry him," and now too, as far as I know, she keeps to this decision. Sometimes I think that it's my daughter's good fortune that her father was not with us. Because it was only in the void that he left with his departure that I could learn to love her. I don't think that I could ever have "grown used" to him, and it's clear to me that his daily presence would have stopped any other presence from growing inside me.

"Do you know what great love gave birth to Columbus?" he asked me one night in Moscow when I, at least, was quite drunk. "You don't know because there is no such story. A great man like Columbus, something as tremendous as discovering America by mistake, is not the result of love. Love has no results."

"And great results don't come from love," I wisecracked in the treachery of drunkeness.

"Something like that, but don't you believe it. It's only Symbolists' talk. Not something really connected to life." At this point I already knew, if I didn't know from the outset, that the ideas he spouted were to be taken no more seriously than his retraction of them.

The Yom Kippur War was the first time that I paid my daughter any real attention. My father put on his uniform on the first day of the war and drove to the staff headquarters to find himself a job in the chaos. My mother plunged immediately into the hospital, and hardly emerged to go home. Talush was deposited with neighbours and

Miriam moved temporarily to Kiryat Yovel to help her sister-in-law who had been left alone with three small children. In September I had started work in Tami's restaurant, Soupçon, and Hagar had started going to daycare, but with the outbreak of war both the restaurant and the daycare were closed, and with all the horror around, I no longer seemed so important even to myself.

I once read a story in an American magazine, maybe made up, about a flood in a Scandinavian mental asylum. According to this story, when the water began rising the catatonics emerged from their paralysis, came to life and began to evacuate the building with exemplary efficiency, ingenuity, and mutual aid. All the way to their new temporary facilities, with the water still rushing behind them, they kept on making merry, sat wrapped in their blankets and sang, threw candies at each other—or so I imagine the scene—and only early in the morning, when they were taken off the truck and led into the new building, did the lunatics return to their lunacy, the catatonics to their catatonia.

Two thousand six hundred soldiers were killed in the Yom Kippur War, Amikam among them, I already knew, and two of my peers from the youth movement, and four members of the kibbutz. Most of my classmates were at the front, Yoash was in Sinai with the reservists; almost everyone I knew plunged into the war, and the whole horror passed me by.

All that happened to me was that I started to think about Hagar, and that too came from a primeval fear. Suddenly the two of us were alone, and with all the unclear information and rumors flying around, I started fantasizing about how I would flee with her to the forests. The forests? Yes, I regret to say that for some reason I saw myself fleeing the shelling with the baby to the forest.

Among other nonsense I thought that it was a good thing she was still breast-feeding, because when the Syrian stormtroopers ran riot in the streets—for some reason I had Syrians in my head—I would be able to lock the door without having to worry about food for her. I remember that I even checked the lock. At the end of all these adventures was of course an emotional reunion with Alek who came to look for us; but until the emotional reunion, I was at least with her both in fantasy and reality.

Someone will have to explain to me one day why people make propaganda for love: we have our heads stuffed with it from infancy, as if this particular lunacy is an important Zionist value. Get ready, get set, here it comes . . . like a flash of lightning . . . your personal earthquake . . . . don't let it pass you by, you too deserve to experience it . . . love at first sight for every citizen!

When I was a child it wasn't so bad: "love" was mentioned almost only at bedtime; "love" appeared in the fairy tales that Yochi sometimes read aloud to us from the passage, when we were all already tucked into bed in our rooms, with our faces to the wall. But Yochi usually preferred stories of a different kind, and it was only rarely that she read us fairy tales.

Later on we discovered Hollywood romances for ourselves, in the movies for adults screened in the dining room and in hidden copies of *Movie World*. The girls read *Daddy Longlegs*, the boys restricted themselves to volleyball. . . . On the door of a cupboard in the dentist's clinic Rhett Butler held Scarlett O'Hara's chin as if he were about to examine her throat, and when I opened my mouth wide Shoshana Damari sang on the radio, "He knew there was no lighthouse on the shore. . . ." On the whole, I think, most of the time we were free of romantic preoccupations. Not like today when the propaganda is more and more pervasive, and every click of the remote control brings you propaganda for epilepsy or some weird jingle in praise of being struck by lightning.

In a thousand years I will never understand why they sell us this stuff: as if emotional epilepsy is something charming and lightning strikes are good for the environment.

The worst damage done by romantic love is the coldheartedness that it creates. Because when love seizes you, however much you struggle and kick, you are no longer capable of truly thinking about anyone else, because nobody else is truly real to you any more.

In 1981 my father had a heart attack, and my mother and Talush and I took turns sitting in the corridor outside the Intensive Care Unit. The day after the heart attack was a Wednesday, and I remember that it was a Wednesday because on Friday I was supposed to go on a trip to the north of the country with Alek, and the main thought in my mind was how I was going to get away now, because as things stood I didn't have an alibi for disappearing for a couple of days, and I had no one to look after Hagar. Ute had gone to visit her parents in Germany with baby Daniel, she was due back the coming Tuesday—you see, I remember everything—and I, with the ice of love surrounding my heart, walked around with a styrofoam cup from the coffee machine in my hand, biting the rim of the cup and thinking, among other things, that if my father died, and they sat *shiva* on the kibbutz, I wouldn't be able to spend any time with Alek.

If there was any logic in the world, the radio would bleep every time the word "love" was mentioned. The censors would blacken the television screen and warn that the material in question is not suitable for children, that it is subversive, dangerous. That anyone who seriously succumbs to this madness is definitely not friendly to the environment. But nobody apart from me seems to see things this way.

MY HAGAR, FOR EXAMPLE

My Hagar, for example, tends to chew on the word "love" interminably, and in recent years she has also developed the irritating habit of remarking "I love you" at the end of every conversation with me, casting the two of us in some American television drama.

This is the recurrent pattern: first she provokes some argument with me on e-mail, and then she calls to say, "Mommy, I just want you to know that I love you."

"Yes. . . . Same here," I echo in embarrassment. And only once I said: "Look, surely we can have an argument without pinning this tail to it. It wouldn't kill us."

"And it won't kill you to hear that I love you. Why is it so hard for you to hear me say it? When I have children, I'll tell them that I love them ten times a day."

"I'm sure you will."

"And I want to make it clear to you that I know that you love me."

"I very much hope that you know."

When she was here over the summer I almost vomited at the

conversations she conducted with her boyfriend on the phone: I love you. I miss you so much. I know you care for your brother. I know it hurts. I wish I could share it with you. More than once she stood opposite me in the kitchen with the cordless phone, she didn't even take the trouble to go to her room, and against the background of the synthetic music of these phrases I cut the cucumbers and tomatoes on the chopping board into tiny pieces so that my daughter would have a proper Israeli salad after a winter in New York.

Hagar sincerely believes that "love is communication," and that "love is above all friendship and shared values," and that "love is growing together"; she recites these theses to me without a hint of irony, and since "Peter's aggressive-depressive silences sabotage their love" she doesn't think she'll marry him, even though for the time being they're not breaking up, either. Peter hurts her feelings, and you don't marry someone who hurts your feelings, right? No, my clear darling, says her mother, on no account should you marry someone who hurts your feelings, even if those feelings sound to your mother like commercially packaged nothing.

ALEK

Alek came on the night of the twentieth of November. At half past ten on the night after the war.

How can I convince myself that love is an insane delusion, when Alek appears at my door in the dark as in a vision?

His face is white as that of a tense clown, and he is wearing something white under his army coat. "May I?" he asks, standing so passively in the doorway. You don't ask "May I?" about something that belongs to you anyway, I thought afterwards, when I drew back to get my breath between heartbeats. My heart had gone completely haywire, it had expanded to alarming dimensions leaving no room for my lungs. Alek let me go for a minute and put his Kalashnikov down on the marble counter. "What are you doing here?" I asked when he pulled me back into his embrace. "What am I doing?" he mumbled to my forehead, and without seeing or hearing—perhaps only from the touch of his lips—I made out the words, "What am I doing here? Apparently trying to be Hemingway."

"No," he added immediately and tightened his grip, "no. That's not it. I was a soldier here, and there's you and the child and Yoash and a few others. It wouldn't be normal not to come." And later on, at dawn, he said too that "as soon as the war began I couldn't stand the anti-Semites. Understand, I'm allowed to hate this country, but what is permitted to Ginsberg is forbidden to an anti-Semitic goy, and Paris is full of such anti-Semites, even if they don't know that they're anti-Semites and they just hate Israel." Only then, at dawn, I discovered that he hadn't gone to Heidelberg at all, and had flown straight to Paris when he left in June.

Heidelberg: One of the most beautiful cities in Germany. Known for its famous university, which was founded in the Middle Ages. Tchernikhovsky and Klausner studied there. I know, I looked it up in Grandma Dora's encyclopedia one Saturday when I traveled to the kibbutz with Hagar to show ourselves and stand the test of gossiping tongues. For five months I had imagined Heidelberg at the foot of the Odenwald mountain range, until I could walk down the cobbled streets in my imagination and make

my way to the river. I sometimes went into travel agencies simply in order
to see the name of the city on a poster. Before I went to sleep I would look
at the atlas and measure the distance in days of walking. And whenever
they said "West Germany" on the radio, I would turn up the volume.
And all that time he had been in Paris.

Alek didn't ask about Hagar sleeping in her room that was once his
room. Not right away. First he led me to bed and sank himself in my
body, and gave me back my body that had as if been taken from me
after the birth. Gave me back my body so that I would lose it under him
and above him and this way and that, and then I would fill it up again
until the tips of my fingers and toes dripped happiness.

"We weren't Jewish heroes," he mumbled when I rested on his
arm, and his fingers dripped with milk from my breasts.

"We weren't?"

"No. My father is a Jewish hero. Official hero. Two years he fought
at Leningrad, you know: blocked the canon with his body. He himself
breached the blockade."

"Where is he now?"

"In the same place, apparently. In Sverdlovsk, Ekaterinburg, where
they killed the Czar."

"And you, where have you come from now?"

Years later, too, when he became a full-time journalist, he wasn't
in the habit of volunteering information in answer to questions of the
who-what-when-where kind. "In the area of the enclave. The Golan
Heights," he answered reluctantly.

"Was it hard?"

"For those who were there at the beginning it was hard. This week they finally brought coats for everyone."

As always happens with him, to this day, Alek opened up time for me and stripped the moment of all its specific attributes. Amikam was dead, that I already knew. The IDF was positioned forty kilometers from Damascus, Golda was conducting talks with Kissinger, Tami's brother was in Tel Hashomer Hospital, Yoash was still serving in the reserves, and in Alek's arms, in the clean smell of his body, I was far away, in a place consisting only of the absolute raw materials. Man, woman, war, baby.

Even when I saw his white face in the doorway I knew that he would not stay with us, but I was like a person whose faith has found confirmation: nature abhors a vacuum, and the vacuum is filled with what fits it. Alek had not left me, and he would never really leave me.

At some point or other Hagar began to whimper and Alek didn't get up with me, he waited; I went to her and waited, dense sweet heart-trembling moments, until he came and stood silently next to the wall over us. I didn't switch on the light, and I didn't need to. I saw everything like a cat in the dark. My vision has never been clearer. Alek was dressed—perhaps he was cold, perhaps he felt it wasn't fitting to enter this scene naked. I think that's what he felt. He stood hugging himself in that so familiar position, and from the armchair I could see his fingers gripping his ribs. Something happened to time, which slowed down and spread out between the beats: Hagar's sucking. My breathing. My heartbeats. His breathing presence in the dark. As if infinity could enter between the beats. I don't have the right words to describe it, but I know for certain that in those moments I wanted nothing, I hoped for nothing, my thoughts stayed still. I was all gathered in, all wrapped up, and it was enough for me to know that the moment indeed existed, and since it existed, it would never ever be denied.

Only when I put Hagar back to bed did Alek come up and stand next to me and reach out to put one finger on her hand, which immediately clenched around it. I didn't dare look at his face, I didn't look until he whispered something and I turned my head to read his lips. "Fingernails," he whispered, "I didn't think of this. Of this I didn't think. I didn't think she had fingernails."

During all the years to come I made sure that Hagar never saw the two of us together, except for the unavoidable moments when she went out to him, on the rare occasions when he came to get her at the house. Does she have some unconscious memory in which this picture is stored? Her mother with an open flannel pyjama top, her father in white, standing together over her crib.

My feet were frozen, and when we got back into bed Alek put them on his chest to warm them. And then he asked me about Yoash. He had a gentlemanly order of priorities. First me, his full attention, then Hagar, and then Yoash. When had I heard from him last? I hadn't heard anything from Yoash, Alek was much better informed than I was. Before he booked a flight to Israel he managed to get him on the phone, and Yoash who was already in uniform left him a key in the regular place under the flowerpot. And the first chance he got to make a call, Alek called Yoash's mother on the farm. Yoash was in Africa, on the other side of the canal, with Brigade 421, they hoped to see him safe and sound next week.

ALEK

Alek stayed in the country for nearly three more weeks before returning to Paris, and from the first morning we established a routine which had never existed before and which was never repeated afterwards. The procedure came into being as if of its own accord on the first day, when Alek went to get his discharge from the army. I took Hagar to her daycare, and from there I went to meet him at Yoash's apartment, where he had settled in the night before, before coming to me. I spent the afternoon with Hagar, and at night when she was already asleep he came to me, knocking on the door and staying for a few hours. But after Yoash returned, it sometimes happened that he came with him and left with him.

When Hagar woke up, he would sometimes come with me and touch her with renewed wonder, but he never picked her up. Even on the one night she spent in my arms with the two men in the kitchen, when she was suffering from a prickly rash. Because of this, when I had to go to the toilet, without giving it any thought I handed her to Yoash, who took her naturally, put her on his shoulder, and was in no hurry to give her back to me when I returned.

Without saying anything, Alek made it clear that he was a guest in our house, and nevertheless he tried to spend as much time as he could with me. With me and with Yoash.

One Saturday I took Hagar to my parents for lunch, and we all made a big effort to create an atmosphere of normality, but nothing was normal. The newspapers were black with mourning notices, the telephone kept ringing with news of friends' sons, and rumors of what had really happened and what had definitely happened, and my father looked as if he had shrunk. He never picked up the phone himself, he just stood there with his eyes fixed on the instrument until my mother handed it to him, and to us he hardly spoke at all. It was his friends who were responsible for the fiasco, and he realized the full extent of the catastrophe more than any of us.

Talush, in a childish track suit already too small for her that for some reason she insisted on wearing, withdrew with Hagar to the sofa, ignoring the three of us, and from the look in my mother's eyes she seemed not to see us at all. On the first day of the war she had closed the diet clinic and gone back to working as a nurse in the wards.

And in the midst of this sorrow, of all this sorrow, Noa Weber sat at the table reeking of sex, silent in idiotic satisfaction, and nobody thought for a moment of attributing her silence to compulsive sexual gratification. On the contrary, they thought that I was with them, depressed to the point of speechlessness by the torrent of bad news, and in fact I seemed so depressed to them that at one point my mother put her hands on my shoulders from behind and said: "Cheer up a bit, Noa. It doesn't help to be depressed. In the end, we won a great victory."

For a moment I was tempted to tell them that Alek was in Israel and that he was really a good guy, one of the best of our boys, doing the right thing by rushing to the defense of the motherland, but I immediately rejected the thought. Alek was not a good guy, not in their sense, and I was already deep in an emotional underground, too deep to be able to conduct a public relations campaign on Alek's behalf.

Two days before, on Thursday afternoon, I had gone with him and Yoash to drink coffee in the Old City. When we came out of the cafe it began to pour, the merchants retreated into their empty shops, but we ran through the water cascading from the awnings, embracing, skipping crazily up the wet steps, eliciting peals of laughter from the spectators, who also seemed to forget the time and events for a moment.

Something was happening between the three of us, and when I thought about it—and I thought about it most of the time—I felt a kind of conspiratorial warmth spreading through me.

In the days preceding Yoash's release from the army I understood the intensity with which Alek related to him. He called up to find out what had happened to all kinds of friends and acquaintances, but as far as Yoash was concerned it was evident that he was really worried, a worry that never left him. "I love him," he said. The best of our boys didn't say such things then.

About the events of his own war Alek was unwilling to talk, and it was only gradually that I gathered information. On the first day of the war he tried to get onto a plane, but reservists from Golani were not a high priority, so it was only on the fourth day that he reached brigade headquarters. For some reason they kept him at Acre for three days, and from there they sent him to Rosh Pina, it's not clear why. In the end he went up to the Golan Heights to escort a convoy of supplies to the enclave, but by that time the worst of the fighting was already over.

I have no idea what he saw and what he did, perhaps he talked about it to Yoash, but with me he just shrugged his shoulders. "We weren't Jewish heroes."

When Yoash came back Alek was the first to notice that there was something wrong, it took me time, and all I saw at the beginning was that Yoash was in high gear, and it was nothing new for Yoash to have attacks of speedy hyperactivity. He talked a lot, he talked without stopping, rapid strings of words, and Alek sat next to him and listened. The words were the same words that everybody was repeating then: Golda, the Chief of Staff, they came in from here, they attacked us from there, the bridgehead, the breakthrough, General Gonen. . . . I didn't pay attention to the exact content and the details of the complaints which were endlessly, monotonously repeated, but after Alek pointed it out to me I began to notice that there really was something wrong with Yoash. He hardly slept, none of us slept much in those days. Alek my insomniac prince never needed much sleep, I made up a little sleep in the mornings, but Yoash was different, he looked like a clockwork mouse which had been wound up and couldn't stop. He would get up in the middle of a sentence and say that he had to go here or there, volunteer unnecessarily to go to the corner store and buy us butter or salt. The Hamida file had been replaced by petitions and manifestos that he had to fetch and return and duplicate in the middle of the night. As if at every moment there was something else that had to be done. Even before, he used to jiggle his foot nervously when he sat, but now it seemed that the agitation had taken over his whole body.

"Yoash had a bad war," Alek said to me, "and Yoash, never mind how he fought and how much of a hero he was, is still exactly like a child. From this point of view, he's a typical Israeli." Infinitely patient, he did not argue with Yoash, but one morning when the two of us were alone in his apartment on Yarkon Street, he said a few things to me, and his mouth, I remember, twisted in a terrifying, or perhaps terrified, anger. "Oversight . . . I can't bear the sound of that word any more. They found themselves a word . . . oversight."

"But there was an oversight, in spades," I objected. Motherhood, the weeks that had gone by without him, the fact of his return, had given me a new self-confidence, and I no longer hesitated to confront him, I even enjoyed it.

"Of course there was an oversight, nobody's denying this, it's obvious. Daddy promised that there wouldn't be war. Daddy told me that war would only begin in the afternoon. . . . They said we'd be attacked at four o'clock. . . . How old are they, tell me, all these people who are writing and talking?"

"So are you telling me that Golda and Dayan shouldn't resign?"

"Of course they should resign, immediately. They're responsible for the 'oversight.' That's not what I'm talking about at all." In the background a festive concerto by Schubert was playing, one of the records he had left behind, and for a moment I felt the old inner surrender setting in. "Unbelievable that these people are Jews," he said. "As if they've learned nothing, and once again Daddy promised, and once again authorities said. It's not normal." And almost instantly a gentler tone returned. "This is Yoash's problem, too, that he has a daddy who makes promises, and that he is naive like most of the Israelis." I identified the area of warmth and approached it: "So what will become of Yoash?" "Yoash isn't right. Maybe he'll become right, but now it's not good. You are good for him, I am too, but a woman is something else. With you he's calm. With you and Hagar. And with me, however hard I try, it's not the same."

These were the most explicit words he said to me, I don't know how explicit he was to himself. In any case, Alek spoke in other ways, too, and in fact all three of us did. I remember that he was standing in the kitchen and peeling potatoes and chopping dill on a plate when Yoash started on one of his tirades. It went on and on, until Alek asked him to take over the peeling and chopping and handed him the knife, and when they changed places he hugged him hard and pulled me too into the embrace. His fingers rested on my cheek, and rubbing up against the smell of the dill I thought, as if in an attempt to reassure: It's all right, I know what you're doing now, what you're trying to do, all three of us know, it's all right.

During all that time, throughout that period, Alek kept close to my face: touching my cheeks, holding them when he kissed me, holding my head and turning it to him in bed. And with the same concentration he looked at Yoash, too, and Yoash looked at me. All three of us, I mean to say, looked at each other far, far too much.

I know what might be said about this. I know what Nira Woolf would say, the same thing that Talush and Tami and all my friends would have said: He found himself a convenient arrangement, that Alek, landing you with his crazy friend and taking the heat off himself. I know that this is the obvious thing to think, I understand it, but it isn't true, it isn't true at all, and anyone who thinks so doesn't understand the intensity. How the three of us were really and truly more important to each other than the whole world.

Even today nobody could persuade me that Alek wanted to pair me off with Yoash, although if anything like that had happened, it would have seemed perfectly natural to him, "the most natural and beautiful thing in the world," in his words. *Inter alia* because the whole notion of sexual fidelity was completely alien to him. I'm not talking about some sixties ideology of free love, Alek has no ideology, certainly not about sex. I mean that the very idea of sexual fidelity seems weird and incomprehensible to him. Not only in relation to himself, but also in relation to me and everybody else. I remember how one of those days I told him about my father and his affairs with the girls in the kibbutz high school—in general we talked a lot more then than before—and I brought this story out as if I was revealing some traumatic family secret. But in spite of my breaking voice Alek missed the traumatic point, and when I reached the bit about leaving the kibbutz—I said that I didn't know to what extent, if at all, our leaving was connected to those affairs—he shook his head dismissively and said: "What kind of people. . . ." And with regard to my father all he said was that he didn't understand men who were attracted to young girls.

"And what about me?" I asked.

"What—what about you?"

"Aren't I a young girl?" "No, you're not. Perhaps according to your age you are, but your age is accidental."

A million years later I remembered this conversation. I had come home from the television studios in Herzliya, where I had heard all kinds of sanctimonious statements about the Lewinsky affair, with the emphasis on the regrettable way in which Hillary had humiliated herself, and late at night, when I was about to remove the make-up and take a shower, Alek called from Moscow. "Lucky my mother goes to bed early, she wouldn't have enjoyed listening to a few of the things I had to say," I said. Alek was silent. He was silent long enough to take the wind of righteous public indignation out of my sails, long enough for shame to begin gnawing at me: who was I to talk, where did I get my nerve from?

Alek was silent and then he said with painful dryness: "I'm not sure I understand what you're talking about."

"What don't you understand?" I held my ground against him or against myself and wiped a layer of makeup off my face. "Don't you understand that the role of the forgiving wife is humiliating?" "I understand that too many people are interfering in something that is none of their business, and in my opinion it is this which is humiliating and hard to forgive. Apart from which, have you considered possibility that the iron lady doesn't care that much what her husband does? This lady rules the world, and also, they say, her husband, so maybe things of interest to other women don't interest her so much. . . . Once, aristocracy knew how to deal with such matters, and nobody made a scandal, but on the other hand, Clinton is certainly not an aristocrat, maybe this is what you are really saying." That is not what I was saying, of course, but neither did it occur to me to come up with a slogan like "the personal is political" or "the President's wife is not only a private person, she is a role model," although these are precisely the kind of things I had said an hour and a half earlier. As was happening more and more in the course of time, I didn't agree with him, I didn't agree with myself, and above all I felt flawed and distorted. As if I had been caught in some falseness or stupid boasting. Everything that formulated itself in my head at those moments had a phony ring. Was this my voice? Was it an alien voice? Which of all the voices I uttered was my own?

"So what's happening in Moscow?"

"Moscow? Like Moscow. A crazy province. It's not clear why God decided to put it at the forefront of the world. And Jerusalem?"

"The same thing exactly." I could hear his smile through the receiver. Sometimes he has the smile of a child throwing off his school satchel, and never mind what had happened a moment before, his smile spreads to my face, too.

YOASH

Alek loved Yoash, he loves him still, and passing between them was like crossing a densely packed energy field. A kind of palpable energy that reorganizes all the particles in your body. Sometimes I would fantasize that I was fucking both of them together. Sometimes when I went up to Alek, and Yoash was there, it seemed to me that it was beginning now, here in the kitchen. In all my fantasies Alek was the initiator, he made all the initial moves and as if offered me to Yoash. And in all of them he went on looking straight at me throughout the act, with the same look.

In May 1995, a million years later, I felt the same vibration of intensity passing between him and Borya. Boris Chazin, a doctor by profession, playwright, journalist, recovered drug addict, occasional trafficker in mementos from the Stalinist era, and election campaigner for Luzkov, is a friend of Alek's, meaning that Alek lived in his apartment for unlimited periods of time, and to this apartment in Yakimanka he brought me as well. Alek doesn't need to explain anything to Borya, and what seemed to me at first socially embarrassing—my appearance in Moscow as a mistress—seemed to him the most natural thing in the world. For a few days he removed himself from the apartment, went to sleep in another friend's apartment, and when he returned and joined us he treated me like a long lost sister. A sister and a visiting Czarina. Out of pride or shyness he refused to speak broken English to me, but somehow it didn't matter. On the sideboard stood pictures of the blonde Ute and little Mark and Daniel in ski suits, and this too did not get in the way of Borya's stammering welcome. Without asking or requesting, the two of them shared everything between them: money, connections, food and drink, Borya's bed while the owner went to sleep on the sofa, Alek's jacket which Borya wore, Borya's cashmere scarf which was wound around my throat, the slippers of who knows which lady placed on my feet with much ado after a little splinter penetrated my toe.

One evening our taxi lost its way in a maze of little streets until Borya located the iron door that hid a fashionable nightclub designed as a communal apartment. Alek in the taxi: "He says it's an amazing place and you have to see it . . . no, he's never been there either." Borya had gathered together a party of twelve people, and at three in the morning, after he had finished ordering us the entire menu—"Pablik Morozov pancakes," "Komsomol girl's ribs," "Pilot amputee," jokes behind which were dishes unlike anything ever tasted in a communal apartment—at three o'clock in the morning we were still reveling there among the blinking lights, to the strains of Eurovision pop songs in Russian.

Alek doesn't dance and Borya didn't dance then, they remained seated at the table, and in the vase standing between them a spray of white lilac changed color with the changes in the lighting. Their faces changed color from white to spectral green to blue, and drunk as I was, even from behind the shoulder of someone introduced to me as a Tartar poet, I didn't lose eye contact with them. They raised white-green-blue glasses in my honor, and in theirs I allowed the Tartar poet to press his pelvis against me.

Borya, Alek explained to me, had sold some French collector a genuine oil portrait of Lenin, Trotsky, and Stalin, and the money he received for the group portrait—how it survived the devil only knows—he quickly showered on all of us, as if it were burning a hole in his pocket. In the shopping arcade next to the apartment, he bought me a fur hat of the expensive kind, a heavy little iron horse which is now standing on my desk, a Bukharan dressing gown, "our ice cream that she has to taste," and a little bunch of white flowers with a sweet, subtle smell. At other times the money was Alek's, or there was no money at all, but nobody ever kept accounts.

In my last three days there the weather suddenly turned hot and stifling, at night too, the pavements were covered with a seasonal shedding of blossoms, and the dusty down gave Borya an allergy attack. With a checkered handkerchief pressed to his fleshy nose he led us to Red Square, to the Tretyakov Gallery and to the graves of saints and sinners in Novodevichy, and during this whole tour of tourist "musts" which Alek had refused to take me on previously, he showered me with jokes about the "New Russia" and funny-horrific stories that "nobody could imagine" and whose truth Alek was called upon again and again to verify.

On the endless escalator going down to the Metro platform it was Borya who held my elbow, and along the avenues the three of us walked arm in arm, with me in the middle. Nikolskaya Street, Kirovskaya Street, Tverskaya Street, Komsomolsky Prospect. In exactly the same way I had walked with Alek and Yoash on one distant Friday night in Nachlaot, and Borya was as tall as Yoash, his gait as ungainly, and his gestures as broad.

In the greasy little kitchen in Yakimanka, rubbing up against each other in the passage to the stove, I furrowed into the heat produced by the contact between them, and at night when Alek lifted me above him with a strong movement, I thought: Now he's going to tell me to go to Borya.

If he'd told me to, I would have gone. And if I had been asked to, I would have remained there with both of them. Hello, Hagar, I just wanted to tell you that I'm not coming home. The time has come for your mother to come out of the closet, and I'm sure that you will accept it in the spirit of American tolerance and understanding. I have a lover in Moscow. I have two lovers in Moscow. One of them is your father, my husband in law and Ute's husband in practice. The second is an occasional drunk and an ex-junkie, and your mother, my dear, is crazy about both of them.

I really did fantasize about staying there with them. With time I would no doubt have found some cleaning agent capable of removing the filth of generations from the lavatory and the bathtub.

The perversity of course lies in the fact that all this time I knew that I wasn't really attracted to Borya; not to Borya himself and not to his shadowed life and his wet face and the hair plastered to his forehead, but Borya just like Yoash was a part of Alek, and therefore to this day I fuck both of them in my imagination.

I KNOW WHAT

I know what the above description seems to imply. I can understand how people might come to conclusions like: So, your Alek is actually a homosexual, he only really loves men. I understand where this apparently logical idea comes from, but it is completely mistaken. Alek is neither a practicing homosexual nor a latent one. There's nothing latent about Alek's sexuality. Nothing repressed or dormant. I know. And precisely for this reason I sometimes dream of turning into a man, so that I could be like Borya and Yoash for him, so I could be with him like Borya and Yoash.

Nothing happened with Borya, nothing could possibly have happened with Borya, but I did go to bed with Yoash in the end. Not on the night that he drove Alek to the airport and Alek sent him back with a bunch of flowers for me, but a few nights later. We did it, and it was definitely nothing to write home about. At first he couldn't even get it up. We were already friends by then, perhaps that worked against us, too, but the main problem was that Yoash was no more attracted to me than I was to him, he simply saw me as part and parcel of Alek.

Late at night, after I got up to feed Hagar and came back to bed, he succeeded in completing while half-asleep what he hadn't managed to do before, but the act did not improve the situation. Alek was no longer there to turn us both on, and for all our strenuous efforts to fan the feeble flame, the fetish lost its spell. For the sake of his honor, out of consideration for the battle-weary state of the warrior, for Alek's sake, or for God knows what reason, we didn't stop, I didn't stop him in the middle, but even as Yoash pushed and pushed himself into me, I felt the old void opening up inside me. And it was only then that I really understood that Alek was gone.

We remained friends, Yoash and I are friends to this day, and as such we can sometimes relate explicitly to the third person who isn't there. "You know, Alek phoned last week, it sounds as if he's living in Moscow semi-permanently. He's renting an apartment there." "What do you say? What, he's not going back to Paris?" "He went back in the summer and stayed with his family for a few months, but for Ute and the boys moving to Russia is out of the question, and it seems to me that Alek isn't too enthusiastic about having them with him all the time either. Tell me, do you have any idea if that maniac ever contacts Hagar? In your next book you should make the murderer someone who doesn't relate to his children. Mark and Daniel don't get too much attention from him either."

Yoash was good to Hagar, and the truth is that she was good for him, too, and it was only when she grew up that the ties between the three of us loosened a little. In many senses he was the man in her life, even more than my father. And even during the two years when he tried to escape from everything and wandered around Australia as a backpacker before his time, he took care to send postcards addressed to the infant who had only recently learned to stand without support. To this day they are preserved in one of her boxes in the storage space under the roof.

NIRA WOOLF

Blood Money came out in 1982, was taken up by the new local papers, and won both exaggerated praise and exaggerated condemnation, which took me equally by surprise. It would never have occurred to me that my manuscript, rejected by two publishers, was "welcome evidence of the normalization of Hebrew literature," it had never occurred to me that I had "appropriated the Palestinian narrative and exploited Palestinian suffering for profit," and I hadn't even thought of Nira Woolf as a "feminist heroine." At that period I had hardly even started to identify myself as a feminist.

Woolf's feminism gave rise to strange reactions, which I might go into more thoroughly one day. The reactions to the first books praised the perfection of the heroine as a fictional creation: her independence, her brilliant mind, her five martial arts and her liberated female sexuality—until, more or less since *The Stabbing*, both of us began to get it in the neck. "Nira Woolf with her big breasts and her convict's cropped blonde hair is actually a man's wet dream," "the blonde Nira Woolf is James Bond disguised as a female lawyer," "Nira Woolf is a product of the male power ethos."

Comments like these, mainly from women critics, but also from men, explaining that my feminism wasn't "true feminism," one of them even stating explicitly that it was "false" because Nira Woolf/Noa Weber "does not offer us an alternative ethos and in fact undermines its development."

But this isn't what I want to talk about now, I want to talk about Nira's sexuality.

I began to conceive Nira in my second or third year in the law faculty, between "Changes in English Law" and "Corroboration in the Rules of Evidence," while the lecturers droned on and on about what we already had written down on our cheat-sheet anyway. At the beginning of our lives together I did not yet make Nira a protagonist in any plot, or even think of doing so, I only played with her in my head as a kind of private amusement, enjoying myself by attributing various virtues to her as the spirit took me. When Hagar complains that Nira Woolf looks more like a Swedish sexpot than any woman lawyer she's ever come across, it doesn't help me to say that my books are entertainments and that the whole thing started as an amusement. But this is exactly how it happened. I looked around me, and as I followed the legal entanglements of Foxy-Dopey-Smarty and the depressing characters trying to resolve them, I invented someone who was the complete opposite. Someone who without any scruples or inhibitions planted a well-aimed kick on Foxy's behind. And who had great legs as well.

My Swedish sexpot, as Hagar calls her—"But why does she have to have such big breasts?" "What do you want me to do? Send her to a plastic surgeon to have them made smaller?"—my Swedish sexpot has a happy, adventurous sex life, and even though I have never actually described a fuck in any of my books, what happens between one chapter and the next is quite clear to everyone.

"The best sex is on the second date," my Diva says to the gloomy pathologist, "it's a law of nature," but in the end she agrees to a third date, as well. Part of the sensation caused by the first books was due to Nira's sexuality. In American literature women were already fucking for pleasure then, consciously or unconsciously, but in Hebrew, a woman who fucked for the sake of it was somehow seen as an innovation.

Never mind all that now, because the point I want to make here is only that I bestowed all this sexual freedom on Nira at a time when I wasn't having any sex at all. A contemporary woman is not supposed to admit to such a disgrace. A contemporary woman is supposed to take care of her sex life in the same way that she takes care of brushing her teeth. And if you don't go to bed with anyone for four years, and you don't even feel the urge to do so, it means that something about you is simply not normal and you should see a psychologist. In the present state of the market, admitting to the lack of a sex life lowers the value of your shares and leads to a heavy loss of prestige. Even between girlfriends who tell each other everything.

Four years of abstinence I had after the miserable fuck with Yoash—that is, if we don't count masturbation as actual sex—and the reason for my abstinence was absolutely clear to me: not the fact that I was tired most of the time, not the technical difficulty posed by being a single mother—even though a few nonentities in the law faculty lived with their parents, some of them at least had apartments or pigsties of their own—and certainly not a "fear of relationships" or any other psychobabble of that kind. I abstained because from my point of view there was only one right body and one right touch and smell: one unique model that had been imprinted in all my cells, engraved in my bones, which made every other contact wrong. On several occasions I had in fact tried to go the way of all flesh, for the sake of my self-respect and release, petting that had failed to ignite any joy in me and had succeeded only in making me feel very remote from my body. As if I were perching on the branch of a nearby pine tree, on the roof of the car outside, on the lampshade, on one of the fat clouds in the sky, and observing myself from there as in a movie. The hands weren't right.

The height wasn't right. And the contour of the hips. The mouth tastes of wine, sweet and revolting. Bob Marley doesn't do it for me. And the wrong things are said in the wrong tone. I, unlike my Nira, escaped not after the second fuck, but after the first one.

Even without these attempts my body seemed rubbed out. And not only my body, but also my soul. As if I had retired from myself and I was now operating mainly on automatic pilot, obeying the instructions of some higher authority. Now go to the photocopying machine. Now you have an hour in the library, concentrate. Now go to the bus stop to pick up Hagar on time, and don't forget to pop in at the grocery store on the way home.

My memory is a trash can, I stuff it with whatever rubbish I like, and the studies which did not demand much thought came easily to me—when I was told to read verdicts I read them, I didn't look for someone with a cheat-sheet, and when I was told to regurgitate the material, I did so. In the human landscape of the law faculty I was an outsider and I felt like an outsider. Female, younger than everyone else, the mother of an infant who woke up at night with an earache, and who had to be provided with dried fruits to celebrate Arbor Day in nursery school. Somehow I managed, and in fact, not "somehow" but mainly thanks to the help of my mother and to Miriam who came to the rescue, but now, from a distance, those years are covered in fog with scarcely a landmark, as if I had walked through them in my sleep.

Two or three times a day, I remember, I would close my eyes, and as a reward for the functioning of the previous hours, I would conjure up Alek. In the library. For a moment or two while Hagar was playing quietly. And it was as if I were retrieving my soul. Even when I was overwhelmed with sorrow.

229 | The Confessions of Noa Weber

TAMI

Tami called in the morning, waking me up after I had gone back to bed. She was on vacation in Eilat with her husband and her three young ogres, the four lunatics had gone to the beach again, her back was burned to a frazzle, the ogres had insisted on going to flay themselves some more, thank God, she herself had stayed behind in the air-conditioned room, and she was in dire need of hearing a human voice actually talking instead of grunting at her in bass. "Are you all right? Were you sleeping?"

"No, of course not. What's the time?"

"Eleven o'clock. Why do you sound so strange?"

"That's what a human voice sounds like, you must have forgotten. That's what happens to a girl who spends too much time with boys."

"Go on, laugh at me. Not everyone gives birth when they're minors, and not everyone has daughters. I saw you in the paper. It was a good interview. How's the book doing? Is it selling?"

"I very much hope so."

"What do you mean 'you hope'? It's a great book. Write us another one. Exactly like this one. I finally realized what you got out of all those trips to Moscow. Dalya and I were already sure that you had a lover in the Jewish Agency, but after this book we decided that it's a lover in the Russian Mafia."

"Benya Krik."

"What?"

"Benya Krik, that's the name of my lover. Benya is a king. The king of the Mafia."

"Benya Krik is the name of someone from the Jewish Agency and not the Mafia. Benya Krik isn't the name of someone you fuck. Benya is the name of an old man from Bat Shlomo. . . . You don't know how I'm dying to get back to work. You don't know how lucky you are that you don't have to worry about holidays any more."

"You just like complaining. Kisses to the boys, or regards."

"Kisses, I'll pass them on. And you're right, on the whole it's fun here. They're coming to clean the room in a minute, you won't believe what a mess the boys have left, at least I don't have to clean it up."

"Look after yourself, have a good rest."

"You too, and write me another book, you hear? So the girls will have something to read when the next holiday comes round."

HAGAR AND MY MOTHER, TAMI, AND MIRIAM

Children are stuck with their parents and as a last resort they don't have any alternative to bonding with them, but Tami and Miriam and my mother—I shall never understand all the goodness they showered on me when I had so little to return. My mother set Hagar in the center of her world, and she remains just about there to this day. And in spite of all her efforts to treat us all equally, she doesn't relate to Talush's twins in the same way, with the same pride and surprising tenderness.

It was only at the beginning of the nineties, when I met a few Russian families, that I realized what a joke Alek had played on us, that indirectly and without any intention on his part he had maneuvered the Weber family into a Russian pattern: the wife works, the wife studies, the wife has important business, and the grandmother suspends her no less important affairs, and takes care of the grandchild. My mother continued working at her clinic, but two or three times a week she finished early to pick Hagar up from her daycare, and in later years from school. My old room at home was turned into a second room for my daughter, with toys "for there" and books "for there," and to this day it remains hers and she keeps things there.

Very late in the day, only after Hagar had left home, it occurred to me that a situation of double motherhood invites all kinds of conflicts, is a recipe for the development of tensions, but the truth of the matter is that I don't remember any tension between my mother and myself. Perhaps I was too drained to be angry or jealous, and whatever she told me about my daughter I accepted. For the most part.

Self-condemnation can turn very easily into a kind of boasting in reverse—look at me, look at me, see what an incredible monster I was—and therefore I have to say that there wasn't a drop of anything monstrous in my treatment of Hagar. I dressed her, I put her shoes on, I listened, I reacted, I thought about . . . I remembered to. . . . When she was small I braided her hair, and when she was in high school I picked her up at the youth movement center when she came back from hikes.

With time I also began to breathe in the smell of her hair, to delight in the warmth of her little body in her pajamas and to admire her sayings. She was a sturdy child, with penetrating logic, and when she learned to talk—she began to speak fluently at an early age—I enjoyed talking to her. You could say that I enjoy it to this day.

One winter Saturday, when Hagar was nearly two, I took her in her stroller to the Old City, and went into the church of the Holy Sepulchre with her. In the hall where the picture of my Madonna hung in one of the niches, a large group of tourists was gathered, and a guide was standing with his back to the picture and speaking to them in German. I let Hagar, who had just woken up, out of her stroller, and despite the Germans I approached the painting, wanting to confirm or refute something, hoping perhaps that something would return to encompass both of us together, but nothing of the sort occurred. Hagar turned her head right and left on my shoulder, the tourists' cameras flashed, and the same place was completely different. Whatever it was that I wanted to check, I wasn't disappointed. There was an athletic, middle aged German woman standing next to me, with pale freckles on her arms and a red-checkered *keffiyeh* covering her shoulders. Hagar weighed heavily on my arms, and when I tried to put her down she arched her back and refused to stand. The guide in his silly hat kept repeating the same word, the only one I recognized. Jews, he said. Juden. He had a stick in his hand, it too was crowned with a hat.

It was a long way back, almost all uphill, I had to get Hagar something to drink, and whatever I had been looking for, if at all, had nothing to do with her and would never have anything to do with her. Because for some reason which I would never be able to explain, Hagar did not belong to Alek, and from the time she was a few days old it was already clear that she didn't belong to him. So obvious was this to me that the relation between them sometimes struck me with a shock of surprise.

Tami: When will you be done in the library? Should we meet in the cafeteria? No, I have a better idea. I'll be in the restaurant this afternoon. Are you picking Hagar up today? Bring her here. Does she still eat soup? We'll find her something without carrots. You look as if you could do with a good bowl of soup, too.

Miriam: The skinny man with the sideburns was here again this afternoon, asking about you, if I know when you'll be back. Now listen to me and believe me when I tell you: study, work, study, work, day in day out, it's no good. A person isn't a machine, and a woman especially has to find the middle way.

Noa: It's not my fault that I haven't got any time.

Miriam: I'll tell you what, you leave the little one with me, all night long, and go to a movie. And don't hurry back. A gift from me.

Noa: With you it's work, work all day long, and you don't go to the movies either. . . . How's Avi? Is he still with that nice girl I met?

Miriam: Don't talk to me about her, I don't want to say anything bad. She's not nice at all, she just wants to butter me up.

Noa: The man with the sideburns isn't nice at all either.

It took a few weeks, but during Hanukah, when Miriam's nursery school was closed and Hagar's daycare was open, we went to the cinema together to see a matinee of *The Godfather*. Both of us groaned in chorus at the sight of the severed horse's head, we both relaxed together in our chairs when Michael finally put two bullets into the police captain—something, not in his appearance but in his body tension, reminded me of Alek—and only when we walked down the street and peeled the paper off the chocolate bar we had forgotten to eat inside the movie theater did I realize that Miriam Marie had understood the movie completely differently from me. She said that it was very sad how Michael had been dragged into a life of crime just because of his family, and how come his mother as the mother of the family didn't have a word to say about the ways of her menfolk?

"Didn't you enjoy watching Sonny beating up Connie's husband?" I knew she'd enjoyed it, I was sitting next to her, but I wanted to hear her say it. "I enjoyed it, of course I enjoyed it," she admitted. "And don't you think it was just?" "Just?" she exclaimed with majestic disdain, "Just? Believe me, if there was any justice in this world, half the men would be in wheelchairs. Including my engineer and including that one of yours, who doesn't pay a penny for his daughter. But what good will it do us to say so?" Suddenly, I remember, I had a tremendous urge to hug her, but hugs weren't part of our repertoire, so I just broke a piece off the bar of chocolate she was holding in her hand and put it in my mouth.

Miriam would read all my books, nobly pass over the passages that embarrassed her, and generously forgive my and Nira's lust for revenge and justice. My books would stand in a neat row behind the glass doors of her display cabinet, and she would enjoy showing people the dedications, but nevertheless I was destined to hear the most accurate criticism of them from her. She would ask about the sales, I would mention that most of the people who bought the books were women, and then she would say consolingly: "It's the same thing in the nursery school when we tell the children fairy stories. You can see how it grabs the girls, and the boys start squirming and making noise right from the beginning. Boys are more into reality. And your books are more naive, like fairy tales."

STUDYING LAW

Alek didn't pay child support, and even if he'd had the wherewithal he wouldn't have paid it, he would simply have given us as much as we needed without keeping accounts. I know it. But the way things turned out, when I needed money Alek didn't have any either, and when Alek's situation improved I was no longer in need.

Before he returned to Paris I said something about thinking of studying law, and that without help from my parents there was no way I would be able to do it, not in the next few years at least. I didn't mean to hint, but for a moment an expression appeared on his face which somehow reminded me of the way he looked standing in the door on the night my labor started. I understood that he was condemning himself for not being able to help and I was sorry for the misunderstanding.

He helped me in another way, however, by his reaction to the story about Aunt Greta. Aunt Greta had announced that she was coming on a visit to Israel to check out her donation to Hadassah, and up to Alek's departure it was not yet clear whether she intended summoning all or only some of us to her presence, and the discussions and conjectures about this question, and about Aunt Greta in general, injected a little of the old vitality into the family. The fact of the donation to Hadassah was unprecedented in itself, because up to now she had totally rejected the state that had robbed her of my father. Not that she denied its right to exist, she simply ignored its existence completely. Perhaps the war had provided her with the pretext for a reconciliation she had desired even beforehand, there was no way of knowing.

To my surprise Alek showed a keen interest in this story, he liked family mythologies, and so it happened that I told him the whole legend in detail.

Aunt Greta was my grandmother's sister, and when my father was a small child they packed him up and sent him by ship from Hamburg to New York to stay with her. His mother, Grandma Hannah, had died, apparently of a complication of influenza, and in a certain, terrible sense it could be said that this was his good fortune, since but for Grandma Hannah's fatal attack of influenza, it is doubtful if my father would have survived and I would have been born.

Aunt Greta's husband, Uncle Haim who was a socialist, "went and killed himself," in his wife's words, as a volunteer in the Spanish Civil War, and he wasn't even killed by a bullet, but died there two weeks after his arrival from dysentery. Uncle Haim's death, and perhaps also the manner of his death, gave rise in Aunt Greta to an impatient skepticism with regard to volunteers in general, as well as the general foolishness of the world, and armed with this angry skepticism she sold her late husband's laundry and devoted herself to bringing up her nephew and to the real estate business. Buying apartments, dividing them up, and renting them out. In 1948, when my father announced that he was going to fight the Arabs, Aunt Greta reacted with disapproval, to put it mildly, and when he met my mother and informed her that he was getting married and remaining in Israel—perhaps one day she too might consider joining him there?—she broke off relations with him. My father went on writing to her from time to time anyway: greeting cards for the New Year, announcements of the birth of his daughters, photographs, drawings made by Talush and me, and various items of family news, to which she eventually began to reply, albeit coldly. Towards my mother, on the other hand, there was no attempt at politeness, only obdurate, unrelenting hostility, and the letters my mother wrote in her broken English were returned unopened. The question now on the family agenda was whether Aunt Greta was about to effect a reconciliation only with the state or also with the wife, or whether perhaps she had no intention of reconciling with anybody, and the visit and the donation to Hadassah were intended only to provoke us.

Alek was evidently fascinated by this story. He said that my Aunt Greta sounded like "someone worth knowing, not at all like an American person," and added that "every family needs one rich Aunt Greta to make life interesting." His lighthearted, literary attitude to something I saw as a complicated family dynamic inspired me after he left to write to Aunt Greta and tell her about myself, about baby Hagar, about my keen desire to study law and about my parents' opposition to this project. Shamelessly, I even hinted that the main obstacle was my mother. This wasn't true, and it wasn't fair, but I simply couldn't see myself working at Soupçon until I managed to save up enough money to finance my studies, and I couldn't think of any other way out. When I wrote my manipulative letter to Aunt Greta, I imagined myself reading it aloud to Alek. I knew that he would find it entertaining and appropriate to the story and character of the rich, tight-fisted aunt, who every family should possess.

When Aunt Greta landed at the Hilton and summoned me into her presence, the plot advanced as expected, but in a style which was, from my point of view at least, surprising. Aunt Greta did not display even polite affection towards the baby I brought with me, then eleven months old, togged out in a party dress, with a single tooth showing cutely when she smiled.

After ordering tea and cake for both of us, without first asking what I wanted, and even before the waiter wheeled the room service trolley out of the room, she opened a thorough, no-nonsense investigation, without any sentiment. Only when in reply to her question I said in careful English that I was "not in contact with Hagar's father," she sighed from the depths of her tough old breast, turned her faded blue gaze towards the view of Nachlaot, and remarked that she didn't know what was happening to men nowadays. "Haim," she said, "had his dreams, but at least he was a man. A real Jewish man. Not like the floor rags you bump into everywhere today who don't know the meaning of responsibility. I can tell you, child, that I personally don't rent apartments to hippies or psychologists." "Hippies I understand, but why psychologists?" I asked, feeling for some reason that I could come to like her. "If I rent to psychologists, men will come to see them," whispered my Aunt Greta in a mysterious husky voice. "Men will come, and you know what will happen then? Those men will begin to whine and wail, and that I cannot tolerate and I will not permit, not in any apartment of mine." She too was quite an accomplished actress. A woman who lives alone for many years, I think, is compelled to adopt a few eccentric behaviors, even if only in self-defense.

When to my surprise Aunt Greta put out her cigarette on the Black Forest cake—perhaps as an expression of contempt for the margarine—all that remained was to sum up, which she did precisely and succinctly. "It's obvious that law isn't for you, and that you, Noa Weber, will never be a lawyer, but as far as it depends on me I will try to help you. And don't ask me why." And so she did. Aunt Greta would pay my tuition, my parents would help with other expenses, and

I would find pupils for private coaching, because a combination of a day job and studying law—forget about it, you can understand that it just isn't realistic.

After she returned to New York I never saw her again, "she flew away on her broomstick and disappeared," as Alek said. Aunt Greta died at Mount Sinai Hospital in the autumn of 1983, on the day that Menachem Begin resigned, after Alek had already left Israel with his family. In her will she left Talush a few pieces of old jewelry, and to me she left her Encyclopedia Britannica together with its bookcase. The rest of her property went to Jewish charities. But even when I stood in line to pay the custom duties on this superfluous encyclopedic legacy, and when I went crazy trying to arrange for its transportation to Jerusalem, I remembered her with affection.

IF I REPEATED

If I repeated this little story about Aunt Greta it's only because it is so pervaded by Alek's spirit that it seems he could have composed it himself. He rejoiced in the concluding scene with the Britannica, and laughed like a child when I described my great-aunt's rental boycott policy: "All according to the rules of the genre." As far as the psychologists were concerned, and their male clients in particular, he and Aunt Greta were of one mind.

Hagar, for example, tells this story quite differently. In the eyes of my daughter, Aunt Greta is "an independent woman who existed before her time and paid the price for it" (how does Hagar know?), and was "one of the many tragedies of Zionism that nobody talks about." One of the first things that my Hagar did in New York was to locate Aunt Greta's grave and recite the mourner's prayer over it (I wonder how the old lady would have reacted to a woman reciting Kaddish, but what does that matter?). In her lectures my daughter sometimes quotes Aunt Greta's story as an example and symbol of the Jewish fate, which is apparently the kind of story that Americans like. I, like Alek, prefer a different story.

IN THE LAA FORUM

Tonight I entered the LAA forum again to check and see if there was anything new. Sandy, Sally, Sara, and Susan were all singing the same old tune. But for the benefit of the girls someone had gone to the trouble of sending in a whole lecture on biochemistry, "to help us become better acquainted with our bodies and understand what's happening to us."

So, everything had begun on the second of July 1972, with a little molecule called phenylethylamine. My brain, which was and is "about the size of a grapefruit," had become addicted to this cunning molecule which stimulates the nerves, and in my case, as with other addicts, common dependency had turned into an addiction because of a "structural deficiency" in the "monoamine oxidase inhibitors."

I understand, girls. Now I understand everything. And nevertheless I didn't understand. Was Alek's melting smile engraved on my phenylethylamine molecules? Had it been engraved there in advance? From the moment I was conceived in my mother's womb? And the touch of his hand, and the smell of his neck, and the smell of his apartment and the smell of snowbound Moscow—are they imprinted on my monoamine oxidase?

If we're talking about a typhoon raging in my neurons, why doesn't the storm subside when the storm god disappears for years at a time? And how can you explain the fact that only one person, present or absent, sets this storm in motion, if indeed it is not the person whom my body craves, but only the storm?

On the second of July I drank of the love potion of Tristan and Isolde. On the second of July I drank bitter coffee mixed with phenylethylamine.

But how does that explain me, me and Alek? And the touch of heaven on the skin, how does it explain that?

Among all the babble of Sandy and Sally and Sara and Susan, among all the drivel of the dope from Detroit, there's one thing I can't find, pardon me, there's one thing missing, and that is the soul. Because in my case, my stupid sisters, it is the soul that begs for a fuck, yes, precisely the soul. Believe it or not, this is my fantastic perversion: it's not my body I want him to fuck but my brain. And it's not the "reptilian brain" that I howl to the wicked moon for him to fuck, but the cortex of the brain.

"Most mammals pet while courting," they write there. But this primate would forgo the petting to her last day, if in exchange she could receive her one and only into her soul.

"To her master, or rather her father; to her husband, or rather her brother; his handmaid, or rather his daughter; his wife, or rather his sister. . . ." In these words Eloise's penylethylamine addresses the castrated Abelard; in words like these the sick molecules inside me cry out when the soul, the soul, the screwed up soul and nothing else addresses the absent one. For then the body and even the emotions are only an instrument and a means to reach what lies beyond them.

I'm sick, forgive me, sick and tired to death. Even my only one would laugh at me.

It was last February, in the apartment in Ordenka, we didn't go out anywhere, we stayed in bed, Alek read a book full of old marks and quoted: "The drive to love is the drive to death," and shrugged his white shoulders and added: "Another one of Soloviev's exaggerations. You asked about him once. He talks about sex if it isn't clear. Anyone who has sex like animal will die like animal, also. I completely forgot those formulations of his." "What other exaggerations was he guilty of?" "You want me to translate for you? I won't translate . . . he speaks about striving for perfection . . . love is from God, is perfection and most close to God, but in order for love to unite with God . . . for that, the whole world order must first be changed . . . the way we understand things." He sat leaning against the headboard, leafing through the pages, and as he spoke his voice and face took on the weary, familiar expression of friendly, consoling self-irony. "Understand . . . I don't know if you can understand, or what it could mean to you . . . we're in year ten, and this man in year ten is saying that in his opinion we should construct the world, our biography, and above all, love."

"Which has no connection to sex."

"Not necessarily. He isn't against sex. But this is already related to the subject of androgyny, the missing half of every one, and also to the question of how ready is the soul. How high soul can lift . . . no, not lift, raise. . . ."

"Rise?"

He smiled. "Something like that."

I took the book out of his hands. "In that case," I said, "come and raise me up." And he raised me, and how, or lifted me, whatever you like, and I definitely rose. Even my only one would laugh at me, I said, but Alek saw and knew and he never laughed.

ALEK RETURNED

Alek returned to Israel in the spring of '77, this time as a journalist, an official observer from the side. He had a job with Radio Luxembourg, he freelanced for a number of European newspapers, and nevertheless you couldn't say that he was "sent" here, because Alek wasn't the kind of person that anybody "sent." In recent years the interest he had once had in Israel is dwindling, and he no longer asks questions and gets angry as he did then, but when he left after the war in '73, it was clear that there was something unresolved in his relations with the country that wouldn't let him be, and it had to be this which prompted his return.

Alek came with Ute. First they lived on Palmach Street, a fifteen-minute walk from me, and then they moved to Musrara, about the same distance in the opposite direction, and I sensed nothing and guessed nothing. It took him nearly two months to get in touch.

When he returned I was already in my third year of legal studies, and ostensibly three and a half years more mature. I am referring to all the behaviors I had acquired by observing the women in the law faculty and imitating them. There weren't many women in the faculty then, and with the exception of one girl in the ROTC, they were all older than I was, and most of them were good girls with fathers who were lawyers or judges. I imitated the way they dressed—clothes from the Old City were out—I imitated the way they spoke in seminars—intelligent and restrained—I imitated their expressions—intelligent and attentive—and I imitated their attitude to politics—that it was for students from other departments, who had time. Once in a while I would run into someone from my other, former life—Dalit from La Mama lived nearby and dropped in to see the baby once, the slimy Hyman would pop up occasionally on Ben Yehuda Street—but except for Yoash, they all seemed as if they belonged to another incarnation. Emotionally anesthetized, with a new, careful persona, I advanced steadily, on automatic pilot, towards goals I did not really desire. I had longings, of course. But the longing was no longer a threat. It could be lived with, the way one lives with a chronic disease; morning and evening you tether it under your ribs, and morning and evening you make all kinds of deals with it. Leave me alone now, and I'll devote myself to you later. Let me be now, and I'll let you loose later. If you just leave off now, I'll unleash you when night comes. I had no doubt that Alek would return, so that in the end it was simply a question of how to pass the time, and I, with my Tatyana fantasy—"not the plain, timorous, lovelorn maiden whom he'd known. . . ."—and my kibbutz education, I simply tried to do it with dignity.

Longings. What is there to say about longings that hasn't already been said? Perhaps only that in spite of all the negotiations and the postponement deals that I made with them, I wouldn't really give them up. The void was Alek's void, the absence wore Alek's form, and therefore the absence was also a kind of presence with which I made love. The touch of his absence. Its clutch.

After he left—I know how ridiculous it sounds—I developed a foolish sensitivity to airplanes, I mean that I couldn't resist looking up to follow their flight. "Airplane, Hagar . . . over there, above the tower, look, an airplane. . . ." But even when she wasn't there I looked.

"And now the international weather forecast. Rome fifteen degrees, fine to partly cloudy. Paris nine degrees, fine and cold. . . ." Perhaps the Boeing was coming from that fine cold weather. In our part of the world it was the eve of the festival of first fruits, my mother had taken Hagar to the kibbutz, and I had forgotten to close the window, and by the time I came home the table would be covered with desert dust.

In the year 1977 I already had a telephone, a gift ordered by my parents which arrived in time for my twenty-second birthday and Hagar's third. As far as I can remember people didn't phone each other much in those days, and the conversations were shorter and more functional than they are today. And perhaps precisely for this reason I was already in the mindset of someone waiting for the phone to ring. For the phone to ring rather than for a knock at the door. From the mailbox, on the other hand, I didn't expect anything; Alek who was fluent in Russian and French, and who read German and English, often said that he was unable to read and write in our language, that it was too frustrating, and it was clear that he wouldn't try.

He said "Shalom" without identifying himself, and I said, "Where are you?" "Where am I? In phone booth on Zion Square, that's where I'm standing now." "What are you doing in Zion Square?" I asked, infected by the smile on the other end of the line. From the tone of his voice it seemed as if we had met yesterday and the day before, as if we hadn't stopped talking, and this was exactly the confirmation I needed.

"It's long story, I'll tell you everything. . . . How are you?" His voice sounded very far away, intermittently drowned out in the noise from the street. "Where have you been?" "Where have I . . . nowhere. I'm here." "It sounds as if you were running from somewhere." "Most of the time I'm running." "What did you say? It's hard to hear. . . ." "I asked how you are." "Fine. . . . All kinds of changes happened . . . plans . . . I have a woman I live with now . . . she's here . . . we rented an apartment in Musrara, I signed a lease this week. When can I see you? It's too long since I saw you." "I'm studying law," I said suddenly as if without any connection into the wind, for that was how it seemed to me, as if the two of us were snatching sentences from a roaring wind. "I'm studying law. In the end I succeeded in getting in. I have one more year to graduate." "Law is good. It's good . . . be so kind to tell me, please, when can we meet?"

All the time I knew that he had other women in Paris, women in long black raincoats, women in aromatic cafes smoking Gauloise, women who lived in attics with pigeons flying from the pediment when Alex went to shut the window. I didn't spend much time thinking about it, I simply took it for granted, and only when I averted my face from another man's kiss the images would sometimes arise. But somehow, in my foolishness, "I have a woman I live with" had never entered my head.

I told him that I would meet him at lunchtime the next day at Fink's Bar. "You want Fink's? Okay, if you want Fink's, let it be Fink's. I'll wait for you there."

Outside it was a heavy summer dusk, I was wearing a long tee shirt with only panties underneath it . . . one remembers such trifles. And when I replaced the receiver I felt a sudden panic at the silence in Hagar's room, and I rushed to her. As if a catastrophe could have happened during this conversation, due to this conversation. . . . But my daughter was sitting on the rug surrounded by her stuffed animals and feeding them with a teaspoon.

In the four years that they lived in Israel I saw Ute twice. The first time, it was the first summer, they were standing together at the entrance to the Jerusalem Theatre, waiting in line for a Friday matinee film show. And a year or two later, also in summer, she came up Ben Yehuda Street and walked past me in the opposite direction. I was with Hagar.

A big, blonde woman, a little taller than I was, yellow hair piled on top of a head held high. A graceful walk, a long neck gracefully bearing her head over her Viking breast. I knew that she would be beautiful, it was inconceivable that she wouldn't be, and in some perverse way I took comfort both in her beauty and in her complete difference from me. She was one thing, I was another. She was one story, I was a completely different one. However strange it may sound, I hardly ever thought about her, and I still don't. A German by birth. Worked here in the Rockefeller Museum. Had two sons with him. Her father, I know, owned a chain of retirement homes in Switzerland, and at a certain stage he offered Alek a job working for him. "Of all things in world, can you imagine me calling some laundry to find out when they're returning those Nazis' sheets?"

Even when Alek began meeting Hagar, and avoided taking her to their home, I wasn't angry, even though I guessed that it wasn't his idea not to take her there. I was one thing, and Ute was a different world, and just as I had no wish to know about her, it seemed natural to me that she wouldn't want to be reminded of my existence.

All these thoughts, all this blocking out, actually came later, in the course of many days to come. But then he said, "I have a woman I live with now," and so I said "At Fink's. . . ."

I detest all those twitters of "he said," "and so then I said," all those little female pecks in words. I detest them when it comes to me and Alek, and in spite of that and just because of that I'll repeat it again. . . .

He said "I have a woman I live with now," to which I replied, "At Fink's," but the words had no connection to the transparent radiance flooding me under my skin. Or the tender liveliness of his voice.

Two o'clock in the afternoon at Fink's was a new despair; not because the "real" Alek paled in comparison to the imaginary one. Not at all. In days to come I developed an intimate acquaintance with the particular despair of meeting the one who is present in your thoughts all the time. The impossibility of collecting all the times into this one time, and the pointlessness of it.

Alek occasionally says: "I remembered you . . ." or: "And then I thought of you, what you would have said. . . ." I myself cannot pick out moments like this, because I remember him and think of him all the time.

I hadn't been in Fink's for over four years, it was still shrouded in the same dim light in the afternoon, with the exotic coolness of the first air conditioner in Jerusalem. The atmosphere of a black-and-white spy movie. When I was already seated opposite him I found it difficult to look into his face, as if afraid of being burnt, and opened with a political speech, of all things, as if it wasn't Alek sitting there. "Do you really believe that?" he asked me in polite surprise when I parroted that now-Begin-was-going-to-annex-all-the-occupied-territories-set-the-Middle-East-on-fire-and-isolate-us-from-the-world. "Don't you?" "Propaganda is one thing and action is another, but when people like you . . . when even you begin to believe in propaganda, perhaps there really is problem. In any case," his voice smiled, "you'll agree with me that a man like Begin who thanks his wife so nicely, and in the language of the Bible what's more, can't be all bad."

"What made you leave the university?" I asked. "Nothing really made me leave, things just took their course. You tell me, what do you think, could you spend whole year debating where Baudelaire is more symbolist and where he is more decadent?" I couldn't because I'd never read Baudelaire. At the table next to the curtained window looking onto King George Street three men were speaking German, they didn't look like tourists, apparently foreign correspondents, or maybe spies. It was quarter past two in the afternoon, and Alek ordered wine.

A silence that lasted too long obliged me to choose between looking at him and talking. "I suppose you want us to finalize the matter of the divorce?" "The matter of . . . if we need to . . . how did you say? . . . finalize? If you say then we'll finalize it. . . . You haven't told me how you are yet."

The next item on his gentlemanly agenda was to ask me about Hagar, and in the middle of an adorable story about how she sat up in her sleep with her eyes closed and said—I suddenly faltered, not knowing if I was trying to endear my daughter to her father, or using her to make me seem sweeter in his eyes. And then Alek, all attention, very carefully, leaned over and took the salt shaker out of my hand.

"Not like this," he said, "no . . . not like this." "Not like this—what?" I protested angrily. "To talk like this, to meet you like this, it's not normal." I could say that it was this sentence that broke me up, or the touch of his fingers on my cheek, or the almost voiceless murmur of "Noichka," but in truth I had come to him defeated in advance, helpless to deny.

The next morning Alek came to me at home, held me patiently when I sobbed over his shoulder with clenched teeth, and came again later in the week, until a pattern of clandestine life was established, if it could be called a pattern at all. Sometimes we would meet every two or three days, sometimes weeks passed without my seeing him, and it also happened that he once disappeared for almost four months. I could never point to a reason for his comings and goings, and when we parted I usually didn't know whether I was going to see him in two or three days or whether weeks would pass again.

What is there to say about the humiliations of being somebody's mistress that hasn't already been said? Actually, perhaps I do have something new to contribute: a kind of gradual recognition that, without any connection to Ute and "I have woman I live with now," Noa Weber needs the underground. That the clandestine procedures of a humiliating secret protect me and my soul no less than they protect him and her, for I could not bear a stranger to see me naked with him, and almost every moment with him feels like nakedness.

Not for a moment did I fantasize that Alek would leave Ute and move in with me. Our meetings left me exhausted, prickly with a cold energy, unable to sleep. From the memory of our first year together I could imagine how staying with him for any length of time would devour me, how there would be nothing left of me, no human image but Alek's. And when Nira Woolf became part of my life, and my life began to take on an identity, and when I already had "talents" and "opinions" and "achievements" of my own, this awareness grew even stronger.

ALEK ASKED

When Alek asked my permission to see Hagar I couldn't deny him, let alone her. But this permission, which I didn't give at once, cut me into pieces, because it obliged me to tell real lies.

And so I roped in as consultants Tami and Liora—the oldest student in the law faculty, who before starting to study law had completed a degree in social work—and even though I didn't tell the truth in this consultation, I needed it. And despite the deception, it helped me.

Me: And you don't think it will be too confusing for her? He's not going to stay here forever. . . .

Tami: The idiot . . . what does he have to see her for in the first place? Just to satisfy his ego?

Me: Believe me I have no idea.

Liora: The problem is that he has the right, from the point of view of visiting rights I mean.

Me: As far as I know him, I don't think that he'll demand visiting rights. . . .

Tami: The idiot . . . the question is what's right, what's good for Hagar.

Liora: What's right for Hagar is for her to meet him, even if nothing comes of it, and even if it's a disappointment. Besides, it's impossible to know what will happen in the long term, with him, I mean, parental competence can change over the years. But even if nothing changes, in my opinion the best thing for her is to face up to reality, because in my eyes at least, the most harmful thing is to live in a fantasy.

Me: Perhaps you're right, but up to now I haven't noticed any fantasy on her part.

Liora: I hear what you're saying, but what makes you think that she would tell you if there was one?

My mother was so horrified by the news that Alek was in the country and wanted to get to know her little darling that when she suddenly rose from her chair I thought that she was going to call my father abroad to get his friends or the secret service to take care of the problem. But she only went to take the milk out of the fridge and broached another subject: "Once he's here already, why don't you finally get divorced from him?" "Because I don't want to go to court with him." "You won't have to go to court with him, Daddy will make an appointment for you with Nelkin." "You don't understand. The apartment is registered under his name, if we go to court we might be left without a roof over our heads." "What are you talking about? What right does he have to throw you out of the house? Nobody in the state of Israel will throw you out of the house." "Tell me, Mother, which of us is studying law?" My mother pursed her lips. "This is what happens when people make a laughing stock of the law," she said with a resentment that I was surprised to discover she still nursed. "At least you've learned your lesson. It's just a pity that the child has to pay the price." And when she resumed her seat and saw my face she added: "All right, maybe it won't be so terrible for her. Because what can already happen? He'll come, he'll see her, and he'll go. That man wouldn't dare make trouble for us."

Miriam realized at once that no salvation would be forthcoming from my father's buddies, the secret service, or the attorney Zachary Nelkin, and took pity on our vulnerability in light of the traitor's sudden invasion. "What does he want to confuse the little one for? Such a good little girl, she doesn't deserve a yo-yo for a father . . . the main thing is that he doesn't start mixing you up again." As opposed to my parents, who firmly denied that love played any part in the story, Miriam saw me as the youthful victim of a harmful teenage love affair. I never mentioned the business of the exemption from military service to her, Miriam respects the IDF and those who serve in it, and I was afraid of losing her respect. "How could he mix me up?" I reassured her. "Believe me there's no chance of that any longer." And I averted my face from her gaze.

I stayed in bed with him until twelve o'clock—it was the summer vacation, the exams were over and only two of my private pupils were still coming, so I had far too much time on my hands—until after twelve o'clock I was with him, and then he left and returned at five to meet Hagar. I planned the protocol of the visit with Liora, who came to support me and remained sitting in the kitchen, and Alek—Alek fell in with everything I laid down. If I had refused to let him meet his daughter, too, he would have accepted that as well.

Hagar's father nodded at Liora, almost bowed to her, and handed his daughter a gift which she did not hurry to open: *The Great Stories of the Ballet.* He was pale, he stood and waited for me to invite him to sit down, he accepted my offer to stay and have "something cold" to drink, as agreed, and I noticed that he had shaved since noon. Hagar, aged four, seemed paralyzed, obedient and paralyzed, and she went out with him obediently for half an hour to eat date ice cream. I watched them from the window as they descended the stairs together. She didn't take his hand, he didn't try to take hers, only went down the stairs by her side with his head lowered, as if he were trying to make himself shorter. My sturdy daughter in a blue sleeveless dress . . . in the middle of the stairs she suddenly turned round and waved to me with a courage that broke my heart. I waved back to her, and then I collapsed onto the marble counter, pressing my ribs against it. I didn't remember, at that moment I didn't think about anything, but a week or two before he had fucked me on that counter. Never mind the counter, to hell with the counter, the counter's not the point, the point is that you're not supposed to fuck like that with the father of your daughter. Not with shouts smothered on a wet shoulder. Not with that kind of desperation, come to me, come, come, take me, take me to oblivion. Not with only you, nobody else but you in the world. And with more, more, fuck me more, fuck me out of my mind.

Not with her father. Not like that.

Am I the only one in the world who distinguishes between the husband and the father?

ONCE WE'RE TALKING ABOUT SEX

Once we're on the subject of sex, this is the moment to say that something in this regard also changed when he returned. The change didn't happen immediately, it came about gradually, in a kind of theatrical building up of suspense; from the start it seemed to me that he had returned with sexual experience, with tricks he didn't have before—he didn't have them with me, anyway—but the sexual experience isn't the point. New movements appeared, in both of us simultaneously, a kind of conscious, coordinated game whose purpose was conquest, mastery and surrender: pinning my arm above my shoulder to the wall, grabbing hold of my hair when I turn my face to the right or the left, pulling off my clothes in one sharp movement, slapping me lightly when I'm on top of him, making me turn my face from side to side, and stopping—always stopping—at the first sign of fear; stopping and waiting for the sign. Hints of violence, symbols of violence, never actual violence. Sometimes marks would appear on my skin hours later, but at the time I hardly felt pain. I loved the marks he left on me, and sometimes I would deliberately provoke him to leave them. They almost always disappeared before the next time. And it wasn't always like that, of course, sometimes it was slow and gentle, too.

Me (in his arms, with him behind me on the mattress in the living room, for some reason we hardly ever sat in the living room): Tell me about Paris.

Alek (into my hair): Paris...Paris is the city of everybody's dreams.

Me: "The city of everybody's dreams" isn't telling.

Alek: So what is telling?

Me: Taking me to one particular place in Paris.

Alek: To tell you about one place...not far from where I lived there is an old cemetery. Baudelaire's grave is there and also the graves of all kinds of other famous people. Tourists like visiting there, once I went in too when I was passing, they gave me a map . . . never mind . . . around this cemetery is high wall, and gate, and next to the gate is rusty iron bell, like a bell should be, quarter of an hour before closing a guard rings this bell. One evening, it was spring when the city is very lovely, two students I knew ignored the bell, and they stayed there on purpose to spend the night next to grave of Baudelaire. I have no idea what they did there, read poems, performed some ritual with candles, maybe without candles . . . no, they would have to have candles, those people . . . Both of them wrote terrible poetry, absolutely shocking, before, and they both continued writing terrible poetry afterwards, too. But if you ask me about Paris, it is a city with the grave of a great poet where trash poets can make a pilgrimage, and even if it's funny, it's still great thing.

Me (smiling): Just once I'd like to hear you say something that isn't a paradox.

Alek (genuinely surprised): I speak in a paradox?

Me: Yes, always (at which point he did all kinds of things to me which I have no intention of describing, and which it makes me moan just to remember).

Alek (afterwards, into my face): That isn't a paradox.

Me (mumbling): The greatest paradox possible.

Alek (meekly): You know. If you say so it must be true. . . .

I said that we were playing a game, and now that I think about it, it isn't clear to me where I got my knowledge of the game from; where did the knowledge of the rules and the movements come from, then when I had not yet been exposed to any pornography, certainly not of that kind. My sexual education proceeded from *What Sex Are We?* to *Lady Chatterley's Lover* and *Fear of Flying*, and none of them included this material. When *Emanuelle* and *Last Tango in Paris* were playing in the cinemas I didn't have time to go to the movies, and I never dared approach the plastic-covered magazines in Steimatzky's Bookstore, so where did I get it from, and why does it seem to me that it was always there inside me? Inherent in the very nature of sexuality?

Nira Woolf fucks gladly, so do I more or less, sometimes, but when I come to the sexy parts in the plot I restrict myself to the cheerful before and the happy after, as if in obedience to Hollywood's Hays Code. Not only because of the embarrassment of the language, and not only because of what-will-my-mother-think-when-she-reads-it, and how will Miriam react, but also and mainly because there is no way I can get around the terrible vulnerability of sex.

A friend of Hagar's came to consult me once, a wild and quite disturbed girl, she spoke tensely about how her sister fucked boys. I've heard this expression from older women, too, and even though I have never used it in my writing, my readers will assume that this is precisely what Nira does: beds them and fucks them. . . . I myself have no doubt that this is what Nira does, only I'm damned if I understand exactly what she does, or how a woman can fuck.

It doesn't matter who rolls onto whom, and who performs the movements, and who pushes whom away afterwards, nothing can change the fact that at a certain moment of this event you are utterly abandoned, vulnerable and abandoned. And it is the man who possesses you, and not you him.

Sometimes my vulnerability was such that I felt I was dying; that's how I felt, as if my soul was departing my body, and in my perversity it was precisely to this that I gave myself up, to the vulnerability and the departing soul, and the ritual abandonment of the body.

Sometimes I thought: he no longer treats me like a child.

The strange thing is that parallel to these developments, to the addiction to vulnerability and sex, my sense of control in the time outside of it increased—control over myself, I mean—until it was no longer possible to see me as that "plain, timorous, dejected / and lovelorn maiden." I polished my opinions until they gleamed, though failed to achieve clarity of mind. With the love and the far out sexual experiences I grew further and further from my mind, or my mind grew further from me, drawing out the distance to the edges of fear, which always disappeared with his touch.

I never refused to meet him, sometimes I would keep myself in suspense and put him off for a week, until after my exams, after the seminar paper—I wasn't even kidding myself—but when we met I was no longer afraid to argue with him, and after I realized that he was sure that I "understood everything," I finally began to open my mouth, and even to use the phrase "I don't understand" to good effect.

Alek: Tell me who was your policewoman.

Me: What policewoman?

Alek: Who came to guard you when I took Hagar.

Me (assertively, it's called being assertive): She's not a policewoman, her name is Liora and she's my friend.

Alek: Sorry, I apologize, do you forgive me?. . . When is she due to give birth, your friend?

Me: How did you know? (Liora was then in her fourth month, her pregnancy was still a secret.)

Alek: You can see on her face. When a pregnant woman is happy, you can see it on her face, also in how she sits . . . . I wish your friend good luck. (She would not have good luck. Liora had a miscarriage in her fifth month, and it would be eight years until she had Asaf.)

I made it clear that I wasn't interested in hearing what he thought of Hagar, out of an embarrassing feeling that if I let myself listen and get into a discussion about her—never mind what was said—I might somehow be betraying my daughter. To this day when he asks me how she is, I tend to be miserly in my answers, and on the isolated occasions when I did say more or let him talk, it left me with a bad taste in my mouth.

Most of our arguments to this day concern the sociopolitical, as if it doesn't really touch us, although how this can be possible when I become increasingly sociopolitical as time goes by is not quite clear to me.

In the summer of '81, before the elections, Alek went to Kiryat Shmoneh without me—I stayed with my father, who was still at Hadassah Hospital after having been transferred from Intensive Care to the cardiology department—and when he returned we argued about Begin again. "Of course he incites, of course he does, what else? I don't deny it, but what I don't understand is why you on the left enjoy it so much, as if he turns you into saints." "Who said we enjoy it? Where did you get that from?" "What do you mean, 'Who said?' Switch on television." In the family and among friends it was agreed that Begin was responsible for my father's heart attack. The day before, I had knelt by his bed to help him put his slippers on. On the plastic chairs in the corridor two old friends were waiting, good people, who had brought us all fruit from the kibbutz. "You switch on the television, look who his people are, look at the characters they drag to their demonstrations." Alek put on his shirt. In a minute we would go into the kitchen and have something to drink, and ten minutes later he would leave. "Lumpenproletariat," he said as he buttoned his shirt, "that's who you mean. You know, I haven't been lazy, I drive all the way up to Kiryat Shmoneh, I go to demonstrations, and I see all kinds, including, you're right, lumpens, real rags, people with no connection to culture. But lumpens, if you don't mind me saying so, you also have on the left. You remember Menachem, who used to come to the house here and burn down museums?" I remembered two. "One of them. He lives now in Paris. I met him, to my regret, and what can I tell you, even if somebody lives in a European capital and associates with Third World and Palestinians, it makes no difference, lumpen is still lumpen. . . . He was with some student, Palestinian, never mind what his politics are, I saw immediately that this is a man with self-respect, who knows where he comes from. Menachem, on the other hand, is completely different story. . . . The way he fawned there, in a minute he would have dropped to the ground and kissed his feet just because he was Palestinian. . . . So they want to burn down museums? You know what? For my part they can burn what they like, let them burn. . . . But for an avant-garde too you need culture."

I didn't understand this speech fully, or why he was so angry—he was only a guest here after all—I didn't know where his anger came from, but I did know that Alek was leaving soon, and even though he was already dressed I still hadn't put a foot out of the sheet. Suddenly, I remember, I detested them all equally: Peres and Begin, Aridor and Meridor, Kiryat Shmoneh and the kibbutzim and the atomic reactor, Shulamit Aloni whose book *Women as People* had opened my eyes, my sociopolitical insulted parents, and that Menachem and this one— all the Menachems in the world, together with all their friends and enemies: everyone who forced me over and over again to stand up and be counted, to take a stand; everyone who made him close his face to me.

In the state of Israel you have to take a stand, in this world you have to take a stand, in this world you are your stand, only sometimes, what can I do, I get sick and tired of all these stands, they turn my stomach and make it hard for me to breathe. Alek never expected me to take a stand, not in that way, and it was I who usually introduced the outside noise, in order to test what? Who?

He looked down at me and then he lay down next to me again. He allowed me to crease his shirt in silence a little longer, but he didn't let me off completely. "Your friend, Miriam, who moved to Ma'ale Adumim, why don't you ask her what she thinks of Begin? Or do you also prefer for the people to keep quiet?" I didn't have to ask Miriam because I already knew. "Miriam isn't an example, in many senses she's even more left-wing than I am, but she has her own personal story, her own private score to settle for what happened to her when she arrived in the country." "And the left doesn't have, right? They don't have private scores to settle, and that's why they're the only ones who know how to understand history and how to make progress. What a pity that there are people like your friend Miriam who get in the way of historical progress."

ON THE BRINK

This is the phrase that comes to mind because that's how it felt then, as if I was teetering on the brink, and sometimes I stumbled. With three or four hours of sleep at night, giddy and aroused to the point of being unable to concentrate, there were moments when objects seemed to lose their solidity, and then I would stumble, and bruised toes and cut fingers were quite a common occurrence then. I would linger with Hagar for a long time on the curb before crossing the street, afraid that I wasn't assessing distance and speed correctly.

Strange how you get accustomed to walking on shifting ground, too. Absorbed in mapping my own inner swamps, I was careful not to arouse suspicion, I adapted my movements to my loosening grip on reality, and the only attention I provoked was of the "you look tired" variety. In a certain sense everything became easier, because nothing seemed completely real except for the hours I spent with Alek—closing the door with a backwards kick, trapping my eyes as I stepped back, not letting them go as he came closer, and when I expected his quick, hard movement, touching me rather with a slow, long one.

When everything becomes a little abstract, the concrete stops resisting you, and movements grow lighter, like those of an astronaut in space. During the weeks when he disappeared I would make up for lost sleep, and somehow or other I must have been born lucky, because even when the phenylethylamine rioted through my brain, my memory went on functioning like a separate disk.

As the end of my last year in the law faculty approached, it was clear that I wasn't a candidate for internship, that no legal firm I knew would take on a single mother as an intern—in those days I don't think the term "single mother" was yet in use—and even if someone would have accepted me, I wouldn't have been able to organize myself to cope with twelve- and fourteen-hour workdays. A few of the women graduates applied to be prosecutors for similar reasons, but I looked for a way out. Armed with a self-confidence that was paradoxically nourished by my new sexual exploits and the dramatic externalization of my sexual vulnerability, and under Alek's imaginary eyes, which turned every test into a trifle and at the same time also challenged me to win, I went to be interviewed for a job with a human rights foundation. They weren't necessarily looking for a lawyer, but legal articulateness and articulateness in general was seen as an advantage, and in the end I impressed them to such an extent that they agreed to keep the job for me and wait for almost two months until I graduated. I worked for the fund for over sixteen years, from the days when a staff of five were crowded in a noisy little office on Aza Street, until 1996 when it had grown into an empire, with a magnificent house in Talbiyeh and professional departments. According to the mandate defined by our donors we were supposed to assist in the development of local organizations dealing with the rights of . . . only such organizations barely existed then. I have had a number of occasions to say that most of the upheavals undergone by Israeli society from the end of the seventies to today can be described by the growth of such bodies, but what is relevant here is that the work consumed me to an extent that I never imagined, and that everything I learned during its course about the reality underneath the reality became a part of my being.

In the beginning I made all the mistakes usually made by beginners. All of us except for Jeff were new at the job, and Jeffrey's American experience didn't suit the situation in Israel. We wasted months enthusiastically and inefficiently monitoring the activities of the so-called "Green Patrol" in their harassment of the Bedouins. At the height of these futile endeavours I found myself driving round the Negev with Yossi Lenk in the vain attempt to identify a stolen herd, as well as conducting furious and no less futile telephone conversations with my father's friends, who naturally denied all knowledge of what I was telling them.

Months were wasted in vain attempts to organize the residents of what was once the picturesque slum of Yemin Moshe, all with the aim of obtaining legal representation for these people who had been evicted from their homes when it was decided to gentrify the neighborhood and turn it into a tourist attraction. During the razing of the Shama'a Quarter to make room for the Cinematheque we compiled a thick dossier, which we didn't know what to do with, and our initial contacts with a few doctors in the Gaza Strip were abruptly broken off, for reasons we were unable to understand. We also had no firm policy at that stage as to whether the occupied territories were part of our mandate or not.

In internal seminars held by the fund I am sometimes called upon to tell anecdotes from those pioneering days: before the era of directors and research assistants, of nonprofit associations and volunteers and organizational consultants, of project descriptions and project funding and spreadsheets, when goals were not yet printed on recycled paper and human suffering was not yet parceled out among us in groups. As greenhorns we let the experiences swallow us up, let them make demands on our time without consideration of working hours, and this was exactly what I needed. I met people, I spoke to people, I traveled to places, the phone began to ring a lot, I made a lot of phone calls myself, and for a change I was doing something that seemed important to me.

The year that I left the fund, when I held down two-thirds of a full-time job and was in charge of a number of well-formulated projects, it happened that I removed a young woman from dealing with damaged children. We were in the car on our way back from Haifa, after visiting one of the hostels whose financing the fund was then investigating, and this young woman, whose name was also Noa, told us how after previous visits to similar institutions she had woken at up night with horrible nightmares and gone to sleep with her daughter. "The strangest thing," she said, "is that after not being able to tear myself away from her all night, after lying next to her and praying to God that nothing terrible happens to her, as soon as she wakes up I haven't got any patience for her. She's a little slow in the morning, she always dawdles in the morning, it's nothing new, but precisely on this morning, I don't know why, I lost my temper and behaved like a monster."

"If that's the situation, it's a sign that the job isn't for you," I pronounced from the front seat. "It doesn't help you and it doesn't help the work for you to get into trouble at home." And the next day, in spite of her objections, she was transferred to working with groups assisting foreign workers.

I was never in danger of over-identification. Suffering, wickedness, stupidity, injustice, cruelty—I learned things about reality that I could never have imagined, but the main feeling simmering inside me was anger, which didn't always explode in the right place, and not always in a helpful way. My father was often an object of my anger, especially in the first years, as if he, as a representative of the "oligarchy," was responsible for Israeli reality and could be called on to account for it.

"Good material for the KGB . . . ," Alek said once, when he picked up one of the illustrated publications of the Agricultural Development Company lying next to my bed. Hagar had scribbled a red beard and mustache on the face of the scientist in the photograph and made red flowers bloom from his test tube. "You want to pass it on to them?" I asked. "What? To whom?" he said, in alarm or revulsion. As far as I was concerned he could have been a spy, I didn't care whom for. I was ready to be his agent, his field worker, taking his questions and presenting them to my father—Alek wouldn't fuck me until I brought him the answers—I was ready to mingle with my parents' friends, to question them and get the required information out of them, to blow the whole rotten system up from the inside.

But Alek said: "It isn't funny. KGB and its informers, Noia, it isn't funny." "Informer" was apparently the worst word in his lexicon, and once we had a nasty argument about it, when in the wake of ideas we were tossing around in the fund I mentioned to him a proposal for a sweeping law making it mandatory to report the abuse of minors, women, and the elderly. "Someone who does something like that, who abuses defenseless people, has no rights and should be shot. I would shoot him myself. But to inform, and even to make this law, that is something else." "You're an anarchist," I said, as if a minute before I hadn't had fantasies of blowing the system up from inside. "I am not an anarchist. You know what? Okay, I am. Better to be an anarchist and to shoot, than for neighbors to start informing on each other."

But this isn't what I wanted to talk about now. I was living with injustice, cruelty, stupidity, and sadism, with this cocktail of the social system, and with the fact that my heart was hardly ever crushed like the other Noa's. The anger got through to me, and I was good and angry with whomever and whatever I needed to be, but I couldn't feel the pain of the victims.

For a considerable part of the time however I did succeed in attaining one thing, and I sought it more and more: the awareness that in this world I and my entire range of feelings were not of the slightest importance, because touching heaven didn't change anything in the real world.

I went on meeting Alek whenever it suited him, he still pushed me to the edge and he still unraveled my heart and sharpened my edges, but in another separate part of my brain I grew indifferent. Not to him, no, never to him, but to myself and to what was happening to me.

One minute I was with him with the blinds closed, with take me, take me already, ready to fall to his feet as long as he took me, and half an hour later with the Association of the Victims of. . . . Or the Committee for the War against. . . . Switching off my face and saying: "Let's hear how you define your aims," saying: "We'll take it up with the board of directors," saying: "But the most important thing is for you to start showing independence." Sometimes I would lay my hand on my skirt, under the table, press a fingerprint left on my thigh to see if I could produce a pain, try to deepen the mark; the desire didn't diminish, but gradually it began to seem worthless.

The heavens could open to me, divinities could manifest themselves to me, my soul could fly out of my abandoned illuminated body, and all this would not change anything in the intermittently disembodied but nevertheless villainous world in which I moved.

HAGAR

I said that the work didn't get to me like it did to others, but in the end I think it may have had an effect on Hagar. I don't mean only that it took up all my time, and that I kept on sending her at the last minute to my mother, to Miriam, to girlfriends; I mean mainly that all the great injustices we dealt with at the fund somehow dwarfed her childhood, which suffered from an excessive sense of proportion. When her mother is going to visit a shelter for battered women or to meet the representatives of an organization for the disabled, a wise daughter—and Hagar was always wise—will not complain about the fact that it is her grandmother who accompanies her to the end-of-the-year party. As compensation, I would talk to her a lot about my work, tell her where I had been, who I had met and what I had done, and she was always interested. Sometimes more than in what was happening at school or in the youth movement.

During school vacations she spent quite a lot of time in the office, where she always asked for explanations about what we were doing, and there was always someone who offered to explain. At the age of nine she inhaled tear gas at the demonstration outside the Prime Minister's house in the wake of the massacre of Palestinian refugees in the Sabra and Shatila camps in Lebanon. At the age of sixteen she was spat upon on Paris Square at the Women in Black vigil against the occupation.

If today my daughter sometimes looks to me as if she is made entirely out of ideas and principles, I have only myself to blame.

If I hadn't met my soul, if not for Alek, perhaps I would have been just like her.

Me: Hello, darling, how are you? What was it like with your father?

Hagar: All right.

Me (carefully, as if absentmindedly, looking for something in my blazer pocket): All right—how?

Hagar: Just all right. But I don't like date ice cream any more, and anyway it's not healthy to eat ice cream in winter.

Me: Why don't you tell him?

Hagar: Next time he comes it may be summer already, and maybe I'll like the taste again.

In the spring of '88 Alek arrived for a short, bad, two-week visit, accompanying a television crew which was preparing a film about women in the Intifada, and he took a room apart from the crew in the Hotel Petra next to the Jaffa Gate. "I've wanted for a long time to wake up in the morning in the Old City." Hagar, who was almost fifteen and very active, accepted his invitation to meet him at the YMCA, and came back to me with the angry conclusion that, "That man is a right-winger, a male chauvinist, and a racist."

"Now that I've met him," she said to Tami who was in a huddle with me in the kitchen, "now I'm really beginning to understand why my mother can't stand men."

Alek to the best of my judgment is not right-wing, chauvinistic, or racist, but there is no doubt that he succeeded in infuriating her with the question: "Is it permitted to tell a feminist girl how pretty she is?" with his tasteless remark about "shots of a Palestinian *yingeleh*," and who knows what else. My little feminist, by the way, was not exactly pretty at that period in her life. Adolescence made her clumsy, her body looked embarrassed, and it was only in the summer before going to the army that she recovered her grace. In any event, I imagine that he was trying in his way to flatter her. I couldn't tell her that her father, too, thought that we were waging a war of Goliath against David, that personal liberty was more important to him than anything else, far more important than national liberation—either ours or the Palestinians'—and that he detested propaganda of any sort; in doing so, I would be giving myself away. And in any case it was clear that the two of them rubbed each other the wrong way: she made inflated declarations, and he deflated them. He could have, should have, restrained himself, but in the end perhaps it was for the best, and when she went to visit him in Paris both of them were already careful to avoid provoking arguments.

Alek is not a father to Hagar, and he is a bad father to Mark and Daniel, the sons of the woman whose children he wanted to sire from the moment he set eyes on her. If Hagar needed something big, for him to bring her the golden-hearted flower, to pluck the moon from the sky for her, I have no doubt that he would do everything in his power and beyond it, that he would turn the world upside down for her sake, and the same goes for his sons, but the daily business of fatherhood is something beyond his comprehension or his capacities. And in any case, it seems that his women and children get along very well without him.

Should I bear a grudge against him for what he deprived his children of? In my opinion I definitely should: men are responsible for their offspring, both parents bear equal responsibility, and so on and so forth, and nevertheless I don't bear him a grudge.

When she was a little girl Hagar tried touchingly to attach me to Yoash. When he raised her to his shoulders she would kick and ask me to hold her from behind, and we would walk down the street like Siamese triplets; she would demand that I phone him now, why not now, and invite him over; she would ask why Yoash wasn't married, say it would suit him to have a baby, and quiz me as to whether in my opinion he seemed "in love."

When she grew older she became more explicit, and when she despaired of Yoash and his eccentricities, she began questioning me about others, especially Jeff. "How long has he been divorced already?", "I think his daughters are really nice, it feels as if we've always known each other," and finally: "If he's such a good friend of yours, why can't he be your boyfriend?" If Tami had asked me the same question I would have replied that I'd tried, "for my sins I've tried, and I really can't recommend it, six out of ten on the Noa Weber scale," but small daughters are not girlfriends, and therefore I replied: "It's impossible and it will never happen because he's my boss." "So what if he's your boss?"

"If you go to bed with your boss your children are born with a squint." Hagar was not amused, to this day she tends to take everything literally and is offended when she discovers her mistake.

This year Alek became the father of a baby girl in Moscow. Dasha, or Dashka, is her name and I know nothing about her mother. Somehow I understood that the pregnancy was unplanned, by him at any rate, and that he sees her from time to time and also supports her financially, but Alek, always the gentleman, did not go into details. Was I upset? And how I was upset, mainly, in some strange way, because the baby was a girl. Ute is big, blonde and ample, I am small, short and relatively dark. Ute is German, European, and I am the Middle Eastern minx. The German woman has sons, and the Israeli minx gave birth to a daughter. Something in this division of roles helped me to separate between the worlds, to separate myself from the other woman, and to remove the sting of jealousy. Ute was one thing, I was another, and whatever there was between him and her did not touch me. And now he had a daughter, like Hagar, with twenty tiny nails, and another young woman who might be like me. How was she like me? And how was she with him? And how was he with her?

We were on the way from Sheremetyevo, on the Moscow Ring Road encircling the city. It was a quarter past eight in the morning, and outside the taxi window was a gray fog so thick that you could hardly see the white of the snow. It was my seventh visit, and when I stood in line for customs I noticed how the airport had changed since the first time I came to him, in 1993.

I was all aroused in anticipation of meeting Alek, but without the fear crawling under my skin that had diluted the arousal of the first visits. No shady character tried to take my bags from me, nobody offered the devil knows what services, and the airport employees no longer looked like gray corpses on leave. In another year or two maybe they would begin to smile and even to wish the passengers a "nice day." *What Did Mrs. Neuman Know?* had already been sent to the printers, and it occurred to me that perhaps in my next book I should bring Nira here, in winter. I would dress her in a black fur like the one displayed in the shop window upstairs. The flat-faced passport controller knew no English, but she took my visa without making me wait nervously, and without fixing her long narrow eyes on me or the computer screen, she stamped it with a hammer blow. Over the loudspeaker system, too, there was not a word to be heard in English, and when I stood in the next line I suddenly felt goose bumps at the sound of the names: "Irkutsk . . . *vosem tridzat.* Habarovsk . . . *vosem tridzat pyat.* Tallinn . . . Samarkand . . .

Vladivostok. . . ." Expanses of cold, imaginary forms of existence, all poured into the airport, and in this heart-rending vastness, present and tangible and standing patiently in line, there was nothing that it made sense to cling to except for the one waiting for me with a flower in his hand beyond the next set of doors.

"They say that at my age a child makes you younger, but what can I tell you, Noia, it's not exactly like that." The taxi driver had a slender neck, suddenly I wondered how the coarse wool of his sweater didn't drive him crazy with its touch, and when he opened the window to move the stuck windshield wiper, he did it without gloves. I had gloves, but Alek didn't, and when he wrapped my hands in both of his, hands no longer young, I was defeated again by the old rebellious helplessness; the helplessness that told me that in all the infinite expanses, in all the infinity confronting me, there was no point in anything, anything except for this. What could I say to him? "Congratulations"? "You're a maniac"? What could I ask? "Is she like me? Does she love you in the same way?"

"Tell me about Borya," I said. "What's he up to? How is he?" Alek leaned back and took out cigarettes for both of us. "Nobody can talk to Borya any more he's become such *pravednik* . . . kind of saint. And his new woman, complete *svyatosha*, with her it's even worse. You know how she answers telephone? You don't know, you can't even guess. The handmaiden of God." "Hello, this is the handmaiden of God?" "Exactly. Even my mother, who knew her mother when she was a baby, even she can't stand it." "So Borya doesn't drink any more?" I asked, and I nestled in his arm, happy and relaxed. "Why not? He drinks all right, but drinking with saints, you know, isn't such a pleasure." And I laughed heartily and felt great love, for both of us.

ONCE I IMAGINED

Once I imagined telling everything to Miriam, to her and nobody else. Perhaps she would have pitied me: Look how he took advantage of your love, you wasted the best years of your life on him and what did you get out of it, tell me? Perhaps she would have said: I felt that there was something wrong in your life, but I didn't want to poke my nose in. Only when Hagar changed her name did Miriam find out that I had been and still was an officially married woman, and my declared indifference to the formalities of the situation shocked her deeply. In her affection for me she had surmised that I had been done some injustice that I didn't want to talk about, and while she was wrong, of course, regarding the injustice, she was right in assuming that I couldn't possibly be truly indifferent to my legal position.

Miriam might have been angry with me: How could he lead you astray like that and how could you let him—she would certainly have been a little angry—but at least she would not have provided me with the telephone number of "an excellent psychologist." For some reason it seems to me that Miriam, more than anyone else, is capable of thinking of love as one of the afflictions of fate.

There was relief in the fantasy of confession. The thought of baring the soul brings relief, but sometimes the price to be paid for that relief is the soul itself, whose life seems to demand darkness.

As opposed to Miriam, I never for a moment thought that Alek was taking advantage of me in any way whatsoever, and sometimes it even occurs to me that the one taking advantage is me.

Last February, when we were already in his apartment in Ordenka, after he had told me about Dasha and after he had made me rejoice from head to toe, I reminded him that on my previous visit he had promised to take me into the refurbished gilded white church three buildings away from us, but he was too lazy to get up. "I'll put on some music for you instead, all night prayers, I'll find the disc in a minute... there you are, with your permission." And then, after all those years, like on Usha Street, like from the record he played me on Usha Street, rose the low male voices—slowly gathering, parting, like walking slowly in the dark, not actually growing stronger or louder, simply bearing stubborn, undefeated, sonorous testimony.

The mattress was very soft, snow went on falling and falling outside the white lace curtain, and between us there was a kind of weariness that sets in after everything is over, like a kind of pity or pardon. When he made love to me, the repertoire of movements had not changed, but the violent demand had disappeared, as if we were becoming reconciled, becoming one. As if becoming one was our purpose on earth.

Alek, one hand under my head, the other on my breast, breathed slowly, perhaps he was sleeping, and I with my eyes open saw visions of white infinity measured step by step, white vales of despair extending without a sign. Then breathing under his hand, slowly and surely I took off, slow and low; as if gathered up in the mist, I glided over infinity. Even if I dived into the white I would be gathered up, even if I dived down I would rise again like mist, even if I fell I would not fear.

When I awoke from the vision I looked from the side at the sleeping cubist profile: a single gray hair bristling from the arc of the eyebrow, thick boyish lashes on a heavy drooping eyelid, and a soft wrinkle shaped like a crescent moon beneath it. I put my hand on his hand lying on my breast, and then I thought: perhaps this man is only a gateway through which to pass. Perhaps he is only matter through which to see beyond matter. Perhaps he is only a stair to another love which no longer needs anyone.

I cannot justify these thoughts, or explain a single word. Matter and beyond matter . . . love which needs no one . . . vales of despair. . . . The yellowish light of a Passover heat wave should be enough to dissolve these phrases. Just saying them out loud should be enough to annihilate them with laughter. Where did they come from? And where did I get the feeling that like a precognition they were always there inside me?

In *Blood Money* I gave the contractor's repulsive brother a mystical turn of speech, like that of the messianic settlers' movement, and all through the plot he breathes a fog of verbal vapors on the reader that covers up the suspect and the murder; in *Compulsory Service* there's Sylvie, a particularly silly soldier who complicates the investigation when she consults spirits and energies. My better judgment cannot bear them and their talk, they truly and instinctively repel me; in the same way, I should be repelled and disgusted by myself, and nevertheless I am not disgusted. Not at the right time, and not to the required degree. Life in the underground lets you do this: fall foolishly in love without having to listen to yourself talking, and without paying the price of shame.

NIRA WOOLF

If I send her to Moscow she'll learn Russian first, which I never did, apart from a few words I picked up from Alek.

Nira Woolf will learn the language in two or three months, perhaps dialects, too, and if I send her into the white and gold church, she will even understand the liturgy sung there in Old Slavonic. Perhaps I'll give her a guide, an intellectual like Borya, who will also fall in love with her, but very soon she'll learn everything there is to learn from this teacher, and from about the first third of the book she will no longer be dependent on him. Mastering the language will come easily to Nira, like the knowledge of immunology she acquired in *The Stabbing*, like the understanding of bank fraud in *Birthright*, like her five martial arts. And studying the map at home will suffice for her to navigate the complex city and to locate herself even when she emerges from the Metro station in the middle of the night at some remote suburb.

Nira Woolf is "more like a fairy tale," as Miriam said, but why shouldn't women have fairy tales of their own? Tales of women who never know panic in the street and the fear of footsteps following them in the dark; legends about heroines who do not fall in love with their teachers and officers, and who are never impressed by rich, strong, mature, famous, tall men.

"It's important for us to have role models to identify with," Hagar lectures me, "but it's impossible to identify with such an unrealistic character." "What about the role models men identify with?" I type indignantly in reply, "Does James Bond look realistic to you? Do Indiana Jones, Van Damme, and Schwarzenegger look realistic to you? Half the men in the movies aren't in the least realistic. Much more than half, almost all of them."

This morning she called me unexpectedly from Boston, I hadn't anticipated hearing from her until she returned to New York. She had just finished reading *What Did Mrs. Neuman Know?* and she didn't want to wait, she had to tell me that this time she had really, really liked it. "Even though you write books for entertainment, the message gets across.... I think it's just wonderful how you managed to get in so much information. . . . You know what? In the last chapter, when Nira gives Svedka the revolver? Even I felt ready to shoot him, that swine, if he couldn't be brought to trial, that is." "She could have brought him to trial," I corrected her slowly, "but the punishment didn't seem harsh enough to her." "That's because the judges are men and the law is made by men, and even now that there are women judges, they learn to think like men." I was glad to hear her voice, but after two whole days in which I hadn't spoken to anyone, even at the grocer's, dragging the words out was an effort. "Did I wake you up? Aren't you on summer time?" Everyone who called me that Passover asked me if they had woken me up, but the truth is that when she rang I hadn't gone to bed yet. "You're not sick?. . . Are you sure you're not sick? . . . Is the holiday hard? . . . Are you eating, Mommy? Are you taking care of yourself? Going out? . . . Are you meeting your friends, or have they all gone away? What about Tami? Is she back yet?" Where are all these worries coming from all of a sudden? I'm forty-seven and healthy, active up until recently, my planner is full of addresses and phone numbers, I am interviewed in the papers, my book is on display in shop windows, and even though Hagar is my only child and I am a single parent, a mother is a mother and a daughter is a daughter and the roles should not be reversed. "I'm fine, just busy writing." "So soon? It used to take you longer to start a new book."

"Just playing with ideas. Now tell me, how does it feel being without Peter for two weeks?"

In the winter of 1980 the fund ceased its activities for a period of three weeks, and everyone except for me flew to the United States to meet the donors and consult with a battery of experts on how to go on, if at all. I composed most of the first draft of *Blood Money* then, on a baby Hermes borrowed from the office.

Ute gave birth to Daniel in November, Hagar was invited to the *brith*—in view of the Viking appearance of the mother, it seemed strange to me that they were having a *brith* at all—and in the following three months Alek disappeared from our lives. From our overt lives, I mean, and as far as Hagar's covert life is concerned I have no idea. She said that the baby was cute, that it was impossible to talk to Ute because she didn't know any Hebrew, and when she was brushing her teeth before going to bed she suddenly asked with her mouth full of toothpaste if we could also have a baby like that, to which I replied "We'll see," even though I had made up my mind never to have any more children. In any case, Hagar with her healthy instincts appeared to have come to terms quite happily with reality.

Serious writers describe themselves as suffering when they write; I, who have no pretensions to seriousness, have never suffered in the course of the work itself, and my difficulties only arise at the stage of publication. Writing held me together when I felt I was coming apart, and solved the problem of time when it began to unravel at the edges. Constructing a plot, like reading, in fact, gives time a direction, and when Nira Woolf began to take action, I was animated by a happy feeling that I too was making progress.

The background data of the story didn't present any problems, they were all taken from testimonies I heard at work before the decision to limit the activities of the fund to this side of the Green Line: the bribes paid to the Military Government, the harassment and frequent arrests, the contractor seen riding in the company commander's jeep, the medic's suppressed evidence, the pen in which the young boys were confined, the scene of the nocturnal burial. . . . The scene of the boys behind the barbed wire and the picture of the night burial annoyed a lot of people.

Nira Woolf already existed in my head before *Blood Money* as an infantile fantasy. In 1974 she solved the murder of the soldier Rachel Heller; in '75 I sent her to the Savoy Hotel as a resourceful hostage; in my night runs, when men bothered me with disgusting lip-smackings, Nira Woolf would fell them to the pavement with one graceful blow, without even stopping. She still does it, and to this day I still summon her to deal with male pests. The mere thought of her helps me to radiate something that sends them packing.

Once Nira Woolf put a man in a wheelchair after he raped an old woman in Ramat Gan and got off with community service; and once I sent her to the High Court of Justice to eloquently plead the case of the people evicted from their homes in Yemin Moshe, and she won. As I said: an infantile fantasy, a completely infantile gratification, but from the moment I sent her into action in a well-constructed plot, the fantasy became a little less shameful. My last doubts concerning Nira, strangely enough, were about her hair, and in the end, after dying it and shortening it and lengthening it, I gave her an Annie Lennox look that was before its time. For some reason I was bothered by this matter of her hair. . . . Now I don't know anymore if her cropped head speaks of fragility or strength, but this was the look I decided on in the end, and this is how she has remained ever since. Forty-five years old, big breasts that won't develop cancer, and a close-cropped, almost shaved, blonde head.

Two publishers rejected the book in letters of one and a half lines. I was prepared for this, what I wasn't prepared for was the extent of the response after the publication, and the way in which people began to identify me with Nira. At fund meetings my colleagues began to make remarks in my presence such as: "Maybe we should get Nira Woolf on the case," or: "Let's not be carried away into adopting Nira Woolf solutions," and on a number of occasions Jeff warned me that, "What we need here is quiet, in-depth work," and, "Forgive me for saying so, but this is a matter that demands exploration and negotiation, not a militant style." As if I had ever given him any reason to doubt my "in-depth work." All of a sudden I needed to prove that I was "serious," that I was "realistic," that I wasn't trying to cut corners and shorten procedures with a kick, and at the same time, to my embarrassment, they seemed to imagine that I actually could take advantage of all the publicity to get things done without going through the proper channels, which was far from being the case. It didn't help for me to repeat that I wasn't Nira and Nira wasn't me, people simply refused to listen; Nira was a symbol, I was seen as a standard-bearer, and for want of an alternative I decided to enjoy playing the role and put it to use wherever possible.

I'm not trying to say, God forbid, that Nira Woolf's opinions were far from my own, and since Nira Woolf acted more than she voiced opinions, I was obliged to formulate the views that justified her actions—which, in the last analysis, certainly did me no harm. Suddenly I was asked for my opinion on oppression in general and in particular, on the state and the individual, on the state and Zionism, on Zionism and women, on women and the patriarchal structure, on women's literature and the representation of women in literature, and so on and so forth—and it seemed that even those close to me attributed a new importance to my words, as if they "represented something."

Nira Woolf improved my financial situation, Nira made me "opinionated"—as people began later on to call any woman who had an opinion—Nira Woolf prompted me to read and think; so that in the final analysis it could be said that I, at least, was empowered by her character. She was born from the voice of an infantile fantasy, but from the moment she began to make her way in the world, she made me into what people today call a "voice."

LITERATURE AND REVOLUTION

My editor, who is more literary than I am, once quoted me something that Schiller is supposed to have said: All women writers write with one eye on the page and the other eye on a man, except for the Countess Von So-and-So who has one glass eye. . . .

With me it's the complete opposite. I never wrote with one eye on Alek, I never attacked him, and with both eyes on the page I was actually free for a while of his imagined gaze. With the years and the additional books I sometimes regretted writing so fast, so that the truce never lasted long enough.

Alek left for Paris in 1982, before the IDF invaded Lebanon, and from my point of view before the publication of *Blood Money*, so that he missed my transformation into a "public figure," and he also didn't read the book. It was only when they sent me the contract—the first, bad one—that I told him I'd written a book, and he was glad for me and congratulated me and came round with a bottle of fine wine. After he had refilled my glass until I was too drunk to return to the office, he asked me to tell him something about the book I had written—even today, with all my experience, I find it difficult to answer this question—and then, when the embarrassment was still new to me, I said something like: 'Well, look . . . it's not actually literature . . . it's more like a thriller . . . with a strong heroine, a lawyer, not exactly a lawyer, not only . . . but a woman with power. My editor says that on the jacket blurb they're going to call it a feminist thriller."

"Feminist thriller is good," he said and smiled and leaned over me and took a cigarette, "thriller is good, and feminist thriller is even better. It's a pity I can't read it." And inserting his hand under my neck he added: "You know what they say . . . in time of revolution the relation of literature to life is a relation of incest."

"What revolution?" I asked, drunk and vague.

"Today this is your revolution, the women's revolution."

A thousand times since then I've used this phrase, "the feminist revolution," and since I was asked, I've learned all kinds of illuminating things about its relation to literature and literature's relation to it. Sometimes now, in an intimate rather than a public setting, when I'm listening to Hagar, it occurs to me that this worn out word, "revolution," explains something in relation to her. In my relation to her, I mean. My darling Hagar is to a great extent the product of this revolution: good, clear-minded, and emotionally focused; and I am a daughter of the generation of the wilderness, not like her. . . . I got stuck in the middle and only half of me has made it. The good half, I say. I look at her in the same way as the hairy Neanderthal no doubt looked at *Homo sapiens*, lurching at a four-legged crouch, and however hard he tried to stand up straight and speak like a human being, he went on blurting out ancient, unintelligible grunts.

Hagar will never ferment underground and poison herself underground, and everything that bubbles inside her rises to the surface and is clarified in the light of day. I should have missed my transparent, enlightened daughter more.

But why "should" I? Who says I "should have"? When she left home for the first time with her boyfriend to do a year of national service in Ofakim, I wasn't sorry. They were like two clumsy, happy cubs, they romped around the house, they talked without stopping, they conducted long ideological seminars in the kitchen. I admit that I needed quiet, that I was tired of clarifying and explaining and answering so many questions at home as well. Afterwards I sometimes missed her. Actually, what do I know about the *Homo sapiens* I brought up? Perhaps she too. . . .

When she was here last summer she fell asleep one night on my bed, and when she was sleeping deeply and breathing quietly, I looked at the curve of her cheek, and for some reason I touched her temple. I needed to feel her pulse, I laid three fingers on her temple, and with the delicate pulse beating on my fingers came a feeling of wonder, both sad and tranquil. What did I know about her? What could I possibly know? But then she turned over and went to sleep on her back.

Another time, I remember, when she was in the army, I came home one afternoon, I didn't know that she was there and she didn't hear the door opening, and when I came in I saw her lying in her room, on her bed, in the place where her father's couch once stood, her wet hair spread over the pillow. The Walkman was lying on her stomach, she was wearing earphones, and on her face packed between them was a strange expression, flickering, illuminated . . . as if she were lit up from within. My daughter lay straight, uncovered, her hands folded on her chest and her eyes closed—seeing what? And suddenly, still and full of light, she looked like him. And then too, fair as the moon, clear as the sun, she was like a miracle.

TALKING ABOUT THE FEMINIST REVOLUTION

Talking about the feminist revolution, Alek good-humoredly called it "your revolution," but at other times, when we weren't celebrating a book, he pronounced it quite differently. Dryly and sarcastically. On the subject of feminism, as on a number of others, he had, and still has, completely reactionary opinions—"How do you know what's good for other women? Why impose the liberation of feminists on all of them? Are women cripples, that you have to fight for their rights?"— but somehow or other we often agreed on specific cases, and if he had been required to beat up some chauvinist bastard, I think that he would have done it without too much hesitation. The absurdity of all this is that in a certain sense Alek liberated me, from dependency on a man, I mean, and when I said that "a woman needs a man like a fish needs a bicycle," it wasn't a complete lie. I needed only the one, and since this one was not there but was nevertheless present, I was freed from getting involved with others. There were times when I wanted to be free of him too, but never in order to free myself for someone else, never in order to make myself available for the "healthy" and "meaningful" relationships so dear to the hearts of the members of LAA.

"Meaningful relationships," "support," and "equality" I had with my women friends, and with Talush who grew even sweeter as she grew up, and for these things I did not need—and I still do not need—a man.

Some time at the beginning of my years of active mistresshood I began to turn into a tramp. Not in the heavyweight league, my way of life didn't permit it, but I definitely turned myself into a serial slut, and I did so quite quickly.

"A nun and a tramp are two sides of the same coin produced by the patriarchal culture," my Hagar would have said sagely if she had known, but what the hell am I supposed to do with these words of wisdom? To lament and confess and grovel and beg for help in reforming my nature? Throw myself out of the window and smash myself up? I won't grovel for help and I won't throw myself out of the window, either.

At the beginning of my years of active mistresshood I started to work at the fund. The fund was a respectable place, but all the meetings and the debates with the groups and the initiatives and the sociopolitical fervor led so easily to sex that it sometimes seemed as if that was their main reason for existence. Later on, when people began confusing me with Nira Woolf, an additional element came into play, with all kinds of idiots seeing me as a challenge; they were eager to prove something to me, they were eager to prove something to themselves. One of them, a community worker I remember particularly—I had tutored him for his final exams a few years before—stood up after the event with a smug smile, proud as a peacock, as if he had just been decorated with a medal for gallantry. Since they were so dumb, these idiots did not always know that it was this they were looking for, but I always knew. It didn't bother me particularly, in a certain sense it was more convenient with them: they wanted Nira Woolf, they got Nira Woolf, and just like Nira I refused to meet them a second or third time—a fair deal, in my eyes at least. And from the sweet, innocent guys I usually, not always, kept my distance.

It was quite a dirty business, all this. It was dirty from the start and it got dirtier. I became a seductress. I became capricious and deliberately impossible. I discovered that men, like dogs, smell each other on your skin and the smell arouses them. Even Alek is not exempt from this doggishness, and part of the ritual violence of the sex then was related to this, too. He never questioned me about other men, he never demanded sexual ownership of me. I have already said, repeatedly— Alek didn't love me, Alek doesn't love me—but just as I can guess the presence of others in his touch, he could guess them on me, too, and the guess spurred him on. To touch me so that no other hands would erase his hands. To kiss me so that no other lips would erase his lips.

As far as sexual morality is concerned, Alek doesn't have double standards, it doesn't even occur to him to connect "sex" with "morality," and anything I or any other woman might do in this area seems okay to him, not because he has convinced himself of our rights, but because this is how he really feels. This is how he feels, and nevertheless, without ever putting it into words, he would come to take back his own. To take back my body and exorcise other bodies from it. When I realized this, I was delighted by the discovery, and I really began to use the others, to fornicate mainly for effect. How much would he sense? How much would I feel? Perhaps it was possible not to feel at all. At the height of this activity it was no longer completely clear to me what I was trying to do: to chase him out of me. To bring him into me. To wallow in others as in a smell in order to make him stick to me or in order to drive him away.

Alek had Ute and I'm sure he had other women, too; in '79 Daniel was born, and I had Hagar and there were others to even the score between us. The more I bled strength between his appearances, the more I needed it. And after he came I needed it in order to regain my balance. Like a drug to counter a drug, it only made me more addicted, and perhaps this is what I really wanted. As if I were performing rites in his honor. For him or against him. I really don't know.

The sex was sex, sometimes better sometimes worse. But sex in itself is nonsense. By the age of close to thirty, with a reasonably attractive man a woman is supposed to know how to enjoy herself, and coming is trivial, so that what distinguished one time from another was only the proximity of despair. Pleasure touches quickly on despair, removes its muzzle and sends it racing towards you, especially when you have sent your soul to perch on the ceiling while you abandon your flesh to its pleasures.

I wasn't trying to disgust myself, I usually chose well; sometimes I emerged into the street afterwards with a light step, which is what I wanted, to walk down the street with a light step. . . . I really wasn't trying to do myself any harm, and nevertheless it seems that I did. The gaze of another was stamped on my soul, nothing was closer to me than this gaze, and only it, in its absence and its presence, was capable of redeeming the sex.

Was Alek the best of them all? My girlfriends sometimes make these cheerful comparisons, and perhaps I should have made myself grade him, too. Alek made my soul manifest to me, he gave me back my soul, he filled my body with my soul without taking his eyes off me, until he made me lose my body. Not always, but often. So what is there for me to grade?

HOMO SAPIENS

I was cheating a bit when I glorified my *Homo sapiens*. Something is lacking in my daughter, something is being taken away from her, but what it is has no name. . . . My better judgement tells me that what my enlightened daughter lacks is only the slavish curvature of the spine, and the Neanderthal superstitions, and in spite of myself I sense a lack in her, and without any justice I see her as not a whole woman. . . . Strange that the more Hagar persists in her enlightened and verbose religiosity, the more she prattles on about "soul," "spirituality," "God," and "love," the more sterile she seems to me. As if she has sterilized the words by removing some secret from them, and in so doing also sterilized herself.

Secret, God, and soul—words that befuddle thought, words that it would be better not to say . . . or perhaps the opposite, perhaps they should be used as frequently as Hagar uses them, until they cause an inflationary spiral, and lead to bankruptcy, used precisely in order to sterilize. Sunlight is the best disinfectant for mystery and nonsense.

Alek, I remember, once spoke about the "mystery of the Russian soul." With ridicule and his lips almost closed he spoke. "Chaadaev, there was once such a man, an adjutant of Czar Alexander, who invented the mystery of the Russian soul, and ever since people who don't really think repeat this endlessly, mainly Frenchmen but not only . . . and with them there is no longer evil plain and simple or chaos for its own sake, because just to be evil isn't nice, but mystery of the Russian soul, this is something else." It was in the spring of 1988, during the bad visit when Alek came and took a room in the Petra Hotel, as if they weren't throwing stones from the Old City walls, and as if there were no merchants' strike, and no slogans painted on the walls and rubbed out and repainted in the alley below, and no white signs on the doors of the shops. He stayed in the Petra Hotel because that was where he wanted to wake up in the morning, and he even bought himself a hookah, I saw it when I came there. He remained in Israel for two weeks, most of which he spent driving around the territories with the television crew he was accompanying, and collecting impressions of his own for his reports for a number of French newspapers. I was busy at the fund, involved in research for *Birthright*, and under the overly observant eyes of an adolescent daughter who knew that her father was in the country. I didn't want her to see or hear when I spoke to him on the phone, so that even the telephone became a problem. When we finally met, after he had already met Hagar, it was cold and bad. A handsome stranger in a thin black turtleneck sweater received me politely, a stranger in a black sweater saw me out of the Jaffa Gate towards evening. That year he let his hair grow, afterwards he cut it short again, but that spring I was met by a curly-haired Alek.

If this is how he wants it, so be it, I thought as we parted, and I imagined a stone thrown at us and me crouching down and making a dash, like Nira Woolf, for the wall and flattening myself against it like a cat. Only after taking a few steps along the outer wall, my knees suddenly gave way beneath me, and I turned back into his embrace in the gateway and with his arm around me back into his bed again.

Before this, with small almost malicious smiles on our faces, we talked about politics, I remember how I protested when he said something about the "Arab mentality," and he retorted with the Israeli mentality and the Russian mentality and from there to the "mystery of the soul." With a politeness intended to hurt we competed to push each other away, and so it seemed to me that it was not the "mystery of the Russian soul" that he was mocking, but Noa Weber, only I, no longer "the plain, timorous, dejected / and lovelorn maiden whom he'd known," imagined that I was stroking a big cat, one of Nira's monsters, fastened one of my jacket buttons, and with affected calm replied: "As far as that's concerned I agree with you completely. You know, when you make a big deal out of the soul it leads people to ignore their actual living conditions."

"You mean . . . like religion is the opium of the masses?" he asked and stretched his tight-lipped smile a little further. "I mean that the assessment of the depths of the soul is greatly exaggerated," I said and adopted Nira's voice, too, the three-hundred-dollars-an-hour voice. "People exaggerate the depths, and the darkness, and the uniqueness of what is to be found inside it. Because tell me, what can there really be in the depths of the soul? Take a hundred people who live in the same society, and you'll find more or less the same garbage in all of them. The same crap stuffed into our brains by the people with the power to stuff things into our brains."

Last February, during my last visit, the same subject of the "Russian soul" came up again. We had returned from a walk along the Kremlin walls and again we didn't go into the church on Alek's street, it had already become a joke between us, not to go into the church again, and when he made me tea I asked him about Borya and his Anna, his new woman, God's handmaiden. "It seems that you're falling in love with the Slavic soul," he said disapprovingly, "and you're not the first. It happens to people who don't understand much about this country." And this time it seemed to me that he was actually saying something about the two of us. No, I didn't fall in love with the Slavic soul, don't worry. I love Alek. I loved him ages before he brought me to the violent, heart-rending, merciless expanses of the country he does not call his. It's his soul I love, and the dark, famished, howling element in mine.

THERE'S A KIND OF LIE

There's a kind of lie in this linear writing which does not encompass all the details. I remember how on the way back I sat withdrawn in the window seat of the plane, how I waited for the takeoff so that I could withdraw into myself and let my thoughts glide, among other things, over this last conversation with Alek. The flight's four hours were not enough. I have already said: love does not need much to feed it. And what of this abundance of small things can be described at all, when I enlarge some picture and it goes on and on subdividing into more and more pictures ad infinitum? Should I focus on his hands holding the tin kettle? I love his hands, I love to watch them when they do something apart from caressing me. When they touch ordinary objects. When he hugs himself. Holds a cigarette between thumb, index, and middle finger. But what can be said about this that isn't totally dumb?

Easier to talk about the mental alertness, the scurrying thoughts, and actually this too is difficult when every thought involving him splits into so many strands that it is impossible to follow them all. I didn't fall in love with the Russian soul, I cleaved to Alek as to the missing half of my own soul, as if it were ordained by the very nature of my being and the very nature of his being, and as if this cleaving was an attribute of matter.

Sometimes at the height of illusion a hallucinatory thought about the last incarnation crosses my mind, as if I have known him in other bodies, men's bodies. . . . Perhaps I was like Yoash or Borya to him, and it was impossible to become whole and complete the cycle then, and only now is it possible, and this is therefore an opportunity for the final incarnation.

For some reason it is easier for me to imagine myself metamorphosing into a man than to imagine him metamorphosing into a woman, and in any case it's only a metaphor. The belief in the transmigration of souls is nonsense.

"There is something about this place that cannot be grasped by normal thought," I said to him then when we walked under the Kremlin. A plane taking off from Saint Petersburg had exploded in the air that morning, and Alek like others had suspicions about it, none of which would be investigated, and he, too, as a journalist, would not investigate them. A local paper reported that Lenin's mummy was putting on weight, and a hysterical, consumptive medium appeared on television that night with a daughter with braids like rats' tails, who was also a medium. Trotsky spoke from the mother's throat, and Zorge the Spy from the throat of her daughter.

Alek laughed and said that I was quoting again. "Quoting who?" I asked. "Lermontov. It's impossible to understand Russia with the intellect. Another sentence quoted by the wrong people at the wrong time. You can say that the Empire of Evil is something the intellect cannot comprehend, and the Israeli intellect never comprehended, but from your mouth it sounds completely different."

By night on my bed I sought him whom my soul loveth. And perhaps it is not him whom my soul loves that I am seeking, but simply my soul.

With the years, I think, I have been purified. Facing him, or on his behalf, for him or because of him, in one way or another, I have been purified. At night, on many nights, I am able to let the longings go, to touch them, and then to dispel them inside me. Able to touch the absence as if it were a presence. Jealousy was never cruel as the grave for me, and for some reason I hardly tasted bitterness. Perhaps it was only for this that he was given to me.

Sometime close to the meeting in the Hotel Petra I stopped sleeping around, which is another way of saying that in all the many years since then I have abstained from other men. I don't know why, or why precisely then, it wasn't a decision because I didn't decide, the need to go the way of all flesh simply disappeared. Not owing to disgust, because I wasn't disgusted, I simply lost the taste for it; if it had disgusted me perhaps I would have carried on.

The urge itself didn't go away, perhaps it didn't even diminish, but like a nun I choose to resolve it, or to rid myself of it, with my own hands. From time to time I still find myself turned on by the idea of a little fling, but everything needed to get there, and in fact also the imaginary act itself, seems like a ridiculous hassle: the smell of a strange scalp, crackling curls, strange breath, wet lips, the wetness of strange lips on my breast, the wrong touch and bodyweight thrusting into me—what is it all for? The body will do what bodies do—but for what?

In my wild decade I gained such a reputation that nobody noticed when I stopped having sex; and of the possibility of finding me a life partner all my friends had despaired long ago. That "Noa needs a man in her life like a fish needs a bicycle" could be a statement of praise or of resignation, but the absence of sexual need and renunciation of the spasms of pleasure is for some reason unforgivable. Did I say unforgivable? So let them not forgive me, and I won't forgive myself either, because what does it really matter? I, if I haven't noticed, am increasingly evading the eyes even of those I invited to hear my confession. Escaping the impediment of words. And it is not their peace that I seek, but a different peace, a peace of my own.

OVER THE COURSE OF THE YEARS

Over the course of the years I kicked out in all kinds of directions in an attempt to "liberate myself from dependency," and what I did definitely succeed in liberating myself from was the concrete dependency. I don't need him to support me. I don't need him to protect me. And I don't turn to him for advice and encouragement, not even in my imagination. Sometime around Daniel's birth I brought up the subject of the divorce again, I even went to the Rabbinate, where they opened a file and set a date for a hearing. And when the date arrived Hagar was sick and I couldn't find a babysitter, and after that we didn't bother to set a new date. If he had asked me, if he had shown any interest in the subject, we would have been officially divorced, he would have married his common law wife officially, and that too would not have made any difference. Today it's clear to me that it wouldn't have made any difference, and perhaps I knew it then too.

The paradox of love is that it enslaves you to one person, and by so doing liberates you from other things. It liberates you to the point of indifference, which increasingly seems to me to be true liberty.

I did not adopt Alek's views, his instinctive detestation of sociopolitical ideology, I still believe in "equality," in "rights," in "social responsibility," and in "justice," only justice is too obvious to arouse my curiosity, and the idea of a "healthy, decent society" doesn't make heaven and earth breathe and animate the world for me. In the end all that remains is the utterly unthrilling work required to get there. Official forms in five copies on recycled paper.

Anger still comes to me more easily than human compassion, and anger still makes reality forcefully present to me, but over the course of the years the anger too has increasingly become an automatic response; and perhaps in this too I have been influenced by Alek, who is never astonished like me by human wickedness.

It would have been reasonable to assume that the dulling of my senses in this respect would undermine Nira Woolf's pursuit of justice, but the truth is that it had no effect on my writing. I have already said that I am not a real writer.

As with the writing so too with the work at the fund, the emotional unresponsiveness only improved the quality of my work, so that if previously I had wallowed in self-accusation for what I called my coldheartedness, I did so for no good reason and without justice.

The problem in leading a double life has nothing to do with

justice—with the proper allocation of emotional resources, with the right investments and fair trade in feeling. Very little feeling can suffice to behave decently and be of use.

The problem with leading a double life is that the everyday part of that life seems to you—not less real, I was always realistic—but somehow less true. As if lacking inner light and seeking a crack through which the light from outside can stream in and rise. . . .

I should have said now: Light . . . what light are you talking about? Neon light? The blinding summer sunlight at noon today? The orange light of the street lamp?

I should have said: A kettle is a kettle and a table is a table, and neither of them needs a light and certainly not a crack.

I should have said it and now I've said it, so what? I'm tired of these wisecracks. Which of course aren't wisecracks but wisdom. But I'm tired of this wisdom, too.

When I resigned from the fund in January of '96, I had the feeling again that I needed to clean myself and my life out a little. This was how I thought of it then, in terms of cleanliness, even though I had no idea of what this cleanliness I was seeking might be. Mainly, I remember, I wanted to talk less. Before this there were days when I had seven meetings in my planner, days when I met dozens of people, and the outside world had begun to make me ill. More and more I felt sickened by so many contacts and so much talk, sick of myself and my talking, and tainted, until I sometimes felt as if a moldy lump was sitting in my throat and incorporating more and more particles of pollution with every additional sentence I uttered.

In the months before I left, Nira Woolf took up most of my leisure hours, but the plot of *The Stabbing* unfolded reluctantly, as if I was serving one more tour of duty in the reserves. In a fit of spite I destroyed one of her monstrous cats, and laid its carcass at the entrance to her apartment. In another fit of spite I decided to leave her at the end waiting for the results of an AIDS test, without telling her that she hadn't been infected. If I said before that the world doesn't need my feelings, *The Stabbing* is one of my proofs, because when the book came out none of the readers noticed the change.

For the second time the movie rights to *Compulsory Service* were acquired by the same producer, and this time too I assumed that nothing would come of it, but in the meantime a handsome sum was about to be transferred to my bank account. The manuscript of *The Stabbing* was handed to the editor. For almost seventeen years I had been putting money into a pension fund. I have an apartment that I can't be thrown out of, my needs are modest, and I could afford to stop working. Hagar, who was planning to go to America and had already applied for a grant which she would no doubt get, expressed reservations: "But what will you do all day?" And I reassured her by saying that now I would have time to research and write in the mornings, which was what I had wanted for a long time—to write in the mornings. Perhaps I would register for a course at the university, I would find a new field of interest, and who knows, maybe I would come to bother her with a prolonged visit to New York, because I had never been there.

When Hagar, not reassured, finally left, I flew for the third time to Moscow, and when I returned I spent two or three months cleaning out and reorganizing the apartment. It was only in the middle of this fit of activity that I realized what I was doing, that I was returning the house to how it had been in 1972. My daughter's room, Alek's room, was turned into my study, and according to the logic imposed by the room itself, my new desk with the computer now stood in the place where his desk had once stood. Hagar's things were boxed and stored in the space under the roof. The picture of the greenish woman was brought down and hung in the newly painted bedroom, and Klimt's watery dead women were taken to Yoash to be reframed and returned to the kitchen. I brought them back on the day that bus number eighteen blew up, the day that bus number eighteen blew up for the second time, and the explosion shook the windows of the house, but I walked down Agrippas Street to Yoash to fetch the picture and continued about my business. I realized what I was doing, but its purpose escaped me, and as I packed and unpacked, moved furniture, took pictures down and hung them up, I enjoyed waiting for the understanding to come. Waiting for something that I felt would come later.

At the age of forty-two and a bit I started life as a semi-retiree. Reading in the morning paper about how we were settling accounts in Lebanon. Reading books in the morning. Going nowhere in particular without a shopping bag or a purse. I didn't disappear from the world or shut myself up in my lair: from time to time I took freelance jobs, which I still do, and wrote applications for support from various funds on behalf of various organizations. I sat on the board of a public committee, and I do a little volunteer work for two non-profit justice-seeking organizations. Family and friends come to visit and I visit them, Talush comes to lie in my bed and get some rest from her twins. On Friday afternoons people often drop by, their children run up and down the stairs, shaking the rail and threatening to fall with it.

My financial situation is stable and my health is excellent. At least four times a week I go out to run, and with time my route has grown longer, so that it reaches the Israel Museum, passes the Knesset, and returns via the Supreme Court. It was on such a night run with my walkman that I heard the news of Rabin's assassination—Hagar was there in the square, I had let myself off going to the demonstration—and when I got home and switched on the television, under the rush of adrenaline surging through me and the flood of phone calls to me and to her, I was still waiting to hear from him.

After the murder, when everyone jumped up to make declarations and beat their chests and point their fingers, and at the fund, too, when people asked themselves where we had gone wrong and what more we could have done, all I wanted to do was retire. Young people, my daughter among them, lit candles in the square and fell on each others' necks in an orgy of shocked and weepy self-indulgence; at the fund people talked a lot of nonsense then about "the youth," they seemed to believe that singing sentimental songs, waving candles, and holding "dialogues" would really bring about a new reality here, and I no longer knew what was true and what was false, everything seemed false to me—or at moments that were far worse, like a kind of banal and uninteresting truth. I would switch on the television then and without turning down the volume I would stop hearing the words. Faces on the screen were distorted as if by crooked mirrors, until for seconds at a time I was overcome by panic at not being able to recognize them. I thought that if I screamed the picture would come right and I would see human faces again, and human beings would start talking a human language that I could hear again—why were they talking to me like this?—but in the end the picture straightened out without my screaming, or I switched it off, and only the lump in my throat remained.

I retired from my job, and at the age of forty-two, for the first time in my adult life, I had all the time I wanted in which to think. But grace did not visit my thoughts. Grace did not come from my thoughts.

ONE NIGHT

One night this week I woke up when I heard him calling me from outside my dream. I had fallen asleep late, at about four in the morning, and apparently soon after falling asleep I dreamt that some woman was chasing me, I was being chased by a woman, and I was hurrying down a winding street behind the Natural History Museum. In the dream I didn't see my pursuer, I didn't know where she would appear from, but I knew that she was chasing me or lying in wait for me, and so I was walking quickly. I walked quickly, but the street kept growing longer and longer, as if it would never end, even though it was still the very same street behind the Natural History Museum, which I knew well and which you could walk down in a minute. In the way you know things in a dream, I knew what she wanted, too. When she caught up with me, the woman would bend down and with two movements she would cut my ankles.

At some stage of my lengthening flight from her I heard him call my name, not in the dream but from outside it, from the room, as if he wanted to tell me something or ask me something, some everyday thing, and that was why he was standing in the doorway and calling me, and when I opened my eyes to answer, I could on no account convince myself that his voice, too, was part of the dream. If his voice belonged to the dream then I was no longer able to distinguish between dream and reality. I couldn't fall asleep again and so I got up and got dressed and went outside to walk around the streets in the direction of the open market.

Before dawn the black of night changed to a deep blue darker than the darkness, though the streetlights were already switched off. There were a few trucks parked on the oily wet asphalt of Agrippas Street, and two men were loading empty crates onto one of them, with a kitten wailing like death beneath it. Next to the roadblock outside the market two border guards stopped me with, "Hey, lady, you looking for us? You lose something? . . ." and one of them held out a floral scarf. For a moment I imagined for some reason that they had pulled it from my neck when I walked past them, but when I left the house I wasn't wearing a scarf, and anyway this scarf wasn't mine and it didn't look like any scarf of mine. I summoned Nira Woolf to my aid, I grew six feet tall and asked for a cigarette, which I smoked in their company. They asked me if I had a problem, and I said that no, I lived nearby in the neighborhood, I wrote at night. A reporter? No, a writer. The taller one said that he had a story, one day perhaps he would write it himself, and the short one said that the market at Passover without pita bread wasn't the same market. The air was warm, with a faint smell of jasmine blossoms and rotting fruit. Stripes of gold-blue were painted above the city when I left them.

This wasn't the first time I had heard his voice calling me: "Noia . . . ." It had already happened a number of times. He never called urgently, he never called sorrowfully, he only said my name, and then I woke.

If I doubt that I really heard him, I will have to doubt the Japanese knife in the dream as well, and also the unshaven border guard who tomorrow evening, actually this evening, will be able to buy himself pita bread.

TEN YEARS

Alek left Israel in the spring of 1982, without guessing that Sharon was about to invade Lebanon and invent a new Middle East for us. So that apart from our two meetings when he was staying in the Petra Hotel, I didn't hear from him or see him for ten years. What does it mean to love someone who isn't there? If it weren't for my highly developed memory, I would say that it is simply clinging to an idea, but the sensual memory that grew stronger as it dwelled on every scene was so vivid and detailed that on no account is it possible to speak of an idea, and in fact it often pierced me more sharply than reality itself.

Perhaps this is how we continue to love the dead, but Alek wasn't dead, and the living Alek gave me strength.

I did not lack for enthusiasms in those years, but all these sometimes even feverish enthusiasms were accompanied by an awareness of transience. As if they were flare-ups that had to be experienced until... until what? I don't know. Until the flammable matter was consumed. Until matter was consumed.

I said to myself that a table was a table was a table, that a wolf moon was only a moon . . . that if there was a purpose at all its name was justice, and that the taste of heaven was my daughter laughing in the sea.

For weeks or months I succeeded in turning ordinary everyday existence into a manifesto and a creed: I believe in one single reality and no other. I believe in doing good: now I have to solve problems in the office, to locate Jeff, to buy meat at the butcher's on the way home, to check if Tami has invited Miriam, too, to remember to say I'm sorry to Hagar. That is the good. But then there was a shift in the weather, a different air blew in, a ray of light vanished, a thin, mean moon hung in the sky, and all of a sudden I filled with that oceanic yearning that absolute justice cannot satisfy.

I missed Alek, his voice, his accent, his concentrated body, the touch of his hand on my face, the way he leaned against the marble counter in the kitchen, today too I fold in half when a concrete memory and a no less concrete absence clutch at my diaphragm, only now I can sometimes rise on a wave and ride with it, and from the height of the wave it seems that my longing for him is only a gateway to some other yearning, to which this yearning happened to attached itself.

What did I want? For what was I yearning? What do I wish for now? I have already said: for some crack in the sky, nothing less. For some crack which will open up to me for eternity. When the absolute will be revealed and everything will be filled with the absolute and the streaming and the sealed light which will rise out of matter. Increasingly I see acts as a way, increasingly I see the body as a vessel . . . sometimes for hours I can feel the light imprisoned inside it, waiting for the light from above which will never disappear again. In this light sometimes for hours I see stones giving birth to stones and trees giving birth to trees.

In Moscow about which I know nothing, in Moscow where I am wordless as a baby and helpless as a baby, I keep seeing this vision of objects without a name and without a background, and there and with him I too with the harsh light inside me give birth to myself as a being without a background.

"Yearning," however "oceanic," is not evidence of the existence of something to yearn for, and the body is not a vessel. . . . I haven't got the strength any more to say everything that should be said, like a reflexive apology after an epileptic fit, and nevertheless here I have said it again.

Like a dog running around in circles after its own tail and biting it, I try to get rid of the delusion that I experience as my soul.

I could have resigned myself to the "oceanic yearning," and in the end no doubt I will resign myself.

I could have resigned myself to the sickness of my secret love.

But what I will never resign myself to, and the reason why I keep tearing at myself and my flesh, is the fact that in my visions there is a guard at the gates of heaven. That a man stands between me and what cannot be described in words.

Even if I stood myself up against the wall, I would not be able to give any comparative description of him, but I can put it like this: if at the age of seventeen, eighteen, I saw him as the wisest of men, Alek of the year '72 seems to me now touchingly young and confused, perhaps like I seemed to him then. Since then I have met wiser men, and especially women, handsomer men and so on and so forth, and none of it matters a damn, because only he in all his appearances splits open the spine of words in me, and only he makes trees burst forth from trees and stones burst forth from stones for me.

If these words have any meaning...the spine of words...what lies beyond...I want to see the stone and the tree and myself bursting forth without him. I have to learn to see them without him.

On the second of January 1991, when the world crossed off days from the American ultimatum, Alek phoned and his voice sounded so close that for the first moment I thought that he was in Jerusalem. He said that what was happening in the gulf didn't look good to him, that Saddam Hussein was totally insane, the West apparently didn't know how insane, it was hard to understand when somebody was totally insane. And perhaps he was worrying for nothing, but maybe I should come with Hagar to Paris?...

Where would he put us up? At his mother's? With friends? Had he talked to Ute about it? I didn't ask. Hagar was in the Negev on a year's national service, I was in bed with bronchitis which may have infected my lungs. I told him that it was impossible for us to come, but it would be all right, perhaps Saddam Hussein was insane but we at least were quite sane in our way. Only after he had repeated his invitation and I had declined it again, he asked if I thought it would interest Hagar to meet her grandfather, and since my feverish head was stuck in Paris, I thought that he was talking about Marina's husband Genia, and that it was to them that he was suggesting we come.

But Alek wasn't talking about Genia but about his father Abram Ginsberg, who had immigrated, it transpired, to Israel at the end of that summer. "Perhaps it wouldn't be too much trouble? He's living with friends now in Kiryat Menachem." "Yes . . . of course," I said still confused, "I'm sure Hagar would be happy to go and see him, it would interest her, I'm sure she'd be happy, but how exactly will she talk to him? Do those friends of his know a bit of Hebrew?" His friends, said Alek, were old and didn't know a word of Hebrew, and apparently they wouldn't learn any now, but Abram might remember something. "Where did he learn Hebrew?" I asked, and then he told me his father's story, or at least the outline that he knew, and it was the most fluent story I had ever heard Alek tell.

Abram Ginsberg was a student at gymnasium, not yet sixteen and already wild and rebellious, when he forged some papers and ran away from Vilna to the Land of Israel. For two years he worked and knocked around here, in the Galilee apparently, before he decided that nothing serious would come of the Zionist experiment and went to join the real revolution in Russia. Others who did the same thing were liquidated or died slowly or quickly in camps and resettlement plans, but Abram survived, it wasn't clear how, "I didn't ask questions, and when I did ask I never got answer, I know that for some time he worked as a truck driver, transporting timber in the North, in the taiga, the devil knows.... Up to the war and after he was on the move most of the time."

Alek was born "in the war, during an evacuation, almost in a railway station," and when his father returned as an "official hero" he joined his wife, her mother, and their son, and "registered in Sverdlovsk. My mother was studying at university, he studied a little at the Agricultural Institute, but then he left again, after the war he had friends in all kinds of places, and my mother met Genia, who had a room in Moscow." Alek was five when they moved to Moscow, and he remembered his father mainly from photographs. "He looked like a real Russian, not like me, completely different from me. You can't tell he's Jewish."

Ten o'clock at night, for over two and a half years I hadn't heard from him, and Alek was giving me the outline of a five-hundred-page novel over the phone, strewn with allusions I couldn't interpret and full of gaps I had no idea of how to fill in. Dazed by fever and pills, under the threat of chemical missiles which Alek's concern made me take more seriously—this time I didn't feel young, healthy, white-toothed, rudely constructive and far from any comprehension of the tragic, as I sometimes felt with him. The history that had devastated other places was coming closer, gathering force as it advanced, and threatening to reach my home.

I told him that I was sick and that when I was better I would go to visit his father. "Sick? What's wrong with you?" He sounded alarmed. "Nothing serious, just bronchitis and a fever." "You're sure it's not serious?" And when I said yes he said: "In that case, I wish I could feel your fever." On the other end of the line I heard him light a cigarette, and in the moment of silence that followed, both of our breathing. "Who are the people he's staying with?" I asked and pulled the telephone under the blanket. "Friends, Yacov Rudin, also a veteran, and his wife Fanny. Perhaps it's hard for you to write down the number now?" "Tell me what it is, I'll remember it. Do you know if they're organized? Have they got gasmasks, plastic sheets for the windows, masking tape? Should we take them something?" "There's no need, really. These people you don't have to worry about, believe me. I just thought it might be interesting." "And how interesting it is. . . ." I said, dizzy with over sixty years of history, "I'd be interested to hear what your father thinks about the Zionist experiment now."

More than two and a half years had passed since we last met, and I still saw his smile as clearly as I heard it in his voice. "Warn the little idealist that she's not going to meet a Zionist activist. I spoke to him on the phone, the most he is prepared to say is that the whole world is in a mess now, and if he already has to die, then better to die in a Jewish mess." "To die in the Holy Land? Is that the idea?" "What Holy Land? For my mother, yes, even though she'll never come to Israel, but for him there's no such concept as a 'Holy Land,' why don't you wait and hear for yourself?"

In the winter of '89 Alek was eager to go to Berlin, he was very interested in Berlin then, but both the newspapers he was writing for then had their own correspondents there, and in the end, after "we didn't stop nagging them," they sent him to Russia, to cover the elections to the Duma and report on what was happening there in general. In the winter of '89—to his mother Marina's horror—he went there for the first time, and then twice more, and on his third trip he found his father, which on the face of things should have been difficult in a country without telephone directories, but in fact "wasn't difficult at all. For years we heard that he was in Sverdlovsk." Immigrants, it appears, have information channels of their own.

Alek arrived in Sverdlovsk a few months before the city took back its old name, and found that his father had already applied for an exit visa and was "sitting on his suitcases." Abram Ginsberg landed in Israel on the night after Yom Kippur.

I didn't ask: "So what was it like meeting him?" or "So what did you talk about?" or "How did you feel?" You don't ask Alek questions like these, but I promised to talk to Hagar and to go with her to visit him when she came home. For the first time in the history of our long-distance relations Alek gave me a phone number where I could get hold of him in Paris, and said that he would phone again during the week.

Since I had to talk to Hagar, the story wasn't confidential, and I repeated it to everyone who came to pay me a sick visit and to everyone who phoned, with a strange enjoyment and without boring myself.

A friend of mine who writes for a local paper said that it was "a great story, only it wouldn't interest anyone, especially not now."

Tami said: "Be careful, it would be typical of that maniac to dump his father on you to look after."

My father said on the phone: "Go know who this man is at all and who he served. If Grandma Dora were alive today, maybe she could have told us . . . a person can go crazy with these characters who've suddenly remembered to sign on as Zionists at this stage of the game." My mother intervened on the other phone and said: "Excuse me, that's exactly what the State of Israel is for, so that anybody can remember whenever he likes." And Talush who was sitting on the armchair next to my bed concluded with: "As long as you don't end up stuck with that old man in a sealed room."

Hagar was the only one who was truly excited, and she phoned every day from her group in the Negev while I was still sick in bed to ask how I was and if I had succeeded in making contact with Abram yet. A few months before, towards the end of summer, she had changed her name to "Weber," and the hostility her last meeting with her father had aroused in her seemed to have subsided as a result. Perhaps the act of changing her name calmed her down, perhaps it was only the symbolic conclusion of an ongoing process, I really don't know. Among the many subjects that we talk about all the time, Hagar keeps her thoughts about Alek mainly to herself, but even so I knew that she was hungry for information about her father, collecting scraps discreetly so as not to alarm me, my parents, and Yoash, and in any case she was already obsessed with "roots" and "identity," and I know that she shared this obsession with all her friends.

In a certain sense it was a story of missed opportunity, a series of missed opportunities in fact. I phoned the number Alek had given me four or five times, and every time a woman answered in excited Russian, which grew more excited every time I repeated, "Alek Ginsberg . . . Abram?" With all her heart she wanted to cooperate, but she couldn't, all she could do was repeat in varying nuances of interrogation and emphasis the two words: "*bolnitza*" and "*bolnoi.*" My fever went down but I was still too weak to get into the car and drive to Kiryat Menachem.

A few days before the beginning of the American attack Alek called again and said that his father had been hospitalized at Hadassah, he apparently needed surgery, but Fanny and Yasha couldn't understand a word the doctors said and Marina was worried. And how are you? Have you recovered by now?

I arrived at the hospital when they were sending everyone they could home to free beds for an emergency. Outside the ER, soldiers were busy building terrifying showers, and a row of gurneys blocked the pavement. From Information they sent me to Surgery 2, at Surgery 2 they told me that the patient in question wasn't with them, maybe he was in Surgery 1, or maybe he was at Hadassah Mount Scopus, I had better check it out. In the elevator were a group of tense reservists who looked as if they were getting ready to jump out and run the minute the elevator hit the ground floor. In the end I found a young doctor who had read a few of my books and recognized me, and then it turned out that they had registered him under the wrong name.

"A rotten leg" certainly doesn't sound like a medical term, but those were the words she used as we stood next to the nurses station. Abram Ginsberg—for some reason they had registered him as "Zaltsburg"—had arrived with "an old wound and a completely rotten leg, which nobody here could understand how he had trodden on all those years, how a person could walk around in such pain . . . some people are made of iron. . . ." They had rushed him to the operating room for an amputation, but, she explained, we had to be prepared for the worst, they may have been too late, because we were talking about an aggressive germ that had spread from the wound. At the moment the patient was in intensive care, unconscious, and the prognosis, to be honest, wasn't brilliant, but with these old guys you can never tell, they're made of different stuff.

I didn't go to see Abram Ginsberg in the Intensive Care Unit. Perhaps they wouldn't have let me in, perhaps they would have. . . . When my father was there they let one visitor in at a time at certain hours. I was still not free of germs, I was still taking antibiotics, I drove home and told myself that I would go back another day.

Abram Ginsberg died on the first night of the missiles, without regaining consciousness; early in the morning they phoned me from the hospital and I phoned Hagar, and Alek again, who already knew. He was in Marina's apartment—it was her number he had given me—waiting with her to hear the news. During the night of the missiles itself, after listening to my breathing in the gasmask and to the pounding of my heart, which was beating faster from fear at the sound of my breathing, I spoke to them both. I spoke to everyone I knew that night, whenever the line was freed, but to Alek I went on talking all night long, so that I hadn't had more than a few minutes sleep when the call from the hospital woke me up.

We buried him at one o'clock in the afternoon. Hagar, brave and stubborn, ignored the police recommendations and the general panic and came by bus from the Negev, but by the time she arrived the funeral had already set out for the cemetery, so we drove straight there.

It had rained heavily in the early hours of the morning, the first serious rain of the year, and the roads were washed and deserted as if it were a winter Yom Kippur. I remember: nervous clouds moved low over the hilltops, pierced by long rays of light, and I drove fast between the tatters of gray and the light. The day before, when it seemed that the Americans were going to eliminate Saddam Hussein with a quick, strong, elegant strike, Hagar and her friends had gone to a Hilula, a celebration held under the auspices of the popular religious leader Baba Baruch, in his home town of Netivot, and she started to tell me about it and suddenly interrupted herself: "It seems so absurd now, the Hilula. Like a minute before the end of the world." "The world's not going to end," I said and put my arm around her shoulders. "Are you sure?" "As far as I possibly can be. But still it would be better if you stayed in Jerusalem. If you're worried what your friends will think, you can tell them you're sitting shivah for your grandfather."

The dwellings of the dead on the cemetery slopes were deserted, as if the last corpse had already been buried here, it took some time until we found the plot, and we found it not by signs but by the distant figures who looked as if they didn't belong there or anywhere else, either. Four black silhouettes, of the undertakers from the Burial Society, and another three people standing next to them, all with boxed gasmasks hanging from their shoulders and protruding from their hips like strange alien growths under their coats. When we approached they had already finished piling earth on the pit and on the one-legged old man made of iron and also perhaps on his amputated leg that had been thrown in for good measure, and a thin man from the Burial Society read in a high, rapid voice *El Malei Rahamim*. O Lord, who art full of compassion ... shelter him for evermore under the cover of thy wings, and let his soul be bound up in the bond of eternal life. ... The Lord is his inheritance, may he rest in peace. Big drops of rain fell intermittently on the loose soil. A mist advancing from the east covered Jerusalem. Yacov Rudin opened an umbrella over his wife and the young woman with them, and only Hagar said Amen with the grave diggers, but when the man from the Burial Society laid a little stone on the grave, we all approached and bent down after him. We ask your pardon if we have not acted in accordance with your dignity ... go in peace ... and meet your fate at the end of days.

When the service appeared to have come to an end, Hagar roused herself, went up to the Rudins and the young woman accompanying them, and explained to them with her hands that we wanted them to stay there with us. The undertakers left, in the silence that descended we heard their van driving away, even though it was parked quite far from us, and my daughter who was then at the beginning of her Jewish development took a Bible out of her rucksack and in a strained hoarse voice began to conduct a little ritual of her own. "A golden psalm of David. Preserve me O God; for in thee do I put my trust," she read, ". . . I have set the Lord always before me: because he is at my right hand, I shall not be moved. Therefore my heart is glad and my glory rejoiceth: my flesh also shall rest without fear." The rain grew heavier, Jerusalem disappeared, the surrounding hills disappeared, and in the mud between the tombstones above the muddy earth of the fresh grave we stood, three strangers in heavy coats and I, listening to a girl's brave voice trembling slightly at the edges as she read: "For thou wilt not leave my soul in hell. . . ."

"All according to the rules of the genre," Alek would have said, but what was the genre we were in? The war had not yet turned into a farce, our flesh was not resting without fear, hell seemed like a real possibility, and Abram Ginsberg had died not of biological warfare but simply of an ordinary aggressive germ.

We returned the Rudins and the woman with them to their depressing apartment block in Kiryat Menachem—later I would see similar housing projects but on a much larger scale in Russia—and I dropped Hagar the good soldier off at the Central Bus Station after in a sudden gesture of good will she had presented the embarrassed Rudins with her Bible. She refused to stay over even one night or even to have lunch with me—"I have kids I'm responsible for, their counselors can't just go off to Jerusalem"—and I went back to bed and the telephone and Alek.

We talked a lot in those first three days of the war, before Tami came up with her two boys from Tel Aviv—Avner hadn't been born yet—and they took over the house. In the nature of things our conversations were bogged down by "events" but nevertheless they were like a magical continuation, and somehow also completely relaxed.

When Hagar was small, she would sometimes crawl into bed with me; and when she grew up, too, when she came home from hikes, or from the army, or evening classes at the university, she would sometimes lie down next to me to tell me something, and fall asleep in the middle. I liked her physical closeness, I liked her smell and sleeping next to her felt good, and my daughter was an excellent excuse not to let a man sleep in my bed. In all my years I've only fallen asleep next to one man, and sometimes his voice leads me into sleep. "Are you already dreaming?" "Perhaps." "Are your eyes closed?" "Yes." "If they're closed, then you're already dreaming." And so he followed me into my dreams.

After the first night of the missiles I hardly felt any fear. Alek sounded as if he had a cold, he laughed and said he'd caught it from me. And once Marina cut into our conversation, and Alek explained that she was asking how her granddaughter was, and then I heard-saw him answering her rather impatiently, after which she left the room.

His voice wrapped the events in his presence and turned everything that was "inconceivable" into a part of the general disorder of the world. The world according to Alek…where in the midst of chaos and helplessness, you can sometimes find a different security and a different consolation.

THE SPINE OF WORDS

Miriam Marie went to Cairo in the spring of '82, and returned looking blooming and astonishingly youthful with a pile of photographs. "This woman was my best friend…and this is her granddaughter…this is where we went to the synagogue…and here, this is the Corniche, you can't see it properly in the picture, this is where we ran away when two boys were following us." Miriam wouldn't have dreamed of returning to live in Cairo, she would have laughed at me if I'd brought up the idea, but the very possibility of "smelling the air again," and the knowledge that the places where she had once walked were still more or less there, took about twenty years off her age.

Aunt Greta came to Israel not in order to make her peace with us, and returned to New York.

Abram Ginsberg came to Israel after he had "crossed too many names off his address book," as his son put it, and Alek himself lost interest in Israel and was living alternately in Paris and Moscow, without making either of these places his.

Around what spine of words can these stories be organized? The victory of Zionism? The failure of Zionism? Post-Zionism? Jewish psychology? A new national reality at the end of the millenium? Hagar tries to organize them for herself in precisely these terms, while I succumb to an attack of nervous boredom whenever anyone opens his mouth and talks to me in sociopolitologish, which has been happening more and more frequently over the years. Government ministers, professors, rabbis, and writers, the man in the street in his capacity as "the man in the street" and the taxi driver in his capacity as "the taxi driver"—all of them chew over reality in sociopolitologish: they talk about "strata," "ethnic groups," "elites," they speak of "cultures," "immigrations," and "populations" which suffer from "complexes" and "traumas." I myself speak in sociopolitologish, and not only to others but also to myself. But there has to be, I know there has to be, another language.

This illusion that people's private destinies can be explained at all; what makes them go and what makes them stay. . . .

What makes them go and what makes them stay? The beating of a butterfly's wings in Korea. An old taste suddenly coming into the mouth. Unrequited love. Hidden rage. Sensitivity to some invisible molecule that was in the air at a particular moment in time. Sometimes a great wind blows up, an evil wind which sweeps people away, and then too there is no point in words, which cannot really capture the victims.

No evil wind swept us away in the Gulf War, which from day to day degenerated into a kind of sticky, hysterical farce, but what happened from my point of view was that in a strange and completely unexpected way I entered a new incarnation with Alek. We became friends. And then I went to visit him in Moscow.

PASSOVER

The last day of Passover ended tonight, with a din of cars hooting for pita bread and falafel. The most vulgar and crowded secular seder of all. With the smells of family and cooking ingredients and scouring kettles. All the smells of the Jewish incense that keep the danger of spring at bay.

Long ago, at the beginning of the holiday, when I had just begun to write, I thought of purifying myself until I concluded with a great hymn of praise to everyday secular reality. To a reality without illusions, to the empty yellowish summer sky, to the Zionism of the soul planting itself in history with the morning paper. When I finish my confession, I imagined to myself, I'll begin to quietly praise. I'll bow my sinful head and sing a modest hymn to the only reality there is: a ray of sunlight creeping over the table . . . a child's hug . . . a loaf of bread . . . the tired eyes of my friends . . . the tired laughter of mothers . . . a pot wrapped in a kitchen towel . . . the voice of the newscaster. . . . Thus, stitch by stitch, I would embroider the fullness and the richness.

Tomorrow they'll be holding the traditional "Maimouna" celebrations at the Saker Garden, two streets below my house. Am I supposed to praise and extol this mass cookout, too, the carcasses of beef, the fullness of the chewing mouths, the melting ice cream and the screeching loudspeakers?

If this is the good, then the good is urgently in need of redemption.

On second thought, it's clear to me that I'll never take Nira to Moscow, not in a fur coat and not in a summer dress. If I took her there it would only be to kill her off, to push her under the midnight train to Saint Petersburg, a development my editor would on no account be willing to accept.

In 1999, when we wandered 'round at night among the fantastically illuminated, newly painted aristocratic mansions, Alek explained that it was the Mafia that had cleaned the streets of the small time gangsters. "Thanks to the big crooks we can walk here in safety." What would Nira Woolf, Lady Justice-for-All, do in this chaotic free-for-all, where even seven martial arts would not help her? And what would I do with Lady Justice-for-All and her martial arts?

In order to get rid of Nira there was no need to drag her all the way to Moscow, it was enough for me to want it, to make a decision, and then I could finish her off right here, in my house.

I enjoyed writing *Voice of a Dead Woman* and *What Did Mrs. Neuman Know?* more than *The Stabbing*. I went to visit Alek, I returned from visiting Alek, we held long and short telephone conversations, I was so aroused that my plots, too, raced ahead on light-footed, quick-tempered sentences. Now I think that with the use I made of incest, slavery, and rape I really did scrape the bottom of the barrel, because what other systematic rage could I provoke within myself? And for Nira and me systematic rage against the "system" is essential; rage with a theory, not simply rage focused on a person.

I didn't stop hating evildoers and detesting evil—Alek: "The easiest thing is to hate the villains"—outbursts of focused anger still make reality vividly present to me, but Nira from her inception aspired to more, and the elimination of the oppressors in her exploits always signifies the possibility of eliminating oppression itself.

Russia put an end to that for me, Alek put an end to it for me, it's hard to say exactly how and exactly what changed in me. . . . It's not that I stopped deriving infantile satisfaction from destroying scoundrels, but that everything seems infantile to me now.

Systematic rage needs a sense of direction: with justice behind you and evil confronting you, forward to progress and down with the system! Down with Western imperialism, death to the patriarchal oligarchy, out with oppressive capitalism, let the ground burn, let a social earthquake topple the class pyramid, let the mighty and terrible heroic God fall from His throne, bring on the Great Mother who nourishes and sustains all living creatures in His place. "Spiritual nourishment," too, as my only beloved daughter says. I don't care, I don't care—more than that, I'll even rejoice. From the bathtub I'll join in singing the anthem. I'll stick my head out of the window and sing as prettily as a tame canary. Second voice, millionth voice, I'll sing in harmony with them if they wish.

But the despair, that other despair, that can't be removed from the skin by the whitest teeth, what will eradicate it? And when the soul, the backward soul, begs for redemption, what will I say to it? Shut your mouth, you're just a fiction? Or will I shut it up with social redemption, because that's all there is?

Even when evil has been defeated and the good has triumphed—when foreign workers are not cheated, and women are not beaten, and the poor are not oppressed—then, too, when justice has been done, man will still be in need of mercy.

MOSCOW

Once upon a time I talked about a short-winded confession without perspective, and about Russia in my ignorance I have no perspective at all. I neither loved Moscow nor hated it. I did not understand this city, where I kept on losing my sense of direction, and whenever it seemed to me that the river was behind us, I suddenly saw it in front of us. I didn't love Moscow, I love Alek, and I loved him there.

We became friends, but that was only "an added layer," as they say, I still loved my master, like a willing slave, and every time he said to me: "It's not normal . . . you should be here now, why don't you come?" I bought a plane ticket, packed a bag and lied to all my friends and relations. I lived from conversation to conversation and from trip to trip, as if on cold oxygen that I stored up in my lungs, and the thought of the next breath, the next call, was intoxicating.

I have seven trips behind me, and I can't say that I've seen much of Moscow. We took walks here and there, sometimes for hours. We ate at little restaurants where they served caviar sandwiches on formica tables, where they were generous with the vodka and stingy with the coarse paper napkins. On a number of occasions, without embarrassment or the need for explanations, he took me to meet his friends; but most of the time he wanted to stay at home and refrained from treating me like a tourist. He says that Moscow can tire you to death. That "anyone who didn't grow up here all his life, his body can't take it," and that without going back to Paris he wouldn't have been able to stand it.

It sometimes happens that when he starts talking he addresses me in French and immediately interrupts himself with "'I don't know already which language I'm talking." Sometimes he loses a word in Hebrew and clenches his fist impatiently, until I find the missing word and offer it to him. From visit to visit the soft "sh" and wet "r" which hardly appeared in his Hebrew once become more pronounced. On one of my visits he was about to fly to Paris to his family a few hours after my departure, his suitcase lay open on the sofa.

In spite of his complaints about the city, Alek stayed there for longer periods from year to year. He installed new locks in the apartment on Yakimanka Street, which he had initially rented for only a few months, exchanged his laptop for a regular computer, collected books in amounts that were impossible to transport—"at that price impossible not to buy."

I was full of energy, and nevertheless I too felt no great need to go anywhere, his view was enough for me. A filthy inner courtyard visible from the kitchen window. Rows of windows in the building opposite, some of them curtained in white lace. One ugly wooden chest. A wall covered in old wallpaper with a pattern of leaves with a single picture hanging on it: a fake icon that Borya had given him, a proper forgery, not a reproduction; a tortured Jesus, golden and big-eyed in the style of Rublev, only Rublev hadn't painted it.

Moscow left me naked. However much Alek tried to explain—and he doesn't tend to explain a lot—and however much I read, I was left without a language and without an opinion, without the usual ability to discuss and make judgements. I have heard about similar sensations from people visiting the Far East, but Russia isn't India, we learned something about it in high school, most of the veteran members of the kibbutz came from there, the language sounds familiar, and so I had a kind of presumption that I was supposed to understand, and this presumption was almost always refuted. The strange thing is that I enjoyed this failure, the alarming difficulty in organizing reality, and the inability to make judgements in general or at all. Helpless and with my mind empty of opinions, very concentrated, it seemed to me that I was stretched by a kind of vibration which was existence itself—the devil knows what "existence itself" means, maybe it doesn't mean anything—but it held intense despair and renunciation and a wild and fearful joy, which expanded inside me, pulsing and stretching my ribs, until I could scarcely contain it.

Moscow left me naked, and I was naked anyway, in a nakedness so terrifying that sometimes I would close my eyes in the childish illusion that for a moment he would not see me. But it was for the sake of this nakedness with him that I kept on coming. Because of the gaze that turns all of me into soul and fills my body with soul, so that I never, ever want to escape from it or perch on the ceiling. Never to be in a place where his gaze can't reach me and give my body life.

Once it happened that we were sitting in the kitchen, and when he looked at me I thought that it was a good thing he didn't love me, because even so it was almost impossible to bear.

It's impossible to exist like this for any length of time. My longest stay was in 1995, eleven days, part of which we were with Borya, and when I returned to the city of J in the hills of J I was like a madwoman gathering her cunning to hide what she sees and hears. Alek spent that summer with his family somewhere outside of Paris, for over four months we didn't speak to each other, in Oslo talks were taking place with the Palestinians, settlers were demonstrating and blocking the roads. . . . Hagar wanted to know what I thought about the "right-wing" Russian immigration—how it would affect politics in Israel, and how the Jewish Agency was influencing the immigrants, and how I explained the fact that a fighter for human rights like Natan Sharansky displayed contemptuous indifference to human rights in the territories? So who do you think will influence him in the end?—and I to the best of my ability talked and discussed and debated, and felt myself growing scabs of words until my skin was as dry as a lizard's, which was the only way I could go out in the sun that was obliterating the city the further we advanced into summer. Jerusalem bleached in the light looked as insubstantial as a ghost town, and the air was so heavy that on my night runs I found it hard to breathe. And precisely for this reason I ran longer, but I obtained no relief even after the effort. I needed the darkness in which I could breathe. And then I began to think, too, of giving up my job at the fund.

ONCE

Once we came out into deep snow from an old monastery whose name

I have forgotten—maybe he never told me its name—he took me there to "see a real Rublev." There were a few cars on the side road, none of the drivers was interested in moonlighting as a taxi, and then he took me to one of those little windowless restaurants which on my own I would never have identified as a restaurant.

"Our Yesus Yosifovich is apparently a blessing the world can't cope with," he said as I tried to re-establish my connection to my frozen toes, and for a moment I didn't understand what he was talking about. "Jesus Christ," he said with a smile. "Yeshua in your language."

"What about him?"

"What about him? What indeed? What do you do with a blessing people can't cope with?" I know when to keep quiet, so I kept quiet, and Alek went on and penetrated my thoughts without foreplay, or after the foreplay of years. "God, as I understand it, can never accept human beings or really understand them, and this led to the mistake of Yeshua. . . . World, as I understand, was created to be different from God, the complete opposite of him, and for this reason there are laws of nature and of morality. But with Jesus what happens is that God entered this world to take part in it, as if he got tired of talking to people about their behavior from distance. As if not only the world needs God for its salvation, but also God needs human beings . . . he needs a place in their souls for his development, which is a blasphemous thing to say . . . but God made a mistake. . . ." I succeeded in moving my toes in my shoes, while Alek ordered vodka for himself and tea for me—I had had too much to drink the night before. "You said that God made a mistake," I said quietly, suddenly aware of the men at the table behind us and the foreign sound of the Hebrew. "Yes. He made a mistake. Because he is God and because of his love for human beings. Love of God is a hard thing. Hard when it enters between people, and Jesus in spite of sacrifice and forgiveness is hardest love of all."

"So was God only mistaken in the timing, or was it a fundamental mistake?"

"Now you asked the big question." Alek drank his vodka in one gulp, and then in an uncharacteristic pose he planted his elbows on the table and rested his chin on his hands.

"I asked the big question, what's the answer?"

"What is the answer? That there is no answer. Maybe there can't be one. Maybe for God there is no such thing as 'timing.' 'Timing' is connected to time, and God and time have a problem in meeting. This is another problem with Jesus, and about this a lot has already been written. And people, too, I think . . . people can be ready in their own time, so there is no one timing right for everybody."

I didn't ask him if he "really believed" in Jesus, because what did it matter? And what did "really" mean?

If I asked him perhaps he would answer dryly that we had gone to Bethlehem together and that he wasn't inspired by a pink doll in a manger. If I asked him perhaps he would say that Jesus was a "symbol," but I already know how close and present and personified a "symbol" can be. "Symbols" sometimes take on flesh in reality.

"What are you doing with me here?" I asked him later, when we were back in bed in the apartment. "What am I doing?" he repeated and pulled me on top of him. "Yes," I said and looked down at his face, and then he smiled and clasped his hands behind his head. "Maybe I have a role. In your life."

"Yes," I said deliberately, "yes, you have. But one day, one day I won't need you any more for . . . all this. I know."

"And then you'll fire me from this role," he said quietly and went on smiling.

"And then I'll fire you from your role," and I smiled, too.

I never asked him why he returned to Moscow. Presumably he had questions that required him to go back to the point of departure, like I needed to return the apartment to how it was in 1972. Only it's impossible to actually go back because in the meantime the continent has shifted.

THE PRIVATE THEATER

I have mentioned my resignation from the fund a number of times, and now I think that in this move too there was a certain dramatization, as if I wanted to impress myself. I felt worn out and grubby, I felt like a stinking old sack of words, Hagar was about to leave home, for years I had hardly had any time for myself. . . . All this is true, but apparently not the complete truth, because there was also the matter of the inner theater, my private theater in which the heroine said to herself: "Get thee to a nunnery," and picked up the hem of her skirts and retired, which is of course ridiculous.

I did not seclude myself in a cave, I did not take a vow of silence, and I did not sustain myself on bits of carobs. I simply started living like a semi-retiree with time to meet for coffee in the mornings. I didn't even stop reading the papers or watching soccer on television.

When the phone rings, I can allow myself not to answer; my parents are well and have gone on a trip—my mother had a cataract removed just before they left, but if they haven't been in touch up to now it means that all is well. Hagar and my friends are all fine, nobody needs me, and I, so it seems to me, no longer need anybody.

And this too in a certain sense is a foolish illusion. I pay taxes, the municipality provides me with water, the IDF guards my borders, and the finger of the Galilee is still perched like a pointed hat atop my pensioner's head. So what have I done, and what have I actually achieved?

With my first trips, coming back was still bearable. Like a mole, like a spy under deep cover recharging his batteries through meetings with his controller, I derived strength from being with him over there, and then I converted that secret fuel into a different energy. At about the third time back the transition began to jar me, each time more and more, and from then on I have found it harder to return to my pensioner's freedom, and after every landing days pass before I am able to see people or be seen by them. This time, for days I let the answering machine pick up my calls, and like the old Alek, I didn't get up when people knocked at the door. Let them think what they will of me. But after that, too, after I have already been out and seen and been seen, reality refuses to return to what it was, and like a famished dervish I am still whirling around his absence. A skin separates me from my shadow, and I am desperate to remove it. I tear and tear in desire for some other place where it will be possible to merge with the shadow. Only at night does it become easier, for then I can abandon myself to the dark; in recent years I have begun to live more and more at night. When I started writing this I thought that I would retrieve the day. Perhaps I was wrong to start.

It happened on the trip before last, the plane was half-empty, but both seats next to me were occupied. I left my seat, and a flight attendant who recognized me from television—that week I had taken part in some argument on prime time—allowed me to infiltrate the business class. She even brought me wine. We were flying low, I think, in the moisture of the clouds, and with the faint vibrating hum of the floor under my feet, cradled in the reclining chair, I was visited by a vision that told me that the plane was not really necessary, and that the metal body was intended only to provide those of little faith with something to cling to, so that they would not be alarmed by the actual possibility, or shocked by it. Floating slowly, the speed hardly perceptible, gliding towards him. . . . How easy it was to glide slowly through the air, how easy, the metal body encompassing me wasn't really necessary, it was only a matter of convention. It suddenly made me want to laugh, this metal body which was only there for the sake of propriety, like a polite gesture, it really amused me and I smiled. This was a convention of travel, and I was availing myself of it, but there was another possibility, too: if the window cracked, if the door was torn off and I was sucked out, I would go on floating just as I was now, I would still float towards him. Because it was only for the sake of appearances that I was coming to him in a metal body. . . . I could have come in the light and the wind, I could have come as vapor and smoke and cloud, changing shape as the fancy took me.

There is nowhere in the world where I can wrap myself in my shadow, there is no such place, and the body is not simply a polite convention . . .

but even so, even so, I will not praise what I have no wish to praise, and I do not wish to praise and I will not praise, I will not praise the metal body.

Even if it's impossible in a cloud, even if it's impossible in smoke, even if it's impossible to walk on water, I will not praise the body.

Alek was waiting passively for me at the airport, a body wrapped in a gray coat, the cigarette in his hand had gone out, and I can swear that he touched me with all of himself as soon as he saw me, as soon as I began to be sucked towards him, when there were still a few steps left, none but a few steps left, only a few steps left.

EPILOGUE, SUMMARY

She won't go anywhere; not to a more monastic monastery, nor to him to be taken to oblivion, because there is nowhere to go.

She won't kill herself in a foolish attempt to float from the window, and she won't crush her Nira Woolf under the engine of a train. Already in the weeks to come Weber will make Woolf dance like a graceful bear in the squares of the city of J and the coastal plain. And she herself will applaud her, clap her hands.

Already in the coming months she will find herself some new job that will take her out of the house on a regular basis, because living like this without any order isn't good for her.

• • •

Something else will happen, something else will happen one night, when a voice calls her from outside her dream. It will happen when a mean, mad orange moon hangs in the sky, and absence calls her name from the threshold. Perhaps her hair will stand on end, perhaps she will want to howl to him like a she-wolf, surely she will howl like the last she-wolf, surely she will arch herself to him when he comes. With eyes of darkness I will be able to see him coming closer, with eyes of darkness I will see his face taking on substance, and the body of shadow becoming tangible like a last need.

Something else will happen one night, when a voice calls, and a crouching body hides the mean orange moon and the sky in the window. Then with eyes of shadow I will gaze at his flesh, and I will rise and hold out arms of shadow to touch him. Like a last need I will shed my body before him, and as from a last need my soul will flee from him. Alone I will pass through the gate.

Outside the sky streams onto the city. Outside the night glimmers and clears. My vision clears of itself. But there is no face between myself and the streaming. And there is no longer a face between myself and the night.

A man will remain behind in my house, in his house, and I will not look back at the gate. It is not him I seek, it is not him I sought, not a man. Wrapped in the streaming I shall go, consoled by the abundance, by the awakening night, in the light of the moon I shall see by myself how the city bursts forth.

Now even if they come to seek my soul, they will not be able to take it.